THE INDENTURED HEART

BOOKS BY GILBERT MORRIS

THE HOUSE OF WINSLOW SERIES

1. *The Honorable Imposter*
2. *The Captive Bride*
3. *The Indentured Heart*
4. *The Gentle Rebel*
5. *The Saintly Buccaneer*
6. *The Holy Warrior*
7. *The Reluctant Bridegroom*
8. *The Last Confederate*
9. *The Dixie Widow*
10. *The Wounded Yankee*
11. *The Union Belle*
12. *The Final Adversary*
13. *The Crossed Sabres*
14. *The Valiant Gunman*
15. *The Gallant Outlaw*
16. *The Jeweled Spur*
17. *The Yukon Queen*
18. *The Rough Rider*
19. *The Iron Lady*
20. *The Silver Star*
21. *The Shadow Portrait*
22. *The White Hunter*
23. *The Flying Cavalier*
24. *The Glorious Prodigal*
25. *The Amazon Quest*
26. *The Golden Angel*
27. *The Heavenly Fugitive*
28. *The Fiery Ring*
29. *The Pilgrim Song*
30. *The Beloved Enemy*
31. *The Shining Badge*
32. *The Royal Handmaid*
33. *The Silent Harp*

CHENEY DUVALL, M.D.[1]

1. *The Stars for a Light*
2. *Shadow of the Mountains*
3. *A City Not Forsaken*
4. *Toward the Sunrising*
5. *Secret Place of Thunder*
6. *In the Twilight, in the Evening*
7. *Island of the Innocent*
8. *Driven With the Wind*

CHENEY AND SHILOH: THE INHERITANCE[1]

1. *Where Two Seas Met*
2. *The Moon by Night*

THE SPIRIT OF APPALACHIA[2]

1. *Over the Misty Mountains*
2. *Beyond the Quiet Hills*
3. *Among the King's Soldiers*
4. *Beneath the Mockingbird's Wings*
5. *Around the River's Bend*

LIONS OF JUDAH

1. *Heart of a Lion*
2. *No Woman So Fair*
3. *The Gate of Heaven*

[1]with Lynn Morris   [2]with Aaron McCarver

GILBERT MORRIS

the INDENTURED HEART

BETHANYHOUSE
Minneapolis, Minnesota

The Indentured Heart
Copyright © 1988
Gilbert Morris

Cover illustration by Dan Thornberg
Cover design by Danielle White

Published by Bethany House Publishers
11400 Hampshire Avenue South
Bloomington, Minnesota 55438
www.bethanyhouse.com

Bethany House Publishers is a division of
Baker Publishing Group, Grand Rapids, Michigan.

Printed in the United States of America

Library of Congress Cataloging-in-Publication Data

Morris, Gilbert.
    The indentured heart / by Gilbert Morris.
        p.   cm. — (The house of Winslow ; 1740)
    ISBN 0-7642-2946-X (pbk.)
    1. United States—History—Colonial period, ca. 1600-1775—Fiction.
2. Winslow family (Fictitious characters)—Fiction. 3. Indentured servants—Fiction. I. Title II. Series: Morris, Gilbert. House of Winslow.

    PS3563.08742I5   2004
    813'.54—dc22   2004012898

This book is for my favorite Cajuns
in all the world—the Neals.
There may be more generous,
hospitable people on this planet—
but I have not found them yet.

KENNY   OPAL
ANDY   JAMIE

GILBERT MORRIS spent ten years as a pastor before becoming Professor of English at Ouachita Baptist University in Arkansas and earning a Ph.D. at the University of Arkansas. A prolific writer, he has had over 25 scholarly articles and 200 poems published in various periodicals, and over the past years has had more than 180 novels published. His family includes three grown children. He and his wife live in Gulf Shores, Alabama.

CONTENTS

PART THREE
VIRGINIA

PART ONE

BOSTON

★ ★ ★ ★

1740–1745

THE

HOUSE

OF

WINSLOW

Martha Jakes
(1702–   )
|
1727 ———————• Charles Winslow
| (1728–   )
Miles Winslow
(1675–   )
|
1715 ———————• William Winslow
| (1720–   )
Anne Hawthorne   • Mercy Winslow
(1690–1727)   (1724–   )
• Adam Winslow
(1727–   )

Gilbert Winslow
(1600–1692)
|
1622 ———————• Matthew Winslow
| (1642–1730)
Humility Cooper
(1600–1660)
|
1660 ———————•
|
Lydia Carbonne
(1643–1737)

Rachel Winslow
(1661–   )
|
1692 ———————• Saul Howland
| (1708–   )
Robert Howland
(1658–1715)

CHAPTER ONE

THE PRINTER AND THE PREACHER

★ ★ ★ ★

Adam Winslow never forgot the momentous events of his thirteenth birthday—the first, his meeting with Benjamin Franklin.

Adam had arrived at his special birthday that morning, and thus had been permitted to make the trip from Boston to Philadelphia with his father. But even these august matters faded; in the years that followed, he always remembered that the famous statesmen had, on that late afternoon in 1740, flirted with his sister Mercy in a most forward manner!

Not that it was unusual for men to find his sister attractive—far from it. Adam had grown accustomed to finding the front yard cluttered with young men on Sunday afternoons, drawn by the bright blue eyes, fair hair, and trim figure of Mercy Winslow. But even at that age, he had heard enough of the famous Franklin to be amazed when the portly printer bowed low over his sister's hand, kissed it with a flourish, never letting his eyes wander too far away from her even when he talked business with Miles Winslow.

They had arrived in Philadelphia at dusk after a schooner trip from Boston to New York, and a two-day buggy ride over rough roads. Adam had missed little of the scenes along the way.

Sitting in the back seat of the buggy with Mercy, he had listened to his father talk to William, his twenty-year-old brother. And when they pulled into the crowded streets of Philadelphia, he sat straight up, taking it all in.

Miles Winslow drove the matched bays against a flood of traffic, which all seemed to be headed west. He was a good driver, but it took all his skill to thread the buggy through the mass of pedestrians, horses, and carriages until he arrived at a two-story frame building.

"What's that sign read, William?" he asked wearily.

William Winslow stepped out of the buggy, peered upward in the fading light, then turned and said, "Benjamin Franklin, Printer."

"Hope he's not gone home yet," Miles said, then added, "Mercy, you and Adam come with us." William helped his sister down as Adam scrambled out; then the four of them stepped onto the wooden sidewalk, pushing their way through the crowd. Miles shoved the door open, giving a grunt of approval when he found it unlocked.

The four entered, and Adam's nose twitched at the exotic aroma of ink and paper. A large press was rumbling, operated by a skinny apprentice who gave them no attention at all. Finally a man wearing an ink-stained apron came out of an inner office. He was middle-aged, somewhat portly, and his hair had receded, leaving a large bald dome over his small close-set eyes.

"Yes?" he said with a nervous smile. "Can I help you, sir?"

"Looking for the printer—Franklin," Miles stated.

"At your service, Mister—?"

"I'm Miles Winslow, Mr. Franklin. I wrote you a letter about printing my grandfather's journal."

"Of course! Of course!" Franklin exclaimed. He appraised the two tall men, both over six feet, noting the bright blue eyes and the blond hair with just a touch of red in the lamplight. The older of the two was in his sixties, the younger about twenty. The girl, he saw immediately, was a beauty, with the same fair hair and astonishing blue eyes. But the young boy was quite different—small and very dark. "I believe it'll be an excellent production, Mr. Winslow, excellent!" He looked at the large clock on the wall and shook his head. "It's a little late, but come into my office for a moment."

"This is my son, William, my daughter, Mercy, and my younger son, Adam."

Franklin acknowledged William with a handshake, Adam with a pat on the head, then turned his attention to Mercy. With a smile he bent over her hand, kissed it, and said, "You are most welcome, Mistress Winslow—you grace our poor city!"

William saw Adam staring at the printer, and when he caught his eye, gave a sly wink, then shook his head. Miles gave Franklin a dour look, but Mercy seemed to enjoy the attention, for she smiled and said, "You are gallant, Mr. Franklin."

He held her hand a moment longer than necessary, then wheeled and led the way into the small office in back of the shop. It was cluttered with books and manuscripts of every sort, piled up on the floor and stuffed into every crevice.

"Do you have the manuscript with you, sir?" Franklin asked, glancing through the door at the clock, obviously anxious to leave.

"It's in the buggy," Miles said, then asked with some irritation, "What's going on, Mr. Franklin? I never saw such a mob as that one out there. Is there a public hanging or some other choice entertainment?"

Franklin laughed aloud, with a twinkle illuminating his brown eyes. "Nothing quite so exciting as that, I'm afraid—" Then he gave a shrug, saying, "Only a preacher come to town."

"A preacher!" William's head lifted sharply, and he asked quickly, "What preacher would draw that kind of crowd, Mr. Franklin?"

"None of your home-grown variety, I assure you, sir! No, this is a British minister. Been making quite a stir in England—quite a stir. Name is George Whitefield."

Miles gave a snort and shook his head in disgust. "I've heard of the fellow. All mixed up with the enthusiasts!"

"I'd like to hear him, Father," William said. "You say he's preaching tonight, Mr. Franklin?"

"Yes, I'm going to hear him myself." Pulling off his inky apron, he added, "Why don't you come along, Mr. Winslow—

and we can talk business tomorrow?"

Miles started to shake his head, but William insisted, "We can't miss this, Father. He's set England on her heels, and he's likely to shake up the Colonies the same way."

"Quite so, sir!" Franklin slipped into a brown coat and quickly took Mercy by the arm. With a smile he held firmly to her, piloted the group out of the shop and turned them west. As they made their way down the crowded street, he explained how Whitefield had landed at Newport a short time earlier. He had made a tour of the coastal cities, and his reputation had drawn thousands.

"Never heard anything like him!" Franklin professed, with a wave of his hand.

"Then you are a Christian, sir?" William asked directly, a keen light in his eyes.

The question seemed to take the famous printer off guard, for he faltered slightly, but then threw his head back and said hurriedly, "Why, I am a believer in a divine power, Mr. Winslow!" Then he changed the subject by pointing at a large building directly in front of them. "There is Rev. Whitefield's pulpit this evening—the courthouse steps!"

"He's going to preach *there*?" Miles asked incredulously. "Aren't there any *churches* in Philadelphia?"

"A great number of them, sir," Franklin nodded. "But many of them are closed to Mr. Whitefield due to his rather harsh remarks about the clergy—and in any case, none of them would hold this crowd!"

He waved a hand at the shifting mass of people that stretched from the courthouse steps way down the streets. Nearly every house showed lights in its upper story, and by the flickering lanterns hanging from the walls, Adam could see people hanging out of most of the windows. Franklin crowded them in as close as they could get, and it was fortunate they were with him, for the people made way, so that he was able to find them a place beside the large landing. William, seeing Adam struggling to peer over the level of the porch, picked him up and stood him up on the ledge.

Just as he did so, a massive door opened and three men

walked out, one of them wearing a clerical robe. "That's White-field," Franklin said.

William stared at the minister curiously, for he had heard much of his work in England from a friend at Yale who had been at Oxford with Whitefield and the Wesleys. John and Charles Wesley had been the founders of a small prayer group called by their opponents "The Holy Club." Wesley had simply smiled and adopted the name, and the small band had grown dramatically. The group had been so methodical in their spiritual discipline that their foes had tacked another name on them—"Methodists"—and this name too had been accepted by the Wesleys.

George Whitefield had joined the group at a tender age, and after an awesome spiritual struggle had found a new experience with God. He had gone forth to proclaim his new birth and to call for a turning away from old dead forms. His preaching had shaken England, producing many devoted disciples for the young man—and almost as many critics. When the doors to the churches had been closed to him, he had gone to the fields, preaching in the open air to thousands. The mention of his name had become a magnetic force strong enough to draw massive crowds in any place he chose to speak.

Now he had come to America, and, if Franklin spoke truly, Whitefield was on his way to turning the Colonies upside down as he had the mother country. William realized his father was opposed to the revival methods that had appeared in the Colonies in the early 1730s, but William was eager for a breath of life to touch the churches, so he looked at Whitefield with tremendous interest.

He saw a neat, undersized man, with a boyish look—a stripling of twenty-five with a pallid face. He was youthful, almost angelic; William could hardly believe that such a youth could shake the nation of England. He had dark eyes, one of them with a noticeable squint, and he looked out over the crowd with such calm assurance that a thrill shot through William.

Then he spoke, and such a voice! There was not a sound from the thousands who stood there, no scuffling or whispering. The voice was like a bell, and although Whitefield was speaking almost in a conversational tone, that organ-like voice carried clearly across the night air, down the streets, every syllable sharp and definite.

For over an hour he spoke, and the crowd stood there, rooted and motionless as statues. His text was "Come unto me, and be ye saved, all ye ends of the earth." The voice carried authority, comfort, command, pleading—and William felt, as he was certain that everyone else in that massive crowd felt, that George Whitefield was speaking to *him* directly!

Whitefield preached the riches of God's mercy; then in closing, he lifted his head and called out, raising that magnificent voice to such a pitch that it seemed as though it would touch the clouds floating high overhead: "Father Abraham, whom have you in heaven? Any Episcopalians?"

"No!" he cried, answering his own question in a thunderous voice.

"Any Presbyterians?"

"No!"

"Any Independents or Seceders, New Sides or Old Sides?"

"No!"

"Any Methodists?"

"No!"

"Whom have you, then, Father Abraham?"

"We don't know those names here! All who are here are *Christians*—believers in Christ, men who have overcome by the blood of the Lamb and the word of their testimonies."

Then he threw his arms up and cried out in a voice that seemed to rend heaven and earth and run through the crowd like a bolt of lightning: "Come unto Him, all ye that labor and are heavy laden—and *He* will give you rest!"

And that was the *second* event that Adam Winslow never forgot about that day—not only did Benjamin Franklin flirt with his sister, but for the first time in his life, as George Whitefield cried out those last words, Adam wanted to know God.

William felt the tremor run through his brother's small frame, and after Whitefield turned and left and the crowd began to melt away, William held on to Adam a moment, asking, "Did you like the sermon, Adam?"

The dark blue eyes of the boy touched his with what appeared to be a pleading look; then a curtain seemed to fall over them like a hood, and he shrugged and said, "It was all right, William."

The tall man stared at his brother, regret mirrored in his face as he put him back on the ground. "We'll talk about it later, all right?"

"If you want to."

But that time never came. William watched for a proper time, but the vulnerable air he had seemed to see, if it existed at all, was hidden beneath a shell the boy assumed. He mentioned it to Mercy, who bit her lip and said, "I've been worried about him for a long time, William. He's so—so *hard*! You've seen it, haven't you?"

"Yes. He shuts himself off from the rest of us." He gave her a quick hug and said, "We'll find a way to get at him, Mercy."

But the next day was very busy. They spent a large part of the morning wandering around the streets of the city; then they went to the print shop where Miles and Franklin worked out the details of the printing job.

"Your grandfather was a Firstcomer, I believe you said, Mr. Winslow?" the printer asked, turning the pages of the thick notebook handbound between brown leather covers.

"He and his brother, Edward, were on the *Mayflower*, and my grandmother as well—Humility Cooper her name was."

"Winslow—Winslow? I've read Mr. Bradford's book, of course. I call to mind Edward Winslow; he was an officer in Cromwell's court, if I'm not mistaken—but I don't recall anyone named Gilbert."

"Well, Edward is quite well known," Miles said. "My grandfather lived to be nearly a hundred. He died at 92, and I remember him very well."

"Ninety-two! Remarkable!" Franklin exclaimed. "How did he die?"

A flash of anger ignited Miles' eyes. "If you want the truth of it, he was a victim of the Salem witchcraft trials!" he answered harshly.

"He was executed in that monstrous affair?"

"Not executed—but he was so weakened by the exposure in prison that he never recovered. My whole family was named—my father, my mother, and my sister Rachel. She's still living in Boston. It was God's mercy that they didn't all die in that affair!"

Franklin was reading a page from the book as Miles spoke of the Salem trials, and he got so lost in it that he finally looked up with a start, his eyes gleaming with interest. "My word, sir! This is a *treasure*! I'm honored that you have chosen to trust me with such a task—quite honored! It will sell very well!"

Miles bit his lip, then shrugged, saying, "Well, Mr. Franklin, I wouldn't mind making a bit of money, of course, but that's not why I want it printed." The printer stared at the tall man seated before him, for Winslow seemed to be at a loss for words. Finally he said in a defiant tone, "We've lost something along the way, sir, and that's why I think it's a book that should be read."

"Lost something, Mr. Winslow?"

"Yes!" Miles Winslow slammed his fist down so hard on the oak table in front of him that they all started. "Those people on the *Mayflower* left England—left all they had really, and they risked their lives for a dream. Almost *half* of them died the first year! Died like flies, they did, and why did they do it? Because they had a dream, sir, and we've lost that vision!"

"You think this generation needs regeneration, I take it, Mr. Winslow?" the printer asked quickly.

"All most people care about these days is making money and building fine houses!" Miles Winslow snorted in contempt, and for the next ten minutes he railed at the younger generation, leaving no doubt in Franklin's mind that there was precious little hope for any of the upstarts in charge of the New World. His children had heard it all before, but there was a force in Miles that struck William afresh, and he found himself caught up with it all.

"What you're saying, Father," he said, "is that we need a revival. Get the people back to God."

Miles nodded, then shot a quick look at his son. "Well, we need that—but not the sort that your Whitefields will bring." That set him off again, so that for the next ten minutes he went on about the sad state to which the world had come.

Franklin, William noticed, found it possible to talk about vellum and printing styles (after Miles finally finished his tirade) while at the same time paying close attention to Mercy. The printer hovered over her, finding more than one opportunity to pat her shoulder and pay her effusive compliments.

"The man's a born womanizer!" Miles said in disgust as he and William left the shop after all the arrangements were completed.

"Oh, I think he's just practicing, sir," William said with a faint smile.

"A man his age with a wife has no business *practicing* that sort of thing!"

"I agree. It's strange, Father, but beneath those smooth manners and for all his interest in Whitefield, I have the impression that the man has no feeling at all about God."

"In that you're right, I dare say," Miles nodded. "He's a clever man—interested in how things work, you know? And I think he's just interested in Whitefield as some sort of freak."

"Yes, I think you've hit it." William stared at his father and shook his head, saying, "I wish I could see into the hearts of men as clearly as you, Father. It's a gift every preacher ought to have."

Miles looked fondly at his son, pride in his fine clear eyes; then his smile turned bitter. "I've not always been so wise about people."

They had been to the harbor to see a ship owner, and now they came back to Franklin's shop. Going inside they found Mercy and Adam in the owner's office. Franklin got up at once and said cheerily, "I've just heard that Whitefield will be preaching in a large field just outside of town. I think we've agreed on the printing job—suppose we go hear the good man?"

"I've heard him!" Miles growled.

"That's like saying, 'I've already seen a sunrise!' " Franklin laughed. "Come along, Winslow; it'll do us both good." He turned suddenly and put his hand on Adam's shoulder, saying with a smile, "I don't suppose I could persuade you to leave this good fellow here with me, could I?"

"Leave my son here?" Miles stared in amazement at Franklin.

Franklin laughed and held up his hand. "Only jesting—but I tell you, sir, if I could have this one in my shop for a year, you'd see a thing or two! Look at this, Winslow!" He turned and picked up a handsome rifle with silver insets in the stock and pointed at the matchlock. "See that? It's a new approach to the art of musket making. I designed that new matchlock system myself."

"Looks complicated," Miles said.

"So it is. I had it all apart, and while your daughter and I were talking, that boy of yours put it together in no time!"

"Adam is very good with his hands," Miles shrugged. He did not say so, but he was disappointed that his younger son was not as good with books as his other children. Being good with the hands was not a trait Miles Winslow valued. He did not notice that Adam's eyes dropped when he said this, but William and Mercy exchanged glances.

Franklin's sharp eyes caught the byplay as well, and he gave Adam's shoulder another pat, saying warmly, "Well, my boy, if you ever need a profession, come to me and I think we can work something out!"

Adam looked up quickly, and seeing the kindness in the eyes of the printer, ducked his head and muttered, "Thank you, Mr. Franklin."

William reached out and ruffled the boy's hair, saying fondly, "Well, now, don't suppose there are many thirteen-year-old boys who get an offer from a great man like Mr. Franklin! Wouldn't be surprised if you don't outshine us all, brother!"

Miles looked at the clock and said sharply, "If we must get preached at by this Britisher, I suppose we'd better get at it." It was not an unkind remark, but it seemed suddenly to William that his father had cut short Adam's little moment of triumph— as if he did not like to hear the boy praised. *I must be mistaken*, he said to himself, for he knew no man on earth kinder than his father.

Franklin joined them in their buggy, directing them to the large saucer-shaped field about a quarter of a mile from town. Whitefield was at one end of it, standing on a stone outcropping waiting for the crowd to gather.

He began his message, and William was amazed to discover that though they were hundreds of feet away, he could hear as if he were standing right next to the man! "Amazing, isn't it?" Franklin whispered. "I measured this field once, the first time he spoke, and by calculation, I discovered he could be heard by thirty thousand people!"

Whitefield spoke first of a work for orphans he was trying to establish in Georgia, and after a brief but moving plea, an offering was taken. After it was over, William heard Franklin grunt, and turning he saw that the rotund printer had a crestfallen look on his round face. Then he laughed and shook his head. "Amazing! Just amazing! I was determined to put a shilling in the box—"

"How much *did* you put?" Mercy asked with a smile.

Ruefully Franklin patted his pocket, saying, "Four gold sovereigns—all I had!"

"You'd better be careful, Mr. Franklin!" she smiled archly. "A little more Whitefield and you may become an enthusiast!"

"I dare say!" Franklin replied. The whole matter seemed to amuse him considerably, and he smiled at his own weakness.

Then the preacher began speaking of hell and the punishment of the damned, and he was so graphic that little cries began to go up from some of the listeners. Directly in front of the Winslows there were two young women, both attractive and well dressed. One of them looked back and saw William, and her eyes took in his handsome features and tall athletic form. Franklin's hand closed on Mercy's arm as the young woman looked back again at William.

As Whitefield's words grew stronger, thundering like a storm over the open field, suddenly a man close to the front seemed to fall in a faint. Mercy gasped; then a woman not ten feet in front of them gave a piercing scream, her body arching as she fell to the ground senseless.

"What utter foolishness!" Miles said between clenched teeth. He turned to go, but just as he did, the young woman in front of them suddenly screamed and began swaying backward. William leaped forward and caught her as she folded up; carefully he eased her to the ground, and as he did so, Mercy felt

Franklin's hand squeezing her arm, and she saw that there was a wry smile on his lips. "The pretty ones always manage to hold off until a handsome young chap is there to break their fall," he murmured so quietly that only she heard it.

Mercy looked at the young woman William was supporting. She seemed to be breathing deeply in some grip of agitation, and Mercy whispered, "You think she's a fake?"

"I never judge people, my dear," Franklin said piously, but there was a smile in his small eyes as he looked down at the pair.

Adam had not missed any of this, but as he looked around, he saw that many were not being "caught" by anybody. Some were on the ground crying, tears pouring down their faces, and many were on their knees holding their hands up to heaven. The boy took his eyes off them and looked at the minister, listening to his words.

"God is angry with the wicked every day!" Whitefield called out, his boyish face stern. "His bow is bent! He will in no wise spare the guilty, and hell gapes for those who will not heed His Word!"

Adam felt lightheaded, and there was a cry somewhere deep inside, but he clamped his lips together and stared stonily at the preacher until the sermon was over.

It ended with a different note, for Whitefield, after holding the crowd over the pit of hell, suddenly changed his tone. Holding his hands toward them, he cried out, "This is a faithful saying, and worthy of all acceptation, that Christ Jesus died to save sinners, of whom I am chief!"

Strangely enough, as he left the themes of hell and judgment and began to speak of God's love, more people were moved to tears than ever!

Miles said suddenly, "Come—enough of this!" And they had no choice but to follow him as he picked his way through the crowd, stepping over some who were on the ground weeping.

William carefully put the young woman's head down on the grass, and her eyelids suddenly opened. "Thank you, sir!" she said sweetly, and her hand plucked at his sleeve.

"You're—quite welcome, I'm sure!" he managed to say, then

rose and followed the others to the buggy.

On the way back, Miles spoke harshly of the wild scene, and then he said, "Surely *you* don't believe in this sort of thing, Franklin?"

For once the face of Franklin was utterly serious. He thought about it, then said evenly, "I am not a religious man—but I am, I believe, an honest one. And I must in all fairness say that it is wonderful to see the change made in the manners of some of our inhabitants. From being thoughtless or indifferent about religion, it seems as if all the world here is growing religious, so that one cannot walk through the town in an evening without hearing psalms sung by different families in every street." He paused and added gently, "Some of it is, I fear, not genuine. But I cannot deny that many lives have been changed for the better as a result of Mr. Whitefield's preaching."

Miles was silent for a few moments, then shook his head. "All well and good, sir, but it could be done as well in a church!"

"Ah, I fear that you cannot put new wine in old bottles," Franklin said with a shrug. "You may discover something about that, William, in your new charge."

William had told the printer that he was on his way to pastor the church at Amherst, east of Boston, and he nodded thoughtfully. "Yes, Mr. Franklin, I may indeed. Mr. Whitefield says that many of our clergy preach an unknown and unfelt Christ. If he is right, we shall soon see."

"You would not have that man in your church, William?" Miles turned to stare at his son, alarm in his eyes. "Why, he will divide the people!"

William Winslow turned to look at his father, but he did not answer for a moment. He seemed almost to have forgotten the question as he watched a red-tailed hawk rise up from the warped branch of a dead tree. Finally he took a deep breath, then looked back at his father. "If this thing is not of God, it will die—but if it *is* of God, I will not fight against it!"

Sitting in the back, Adam listened to his brother and his father, and he was afraid, for never had he heard *anyone* stand up to his father!

Then he felt an arm go around his shoulders, and he looked up to see Mercy looking at him with a gentle expression in her eyes. She said nothing, nor did he, but as they rolled along, he was very glad that she had put her arm around him.

CHAPTER TWO

THE WINSLOW CLAN

★　★　★　★

The Winslows arrived in Boston on Saturday, their ship dropping anchor in the late afternoon. The pulsing trade of the busy city was symbolized by the forest of masts in the harbor, for the invention of the Yankee Schooner in 1713 by Captain Andrew Robinson had brought faster travel and a boom in commerce. Masts were the product that linked the great American forests with the ocean, tying the New England colonies to the rest of the world. A good mast 100 feet high could bring as much as ninety pounds sterling on the market after it had been cut in deep snow, dragged behind oxen from a forest, then floated downriver to a shipyard.

"Good to be home!" Miles grunted, leading the group down the gangplank. He paid no attention to the tangle of sloops, schooners, whalers and fishing ketches, but Adam's dark eyes were everywhere, taking in the scene and reveling in the smell of fish. He gazed at the sedan chairs and brightly painted wagons of red, yellow, and blue along the streets, and the signs of taverns and shops fascinated him.

"I'll miss all this, I suppose," William murmured, gazing out the carriage window at the busy marketplace. "Amherst is quite a tame little village."

"I wish we were *all* going with you!" Miles said sharply, giving a contemptuous wave of his hand at the busy streets. "Be better off to get away from this Babylon of a town! For two pence I'd sell out and move to the backside of Virginia!"

Mercy caught the sudden look William shot at her, and shook her head slightly. They both had realized long ago that their father would never leave Boston—not as long as Martha lived. *He'd really like to do it!* William thought, caught suddenly by the sadness in his father's eyes. *Just sell out and go to the wilderness—but it's too late for him.* The happiest days of his father's life had been those years when he'd accompanied his own father, Matthew Winslow, on long trips to the west, establishing the fur business that had prospered the family. Miles had loved the woods, the lost trails and the cathedral-like quiet of the timbered woods. *He used to talk about that all the time—and how he'd do it again someday*, William thought. *But that was when Mother was alive—he's given up on all that now. Martha's burned all his dreams!*

It was almost dark when they pulled up in front of the large white house, a salt-box style with two stories in front, and the roof sloping down sharply in the rear over the kitchen and storage rooms. The ground floor was composed of four rooms—parlor, dining room, library and kitchen. Above, on the second floor, there were four bedrooms with sloping ceilings. Below was a cellar for storage, and just behind the kitchen, with a door opening into it was the woodshed—a dark, roomy place in which a whole winter's supply of wood for heating and cooking might be kept.

The town had not yet caught up with the house, which stood alone beside the dirt road surrounded by large locust and poplar trees. Behind the house was a garden, an orchard of pear trees, a stable, and a press for making cider. A dovecote and a dozen beehives were just behind the garden.

"I see Rachel's here," Miles remarked, waving toward the buggy drawn up underneath a large oak. The sourness that had marked him earlier was replaced at once by a smile, for his sister was a treasure to him. He pulled the team to a halt and got out of the buggy quickly. A short, strong-looking black man neatly dressed in brown homespun came running out of the stable, a smile lightening his dark face.

"You home, Mist' Winslow?" He took the reins and added, "Miss Rachel here!"

"Put the team up, Sampson," Miles said. "Did Saul and Esther come with my sister?"

"Yas, they's here, Mist' Winslow—come early dis mornin'. And Rev. Chauncy, he here, too."

Miles led them around to the front of the house.

"You're late, Miles," Martha Winslow said sourly. She was an imposing woman, somewhat heavy in figure, but her face was sharp-featured. Her brown hair revealed no sign of the white that marked her husband's, and her slate-gray eyes 'lashed with displeasure. She had a thin, hawkish nose, and her lips were rather thin and narrow, a small mouth for such a large woman.

"Ship was late," Miles explained with a shrug. The two made no gesture of affection, and he looked over her shoulder toward the parlor. "Rachel's here?"

"We're waiting for you in the dining room; the food's getting cold."

Miles moved past her and gave a nod at the others, saying, "Hello Saul—Esther." Martha gave a sharp look at Adam, who was slowly moving indoors, and said sharply, "You're not eating with those filthy hands, Adam! Go wash!"

As he scurried toward the kitchen, Mercy and William followed their stepmother into the dining room where their father was embracing a woman with pure silver hair, saying, "You're looking more beautiful than ever, Rachel!"

William could not help noticing that his father was much more like a loving husband with his sister than with his wife, and he saw the bitter twist of Martha Winslow's small mouth as she took in the scene. "Sit down, Miles," she said sharply. "The food is cold."

Miles stepped back, his fond glance resting on the face of Rachel Howland. She was eighty years old, but her back was straight as a ramrod, and her eyes, bright blue, unfaded by the years. She was wearing a simple gown of blue silk that matched her eyes, and somehow it made Martha's ornate dress look cheap and overdone.

"I've missed you, Miles," Rachel said quietly. "How was the trip?"

"Fine! Franklin will do us a good job, I think." He felt the pressure of his wife's eyes then, and moved to shake hands with the short, portly man dressed in a somber suit, who had risen. "Pastor Chauncy, I'm glad to see you."

"You're just in time, Miles—I was about to eat your dinner!" Charles Chauncy was thirty-seven years old, and as pastor of First Church, Boston, was one of the most influential men in the colony. The office of the minister, while not as prestigious as it had been in the days of Bradford, was still a potent force in the political as well as the theological arenas of the day.

They all sat down, and as the food was served, Miles gave them a report of their dealings with Franklin. Even Chauncy was impressed with this, for the printer was one of the best known men in the Colonies. "It will be an edifying work, Miles," the preacher said, pausing between bites long enough to comment. "Your grandfather and the others on that ship were a different breed of men—yes, sir, a wonderful group."

"We heard Mr. Whitefield while we were there." William's face was smooth, and he looked very innocent as he added, "He preached most powerfully, Rev. Chauncy."

"No doubt!" Chauncy's face turned red, for he had gone on record from his pulpit condemning Whitefield and the revival that had swept the Colonies in the early thirties as spurious, and more than once had come close to consigning the whole thing to the devil. "I suppose people were wallowing all over the ground—as usual?"

"Tell us about it, William," Saul Howland said with interest. He was Rachel's only son, and along with his sister, Esther, constituted the only family that Robert Howland had left at his death. Saul was a thick-bodied man of medium height, with his father's heavy features, while Esther looked much like her mother. Saul was thirty-two, a rising businessman, much sought after by the mothers of Boston with marriageable daughters. Neither of them, to Rachel's quiet sorrow, was devout in his Christian commitment. They were worldly and ambitious, though they attended church more or less regularly.

Miles said brusquely, "Oh, it was the usual sort of affair, Pastor—preaching in the open field to a mob of the lower classes. Of course, the man is an orator—never heard a better voice!"

"It's his theology I'm worried about!" Rev. Chauncy snapped. "He's made a name for himself in England by attacking the clergy, and I have no doubt he'll try the same tactic here!"

"Oh, he's already done that," William said cheerfully. He helped himself to a slice of boiled beef, cut off a bite and put it in his mouth. Chewing comfortably he went on. "Mr. Whitefield has let it be known that at Harvard—and I quote—'Its light has become darkness'!"

"Why, the man's a heretic!" Chauncy sputtered. "He'll not preach in Boston!"

"I understand from Mr. Franklin—who's quite an admirer of Mr. Whitefield, by the way—that we will be honored by a visit in the not too distant future." He sighed sadly, adding, "I'll not be able to hear him, for I'll be at my church by then."

"Why do you dislike the man so, Reverend?" Esther asked curiously. She had no interest in theology, but everyone was talking about the sensation of Whitefield's preaching, and she longed to see the spectacle.

"Why, the man says that most of the clergy do not even know Christ! And he insists that everyone in the church must have what he calls *a new birth*! Makes little of baptism, good works, communion!" He gave William Winslow a sharp look, then said pugnaciously, "Your church is very close to North-ampton—you'll be seeing something of Rev. Jonathan Edwards?"

"Why, I trust so," William nodded.

"He's an able man." The words were not unkind, but there were marks of anger on Chauncy's face, and he suddenly burst out, "*He's* responsible for the whole thing! It was in his church back in '32 that the whole miserable business of *revival* had its start."

"He's quite a scholar, Pastor," Miles said evenly. "None better in the Colonies, I hear."

"Oh, as to that, Edwards is quite brilliant—but he has some wrong ideas. I suspect he's an enthusiast."

The word *enthusiast* was much used at the time, and never with a good connotation. England in the eighteenth century was immersed in the age of reason, and any expression of emotion was frowned upon as being *enthusiastic*. In the course of the Wesleys' work in England, some followers had gone too far; every movement had some of these, of course. But now, simply to name a man such in religious circles was enough to classify him as an irresponsible character incapable of reason and on the brink of lunacy.

Men like Rev. Chauncy had forced the Wesleys and White- field out of the churches into the streets. They saw the revival as a threat to their offices, and were contemptuous of the emo- tional content of religion.

"Nothing but a bunch of hysterical women!" Chauncy summed it all up, then took a huge draught of ale from the silver tankard beside his plate. "Troublemakers, William—have noth- ing to do with Edwards if you can help it!"

Suddenly Martha Winslow interrupted the minister, saying shrilly, "Adam—let me see those hands!"

Every eye turned toward the boy, who was shoveling his food into his mouth methodically, paying little heed to the table talk. As he felt the weight of so many eyes, a flush darkened his tanned face, and putting his knife down, he slipped to the floor and moved reluctantly around the table to where Martha stood to her feet glaring at him.

She snatched one of the boy's hands, peered at it, then cried, "Filthy! You won't eat at my table with hands like that. Go wash again, and then you may go to bed! Why can't you ever be clean like your brother Charles?"

Adam cast a look at the young boy sitting next to Rachel, and said nothing. His stepmother took that as an act of sullen rebellion, and twisting him around, propelled him toward the door with a strong hand. "If you go to bed with those black hands, I'll have the hide off your back!" she said, giving Adam a nudge out toward the kitchen.

"I think it's tar on his hands, Mother," Charles said with a smile. "Soap and water won't take it off."

Charles Winslow, Miles' only child by Martha, looked very

much like all Winslow males—which is to say, he was very hand-some. One year younger than Adam, he was already taller, and his thick shock of reddish-blond hair and bright blue eyes drew attention everywhere he went.

"Maybe you'd better go help him with a little turpentine, Charles," Rachel suggested with a smile.

"Yes, ma'am, I will."

William watched his father, who did not take his eyes off Charles; he shook his head almost imperceptibly, then looked up quickly to see that Rachel had seen and understood. She had talked to him once about his father, and he had never forgotten it. He had been fourteen years old and had made some remark to his aunt about how strict his parents were on Adam.

She had put her hands on his shoulders and looked into his eyes, saying, "William, you are very sensitive. I am going to tell you something about your parents. I want you to remember it and I want you to say nothing to anyone. Do you understand?"

"Yes, I promise," he had said.

"Your father," his aunt had confided, "loved your mother to distraction. He worshiped her, William—maybe too much! And when Adam was born and she died bearing him—why, I hate to say it, for I love your father—but he blamed Adam for her death."

"But that's not fair!" William had protested.

"People are not always *fair*—even good men like your father! But there's more. He was so lonely after your mother died that he made a mistake. He married your stepmother. She is not a woman who can make your father happy, and as soon as she found out that he would never love any woman in this world but your mother, why, she became bitter. I can't exactly blame her—but it has made your father unhappy—and since you and Mercy are both too old to whip, she takes her unhappiness out on poor Adam."

"I know. She beats him all the time, Aunt Rachel."

Rachel had taken his hands then and looked up at him, for he was already taller than she. There was a break in her voice and sorrow in her eyes as she said, "Adam needs your help and your prayers, William. He isn't quick with books as most Wins-

low men have been. He looks much like my mother, Lydia—
your grandmother—and that endears him to me—but not to
Miles, I fear. Help him, William!"

William looked at his aunt, and saw a fierce compassion. He
nodded to her, making a silent promise to do his best for the
boy.

Charles found Adam in the kitchen scrubbing listlessly at
his blackened hands with a sliver of lye soap. "You'll never get
that stuff off with water," he commented. He went to a shelf and
pulled down a brown glass bottle, pulled the cork out, sniffed
it, then said, "Try this turpentine."

"All right." Adam seldom questioned anything that his
younger brother said, and he obediently cupped his hands. He
was not surprised to see the pungent liquid cut into the dark
stains. "That's what it took, Charles," he said. "I wonder I didn't
think of it."

"Where'd you get all that tar on you?"

"On the ship. The sailors let me help them tar the ends of
the ropes. I wish you could have been there. You feeling better?"

"I'm all right. Tell me about the trip." Charles sat down and
listened as Adam, in his slow manner of speaking, told him
about everything. Scrubbing methodically at his hands, he told
about the voyage and the events in Philadelphia. Charles pulled
a stool up close and said nothing, for he had hated to miss the
trip. His mother said that he had a cold, but he was certain that
she just wanted to keep him at home with her.

Adam was slow of speech, but he told a story strangely well
for a boy with a reputation for being mentally slow. Sometimes
he had to search for words, but he made it come alive for
Charles—the pushing, pulling crowds who listened to Whitefield, the smells of unwashed bodies, the crying of the women,
and the solid *clunk* of a head striking the earth as a man fell down
under the spell of the preaching.

"Sounds like fun," Charles smiled. "Tell me some more."
He looked at Adam's hands and said, "That's good enough. Why
didn't you think of turpentine yourself, Adam? You've used it
before."

"Don't know. Just didn't think."

Charles was irritated. "You're so good at some things—and so dumb at others! If Mother had beat me as much as she has you, I'd think of ways to get out of it. That's the difference between you and me, Adam. Why, Mother's thrashed you a dozen times for coming to the table with dirty hands, and here you do it again! I take better care of myself than that!"

Adam looked ashamed and mumbled, "I just got to thinking and forgot, Charles." Then he looked up and said humbly, "You don't ever forget anything, do you? Wish I wasn't so dumb!"

Charles shrugged, saying, "You're smart enough in everything except books—and learning how to watch out for yourself. All you have to do, Adam, is find out what people want and give it to 'em. Then when you get big enough, you can tell 'em to jump in the river! Now, tell me some more about the trip."

The adults had moved to the parlor, and the talk soon turned to business. Saul was saying, "Uncle Miles, you ought to get out of the fur trade. I know your father made a lot of money, but it can't last."

"I'm doing all right," Miles grunted. He stretched his legs out and said, "Rachel, this boy of yours may get rich, but tell him to leave me alone."

Saul shook his head. "You've not looked at it in the right light, Uncle Miles. Sooner or later you're going to go broke— and Mother is your partner."

"Why should we quit the fur trade? They're still buying furs in England, aren't they?"

Saul had a didactic streak in him; he loved to inform people. He leaned against the fireplace and began a lecture on the fur trade. The fur trade was based on beaver, he informed them. By the 1600s fashion had decreed that men should wear large hats of felt, and beaver fur was the best. The skin itself was not used, but the short underfur, the so-called "beaver wool," was stripped from the skin and formed into a hat by the felting process. And by the end of the 1600s New France was exporting about 150,000 skins a year, while New England sent only about 8,000.

"And there's your problem, Uncle Miles," Saul concluded with a wave of his hand. "Beaver and all kinds of fur are getting more scarce all the time."

"Then we'll send our trappers farther west," Miles said.

"Ah, but you won't be able to do that—because France won't permit it. We've just had two wars over that territory in the Ohio River Basin—and mark my words, we're about to have another!"

"I don't believe it," Miles said in a bored tone.

"You'll see! Martha, you'd better talk to your husband. In a few years you'll be broke if he doesn't change his profession."

"I've already talked to him," Martha said, shooting a dour glance at Miles. "We ought to get into the plantation business— tobacco, perhaps."

"We have to have slaves for that," Miles objected.

"What's wrong with that?" Martha shot back. "In Virginia the Hugers, the Lees, the Washingtons—they all have slaves, and I think they're good churchmen, are they not, Pastor?"

"Yes, indeed!" Chauncy nodded. "Leaders in the community."

"Tobacco is a bad thing." William rarely said much about business, but he felt strongly about this one matter. "It just about ruined most people in Jamestown! It's a one-crop system and it makes the ground worthless. If you want to farm, don't go to tobacco. And you don't have to go to Virginia. There's good land right here in our own colony."

They argued about the matter for an hour; then Rachel suddenly got up and stretched her back. "Well, if you want to get out of the fur business, Miles, and go to farming, it's all right with me." She turned a smile on her brother and went to pat his arm fondly. "It's all going to burn anyway, isn't it?"

Miles laughed and hugged her, saying, "Yes! That's what Grandfather would have said. He didn't give a bent pin for anything in this world—had all his treasures in heaven, didn't he, Rachel?"

"But God prospers the righteous, Miles," Martha reminded him sharply. "Being poor is no virtue, is it, Pastor?"

"I shall preach on that very subject next Sunday, Mrs. Winslow!" the rotund preacher said with a smile. "Miles, you be there and take some good spiritual advice—and listen to your nephew. He's a sound man—though he is somewhat lax in his church attendance," he added with mock severity. Then he made his thanks and departed.

Rachel, Saul, and Esther left soon after, but Rachel went off first to find Adam before she left. She said goodbye to him and to Charles, giving them both a gold coin. She kissed them both, then said, "Adam, you come to stay with me soon, you hear? I have lots of things that need fixing, and you're the man to do it! All right?"

After she left, Charles said enviously, "Aunt Rachel sure does think a lot of you. Wish she liked me half as much!"

Adam stared at him in amazement. "Why, she likes you as much as she does me!"

"No, she don't," Charles said regretfully. He looked at the gold coin and added, "You can get more of these out of her, Adam. If you'd just learn to butter her up, why, she'd give you 'bout anything you asked for!"

The idea had never occurred to Adam, and he stared at the coin in his own hand, pondering the thought. Then he shook his head, saying, "No, she doesn't like me more than you."

Charles looked at the dark face of his brother with disgust. "You *are* dumb, Adam! You gotta learn to watch people and when they can do you some good, why you gotta play up to 'em! It's the only way to get what you want, see?"

Three days later, William left to go to his new charge in Amherst, but his departure was marred by a rare scene with his father.

He had packed his clothes and Sampson was loading the trunk into the buggy when he heard his father's voice raised in anger. Descending the stairs, he saw Adam standing in front of the older Winslow, who was holding a heavy crop in his right hand.

Miles was saying, "You have been nothing but a lazy drone with your books, boy, and I'll not have it! There's never been such a thing as a stupid Winslow, but you seem to be just that! Now, you did not do this Latin—why not?"

Adam's answer was slow, and William's heart went out to him. "I—I can't do Latin very well, sir—"

"Nonsense!" William caught a glimpse of his father's face, and he saw it was swollen with rage—something quite unusual.

"You shall learn what it means to work, and I've had enough of your loafing at the forge and in the shop! Do you hear me?"

"Yes, sir."

The very submission of the boy seemed to anger Miles even more, and he grabbed his arm, whirled him around and began to strike him viciously across the back with the crop, breathing heavily with each stroke.

William hurried down the steps and through the front door, his face pale and his lips drawn. He took ten paces across the yard, then his eyes met those of Sampson. The black man did not say a word, but every time the whip fell, his eyes seemed to blink.

William stood there, listening; then suddenly he whirled and dashed into the house and into the parlor. He grabbed his father's wrist and held it in a strong grip, saying, "Sir! That's enough!"

"What's that?"

Miles stared at his eldest son's face, not a foot from his own. He would have been no more shocked if the roof had fallen, for William had never once in all his life challenged his father's authority. But he did so now, and Miles grew suddenly furious. He pulled to free his arm, but it was held in a steely viselike grasp, and he was shocked again.

He knew, of course, that he was getting on in years, and William was a strong young man. But now as he stood there, helpless in the unyielding grip of his son, he knew what it was to grow old—and it angered him even more.

"Sir! You are my son!"

William did not raise his voice, but it carried a steely note, a toughness that Miles had heard in that of the boy's great-grandfather, Gilbert Winslow—a voice he had heard and admired.

"So is *this* your son, Father—and you are beating him as if he were a slave!"

Miles bit his lip, and his own face lost its angry glow. "I— was simply chastising the boy, William."

"You were beating him as if he were a grown man, sir, and I must say, for the first time in my life, I do not admire my father!"

"William. . . !"

Miles' lips suddenly trembled, and he looked down at Adam's face, taking in the pinched lips and the misery in the dark eyes, so unlike his own, and he was ashamed. Those dark eyes suddenly brought back the memory of his mother—Lydia Carbonne, and he bit his lips. She had been a cheery woman, dark with French blood, and beautiful enough to win the heart of his father, Matthew. He thought of her dark beauty and looked down, seeing something of it in the face of this undersized, silent son of his, and he turned away from both his sons, his eyes suddenly blinded by tears.

William at once put his hand on his father's shoulder and said, "Try to remember—he's only a boy. And he's *different*, Father. But he's a good boy!"

Miles stood there for a long moment; then he said without turning, "You were right to stop me, William. I—I will be more thoughtful."

"I'm sure you will," William replied, then added, "you've been a wonderful father, sir, and this affair does not mean that I admire and love you any less."

Miles wheeled and caught at the hand William put out to him. Gripping it strongly, he said, "I *will* do better, William!" Then he turned to look down at Adam, saying, "I was wrong, Adam, very wrong."

Adam turned slowly. He had not flinched when the whip was falling, but he seemed to be hurt by hearing this, and he muttered only, "No, I didn't do the work—I'm sorry to be so stupid."

William nodded at his father over Adam's head, approval in his eyes. He smiled and said, "You two must learn to pull together!"

"We will try, won't we, son?" Miles said, tentatively putting his hand on Adam's shoulder. "We'll try!"

Adam said nothing, but there was a light in his dark eyes as he turned to look at the hand on his shoulder.

William said quickly, "Well, I must go!" He wheeled and made his way out, but turning at the door, he took one more look at the pair, the tall man with his hand on the small boy's shoulder, and he smiled as he left.

Sampson was waiting at the buggy, holding the reins, and there was a strange expression in his face. He did something he'd never done in all his life—he put out his huge black hand, and William took it without thinking. Then the black face broke into a smile, and he said, "I thank you, Mist' William!"

"For what, Sampson?" William asked in astonishment.

The black man nodded, gave a powerful squeeze to the other's hand, then said, "Jes' fo' being whut you is!"

As William rode away, he wondered at the scene, for it seemed little short of miraculous to him that his father could change so abruptly—but he had prayed much and, being a simple man of faith, he said fervently, "Thank you, Lord—and let Father know the joy of making a man out of Adam!"

CHAPTER THREE

DISGRACED!

★ ★ ★ ★

Miles was indulging himself in feeding his flock of black banty chickens on a crisp September morning. He had purchased the original pair at the dock from a dark-skinned woman arriving on a schooner, and since she spoke no English, he had no idea of the origin of the birds. Their shiny ebony color had caught his eye, and he had been pleased to find that they bred well and that their flesh was far more tender and delicious than the tough speckled variety he used for his table meat.

"Chick—chick—chick," he called, and as he tossed a handful of grain to the ground, the small, noisy birds came running to him. As they pecked at the grain, he counted them, and was delighted to see that there were still eighteen hens and six jaunty roosters with brilliant red combs. He nodded to himself, deciding that it would not be too risky to have one of the plump roosters for supper. He knew of six nests containing the tiny greenish eggs, and if a skunk or a blood-thirsty weasel did not get loose, and if no other natural disaster occurred, it seemed as though God would prosper the flock so that he could not only have enough of the succulent dish for his own table but develop the species for sale as well.

"Black Winslows!" he said with a smile. "Now that would

be something—to have this breed all over the country with the Winslow name!" He tossed another handful of grain and glanced across the yard. A steady thumping sound had started, and he saw Adam driving dust from a multi-colored carpet hanging on a line. "Be careful with that thing, Adam," he called out. "You know your mother treasures that carpet more than her assurance of heaven!"

Adam looked up, smiled and called out, "Yes, sir. I'll be careful."

We're doing a little better, thank God! Miles thought with some satisfaction. Ever since William had spoken so strongly to him, he had been very careful with the boy. He had noticed for the first time that though Adam was slow with books, he was a worker, never stopping until the job was done. Miles had been forced to take note also that Charles, for all his intelligence, was the opposite; he gave short attention to his chores, half-doing them and avoiding them as much as possible. This discovery had precipitated a family quarrel, for when he had caned Charles for neglecting his work, Martha had interfered with a burst of anger more fierce than he had ever seen in her. An armed truce was now in force that made meals most unpleasant, and Miles was forced to notice how merciless and strict his wife was with Adam.

As he threw the last of the corn to the chickens, a horseman galloped down the road and, seeing him, pulled his small roan up and dismounted. "Sampson!" Miles called out to his slave as he went to meet the visitor, "Tell Clara I'll have one of these Black Winslows for supper."

"Black Winslows?" the tall black man asked, scratching his head. "Wat in de world is dat, Mist' Winslow?"

"Black Winslow—that's what I'm naming these chickens."

Sampson suddenly laughed and nodded, "Yessuh—I tell her—but I thought *I* was de onliest black Winslow round dis' place!" The thought tickled him, and he went off chuckling at his wit.

"Hello, Henry. Come in and we'll have some tea."

"Can't do it, Miles." The man who stepped forward to take Winslow's hand was very short, but wide as a church door. He had a round red face and when he took off his hat to wipe his brow, he exposed a vast expanse of skull, having only a thin fringe of reddish hair around his ears. "You see this article 'bout George Whitefield in the *Boston Newsletter*?"

"No—but I can guess what it says." Taking the paper from Henry Whaley, his closest neighbor, Miles read the item:

> Last Thursday Evening the Rev'd Whitefield arrived from Rhode Island, being met on the Road and conducted to Town by several Gentlemen. The next day in the Forenoon he attended prayers in the King's Chapel, and in the afternoon preach'd to a vast Congregation in the Rev'd Dr. Coleman's Meeting House. So great and unruly was the crowd that what should have been a prayerful congregation was in fact a turbulent mob. When Rev'd Whitefield was advised that five persons had killed themselves in illadvised leaps from the gallery, he decided the Commons might be safer, and there he spoke to a multitude numbering twenty thousand.

Miles shoved the paper back at Whaley in disgust. "I can't believe people will go out after such things!" He lifted his voice and called out, "Adam, that's enough! You're going to put a hole in that thing. You can go down to Farmer's and pick up those hinges for me."

Adam tossed the beater down and ran out of the yard, leaving the two men talking. Ned Farmer's blacksmith shop was a mile and a half away, on the road toward town, but it was his favorite spot in all the world, so he sped away before his father had second thoughts. His sturdy legs pumped steadily and he stopped only once to get a drink from a cold spring that bubbled out of the ground. As he bent over, his coal-black hair fell over his eyes, and he tossed it back with a sudden motion of his head. He hated his black hair and dark skin, and had cut his hair clean to the skull when he was only five. The fair hair and the skin of the rest of his family made his own dark color stand out so that he felt like an outsider.

Ned Farmer was pumping the handle of the bellows as Adam entered the low building that housed the forge. He was a squat man with huge arms and a pair of soft brown eyes peering out of a square, brown face. "Ah, now, here's me helper!"

he grinned. "Give us a hand, will you now, Adam?"

With a quick nod, Adam took the handle, and with practiced, even strokes forced air onto the coals till they glowed yellow, then red, and finally when they were almost white, Farmer took a pair of tongs, plucked a long glowing strip of metal, and carrying it to the anvil began to hammer it with mighty strokes that sent a shower of sparks across the shop.

Adam left the bellows, and getting so close that some of the hot sparks landed in his hair, he watched intently as the blacksmith flattened out the glowing iron. Then he took it up with the tongs and plunged it into a barrel of water, making a sizzling sound and causing steam to rise.

"Well, now, I'd guess your father wants them hinges, don't he?"

"Yes, that's what he sent me for—but can I do some work first, Mr. Farmer?"

"Well, just a bit, maybe. Get them tongs and fish one of them small strips—but let me soften them a bit." As Farmer pumped the bellows he watched the face of Adam Winslow with affection. He'd never seen a lad so anxious to work with iron! Since his father had brought him to the forge as a very young lad, he'd spent every free moment with the blacksmith, and now the boy knew more about metal craft than most men. Farmer's own son had shown no interest in the trade, and now he thought, *Too bad he's not my boy—I'd make a fine smith out of him! He's got the knack.*

Without being told, Adam drew a strip of white-hot metal from the coals, picked up Farmer's smallest hammer and began to beat it with even strokes. The hammer was too big for him, but the smith noted that he held the piece firmly and the hammer fell evenly—not too hard, not too easy—on the metal, and when the piece hardened, Farmer picked it up with the tongs and said, "That's a good job."

Adam's face flushed with pleasure, and Farmer wondered that the son of a wealthy merchant could be so pleased with the praise of a humble workman like himself. He had no idea how little of that sort of thing the boy got at home.

Adam stayed as long as he dared, helping the blacksmith,

and if Miles had heard how freely he talked, he would have been amazed, for at home the boy was taciturn. When Farmer mentioned going to hear the preacher Whitefield, Adam related his experience in Philadelphia, and the large man took it all in. Finally he said, "I never heered nothing like it, Adam! Never! To tell the truth, I allus believed I was a fair sort of man. Good to my family, honest with people." He ran his hand over his face, and shaking his head, he grinned and said, "Well, Mister Whitefield knocked all *that* outta me! Just a no-good sinner, that's what I am—or was!"

Adam stared at him. "What did you do, Mr. Farmer?"

The blacksmith looked embarrassed and bit his heavy underlip before he answered. "Well, I don't rightly know, boy, but when that man told me to repent and throw myself on God's mercy, I done it!" He looked up with wonder in simple dark eyes and said, "I tell you, I called out, and it was like I got hit right between the eyes with a sixteen-pound sledge!"

"You fell down?"

"Right enough, I did!" Farmer shook his head slowly, and then he added, "I been in church all me life, man and boy, but I tell you when I called on God, it was the *first* time I ever really had any notion that He was *real*—and I ain't been the same since!"

Adam was taking it all in with wide open eyes, and he said, "Mr. Farmer, when I saw all those people falling down in Philadelphia—I thought it was put on. But if you say it's real, then I guess it is."

The muscular hand of the smith fell on Adam's shoulder, and tears appeared in his eyes. "It is real, boy! I don't rightly understand it, but since that time, it's been like Jesus Christ hisself has been right beside me—just as real to me as you are!"

Ned Farmer was not an emotional man, Adam knew, and he saw that he was embarrassed by his own display, so Adam smiled and said quickly, "I'm glad for you, Mr. Farmer."

"Well, here's the hinges, Adam."

The boy took them; then his eyes fell on a pipe sticking up out of a barrel of junk. "What's that, Mr. Farmer?"

"That? Oh, Squire Mason had me make him some of them—

got something to do with a new-fangled way of farming—I dunno' what."

Adam went to the barrel and pulled out the pipe, which was about thirty inches long and nearly two inches in diameter. He stared at it, his brow wrinkled in thought, and then said, "Could you put an end on this, Mr. Farmer—and put a hole in it?"

Farmer laughed out loud, then asked, "What in the world you got in that brain of yours, Adam? You going to be an inventor like that Mr. Franklin?"

Adam said evasively, "Oh, just an idea."

Ned Farmer was somewhat of a tinker and an inventor himself, so he chuckled and took the pipe from Adam. "Let's see, seal up the end? Why, that's no trouble—I'll show you." He made an end for the pipe, and showed the boy how to attach it, then asked, "A hole in it?"

"Yes, right there—just a little hole."

In no time, the job was done, and Farmer cooled it in the barrel, then handed it over, saying, "Can you carry this thing and the hinges, Adam?"

"Oh, sure—and thanks a lot, Mr. Farmer."

"Let me have a look at the great invention when it's all done, boy, and don't forget your poor old friends when it makes you rich and famous!" he called out as Adam sailed out the door and headed for home. He shook his head as he went back to his work. *Sure will be the ruination of a good blacksmith to make a scholar out of that one!*

"What's that thing?"

Charles had come into the small building used as a combination shop and storage house to find Adam busily working at something on the work table. There was an injured look in Charles's eye, and for some reason he blamed his brother for the thrashing he'd gotten from his father. Adam glanced at him, then shrugged, "Oh, just an idea I had."

Charles peered at the iron tube that Adam had wedged fast into the top of the workbench. "You're always wasting your time making stuff," he grunted. "What's this supposed to be?"

Adam shifted his feet, reluctant to speak, but when he saw

that Charles was not going to leave, he said, "Well, it's a cannon."

"A what?"

"A cannon." Adam's dark eyes glowed, and he began to explain the mechanism to Charles. "Look, a musket is nothing but a tube with one end plugged up. Well, I saw this piece of pipe at the blacksmith shop, and Mr. Farmer let me have it."

Charles gave a disdainful sniff. "You can't make a cannon!" Although he surpassed his older brother in many ways, he had no head for mechanical things, and it irritated him to be outdone. "That things's just an old piece of pipe, and you're making believe like you always do."

Adam shook his head stubbornly, insisting, "Well, it ain't a *real* cannon, but it'll shoot. Look, when they shot the cannons off over at the fort, I watched 'em. All they do is put some black gunpowder down inside; then they put the cannon ball on top of that."

Charles tried not to be impressed with Adam's knowledge. "Oh, sure, but how do they make it go *off*?"

Adam smiled, and said, "I watched them and they stuck a flame down in a hole in the back—and there's the hole we put in this cannon, me and Mr. Farmer." He pointed to the small hole in the rear of the pipe, and his eyes lit up. He grinned and said, "This cannon would make the biggest noise you ever heard, Charles!"

"Well—" Charles tried to find something nasty to say, and finally blurted out, "You don't know that! It's just an ol' piece of pipe!"

"Is not!"

"Well, if you're so smart with your dumb old pipe, why don'cha shoot it off then?"

" 'Cause I don't have no gunpowder," Adam shot back. "If I just had some black powder, you'd see something!"

Charles suddenly grinned "I'll get you plenty of powder," he yelled. "I know where Father keeps it—and I'll get some of his musket balls, too!"

Adam was shocked. "You better not! You know he told us not to fool with his guns and stuff!"

"How's he going to know?" Charles shrugged. He was still angry with Adam, and he turned, saying "I'll get the powder then you'll see your old pipe is nothing at all!"

Adam was afraid, and he hoped that Charles would change his mind—but he knew his brother too well for that. In five minutes Charles came out of the house carrying something in his hands. He entered the shop, dumped a powderhorn and a leather pouch containing musket balls on the table.

"There, Big Mouth!" he grinned. "Now, let's see your big ol' cannon do something!"

Adam shook his head, looking down at the powder and balls. "I can't use these, Charles. Father would—"

Charles snorted and struck Adam on the shoulder. "You're not only *dumb*, you're a *fake*, too! All this stuff about inventin' things—you can't really do any of it!"

Adam's dark eyes suddenly lit with a rare flash of anger, and he snapped, "You're a liar."

"Well, prove it!"

"I will!"

Adam grabbed the pipe and began strapping it to a section of round wood about six inches thick and two feet long. As he tightened the leather thongs, Charles asked, "What's that?"

"You don't think I'm gonna *hold* this cannon and shoot it, do you? I gotta have a gun carriage."

He finished lashing the pipe down, then picked up the unit with a grunt. "Bring the powder and balls," he commanded.

Charles obeyed, and followed him out the door. Adam struggled as far as the tree line that was beside the house, a hundred-yard strip of oak and poplar separating the pasture from the house. "We gotta get away from the house," he grunted. "It's going to make a big noise!"

"What you gonna shoot at?" Charles asked. He forgot his irritation and began to enter into the spirit of the adventure. "Let's have a target." He looked around, and spotted a large section of the light gray canvas covering up some equipment next to the carriage house. "I'll get us something."

He ran to get the piece, and by the time he got back, Adam had dug a trench in the loamy soil with a stick and had planted the log which served as a mount for the "cannon." "Stretch it across those saplings, Charles," he called out, his face intent. "No, farther back than that!"

Charles retreated into the stand of trees and put the canvas across several small saplings, then came back. "Let's load 'er up, Adam!" he urged.

"Sure! Look, I'll tilt it back and you pour powder in." He took the pipe in both hands and lifted the end into the air. Charles took the powder horn and dumped the entire contents down the pipe. "Wait a minute—that's too much!"

Charles grinned at him. "Thought this was a *real* cannon, Adam!" He took the leather sack and emptied the contents down the tube and said, "That ought to do it."

Adam said with a worried look, "That's a lot of powder, Charles!"

"You scared to shoot it?" Charles jibed. "Then *I'll* do it!"

They argued about who was going to touch it off, all the while maneuvering the piece to aim at the canvas target. Finally, they were satisfied, and then Charles said with a sudden blank look, "How are we gonna shoot it? You have to have fire."

"Sure, you do," acknowledged Adam. "I'll go get a spark from the kitchen stove." He darted across the yard, scattering the black chickens as he ran. There was always fire in the kitchen stove, and he went into the wood room and brought out a large pine splinter. Raking the coals back, he stuck the splinter into the stove and it burst into flame almost at once.

He left the house and made his way across the yard, shielding the flame with his free hand. When he got back to the trees, he looked down at the cannon, and suddenly he said, "We better not do this, Charles."

"You scared?" Charles taunted.

"Well, a little bit. You put so much powder in, it could just blow up and kill us—and besides, if Father finds out we've used his powder, why, *he'll* kill us!"

Charles snorted, "You trying to back out, Adam?"

Adam moved behind the cannon. "All right! One of us will need to put his foot on top to keep it from kicking up, and one of us has to shove this fire down the hole."

"I—I'll—put my foot on it," Charles decided, but his face was a little pale. He gingerly put his foot on top of the pipe and looked at Adam. "Well, go on—do it!"

Adam didn't want to do it—yet at the same time, he did. He almost threw the splinter down and stamped it out, but the pale sneer on Charles's face told him that he'd never hear the last of it. Carefully he moved to one side, knelt, and held the tiny flame over the hole. Then with a sudden burst of desperation, he thrust the splinter into the hole.

There was a short sizzling sound; then the cannon bucked wildly, skipping out from under Charles's foot! The explosion deafened both of them temporarily, and they fell backwards with their eyes shut tightly.

A stillness followed, and Adam rolled to his feet, followed by Charles, and he yelled, "Look at the target!"

The canvas had been blown almost off the saplings, but they could see at once that it was riddled by dozens of holes.

"What a cannon!" Charles yelled back, and the two of them started running toward the tattered canvas. Picking it up, they looked at the holes, counting them. "Boy, we sure got us a good cannon here!" Charles cried excitedly.

Adam started to reply, but suddenly there was a cry from the house. Both boys wheeled around, and they saw their parents running out of the back door, closely followed by Sampson and the household servants.

Charles gasped. "We hit the house! Come on, Adam! We gotta get away from here!"

Charles took off running into the woods, but Adam stood fixed to the spot. It never occurred to him to run, and with his heart beating in his chest for fear, he stepped out of the woods and made his way toward the house.

The musket balls had plowed through the canvas, a few of them had lodged in the trees on the edge of the tree line, but most of them had swept the yard.

As Adam slowly walked across the yard, he saw his father standing in the midst of a dozen dead black chickens. A few others were flopping all over the yard uttering plaintive clucks.

Adam could not bear the look of sorrow and anger on his

father's face, and lifted his eyes to the house, where he saw that one of the expensive glass windows, which had been shipped all the way from England, was shattered, and there were round holes all along the sides of the house.

Then he saw his stepmother standing beside the rug she'd inherited from her grandmother. She stood there staring in disbelief and shock at the holes that let the sunshine through in tiny bars.

Adam heard his father's voice calling his name in anger, and the fear in him was so strong it robbed him of his strength. He stood there with his face down, pale as a ghost, and he knew that his father was standing over him, yelling.

He looked up once and saw his father's face twisted into an ugly mask; not being able to look at him, he shifted his gaze away. He saw his stepmother, her lips like a knife, take one look at the rug, then stoop to pick up something. She straightened up, strode over to his father, and raised her arm, revealing the carpet beater in her hand. It was a heavy piece of rawhide, blunt and dry, with sharp edges where it had aged.

Martha Winslow drew her arm back, and Adam saw his father's head twist, heard him cry out, but it was too late. She was a big woman, strong and quick. The beater whistled through the air; then he felt something like fire and ice together. For a second, it did not hurt, but then the agony tore through him. His hand leaped to his face, and he felt the raw flesh on his cheek and neck.

"Martha! No!" Miles cried out in shock. He ripped the beater from her hand and threw it as far as he could. Then he knelt beside the boy and said with a trembling voice, "Let me see, Adam."

He lifted Adam's hands away, and then he stopped breathing—as though he'd been kicked in the stomach by a mule. He rose and cried, "Sampson, get the buggy hitched—quick!"

"Yessuh!"

Adam knew that he was badly hurt, but he did not cry. In a few minutes he heard his father say, "You drive, Sampson—I'll hold him. Whip them up—to Dr. Stone's!"

Then he heard his stepmother's voice, but Miles snapped

coldly, "Get your hands off this buggy! Whip them up, Sampson!" The servant obeyed and the buggy leaped forward.

Adam remembered one thing about that wild ride, and it was not the pain in his face. It was the first—and last—time in his life that his father ever held him in his arms!

A month later Miles took Adam aside and told him he'd be leaving. They were in the parlor, and Miles saw that the stitches had done fairly well, but Dr. Stone had said, "He'll always have a scar, Mr. Winslow." His manner had been harsh, for he was sure, Miles realized, that *he* had struck the boy.

Now looking down, he saw that the puckered marks of the scar, which ran along the boy's lower cheek on the jawbone and continued across the neck, would always be a symbol of his own failure.

Martha and he had been farther apart than ever, and he had seen that it would be impossible to have Adam at home. Martha hated him and would make life unbearable.

"Adam, I've decided to send you away."

Adam looked up quickly, despair in his eyes, but he said nothing. He had said practically nothing for a month. When Charles's part in the business had come out, he'd said, "It wasn't his fault. If I hadn't made the cannon, it wouldn't have happened."

"I know things have been hard for you, but I think you'll like your headmaster." He waited for Adam to ask who it would be. When there was no response, he said, "It'll be William."

Adam's head shot up and some of the bleak despair left his face. "I'm going to live with William?"

"I thought you'd like that," Miles grinned. Then he sobered, "You'll study with him—and you'll study Latin with Mr. Jonathan Edwards—in return for which you'll chop his wood."

"I'm to stay there always?"

Miles put his hands on the sturdy shoulders, and his voice was gentle as he tried to explain, "There's no happiness for you in this house." *For any of us!* he nearly added, but did not. "William has a nice house and a housekeeper. He tells me there's a workshop and a good blacksmith who likes boys. I—I haven't been as good a father as I should, Adam." He paused and with an effort went on. "You are not a bookish boy—but you have a genius. Despite all the bad things about the cannon—you *made* it—and I'm very proud to have a son who is gifted in that way!"

Squeezing the boy's shoulders lightly, he spoke softly, "I'll take you tomorrow. Say goodbye to Charles—and to your mother."

Adam saw his father had trouble saying all this, and he whispered, "I—I'll miss you, Father!"

After the boy left, Miles cursed himself. *Why didn't I hold him when I said goodbye? Why didn't I?*

CHAPTER FOUR

A LITTLE LATIN

★ ★ ★ ★

"Well, Adam, it's time for your first Latin lesson with Rev. Edwards."

Adam's first two weeks with William at Amherst had gone quickly. Although he had missed his sister, Mercy, he had adjusted to his new life far better than his brother had expected. But as the two sat at the breakfast table eating the fried ham and scrambled eggs that the housekeeper, Mrs. Little, had set before them, a cloud fell across the boy's face.

"Do I *have* to, William? Can't you teach me?"

"No, I can't. In the first place, Rev. Edwards is the best Latin scholar in the country, and in the second place the arrangement is already made for you to chop his wood in exchange for his teaching. But I've got a surprise for you that ought to make the whole thing much easier. You eat all that breakfast, and you can have it."

William watched Adam surreptitiously, wondering not for the first time if they had done the right thing by the boy. He had been shocked and angered when Miles had brought Adam to him a month earlier, the scars on his face and neck red and not fully healed. It had been hard for his father to put his feelings into words, but William had seen the resentment in his stepmother years earlier, and when Miles had pleaded with him to take the boy, he had agreed at once.

And it had worked well—indeed, he had never seen Adam so cheerful. The scar on his face was still red and angry, but there was a peace in the boy's face that had been missing.

"We're going to be two old bachelors, Adam," William had told the boy after Miles had driven away. "We've got this big old house, and you've got a room all your own. We have Mrs. Little to cook for us and clean up after us. Mr. Little, her husband, is a fine blacksmith—even makes rifles—and he'll be glad to have you help him. We'll get a dog and hunt a bit. We'll also catch some fish out of the stream down the road. Why, it's going to be fun!"

Well, it's been good for the boy, William thought as Adam finished his breakfast. *He was wound tight as a spring when he got here—but he's lost a lot of that. I think being around Edwards and his children will do more for him than anything else—maybe help get that defensive set out of his back!*

"I'm all finished," Adam said.

"Right! Now, let's get to that surprise!"

He put on his coat and led Adam outside to the barn. Opening the door, he commanded, "Now, close your eyes and don't open them until I tell you!"

He threw the door open, went inside and drove out his own horse and the small reddish mare he'd bought from Samuel Sinclair. Then he stepped outside, saying, "All right, you can look now."

Adam opened his eyes, and when he saw the horse, he looked wildly at his brother and whispered, "That's—that's not for *me*, is it, William?"

"Well, I can't ride *two* horses, can I? It's yours, Adam—and happy birthday. Remember your last birthday in Philadelphia?"

Adam nodded and reached his hand out, and the red mare came slowly toward him, then licked his palm. Adam did not look at his brother, and there was a break in his voice as he said, "Thank you, William!"

"Man ought to have his own horse, Adam." William knew how to please a boy, and soon the two of them were saddled and riding down the road headed for Northampton. It gave the man a great deal of pleasure to watch his younger brother as they tried out all the mare's gaits along the way.

It was only an hour's ride to Edwards' parish, a busy village with six hundred parishioners living in the area around the church, a fine frame building with a high turreted roof. Going past it, William led the way to a simple foursquare house bounded by a slab fence. Most of the houses in the village were unpainted, but the minister's was a chaste white with red trim and jaunty green shutters.

The pair dismounted, tied their horses to a post, and as they walked onto the porch, the door opened and a man stepped outside. "Well, William, you're here early."

"Your newest scholar can't wait to get started, Reverend. This is my younger brother, Adam. Adam, this is Rev. Jonathan Edwards, your new Latin teacher."

"Good morning, young man!" Edwards stepped forward and put his hand out, gripping Adam's hand firmly. "You are *most* welcome!" His piercing eyes took in the boy; then he laughed and said, "I suspect you'll not mind that monstrous woodpile out back so much as conjugating Latin verbs!"

"He's a hard worker, sir," William stated. "But if your Latin lessons are as hard for Adam as your theology lessons are for *me*—why, I pity him! I couldn't make head nor tail of this book you gave me!"

Edwards laughed and said, "Well, well, we have time this morning to spend on that old demon of Antinomianism! Let me introduce Master Adam to his woodpile and you to the writings of Mr. Sewell."

He stepped off the porch and led them around the house, pausing to wave a thin hand at a pile of logs strewn over the ground. A set of cross trestles for holding them, several rusty saws scattered on the ground, and a variety of wedges and mauls completed the picture. "There's your wood—and I trust you will take better care of the equipment than *I* do," Edwards remarked. "Suppose you spend the morning on this while I read with your brother. Then this afternoon, I'll see what sort of scholar you are."

The two men left, and Adam picked up the saw and felt the teeth. Finding it to be dull, he walked over to the small shed a few feet away from the house. Tools were strewn everywhere in a careless fashion, and he spent an hour sharpening the saw with a rusty file. He did the same for an ax and for the two splitting mauls. Then he spent the rest of the morning cutting the logs into short sections.

Adam liked to cut wood. It gave him pleasure to run a sharp saw across the log and feel it bite down; soon he had cut a stack of two-foot-long logs. Splitting was even more enjoyable. The air was cool, and the beech he split divided as splinterless as a cloven rock. He had the gift of letting his mind go as he worked, his hands and body operating with machine-like precision while he thought of pleasant things—mostly that day of his new horse and what fine things they were going to do.

The hours sped by, but he had no sense of the passage of time, and it startled him when he heard a voice say, "Oh, my word! Look at the wood that young man has cut!"

He turned quickly to see Rev. Edwards and William standing there watching. They had been watching for some time, Edwards fascinated by the easy way Adam split the wood. He was an indifferent woodsplitter himself, and it was a mystery to him how the boy never seemed to strain, but the ax always fell exactly where he wanted it to.

"I told you he was a worker," William smiled. "And if you have anything broken, he's likely to be able to fix it for you—a real gift with his hands, sir."

"Plenty of that around here, William," Edwards sighed. "I'm not very good in that way. Well, let's wash up, Adam. Mrs. Edwards has fixed us a nice lunch."

A small porch was attached to the rear of the house, where they washed their hands before going through the oak door into the long room that served as a kitchen. "They're waiting for us. I fear we're a little late." Edwards led the pair into a low-ceilinged room with a large window on the long outside wall letting a stream of golden light fall on the white tablecloth that graced the rectangular table.

"I'm sorry to be late, my dear," Edwards said at once. He

walked to a place at the end of the table and introduced Adam. "This is my newest scholar, Mr. Adam Winslow."

William pushed Adam into a chair to his right and the boy gazed in amazement at what appeared to be a sea of girls! Actually, there were only six, including the beautiful woman sitting to Edwards' right, but every eye was fixed on him, and he ducked his head and felt his face burn. He knew that made the fresh scar stand out starkly, making the situation worse.

"You are very welcome, Adam," the lady greeted quickly, seeing the boy's embarrassment. "But you'll have to pardon our daughters for staring. Girls, tell our guest your names and how old you are."

"I'm Sarah—age twelve," the largest girl said at once.

"And I'm Jerusha—ten."

"Esther—nine years old."

"Mary. I'm six years old—how did you get that scar on your face?"

"Mary!" her mother reprimanded sharply, "I've told you not to ask questions. You may leave the table!"

Adam's hand reached up and covered the scar with an instinctive motion, and a quick anger shot through him. But when he saw tears form in Mary's eyes as she slipped to the floor, he said impulsively, "Oh, don't make her go, please! I—had an accident, but it's better now."

"Very handsome of you, sir!" Edwards interposed quickly. "You'll soon discover that Mary is somewhat impulsive, Adam! Now that's Lucy, age three and here you see young Timothy, age two—the only boy among this troop of females!"

"He'll be spoiled by all these older sisters, Rev. Edwards," William said.

"No doubt! I was the only boy in my family. Had *ten* sisters and they all spoiled me." Then without a pause Edwards suddenly offered up a blessing over the food, and they began at once to eat.

"I can tell you, Mr. Winslow," Sarah Edwards stated as she passed the fresh hot bread, "those sisters of his did spoil him. He's not gotten completely over it to this day!"

"My sisters were all tall, and Father used to say he had sixty feet of daughters!" Edwards remarked, then turned to listen to what Jerusha had to tell him.

It was a strange meal for Adam, for while the children never interrupted the adults, they were encouraged to take part in the conversation. He picked at his food, and once when Edwards made a little joke, with the last line in Latin, even Mary laughed! It made him feel stupid, and he wished he could go back and split more wood.

After the meal, however, Edwards asked, "Now, sir, would you go with me to my study? We'll see if your brain is as strong as those sturdy arms of yours!"

Adam gave a despairing look at William, who threw him an encouraging smile, and followed the minister out of the dining room into a small study down a narrow hall. The walls were lined with books, and the single large desk that took up most of the room was piled high with neatly organized papers.

"Sit there, Adam, and read me a little of this."

Adam took the book gingerly and opened it. His heart sank when he saw that it was a book he'd never seen, and for one moment his mind went completely blank—he could not have read one word of it if it meant to save his soul.

Edwards' penetrating eyes searched the boy's face, and he said quickly, "You know, before we start, I have a book here that I have not read myself, but it's just the sort of thing a handy young fellow like you would probably like. Let me get it." Standing to his feet, he reached up and pulled down a plainly bound reddish book, opened it then shook his head. "I never can quite grasp how these things work, Adam. Perhaps you can give me a clue."

He put the book down in front of the boy, and Adam saw on the opened page a very fine mechanical drawing of a pistol. He picked it up eagerly, never dreaming that William had told Edwards of his interest in such things, and said excitedly, "Oh, this is a good drawing, sir! Look, this is the frizzen, and this part here is the pan. . . !" He kept his eyes glued on the book, his finger tracing the lines, while Edwards' kind, luminous eyes watched carefully.

"So that's the way it works, Reverend," he finished at last.

"My, you're so quick at that sort of thing! And you've made even a poor mechanical mind such as mine understand it! Well, let me show you how this page of Latin can be almost as easy for you as that drawing."

Then with easy patience, Edwards drew the boy's attention back to the book, and soon Adam found that he *did* remember some of it, and by the end of an hour, he was doing better than he had dreamed. He did not understand how much that was due to the skill of the tall man in front of him, who said at last, "Why, you did very well, Adam! Very well, indeed!" He got up, and smiled, leading Adam to the door. "You need a great deal of work—but then I've got a great deal of wood, so by the time the woodpile is gone, you'll be reading Tacitus like a scholar!"

"I—I never thought I'd—" Adam broke off and the minister finished his sentence.

"You never thought you'd like Latin? Well, you'll find a great deal to like in this world, my boy. It's a great world the Lord has made for us to study, and I can see you're not going to let much get by you!"

When they stepped back into the main part of the house, they were met by a conspiracy. Mrs. Edwards put her hand on Adam's shoulder as she spoke to her husband. "No more wood-cutting today! The girls have to have a ride on Adam's new mare." Then she put her arm around the startled boy, who had never been hugged by anyone except Rachel and Mercy, and she said warmly, "Happy birthday, Adam!"

"Birthday, is it?" Edwards smiled. "I didn't know that! How old are you?"

"Fourteen, sir."

"Well, many happy returns—but you are trapped, sir, trapped! No escaping these women—so go give them a ride. The wood can wait for another time."

Adam went outside, and William asked, "How did he do?"

"Oh, very well for a beginning—but his heart is in science."

"Yes, and Father could never understand that. I appreciate your interest in the boy." He hesitated, then taking a plunge, told Edwards the problems Adam had at home.

Edwards frowned, then remarked, "Usually, it's best for a

boy to be at home, but this is an exception. He will be better off here."

Outside, the object of their conversation was besieged, every young Edwards claiming the right to ride the mare first. Finally Mary said, "Me first, Adam! You stood up for me at dinner, so you have to let me ride first!"

Adam stared at her bewildered, but he was to learn very quickly that Mary Edwards had a gift with words, and that she was quite likely to get her way even if her logic was sometimes a little fuzzy.

He lifted her on, swung up behind her, and the mare moved obediently down the road. "What's his name?" Mary asked.

Adam laughed suddenly. "It's not a he—and she doesn't have a name. I just got her this morning."

Mary turned around and stared at him in astonishment. "You've got to give this poor horse a name, Adam."

"There's no hurry."

"Yes, there is! And I'm going to help you—I can think of lots of names!"

"I don't need help to name my own horse!"

"Yes, I can think of better names than you can," she cried out, and then she began kicking her heels against the mare's sides, calling out, "Faster! Faster!" She was not satisfied until they galloped at a fast clip down the road.

All afternoon he took the Edwards' children on short rides, and in doing so he learned their names—and he found out that they were all very intelligent. But it was a fine time for him as well as for them, and when William came up and said, "Time to go home, Adam," he was surprised at how quickly the afternoon had gone.

The Edwardses lined up to bid them goodbye, and Mary scurried over to Adam and threw her arms around his neck, pulling him down to whisper in his ear.

"Her name is Abishag!" she said fiercely. Then she kissed his cheek and murmured, "I'm sorry you got hurt."

They left, and the arrangement was made that Adam would ride over three times a week for his lesson and to chop wood.

"How'd you like the family?" William asked on the way home.

"All right."

William was accustomed to his brother's taciturn ways, but he saw the glow on Adam's face. "You'll have to think of a name for your mare," he remarked carelessly.

They said nothing until they were almost home, and then as they slipped to the ground, Adam reached up and stroked the mare's velvety nose.

"Her name is Abishag!"

William's eyes blinked in surprise, and then he smiled and went over to pat the mare's neck. "Well, one thing about a name like that—you won't find any other horses with that title!"

CHAPTER FIVE

A FAMILY AFFAIR

★ ★ ★ ★

"Adam, how long will it take you to get ready to go to Boston?"

"Boston?" Adam was sighting down the barrel of a long rifle, carefully bringing the tiny silver bead into the lowest spot of the rear notch until it was aimed on the eye of one of Little's fine cows, a quarter of a mile away. He snapped the trigger, grunted with satisfaction, then glanced over at William, who had come into the blacksmith shop late in the afternoon. "You're all excited about something," he remarked, taking in his brother's flushed face and bright eyes.

"I've got a letter from Father." He extracted a rumpled sheet from his pocket, smoothed it out and read: *I've agreed on a price with Hunter. Bring Adam to Boston with you and the papers will be ready. You can have your own way, I suppose, about Oxford.*

Adam wrapped the rifle in a piece of soft leather, then turned to face William. There was something slow and methodical in his movements, and though he lacked three inches of his brother's height, there was a thickness and breadth in his torso that William lacked. His chest swelled against the homespun shirt, deep and very broad, and there was a suggestion of power in every move he made. His thighs were heavy and his thick wrists and forearms swelled the sleeves of his shirt—the product of three years at the forge swinging a ten-pound hammer.

"What's this all about, William?" His voice was quiet, his words slow and even. "I don't want to leave right now—need to work on this breech mechanism some more."

"Oh, you'd never be ready to leave this smoky forge!" William gave a half laugh, then sobered, saying, "Two things, Adam. First of all, Father's going to buy the Hunter place, and I suspect he wants you to have a hand working it."

"I'd rather be a blacksmith, William—and I don't know all that much about farming."

"You can learn, can't you? And I've been wanting to go to Oxford to do some study for years. So now Father's agreed to finance me for a year. Come on, Adam, let's get ready so we can leave early in the morning. I'm packing all the things I'll need at Oxford, and that'll include a trunk of books."

He turned and Adam followed him out, but there was a stubborn look on his square face. As they mounted up and started for the house, he thought about the letter, but he said nothing until late that night after William's things were packed.

When everything was ready, he stated, "I'll go with you to Boston, but I don't like the idea of working on that farm."

William considered Adam's sturdy form, and after a moment replied, "It could be a good thing for you."

"I don't want to be a farmer, William. I want to be a blacksmith."

William stared at him, then smiled. "You've changed a great deal in the last three years, Adam. You've done well studying with Mr. Edwards, and Little says you've got the best hands of any man he ever saw for work at the forge—and I guess you've become a pretty stubborn young man as well."

Adam shifted uncomfortably. "I don't want to be quarrelsome; I think I can be good at making things, but not much good at farming."

William shrugged and said, "Well, you can explain it to Father, not me."

The next morning they pulled out early, the buggy piled high with William's luggage. "I've got to take this box of books to Edwards, Adam."

They pulled up in front of the house, and William left Adam in the buggy while he took the books inside. As he went in, Mary came sailing out like a whirlwind. She swarmed up the side of the buggy and began chattering at once like a magpie.

"Why didn't you come last Wednesday like you said, Adam? I waited all day, and then I had to try to go find those eggs all by myself—and I *did* find them, too!—all except the woodpecker. Let's go get that one now, Adam! I know right where it is. . . !"

He smiled down at her, marveling how her tiny ten-year-old frame could hold so much energy—and how that head could hold so much knowledge. She had attached herself to him like a leech since the first day three years ago when she had named his mare, and he realized that her talkative way and unbridled curiosity had been good for him, especially in the first months at Amherst.

As she chatted on, he watched her mobile face and intent eyes, startled somewhat to think of how many of his memories were connected with her.

She had led him through a thousand paths in the woods around Northampton seeking birds' eggs for her collection—she chattering like a squirrel to his silence. Many times he had spent the night at her home, sitting at the feet of her father, leaning against her as Edwards told Bible stories. Every time he attended church at Northampton or went with William to a nearby church where Edwards preached, Mary always wedged herself beside him.

He thought suddenly of his first real fight, a bloody, awkward brawl with a tall, rawboned youth named Landon. He had made Mary cry, and the two of them had fought until neither of them could stand!

He had been with Mary that morning in Enfield when her father had preached a sermon with the frightening title, "Sinners in the Hands of an Angry God," and Mary had clung to him with fear as many of the hearers fell to the floor shaking with terror! He had been badly shaken himself, he thought with a sudden grin, but he had not let her see it.

"I can't go with you today, Mary," he interrupted her steady flow of words. "I'm going to Boston with William."

"Boston? Why? When are you coming back?"

"Don't know," he answered. Looking up, he saw William hurrying out of the house. "I guess I won't be gone too long. Maybe I'll be back day after tomorrow. Then we'll get that egg from that redheaded woodpecker. Jump down now!"

She threw her arms around him, delivered a moist kiss on his cheek, then hopped down like a grasshopper, calling after them as Adam whipped the team into a trot, "I'll see you Friday! Don't be late!"

William looked at Adam with amusement. "That child dotes on you, but you shouldn't have told her you'd see her Friday."

"Why not?"

"Well, Father's business may take longer than you think."

Adam gave a rare smile, his teeth bright against his heavy tan. The long white scar across his face and neck puckered slightly with the movement of his jaw. "Won't take long for me to say what I've got to say, William. How long does it take to say 'No thank you'?" He touched the team with his whip, leaned back and shook his head, saying, "You'll be on your way to England Friday—and I'll be hunting a woodpecker egg!"

"When was the last time you were home, Adam? Last year?"

Adam had drawn the buggy up in front of the house and was getting out as William asked the question. He thought quickly, then said, "No, it's been nearly two years."

"So long as that?" William shook his head, and as they mounted the steps, he murmured, "That's too long, Adam. Father's getting on—we're going to have to come home more often."

Adam could have replied that he had not been invited, but he said nothing. He stood there as William knocked, and when the door opened, the sight of his father shocked him.

"Come in, come in!" Miles took them both by the hand, and to Adam the bones felt thin and brittle as the bones of a bird. His father had lost much weight, and his stoop was so pronounced now that he was little more than Adam's height. There were brown spots on his face, his cheeks were sunken, and his rheumy eyes gave the picture of a man in bad health. *He's sixty-*

nine years old, Adam thought, and he could only say briefly, "How are you, Father?" so great was the shock; the last two years had changed Winslow from a healthy man to a sick one with the smell of death about him.

"William! Come in here—and don't waste any of your preaching on me!" Charles stepped forward, his eyes sparkling, and after shaking William's hand, he turned to Adam. His eyes narrowed, and then he smiled. "Why, you've become a man, brother! Look at those hands!" he grinned. "Strong as vises, I'd say!" But he seemed glad to see Adam and gave him a hearty shake.

"Hello, Charles."

"Adam—It's been a long time."

Adam looked into the eyes of Martha Winslow, seeing that she was not changed. Indeed, she looked stronger, if anything, as if somehow she had drawn all the health and strength out of her husband for her own use. Her eyes, he saw, suddenly fixed on the white scar that ran along his jaw and he smiled, saying, "Hello. You're looking well."

"Thank you," she replied quietly. "Come in and sit down, both of you. You must be tired."

"I'll send Sampson after Rachel and Saul," Miles said. "They're required for this business." He left the room, and William remarked quietly, "He doesn't look well."

"He was bad a month ago—ague, I think it was," Martha nodded. "He hasn't been able to get his strength back." She turned, saying, "Come into the kitchen. I've got something for you to eat."

As they ate, Charles sat across from them, full of the news of Boston. "Did you know I'd been working with Saul, Adam?"

"William told me. Do you like business, Charles?"

"Yes!" Charles looked far older than his sixteen years, and as he spoke it was clear that he was intoxicated with the world of finance. His blue eyes flashed and his hands cut through the air with eloquent gestures as he told a story of how he had, with the help of Saul, been able to pull off a very successful deal in furs from Canada. Adam understood little of it, and he was depressed to think how much Charles knew and how little he had learned since he had left home.

They had just finished eating and had risen when they heard voices. Rachel came to greet them. "Adam! You've grown so much!"

"Not so tall as Charles, Aunt Rachel," he smiled. She looked more fragile than he remembered her, and the lines around her eyes were etched more deeply, but there was still a vitality about her that was missing in his father.

Saul advanced, gave Adam a critical look, then remarked with a smile, "You look strong as a bull, Adam. It's good to see you."

He made his reply to his cousin and to Esther; then Miles entered, saying, "Let's go into the parlor. I've got a lot to say."

Adam followed them into the parlor and sat near the window on a straight-backed chair as his father took a stand beside the tiger-striped oak table in the center of the wall and looked around the room. His voice sounded a little weak, but it grew stronger as he spoke.

"It's good to see you—all of you. It's been a long time since the Winslows have been together—and I regret it. A family is the best thing on earth next to God, isn't it? And we've wasted some time."

He paused, then shook his head almost imperceptibly. Looking across the room he continued: "William, this meeting is for you and for Adam. The rest of us have done a lot of thinking and considerable planning. I've called us all together so that we can agree on which direction the family business ought to go. Saul's been talking a lot about making some changes, and perhaps we ought to listen to him. Saul?"

Saul looked around but did not stand up as he said, "We've done very well, I think, for the past few years. Uncle Miles did a fine job of getting the fur business established. But these are new times, and if we survive, we're going to have to adjust."

"What sort of changes do you have in mind, Saul?" William asked.

There was a line of concentration around Saul Howland's eyes. He had always been a serious man, and was so much older than his cousins that they had always looked upon him as the businessman in the family. Now he stated carefully, "Basically, we ought to guard our interest in the fur trade by expanding as much as possible into the Ohio River Valley—but there's a danger in that. The fur is plentiful, but the French are going to give problems."

"You think there'll be a war?" William asked.

"Yes, I do, but nobody can say how soon. Fur's a good business, so we need to keep our interests going. But we must diversify." He turned suddenly and smiled at Charles, saying, "Charles has been a godsend! I've never seen a young fellow who caught on to business so quickly. Tell them about the ideas we've been working on, will you, Charles?"

It was clear that Saul was grooming his cousin for leadership in the family, and Charles was equal to it. He stood up and said easily, "Of course, these are all Saul's ideas, but they make sense. What we plan to do is buy land and develop it. There's no way that the price of land can go *down*, and we can protect ourselves against any reverses in the fur trade." He went on smoothly, speaking with a confident grace, and Adam was amazed at how his brother had matured.

Charles drew out a map, pinned it to the wall, and pointed at several spots that had been considered. Finally he said, "There are two plots that Saul and I think will be safe and profitable. The first one is here in Virginia." He pointed to a spot on the map, saying, "It's cheap land because it's not really developed, and we can get it for almost nothing. The owner's in trouble and has to sell." Then he moved the pointer to a spot east of Boston. He gave a wide smile, looking at Adam. "Adam, you ought to be interested in this—as a matter of fact, you've probably been over most of it hunting, from what William has told me."

"That's the Hunter place?" Adam asked. "It's pretty run down, Charles. Gone back to woods—and a lot of it's in timber."

"You know it, do you, Adam?" Miles asked, giving his son a sharp look.

"Yes, sir. Everybody knows the place."

"Well, William is going to Oxford," Miles told them, then smiled briefly, adding, "Nobody expects you to be a businessman, William, and I'm glad that we've got a Winslow preaching the Gospel. Edward would have been very proud of you—and

Grandfather Gilbert, too." He paused as some memory rose out of the past, swept across his mind; then he shook his shoulders and stated decisively, "Adam, Charles is going to go to Virginia and start our work there, and we would like you to learn to operate the Hunter place."

Adam grew still, always awkward when called upon to say anything in public. He knew that what he was going to say would sound ungrateful, and yet he could think of no way to agree.

"I—I'm not cut out for farming," he said, then hastened to add, "I've seen enough of that life to know that you have to have a gift for it—and you have to like it."

Martha's lips tightened, and she snapped in a waspish tone, "You ought to be *grateful* for the opportunity—but you always were an unthoughtful boy!"

Saul silenced her with a look, and answered, with just a trace of displeasure in his voice, "It's a trade, Adam. A man can learn it, as he could anything else."

"I think, Saul," Rachel said quietly, "that Adam is right. We don't want a man there whose heart's not in it. He would please neither us nor himself."

"But, Adam, you have to have a profession," Charles argued. "And we're not talking about just being a farm laborer; it will be the family business—*your* business, actually. You can get rich if you work at it."

Adam felt the pressure growing and he looked around, seeking assurance, but even William offered no encouragement. He said, "I want to be a blacksmith," he stated firmly. "It's what I'm good at."

"You can do that, too, Adam," Miles affirmed. He looked across the room at Adam, and there was a plea in his tired old eyes. He knew that he had failed with this strange dark son of his, and he knew that he had little time to rectify the mistake. "I ask you to do this thing, Adam, for the family, of course—but it's really *you* I'm thinking of."

It touched Adam suddenly, this plea coming from his father who had never asked him for anything. They had not been close, but now he saw that his father was reaching out for some way to help, and doing so in the only way he knew. And he longed to agree, but he could only say, "Father, it wouldn't be good for me *or* for the family if I did this."

The pressure grew, and for fifteen minutes Adam was urged to follow the line pointed out by Saul. Martha finally sniffed and said loudly, anger rising in her voice, "Well, I'd think there'd be a *little* gratitude in you, Adam! After all, it isn't as though you had a great deal of talent! Heaven knows we've all worried about what would happen to you if you had to take care of yourself!"

Then Rachel stood up, her thin face drawn with anger. "All of you, be quiet!" Esther and Saul looked at her with shock, and even Martha blinked. Rachel rarely raised her voice, but when she did, it was like a storm cloud, and there were none in the family who cared to confront her when she was roused.

Going over to Adam, she put one hand on his shoulder, raised his face with the other. Her eyes were bright with indignation as she spoke, "Adam, do what you want to do!" She leaned over and kissed him, and her kiss burned like fire on his face.

Then she stood up and stared down at him. "Let me suggest this—and you tell me to mind my own business if you don't like it, all right?"

He smiled suddenly and said, "All right, Aunt Rachel."

"Most of the farming today is done with tools that haven't changed since Gilbert Winslow got off the *Mayflower*, isn't that right? Well, why don't you make better ones, Adam?"

He stared at her in bewilderment. "Me? Make better farming tools?"

"Well, as I remember it, you've spent most of your life making things—the cannon, for example?" She laughed as his face burned with shame, but she cried out, "What's the matter? The thing worked, didn't it?" Suddenly Miles laughed loudly—a rare thing, indeed. "Certainly it worked! Nearly wiped out a whole species—the Black Winslow Banty!"

William joined his father in laughter, then suddenly stood up, his face alive with excitement. "Why, of course! Why didn't I think of it? You can do more good that way than doing the work yourself, Adam. I'll bet you've got a dozen ideas right now about how to make a better harrow or a new way to cut brush quicker with some kind of a new blade? Isn't that right?"

Adam suddenly was filled with excitement. "Why, I can do that!"

A murmur of pleasure ran around the room; Miles stepped over and put his arm around Adam, an act that embarrassed both of them, and stated, "That's it! We'll get a good overseer—and you can oversee *him*—and *make* all the inventions you want!"

"And keep on with the gunmaking, too," Charles laughed. "When a war comes, there's nothing like a munitions-maker to make a family rich!"

They all laughed, and for the first time in his memory, Adam felt like a member in good standing of the Winslow clan!

A week later, William and Adam stood at the rail of the schooner *Rosebud*, watching the coast of America grow dim. Adam had gone back to get his clothes. His assignment was to go to England, to spend three months studying the most advanced methods of farming, and visit as many manufacturers of farming equipment as possible in that time.

Now William remarked, "Well, brother, life is odd, eh?" He laughed and clapped Adam on the shoulder, adding, "You thought you'd be looking for a woodpecker egg—but here you are on the high seas—a businessman!"

Adam rubbed his jaw ruefully. "Mary will never forgive me, William! When I went back to get my clothes, she gave me fits for leaving her!"

"She's a bright girl," William smiled. "But it'll only be a short time, and she'll have you back again. Charles will have the house ready for you and an overseer hired. He's a brilliant young man, that brother of ours!" Then he squeezed Adam's muscular arm and laughed, "But I'll bet he can't bend a horseshoe or make guns like you!" He looked at his brother and added gently, "I know you're a little afraid of all this new responsibility—but you can do it, Adam. In this New World we don't have a long time to be children—girls are married at fifteen, and boys, not much older. It's a new land, and we've got to grow up in a hurry." He would have said more, but finally he merely smiled and put his arm around Adam's shoulder.

The land dropped out of sight, and the two walked slowly around the ship, coming to the bow. Standing there peering into the misty distance, Adam mused, "It's a long way to England, isn't it, William?" Then he leaned on the rail and murmured, "Mary told me to get her something pretty in London. Wonder if she'd like a doll?"

"As smart as that one is, you'd do better to get a set of reference books!" William laughed.

"No, a doll would be nice," Adam decided with a gentle smile on his broad lips. The two stood close together staring across the deep waters, each seeing a vision of his own.

CHAPTER SIX

MOLLY

★　★　★　★

"I hate to abandon you like this, Adam," William told his brother for the third time, a worried look on his face. He stood blocking the door of the coach. The driver had already called down twice for him to get in. He bit his lip nervously, looked around at the hustling mass of humanity that filled the Cheapside Street, then grabbed Adam's arm. "I *must* go to Oxford— but this is a wicked city, and a country lad like you could be easily taken in!"

"Get on the coach, William!" Adam grinned. "Every night since we've been here you've kept me awake warning me about the dangers of this iniquitous place. I promised to trust no one— *especially* handsome females with painted faces!" He laughed aloud at the alarmed look on his brother's countenance, then gave him an affectionate slap on the shoulder. "On with you! I'll be in no danger. I'll be looking at farms and factories; there'll be no tricksters or fancy women in *those* places!"

"Be you goin' or not?" the driver yelled, leaning over the edge of the coach, his yellow face wrinkled with impatience. "Either get yerself in—or get out of the way!"

"You have my address!" William yelled, as he piled in and the coach rolled off. "Write often, Adam—and don't forget to go to church!"

Adam waved, then turned and made his way down the busy streets. He had been afraid of the city at first; it was so big and boisterous, but as he threaded a path through the vendors that cluttered the walks and spilled over into the narrow street, he was seized by a spirit of freedom that was intoxicating. There was no one to tell him what to do, and for the first time in his life he was responsible to no one except himself.

They had disembarked from the *Rosebud* four days earlier after a fast crossing, and had found a room for Adam in a two-story half-timbered house near the center of the city. That same day they had gone to the bank, Lloyds of London, and presented the letter of credit. The funds were in two parts—one sum for William to draw on for his expenses at Oxford for the year, the other for Adam.

"I feel strange with all this money, William," he had said as they left Lloyds. "Three hundred pounds! That's a fortune!"

"It won't seem like it if you buy all that new-fangled farm equipment, though. Saul expects you to get good value for that cash."

The plan had been laid out for Adam. He was to buy as much equipment as he could and have it shipped to the two plantations, but there had been objections from Esther and Martha about his ability to handle money. Miles had raised his head and spoken with a tone of finality: "Adam must learn to handle business, and there'll be no more said about it!"

As Adam made his way to the first of the factories he planned to visit, he felt again the warmth that had flooded him at that moment. He had not known until then how much he had longed for the approval of his father. Now dodging carts and coaches that thundered down the street, he vowed he would not let his family down. He passed by men, women, and children— some dressed in the sooty rags of chimney sweeps, others arrayed in the gold and gaudy satin of the aristocracy. Porters sweated under their burdens, chapmen darted from shop to shop, and tradesmen scurried around like ants pulling at Adam's coat as he fought his way through the human tide that flowed and ebbed on the street.

He found the factory on the edge of the city, and the owner

was not too busy to show him around. It came as something of a shock to Adam to see the primitive methods used in the production of the equipment, and he thought with a start: *Why, I could do as well as this—better!* But he only looked, made notes, and thanked the owner.

Adam visited two other factories that day, finding one of them to be quite advanced. He stayed until late afternoon, making drawings, and by the time he made his way back to Cheapside, he was hungry. He went in to a small, smoky inn called "The Eagle" for a meal. He had eaten with William, and devoured a steak and kidney pie with gusto.

As he left The Eagle and started back to his room, a voice startled him—a tiny, thin voice that came from his left.

"Sir? Will ye buy a handkerchief—only five bob!"

A young girl not more than ten or eleven years old stepped out from the overhanging shadow of an apartment. She held out a fragment of white cloth, but he shook his head, saying, "I don't need any handkerchiefs, Missy, thank you." Already hardened to the infinite pleas of vendors and beggars, he would have passed on, but she took a quick step forward. There was a note of panic in her small voice as she pleaded, "Oh, please, won't yer tyke a bit of fancy work to yer lady, sir? Yer can 'ave it fer four bob!"

He looked down at her, intending to shake her off, but paused when he saw the fatigue in her face. She had large eyes that looked gray in the fading light, and the smudges under the lower lids made them look larger. Her face was thin, her lips drawn with either pain or fatigue, and the finely-etched planes of her face with high cheekbones and a sweeping jawline did not seem to go with the ragged clothes that hung on her thin body. Most of the young beggars had faces blunted by ignorance and eyes dulled by the monotonous life of poverty they led; this girl, for all her rags, had something that was delicate and sensitive.

"I don't have a lady, Missy," Adam said gently; then suddenly she reminded him of Mary Edwards back in America, and he put forth his hand to pat her head the way he had often done with children.

"Don't—!" the girl cried. Dropping the handkerchief, she

threw her hand up over her face, cowering back against the wall.

Adam stood there staring at her, then an anger flared up inside and he bent to pick up the handkerchief. It was a finely done piece of work, now stained where it had touched the filthy sidewalk. He looked at her, then reaching into his pocket, he drew out a coin and held it out, "I'll take the piece, Missy."

She dropped her arm, swallowed convulsively, then stepped forward to take the coin. "I—I ain't got no change—"

"You can keep it, Missy." He looked at it, then lifted his eyes to her face. There was a sudden relief in her features, and he suspected that she had saved herself from a beating by the sale. "Did you make this? It's very fine."

"Oh, me mother made it, mostly—but she's a' teachin' me."

Darkness was falling fast, so that he had to lean forward and strain to see her features. "It's getting dark, Missy. You'd better get home."

"Yes, sir, I be goin' now." She looked around at the man now made faceless by the dark, and asked in a tiny voice, "Sir, be yer goin' down ter 'auberk?"

Adam's rooming house was in Hauberk, and he nodded. "Come along." As she fell into step beside him, he adjusted his steps to suit her. Glancing down at her as they walked, he wondered that such a small girl was allowed to roam the streets of a city. "How old are you, Missy?"

"Ten, sir."

"My name is Adam Winslow. What do they call you?"

"I'm Molly."

He found out that she had two brothers and three sisters, and lived in a run-down section filled mostly with the very poor. When he asked her what her father did, she said with a shrug, "Oh, he's a bricklayer—only there ain't no work nowadays."

They left the main business district, then coming to a side street that led off from Adam's street, she said, "I live down here aways. Thank you, sir."

"Oh, I'll see you home, Molly," Adam replied quickly. She did not protest, and led him down a street that degenerated quickly into a gin lane. The houses were decayed, held up in some cases by long poles. Derelicts stumbled along, bleary-eyed and loose-lipped. Several times along the way, men dressed in rags shambled out of the shadows and approached Adam, eying him slyly. They did not miss, however, the strong, muscular figure nor the direct stare in his dark eyes, and offered nothing more than a plea for money, which he denied.

He wondered grimly what could protect a child like the one beside him, and he realized with a shock that his little world in Amherst where children were safe on the streets lay thousands of miles away. London was a world of predators, feeding on strangers—or on one another when there were no other victims.

"There's me 'ous, Mr. Winslow," Molly said. The two-story house she led him to faced the street and, like the others, was in a state of decay. A strong smell of garbage and sewage rose from the trench in the middle of the cobblestoned street. A single lantern cast feeble yellow beams over several young children playing in the front. A woman who was leaning against the wall straightened up as the two approached, calling out "Molly?" in a thin voice.

"Aye, Ma, it's me," the child answered. Adam paused in the street, and heard Molly say, "This 'ere gentulman, Mr. Winslow, 'e bought the nice lace, Ma. And 'e lives in 'auberk, so 'e let me walk with 'im."

"Why, thank you, sir," the woman said. "It's late for a little one, and that's a fact."

"Glad to be of help," Adam replied. He touched his hat, a gesture that brought a sudden quick look from the woman, as if she had forgotten such manners existed. He turned to go, but she stalled him, "Mr. Winslow? I—I wonder if you be needin' any cleaning done—or like your clothes done up nice and clean?"

"Why. . ." Adam paused, then before he could answer, he was interrupted by a raspy voice.

"Wot's this now!" A thick-bodied man, tall and hulking in the dim light had come up from somewhere down the street to take a stand behind Adam. He had a loose-jawed face with piggish little eyes, and there was something threatening in the way he stood there, his arms held out from his sides and his massive fists clenched.

"Tom! This is Mr. Winslow—he just bought one of my pieces from Molly—and I was just askin' him if he had any cleanin' to be done!"

The woman's voice was threaded with fear. Her hands twitched nervously on the shawl she held as she stepped forward to put herself between her husband and Adam.

The man paused, relaxed his fists, and a loose smile spread across his face. "Oh, yer bought somethin', is it? Well, let's 'ave the cash!" Molly held out the coin, which he took. Holding it up to the light and grunting with satisfaction, he slipped it into the pocket of his vest. "Now, that's 'andsome of yer, sir."

"Not at all," Adam shrugged. "It's very fine work."

"Ah, yer ain't from 'ere, then? America, I tyke it? Burns is me name, Mr. Winslow—Thomas Burns. And be yer 'ere fer long?"

"Three months, more or less."

"Aw, now, Mr. Winslow, 'ow is the brick business in the Colonies, do yer say?"

"Very good. Quite a bit of construction in Boston."

"Do yer tell me that?" Burns said in surprise. "It's been in me 'ead to try me luck over the waters. This 'ere place is dead, it is! Nothin' fer an honest workman!"

He laughed and came forward to stand toward Adam; he was of average height, but massive as a draft horse. The gin on his breath was a raw stench in Adam's nostrils as Burns said, "Well, I got me some business, Mr. Winslow. Yer let me little woman do yer cleanin', yer see? And later me and you can talk some more about workin' in the Colonies, yer hear me now?"

Adam took the huge paw the man held out, and instantly found his hand collapsed beneath the power of Burns' grip! He caught his breath, leaned forward against the pain of it—then tightened his own grip. Burns was peering at him out of a pair of muddy eyes, and Adam realized it was an old trick with the man—but he closed his hand and Burns' mouth sagged open as Adam began to exert power. The sinews of his forearms and fingers had been transformed into flesh as hard as the iron they had wrought on the forge, and Burns was out of condition. Slowly the balance shifted, and Burns, instead of crushing

Adam's hand, found his own caught in a viselike grip that was paralyzing his nerves. Pain began to run up his arm, and he wrenched his hand away with a mighty effort, then stood there glaring down at Adam.

"Be glad to talk to you any time, Burns," Adam offered without a sign of exertion in his face. "Mrs. Burns, my room is with Mrs. Havelock—next to the green grocers. I won't have much cleaning, but you're welcome to do what there is."

"I'll be by every Tuesday, sir," Mrs. Burns said.

Adam said goodnight, turned and made his way home. He went to bed at once, but could not go to sleep. Too much was happening, and he lay awake thinking of the factories and the machinery he had seen, trying to plan ways to improve the equipment.

Finally he dropped off to sleep, but tossed fitfully, dreaming of the events of the day. Several times he seemed to see a pair of enormous gray eyes and hear a reedy voice saying, "Oh, please, sir, won't yer tyke a bit uv fancy work to yer lady, sir?" Finally he woke up, remembering how Molly Burns had flinched from him; he thought of the massive hands of Thomas Burns leaving their marks on the child, and anger ran so strongly through him, he could not sleep for a long time.

11 November, 1744
Dear Father,

I have seen in the past three months practically every factory in central England that makes any sort of farming equipment, and have made up a list of such machinery along with the prices for your consideration. There have not been very many, but there are a great number of gunsmiths, and I must confess that I have spent much time there!

I have not missed a single Sabbath going to church, but I must say that the preaching here is frightful! I know you are opposed to Mr. Whitefield and the Revival, but if you had to sit through one of the sermons delivered by Church of England pastors, you would perhaps change your mind.

I have made few friends here and am looking forward to arriving home. I have taken passage on a small freighter, and should arrive home by the first of the year.

Your devoted son—Adam

Adam sat back in his chair, arched his back, and thought how difficult it was for him to write to his family—and how easy it was for him to write to Mary. He took a fresh sheet, and with a sudden laugh thought, *I'm about on her level, I suppose! I wonder if I'll ever be able to talk to adults?* He began the letter, which, unlike the one to his father, ran several pages. The mails were so slow that he never expected answers; thus his letters amounted to a journal. He had included descriptions of the vivid side of London life for Mary, and had taken pleasure in letting his experiences reshape themselves on paper for her eyes. He was unaware of how he used the child for a sounding board, a confidant on whom he could try out his ideas—one to whom he could speak freely with no reservations.

He wrote steadily for over an hour, then put the quill down and leaned back to read the letter. He was surprised to discover (not for the first time!) how much of his thoughts were taken up by the Burns family. The week following his first meeting with Molly, he had told Mary in an earlier letter, she had come to his door for his washing. He had invited her in, then while gathering up his scarce wardrobe for washing, he had encouraged her to talk. She had been more open than on the street, and it ended by their having tea together. Then he had told her stories of America, which she delighted to hear.

She was, he discovered, quite ignorant, but not stupid. Her questions were sharp, and a voracious appetite for learning lay beneath the surface. He had read to her from some of his books, and her face was a picture of contentment and delight as she sat there in his straight-backed chair drinking it all in.

He put some of his feeling about the family into his letter to Mary:

> I have told you quite a bit about the Burns family. I know all the names of the children by now. Molly is your age, but you would find her quite ignorant. She cannot read a word, but she delights in books. I wish she could spend some time in your company, Mary, for she is a warmhearted and loving child who could do well if she had the opportunity.
>
> Alas, there is no chance for that! Her mother is a good woman, but worn out with work and dominated by her hus-

band. I can say nothing good about *that* one, for he is a brute who lives on the labors of his wife and children. Worse, he mistreats them frightfully!

I have seen the bruises on Mrs. Burns and on the children, and pray that I will never be present to witness the thing! I had an awful battle once with a man who was mistreating his dog, and I do not think I could stand to see a woman or a child beaten!

Keep me in your prayers, and remember me to your parents and your dear sisters and to Timothy. I long to see you, and when I return the first of the year, I will expect to go egg-hunting with you, though the snow be five feet deep!

Your friend and admirer, Adam Winslow

William's black robe billowed in the cutting December wind, making him look like a monstrous bat fluttering across the grounds of Oxford. He broke into a run, casting off his dignity, and reached the relative warmth of the vine-covered three-story building where his quarters were. Climbing to the top story, he shoved his way into the room, then stopped dead-still. A fire snapped in the fireplace and Adam stood there beside it, his face a patchwork of blue bruises and half-healed cuts.

"Adam! What in the world happened to you?"

"I was in a fight." Adam smiled but that was painful, for one of the cuts ran from his cheek right across the right corner of his lips, so he said with a grimace, "You were right about London, William. It's a dangerous place."

"Sit down, and I'll make some tea while you tell me about it." William nudged his brother into a chair and picked up the brass kettle. "Was it highwaymen—or what?"

"It was a monster named Tom Burns!"

William paused, shooting a quick look at Adam. "The father of the girl you've taken under your wing?"

"The same." Adam leaned back and there was a fire in his dark blue eyes that matched the glow of the coals in the grate. "I've told you he mistreated his family? Well, up until two days ago I'd only seen the bruises on Mrs. Burns and on the children. But I stopped by there on my way home last Tuesday, and that's when it all happened."

"He was cruel to his wife?"

"He knocked her against the wall with his fist, the rotter!" Adam stormed between clenched teeth, his face contorted with the memory. "He was drunk, of course, as he usually is. Up till then he'd behaved himself around me. But he'd lost some money gambling, and I was just leaving when he came roaring in, demanding more from his poor wife! When she gave him the few small coins she had, he doubled up his fist and struck her in the face, cursing her for not having more!"

"That must have been hard for you, Adam," William remarked. He listened intently, saying little as his brother went on. There was, however, a deep anxiety in him, for he knew that any Colonial that got into trouble with a citizen of England was in danger of prosecution. He handed Adam a cup of tea, then sat back waiting for the rage that filled the young man to pass. "What happened then?"

"Well, I saw red—so I started to leave, but then he took Molly by the arm and started shaking her so hard I thought her neck would break! I grabbed him and pulled him away—but he almost knocked my head off, William!" Adam touched the cut on his mouth and said, "It's a wonder I've got a tooth left in my head! The man's a bull! He knocked me right out the front door, then came roaring out to finish me off!"

"I would guess you went at it with him?"

"Well, I really think he would have killed me, William. Fights in that part of town turn into kicking matches, and I reckon he'd have kicked my head off if I hadn't fought him."

"He's a big man, you say?"

"Tremendous—not tall, but strong, you know, and very *slow*! Quite out of condition, and I began to give him a few belts in his belly; that slowed him down! But it was a brawl, William! Lasted over half an hour, and we cut each other to ribbons!"

"What about the law? Did anyone fetch a sheriff?"

Adam laughed shortly. "That's not their style, William! No, everybody on the street came to watch, but no law."

William sipped his tea, then asked, "Well, I take it you didn't agree to be friends after it was over?"

"*He* didn't agree to anything!" Adam's face showed a grim

pleasure, and he even chuckled. "It's hard to *agree* when you've been beaten unconscious! I was just about as bad off, to tell the truth, but I staggered home and had to stay in bed all day, I was so stove-in! You ought to see what my ribs look like!"

"Well, what's next?" William asked.

Adam slammed the cup down, then stared his brother in the face. "I can't tell you—because you'd tell me not to do it!"

After a long period when William reasoned with Adam, he finally discovered that Mrs. Burns had come to his room in terror. She had told him that her husband could not move from his bed, so badly was he beaten, but he had sworn that he would beat her and Molly to death when he was able to get up. And she had asked Adam to take the girl away!

"Take her where?" William asked sharply.

"Anywhere so long as that monster can't find her!"

"That's kidnapping, Adam—a hanging offense!" William snapped. "Get it out of your mind!"

"Well, I can't do *nothing*, can I?"

William put his cup down and said quietly, "I'll go back to London with you. We'll see. I have a few connections here at Oxford—influential men. Maybe they can help. But what a man does inside his house is pretty hard to regulate, Adam. There's no law against a man beating his wife and children."

Adam's eyes were hard, harder than William had ever seen them. It was not the gentle boy that William had grown up with who stood there glaring into the fire! No, this was someone he had never seen before, and it sent a streak of apprehension tingling along his nerves as he saw that Adam was not going to be talked out of this. He breathed a quick prayer, then said, "We'll do something, Adam. God won't let us down!"

But God did let him down, or so Adam thought bleakly two weeks later. His ship was due to sail in less than five days, and he had spent most of that time trying to work something out for Burns. He had let the paper work on the machinery go, spending all his time either going around to lawyers with William, or hanging around the street where the Burnses lived, trying to keep some sort of watch over the family.

But nothing had come of it. William had said in despair, "Adam, there are some things in this world that we just can't change, and this is one of them. You'll just have to accept it!"

William had gone to see a judge who was a son of one of the dons at Oxford, hoping that perhaps he could offer a solution, but not having any real hope.

Adam walked around the streets, ignoring the biting cold, and finally, he set his jaw and stalked up the door of the Burnses' house. Mrs. Burns' eyes widened as she opened the door, and she tried to keep him out, "Go 'way, Mr. Winslow! You'll just make him worse!"

"I've got to talk to him! There'll be no trouble! I think I can help."

She opened the door, a weak futility on her thin face, then led him to the small room off the rear of the main room. All of the children were in the large room, huddled beside a small fire kindled in the grate, and he smiled at Molly as he passed.

When Tom Burns looked up from where he lay in the bed, a light blazed in his dull eyes, and he sat up with a groan and a curse, but Adam cut him off sharply. "Shut your foul mouth, Burns!" he snapped and when he moved close, Burns' huge bulk shrank back in sudden fear.

"You leave me be, Winslow! I'll have the law on yer!"

Adam picked up a chair, placed it firmly beside the bed, then sat down in it, staring straight into Burns' face. "How would you like to have a large sum of money, Burns?"

The question caught the big man off guard, but at once a crafty light leaped into his muddy eyes. "Well, I guess yer see you wus in the wrong!" He rubbed his hands together with satisfaction and began to say, "Now, I figure—"

"Shut up!" Adam snapped. "I will make you an offer, and I will make it only one time. If you don't agree at once, I will walk out of here and you'll never see a penny. I won't bargain, you hear me?"

"Wot's yer offer, then?" Burns asked sullenly.

"Two hundred pounds cash."

It was practically all the money Adam had, and it would be a direct violation of his trust. He dared not think what Saul and

Charles would say, but he had no other choice.

"Why, that ain't enough—"

Adam got up instantly and made rapid strides to the door. Burns saw a fortune slipping through his hands, more money than he'd ever seen, and he cried out loudly, "Wait now, don't go runnin' off, Winslow!"

"Yes or no—which is it?"

Burns saw the square jaw of Winslow set firmly, and the light in those cobalt blue eyes told him there would be no bargaining. "Well, yes."

Adam came back and sat down. "Now, this is the way you will get the money, and once again, I will not bargain! I will give you one hundred pounds in cash. I will leave the other one hundred pounds with a reliable party in this city. You may do what you please with the first hundred, but the second hundred will be closely supervised by a man I will choose. He will see to it that the money is doled out over a period of time for food and clothing for your family. He will be certain that it is spent for that and not on gin for you. That is the bargain. Do you agree?"

Burns could hardly bear the thought of his family spending money for food when he could use it for gin, but he saw that he had no choice. "All right, I agree."

Mrs. Burns said suddenly, "He'll beat the girl, Mr. Winslow!"

"Shut yer mouth!" Burns screamed. "I'll show yer—"

"You see?" she said in a rare defiance. "He'll have to let us have the food, but he'll beat me and Molly. You'll have to take her away or he'll kill her."

"I intend to do just that. Burns, in exchange for the two hundred pounds, you will sign a paper—"

"Wot kind o' paper?" Burns' eyes squinted in suspicion.

"A paper saying that for ten years Molly is a bound girl," Adam stated.

"Wot's that mean?"

"It means that for ten years she'll be under an obligation to serve me, but at the end of that time, she's free." Adam realized that Molly would have to be protected until she was grown.

"Take her to America, Mr. Winslow!" Mrs. Burns cried, tears

making a track down her cheeks. "She ain't got no show here! Maybe she can be somebody over there!"

The room was small, but when Adam raised his voice and called the girl, Molly came at once into the room, her eyes enormous in her pale face.

"Molly, would you like to go to America?"

She stared at him, and after casting a furtive glance at her father, she whispered, "Will I belong to you?"

"No!" Adam said sharply. "You'll belong to nobody! For ten years I'll be responsible for you; then you'll be old enough to make up your mind what to do. But until then, you'll work in the house for my family—and you'll learn to read and write."

That brought her head up, and a light came into her fine gray eyes. "Yes, sir, I'll go with you! And what is it I'll be?"

"A bound girl, Molly. That means a servant, but one who can't quit for a certain length of time." He rose and went to her, putting his hand on her thin shoulder. "You can't leave me for ten years—so be sure you want to do it."

Molly Burns looked around the small, dirty room, stared at her father, who was glaring at her with resentment, then looked up at Adam.

"I'll be your bound girl, Mr. Adam—for always!"

The *East Wind*, a three-masted schooner, swayed with the swell of the outgoing tide as Adam led Mrs. Burns and Molly up the gangplank. As they stepped onto the deck, a rattling of chains followed the bosun's shout: "Weigh anchor! Hearty, now!" There was a patter of bare feet on the wooden deck as topmen began to pour out of the depths of the ship to take station for setting sail.

"You'll have to be quick, I'm afraid," Adam said. He could barely see the worn face of Mrs. Burns in the heavy morning fog, for she wore a shawl over her head and kept her face averted. "I'll wait over there by the ladder."

Molly watched him go, and the strangeness of the ship frightened her. She put out her arms, and as her mother put her thin arms around her, holding her fast in a way she had seldom done, great sobs welled up in her throat, and she cried with her face buried against her mother's bosom, "Ma! I don't want to go! I'm afraid!"

The words seemed to rive the heart of Mrs. Burns, and her thin body trembled, but she said, "It's what you must do, Molly." She held the frail body of the child close, and heroically choked back the sobs that rose to her own throat. "Mr. Winslow, why, he's going to take such good care of you! He'll be so kind to you, Molly!"

"But I'll miss you, Mama! I won't have *anyone*!"

"Oh, but you'll have Mr. Winslow, and ain't he told us about his good brothers and sisters who'll take you for their own? And just think, Molly, in no time you'll be comin' back here for a visit—and you'll be wearing new clothes. Mr. Winslow says you'll learn to write too—and it'll be grand!"

She knew in her heart that it would not be—at least the part about Molly coming back. Such travel was expensive, and she was well aware that this was the last time on earth that she would ever hold her child to her breast. The tears burned her eyes, and she had to struggle to keep the agony out of her voice, but she squeezed Molly hard, then dashed the blinding tears from her eyes, saying, "Well, now, I'll have to go—but we'll be writing, won't we now?"

"Mama! Don't leave me!"

They stood there, holding each other until a cry came from the bosun, "All visitors ashore!"

Then Adam came to stand beside them and with a subdued tone, said, "It's time, I'm afraid."

Mrs. Burns slowly released her daughter, but Molly wildly threw her arms around the woman, crying, "Mama! Mama! Don't leave me!"

"Take her, Mr. Winslow!" she cried out. "Take her!"

Adam's own eyes were moist as he reached out and unwound the thin arms of Molly from her mother. For a terrible moment he felt that this was all wrong—that he had interfered in a matter that would lead to a tragic end.

But it was too late now, so he pulled Molly away, and Mrs. Burns gave one final cry. "My baby! God help my baby!" After kissing the girl, she turned and ran blindly across the deck to the ladder, where a sailor helped her down.

Molly struggled wildly, crying out, "Let me go! Let me go!" But then as her mother's form disappeared into the fog, she threw her arms around Adam's neck and, shutting her eyes, held on with all her might.

The bosun called out, "Set sail! Set topsails—set the gallants! Set sail for the voyage."

Holding the child tightly, Adam whispered in her ear: "Don't cry, Molly! Please don't cry! We're setting sail for a new world—and I'll take care of you always—I promise!"

"Will you, Mr. Adam? Will you?"

She moved her head back, and as he looked into her tear-stained face, into the clear gray eyes, she said, as if it were a vow to God made on the altar: "I will take care of you, Molly—always!"

As she clung to him, the ship moved under them, heading out to sea—to a new world.

CHAPTER SEVEN

THE HOUSE OF WINSLOW

★ ★ ★ ★

"Mist' Adam! Look at you now, all back from 'cross de wa-tuh!"

Sampson was waiting at the wharf as Adam stepped out of the dory that brought him ashore from the freighter. His teeth shone in the black expanse of his broad, black face as he reached out and lifted Molly out and placed her down carefully, saying, "And whut's dis you done brought home wif you, Mist' Adam?"

"This is Molly Burns, Sampson." He saw the girl looking up at the large black man with fear in her eyes, and leaping out, he said, "This is one of my best friends, Molly. His name is Sampson." He looked at the buggy and stated, "I didn't expect you to be here."

"Oh, Mist' Miles he been chompin' at de bit fo you to git home! We heard that yo' ship was sighted yesterday, so he sent me go fetch you."

They made several trips getting the luggage to the buggy before Adam lifted Molly into the seat, then sat down beside her. As Sampson clucked to the team and they started up at a brisk trot, he asked about the family, but hardly listened as Sampson rambled on.

What am I going to tell them? What will they say? he asked himself, as he had every day since he'd signed the papers with Burns and forked over the money in his trust. It had seemed so right then, and home and the family so far away, but now as they progressed steadily through Boston and turned down the pike toward home, a blind panic overwhelmed him.

"Is anybody at home, Sampson?"

"Oh yas. I went by and tol' yo' aunt—so I reckon de whole bunch is waitin' fo you, Mist' Adam. I guess you feels mighty big, goin' over de watuh and bein' a big businessman! Yo' father is sho proud, I tells you! He talk about you jes' about every day you been gone—says you gonna be a big plantuh and make lots of new stuff. He proud as I ever see him!"

Adam's heart sank lower and as Sampson rattled on, telling how everyone was looking forward to his return, misery settled down on him like a heavy cloud. As they came in sight of the house, he had one wild impulse to grab the lines from Sampson and drive the team in the opposite direction, but he knew he could do no such thing.

Sampson drove the team into the yard, but Adam said, "Sampson, pull into the barn."

"What I do dat fo?"

"I want to go in alone. You stay with Molly in the barn for a little while." Sampson obeyed, and Adam jumped down, saying with a smile he didn't feel, "Molly, I want to talk a little to the family. You don't mind staying out here with Sampson for a little?"

Molly took a long look at the black man, who smiled and patted her hand, saying, "Why, me and Miss Molly, we do fine, Mist' Adam! Won't we, now?"

She evidently found some assurance in his kind face, for she smiled and said, "All right, Mr. Adam."

"I won't be long." He went around to the front steps, and when he walked up onto the porch, the front door opened and his father stepped out to greet him with a smile.

"Welcome home, Adam!" he said smiling broadly as he took Adam's hand in both of his. Pulling him into the house, Miles urged him down the hall, and then almost pushed him into the parlor, saying, "Well, here he is!"

Except for the absence of William, all the family was there, and for one brief moment, Adam experienced a striking feeling that he had been in this place, doing this same thing before. Then he was met by his aunt who hugged him, as did Mercy. Saul and Charles both gave him a hearty handshake, and even Esther seemed glad to see him. Only Martha did not advance; she stood against the wall, giving him a nod and saying briefly, "I'm glad you had a safe journey, Adam."

There was a bustle as everyone tried to talk; then Saul said loudly, "Quiet, everyone! I can't hear myself think—and poor Adam is quite overcome with all this attention."

"Right you are, Saul," Miles smiled. "Sit down, Adam, and we'll fill you in on what's been going on here."

"Yes," Charles agreed, "and then we can hear what great things you've been doing to boost the family fortune."

For the next half hour Adam sat listening while they rehearsed the details of business that had taken place over the past three months. Basically, the news was that everything had gone very well. The plantation in Virginia had been purchased, and Charles was going to go and begin operations in a month. "I'll have one of Saul's best managers to go with me," Charles smiled. "Really to keep me out of trouble, I suppose."

Rachel said, "The house in the Northampton property has been made ready." She looked tired, but there was a gleam of excitement in her eyes as she told Adam the details of the matter. A good manager had been found, and he would be able to teach Adam the business of running a plantation very quickly.

The talk ran on briskly, everyone excited, and all too soon for Adam, Miles said, "Well, so much for our news, son. Now, let's hear what you've been doing."

"Right!" Saul agreed. "We have to make arrangements to get the equipment moved. It came with you, I suppose?"

Adam cleared his throat, which was suddenly dry as dust. Looking around the circle of smiling, expectant faces, he could think of nothing to say. Somehow he had thought that when he faced his family, he'd be able to explain his conduct in a satisfactory way. Looking around, however, his heart sank, and he knew there was no way that he would ever make them understand.

He had only one hope, so he began to speak, going into great detail about the equipment he'd seen in England, explaining at great length how primitive most of it was. He took so long at this that Saul and Charles gave each other an impatient look; even his father began tapping his foot against the floor as he did when he grew restless.

Finally Adam stood up and said desperately, "You know, sometimes plans change. I mean, we start out to do something, and then when circumstances jump out at us, why, we have to act differently, you see?"

"What are you trying to say, Adam?" Miles asked, staring at him strangely.

Charles expelled a deep breath and said, "You've been up to something, Adam! What is it?"

Adam's face burned, and he saw no encouragement except in Rachel's eyes, and even she looked tense. He replied finally, "I—I've had to make a few—adjustments, you might say—to what we planned."

"What sort of adjustments?" Martha's voice shot out. "You haven't lost that money gambling or something like that, have you?"

"Adam would never do that!" Mercy said instantly. She had been seated to Adam's left, out of his line of vision, and now she came to stand beside him. Placing her hand on his arm, she looked up into his face with trust shining out of her eyes. "Tell me what it is, Adam. I know you did what you thought was right."

That faint encouragement drove Adam to action. "I've got to go outside and bring something in. I'll be right back!"

He left the room at a run and cleared the porch in one jump. Entering the barn, he called out, "Molly! Come inside with me!"

She came to his side, and he grabbed his brown leather case with one hand, took her small hand with the other, then made his way back. "Don't be afraid, Molly," he said, although his own heart was beating fast.

"I won't be if you stay close," she said. Then she asked, "Is something wrong, Mr. Adam?"

"Just a little family problem." He opened the door, led her

down the hall, and into the parlor.

"Adam!" Miles stood to his feet with a gasp, his eyes locked on the child.

"Father, will you sit down and listen for a few minutes? Then I'll answer all your questions." Adam was relieved to see him sit down, but there was doubt in almost every face. He said, "Molly, sit right there, will you?" When she went over hesitantly, Mercy moved over and pulled her down onto the couch with a smile.

Adam opened the brown case, and pulling the papers out, selected one. He went to the oak table, spread it out, and said, "I want you all to see this."

They gathered around and stared down at a beautifully executed drawing of some machine with a great many intricate parts. "Why, that's a very good plan, Adam!" Rachel exclaimed. "I don't know what in the world it is, but the drawing is so good. Who drew it?"

Adam replied quietly, "I did. I've taken a few drawing lessons from a builder at Amherst. It's a machine designed to plow between rows. See, you can do four rows at a time instead of just one."

"Was this one of the machines you saw in a factory?" Saul demanded.

"Well, it's *like* one they had," Adam shrugged. "I made a drawing, but the one there only did two rows, so I drew this one. If you hitch a second team, you can double the number of rows—get finished in half the time; the labor is the same."

"How much did this machine cost?" Charles asked.

"They wanted fifty pounds."

"Fifty pounds! That's a lot of money!" Saul shook his head. "We'll do better with four plows and four slaves."

"I don't know about that, Saul," Rachel remarked. "You can hire one good white man pretty cheaply. What else do you have there?"

"Well, there's this automatic churn." He found another drawing and laid it out. "Instead of sitting there jogging a plunger up and down, you put five or six urns in a row and with this overhead arm, you can agitate all of them at the same time.

You could even hook it up to wind power and do the job with no human labor at all."

"How do you know it will work?" Martha demanded. "Have you ever seen one of the things?"

Adam stared at her. "Why, no, but why wouldn't it work? Just look at the drawing."

"I'd like to know what you have actually bought with the money we sent with you!" she stated grimly. "All these pictures are very pretty, but none of them will get a crop in the ground!"

"How about it, Adam?" Saul interjected quickly. "You're covering something up—and I'd guess it has something to do with that girl."

Adam saw that he couldn't hide it any longer, so he said, "I have a list here of machinery that could be used—and the total of it was over a thousand pounds." A mutter went up at that figure, and he said loudly, "I added up what it would cost to *make* those tools—and it comes to a little over two hundred and fifty pounds."

"Why, you're not saying you can make these things yourself, are you, son?"

Adam nodded and his square face was stubborn in the lamplight. "Yes, that's what I'm saying. Give me time, and I can make all of them—and most of them better. And we can even make them to sell. There's money to be made in that."

"I want to know what you did with the money you took with you." Martha's face was adamant, and she looked around adding, "I think he's lost it or thrown it away."

Rachel came to stand beside Adam, saying quietly, "Who is this child, Adam?"

He went over to stand beside Molly, and as she rose, he explained the whole thing. When he was finished, Martha's face was livid! "You spent our money on that ragpicker!"

"Martha!" Rachel spoke sharply. "Watch your tongue!"

"This is my house and I'll say what I please, Rachel! I knew you'd stand up for him, but I'm telling you what I've said all along, and that is that he's a fool!"

Miles looked totally defeated, his face gray with strain and disappointment. Adam's heart grew sick as he looked at his father, and he could say nothing.

A frightful argument ensued, raging for over an hour. Saul, Esther, Charles, and Martha argued bitterly against Rachel and Mercy. Miles said little, but sat down in a chair, his head slumped over his chest.

Finally Adam shouted, "Listen to me!" His tone startled them, and with a pale face he said, "You'll get the money back. I can get a good job at a forge in Philadelphia. Mr. Franklin will help me."

"We need it now!" Charles growled.

"Yes, it'll take you years to earn that much," Saul spat out in disgust. "I suppose we can put the girl out to work somewhere—try to get some of the money back."

Adam stared at him, then looked around the room. Finally he said quietly, "You know, I've never been much good for anything. Never did well at books. The rest of you are all good at things. But I've always been proud to be a Winslow. I always had that, even though I wasn't much myself." He started to say more, but changed his mind. He reached down and took Molly's hand. "Tonight I'm ashamed to be a part of such a grabbing, selfish bunch of heathens!"

He started for the door, but suddenly Miles called out, "Wait!"

Adam paused, turned to look at his father, who had risen and was staring at Molly with a strange look in his old eyes. He was quiet for so long that they could all hear quite clearly the tick of the clock in the hall. Finally he began to speak, his voice reedy at first, but growing stronger.

"I was just thinking of my grandfather. Remember him, Rachel?"

"Yes!"

"He told us so many times about the poor, half-starved crowd that stumbled off the *Mayflower*! None of them rich. All poor, but all hungry for a new way of life. I was thinking about that poor boy that died in his arms just as the ship came in sight of the new land. What was his name, Rachel?"

"William Butten," Rachel said quietly. "Yes, I've heard that story."

"Yes, poor boy! Risked everything to see a new world—then died without setting foot on it." Miles spoke softly, but his words held them all in place; even Martha could not move, so intense was he. "Grandfather told it so well! How the sky was gray as ashes, and the cold wind swept the deck. There were only a few harsh cries from the gulls. And just before William died, John Bradford stood up on the deck and cried out with a loud voice— like an Old Testament prophet, Grandfather always said!—and he had the words memorized: 'One day our children will say, "Our fathers were Englishmen who came over this great ocean and were ready to perish in the wilderness. But they knew they were pilgrims, and he saved them!" ' "

"That's what he said!" Rachel whispered.

"Well, I'm glad he's not here tonight—to see what his descendants have become!" Miles struck his thigh with a thin hand and rose to his feet. "God help us, we've become so money hungry, we can't spare a few pounds for a poor child to have a new life in this country! If we've come to that, I'm ready to die and get out of it all!"

"I think we can spare the money, Miles," Rachel said softly. Her blue eyes were bright and there was a defiance in her voice that made Saul drop his head. "Don't you think it would be good to support Adam in his generous gesture, Saul?" she prodded.

He swallowed, and his voice sounded hoarse as he nodded. "Of course, Mother! I—I wasn't thinking."

"Charles?"

Charles towered over Rachel, but his face suddenly looked weak; speechless, he only nodded.

"Martha, what about you? If you feel you must have the money, I will pay the entire sum into your hand to do with as you will."

Martha stood there stiffly, her face gray, every bone in her body stubbornly resisting Rachel. She cast a baleful look at Adam, but one glance around the room told her that she had no choice. As gracefully as she could, she nodded and said, "I will agree to stand with the family."

"I thought you might!" Rachel said, irony like a silver blade in her words. "I need not ask you, Mercy, so we all say to you, my nephew Adam—" She turned and went to him, reached up and kissed him on his cheek, then said, "Well done! A real son of Gilbert and Humility, Firstcomers!"

Adam could not believe what was happening! He stood there, unable to speak; then Rachel put her arms around Molly, smiling tenderly at the child. "Molly, you are far from home, but I hope you will let us be a family to you. Would you do that?"

Molly had been shrinking into a little ball, frightened by all the arguments and harsh words. She stared up at the beautiful lady in silks, and seeing something in her face, nodded. Rachel stooped down and looked into her eyes. "I'm very much afraid you're going to have to kiss your new aunt, Molly!" And the child, frightened and confused, felt safe and secure for the first time as Rachel Howland enfolded her.

The arguments and accusations seemed to fade in the light of that which was good and compassionate. Slowly the family members left, some only too happy to get away—especially Saul and Esther. Charles did not leave, of course, but after saying a few words to Saul, he went to his room, chastened and somewhat sullen.

Miles and Mercy stayed for only a brief time. "Would you like to leave the child here with us, Adam?" Miles asked.

Adam felt the alarm in Molly's eyes, but said quickly, "No, I think I can persuade the Edwards family to have her, Father. She'll learn a lot from those children."

Miles seemed relieved, and added, "That sounds like a good plan. And your ideas, son, are good!" He stared at Adam, shook his head and then gave a half laugh. "We Winslows have a devil of a time with our sons! Your great-great-grandfather tried to make a minister out of Gilbert, and it was nearly the ruination of him! I've been stupid about you, thinking only about a bookish sort of way to get ahead, but I see this gift for making things that God has put in you—it's real, son, and if I live long enough, I expect to hear much good of you."

Adam could only nod, and then Mercy said, "Molly, why don't you sleep with me tonight? I've got this big bed and we can be warm as toast!"

As she led the child away, Molly turned and ran back to Adam. Looking up at him, she asked uneasily, "Am I still your bound girl, Mr. Adam?"

Adam smiled down at her, touched her smooth cheek. "Of course, you are! You have to put up with me for ten years, child!"

She smiled and said quickly, "I don't mind! Really, I don't!" Then she turned and followed Mercy out of the room.

"A sweet child, Adam!" Miles remarked quietly. "I'm proud that you fought for her. It's what a Winslow man should do—and what my father and his father would have done!"

"It's what *my* father did, too!" Adam said quickly. "If you hadn't jumped to my aid tonight, why, I don't know what I would have done, sir!"

Miles' old eyes suddenly dimmed with tears and he turned hastily away. "Do you think that, Adam?" he asked tightly, not trusting his voice. "Why, that makes me feel very proud—very proud, indeed!"

Adam reached out and, hesitating, put his strong hand on his father's thin shoulder, and felt it tremble beneath his touch. He said quietly, "Why, you're all Winslow, sir! I am very proud to be your son—and a small part of the House of Winslow!"

Miles Winslow stood there for a moment, savoring the feel of his son's hand on his shoulder, and then he said in an unsteady voice, "God bless you, my boy! God bless you in all your ways!"

Then he pulled away suddenly and left the room, and Adam stood there alone. Finally he looked at the crest on the wall over the sword that Gilbert Winslow had carried off the *Mayflower*. He touched the keen blade, then stared at the coat of arms: a mailed fist clenched against a diagonal stripe of blue on white, and the single word *fidelis*—"faithful"—at the base.

He stared at the shield for a long time, then turned and walked away, thinking mostly about Gilbert Winslow, the Firstcomer. As he walked, he pulled back his shoulders and raised his head with pride.

Upstairs as Molly lay under the heavy comforter that smelled like lavender, she asked suddenly, "Miss Mercy, do yer think I can learn ter read?"

"I'm sure you can!"

There was a long silence, and then Molly asked another question: "Miss Mercy, Mr. Adam likes me now, but will 'e like me when I'm growed up?"

Mercy laughed quietly but said quite seriously, "Yes, dear, I think he'll like you very much indeed!"

Sleepily the voice came one more time.

"That's good—'cause I like 'im better than anybody!" And then Molly Burns, the bound girl with the indentured heart, dropped off into a deep sleep.

CHAPTER EIGHT

"How Much Trouble Can One Small Girl Be?"

★ ★ ★ ★

"There's your new home, Molly." Adam pointed with his buggy whip to the two-story frame house that seemed to nestle in a grove of blackjack oaks beside a large, open field. When the child didn't answer, he looked down and saw that she had fallen asleep. She had a firm grasp on his coat with one hand. *Poor child!* he thought. *She had little enough in London, but at least she wasn't among strangers!*

He drove up to the front of the house, and when he said "Whoa!" to the team, Molly stirred, then sat straight up, staring out at the house. "Is this 'ere the 'ouse, Mr. Adam?" she asked.

"Yep. Come on, let's see our new home." He jumped to the ground and as he picked her up and set her down, he thought, *She's so tiny—I'll have to see she gets lots to eat.*

"Let's see our new home, Molly." As she took his hand quickly, he looked down at her with a smile. "I've never seen the place inside either."

She stared up at him solemnly, then said, "Ain't it funny t' 'ave a 'ouse you ain't never seen?"

"Well, Aunt Rachel said she made sure it was fixed up nice,

and there's got to be a couple here somewhere—the overseer and his wife. Doesn't seem to be anybody here, though."

They walked up to the door, and when nobody answered his knock, he opened the door and led Molly inside. They found themselves in the middle of a wide hallway with a set of stairs to one side leading to the second floor, a door to the left, which they found led to a large parlor, and at the end of the hall a massive kitchen and larder.

They went upstairs and he saw with satisfaction that beds were made and there was firewood by the small fireplaces, which two of the bedrooms had. He grinned at her and said, "Which bedroom do you want? This one?"

She stared at him wide-eyed, then her gaze swept the room in doubt. It was a small room, not more than ten feet square, and the ceiling sloped sharply toward the outer wall. The only furniture was a small bed, a washstand, and a small trunk, but there were plenty of wooden pegs in the wall for hanging clothing and a red rug lay beside the bed. She stared up at him, her gray eyes filled with awe. "Aw, Mr. Adam, this ain't *mine*?"

He laughed, glad to see that she was happy. She had been very quiet on the voyage home, so quiet that he became anxious about her, doubts about the wisdom of his decision filling his mind. And it had not helped when Charles had stared at him with pity in his light blue eyes, thrown up his hands in disbelief and said, "Adam! Only *you* would do a thing like this—bring home a girl practically off the streets! Why, you don't have the faintest idea of what to *do* with her, do you now?"

The truth in Charles's words had disturbed Adam, but now as he saw her mobile features light up with pleasure, he felt somewhat better. "Of course, it's yours, Molly! Now I'll bring the trunks in, and we'll get unpacked. Then we'll go see the minister, Rev. Edwards."

As they went downstairs, they heard the back door slam. "That must be the overseer," Adam said, but it was a woman who emerged from the kitchen. "Mrs. Stuart?"

"Yes, I'm Beth Stuart," she nodded. She was a large woman in her thirties with glossy brown hair and sharp eyes. He also noted that her left hand was deformed, bent into a permanent fist. "Mr. Winslow?"

"Yes, and this is Molly Burns."

"Ah, yes." A light appeared in Mrs. Stuart's eyes as she looked at the girl; then she nodded at Adam. "Seth and me have the place all ready. We been expecting you."

The front door opened and a short, skinny man with a red face and a thick mop of sandy hair staggered through the door with a large trunk. "This is my husband, Seth. Mr. Winslow and Molly Burns."

Seth Stuart dropped the trunk with an alarming crash, came forward to shake Adam's hand. He was older than his wife, in his late forties, and his grip was almost as powerful as Adam's own.

"Weel, now, Mr. Winslow, I dinna expect ye today, but welcome hame!" He had a Scottish accent and his merry blue eyes looked down at the child. "Molly Burns, is it? A gude Scottish girl ye are indeed!"

"Molly is going to be your helper, Mrs. Stuart," Adam said. "While your husband and I are taking care of the outside work, you and Molly will take care of the inside. I think you'll find Molly a good hard worker." Saul had hired the Stuarts, and from the looks of them, Adam decided, he could not have done much better.

"I know we'll be good friends, Molly," Mrs. Stuart said, going to the child and putting her hand on her shoulder. "I've never had a little girl of my own. Maybe we can teach each other some things, all right?"

Molly looked up at her, and the reserve that was a part of her character lasted only a second, then she smiled and said, "I wants to learn 'ow t' work, Ma'am." She had been tense, her lips tight, for the whole journey had been a nightmare for her in some ways. To leave her home with a man she scarcely knew had been frightening! She had not had much joy in her hovel of a home in London, but fear had lain in her heart ever since Adam had taken her on board the ship. She had slept little, eaten little, and even the warmth of Rachel and Mercy had done little to give her heart any peace.

But Beth Stuart's kind face encouraged her, and when the large woman said, "I'll help you get settled, Molly," she went upstairs with something like a light heart for the first time since she'd left England.

"Your wife is good with the child," Adam remarked as they went out to get the luggage.

"Aye, we never had any of our own," the overseer said sadly. "It'll be good for her to have a young one to fuss over."

Adam shared a few of the details of Molly's hard life with Stuart, and added quietly, "I want to see the child get a good start—a good education and everything."

"The gude Lord bless ye fer it, Mr. Winslow." He nodded and said with satisfaction, "It's glad I am to be workin' for a Christian man!"

Adam cleared his throat nervously and said, "Well, my family are Christian, but I guess I'm not much of anything myself."

"Do tell me!" Stuart said in surprise. "I thought you studied under Rev. Edwards."

"Well, a little Latin, Seth." Adam changed the subject and asked about the farm, and after they unloaded the luggage, they left Mrs. Stuart and Molly to unpack while they walked over the property. The scrawny Scot had been there only a month, but he knew all six hundred acres of it—not only the cleared fields, but the springs, the timber and even where the best hunting could be had!

"Seth," Adam said finally, as they made their way back to the house, "I might as well tell you now that I'm no farmer. I guess you know more about it than I ever will."

"I'd not be too quick to say that. . . !"

"This is mostly my family's idea, and if it works, it'll be your doing. We might as well understand each other right now." They paused, and Stuart saw that his young employer's dark blue eyes were about as intense as any he'd seen. "You do the farming, and I do the rest of it. Mostly I'll be working on machines and keeping things up in that way."

"Weel, if you can do that, we'll maybe make a farm of this place, Mister Adam!" Stuart had been apprehensive about the whole matter, and had said often to his wife, "We may be movin' on, lass. If the new owner's not a man of sense, we'll have to leave." Now he saw that Adam Winslow was his kind of man, and his intelligent eyes warmed in a smile. He stuck his hand out, saying, "It's not going to be easy, mind you, for the place is run down something fierce! But give us a few good years and some willin' hands, and we'll make this farm something to notice!"

Inside the house, Mrs. Stuart had helped Molly fix up her small bedroom, noting how scanty the child's wardrobe was, and making a firm resolution to remedy that. Then she had led the way to the kitchen and was pleased that as she prepared a noon meal for the men, the girl was anxious to help and quick to learn.

Beth had noticed that Molly got more nervous as noon approached, but said nothing. Then, as she expected, the girl spoke out her fear. "Ma'am, Mr. Adam, 'e says I gotta go to the minister's 'ouse to learn me letters."

"Well, now, that's fine, isn't it? Everybody in the parish speaks well of Mr. Edwards."

Molly's brow knitted, and she picked at her blouse nervously; when she looked up there was fear in her clear gray eyes. "I don't wanna go there."

"Why not, Molly?"

She ducked her head and said nothing. Then she finally looked up, there were tears in her eyes. "I—I'm *stupid*—and they're all so smart—" She bit her lip and then said with anger, "And that 'un called *Mary* is the wust!"

"How do you know that, child?"

"Cause Mr. Adam, 'e's allus gabbin' about her, 'e is!"

Mrs. Stuart knew little about Molly's past except what few facts she had learned from the brief history the child had given her while they were working. She had sharp eyes, however, and it was obvious to her that Molly Burns had fastened on to Adam Winslow, and this "Mary" was clearly seen as a threat.

She started to speak, then heard the men approaching, so she said only, "Now, you just wait, Molly! Mr. Adam is very proud of you, and I hear that the Edwards children are very nice."

There was time for no more, but there was a rebellious set to Molly's posture. Adam said while they were eating, "We've got plenty of time to go over to Rev. Edwards this afternoon, Molly. I know you must be tired, but I want you to meet them. I'm sure you and the girls will be great friends—especially Mary!"

Mrs. Stuart gave her head a quick shake and thought, *Don't do that, Mister!* But she saw that Winslow was smiling happily and had not the slightest concept of how desperately the English child clung to him. *He's a good young man*, she thought, *but he's a bit thick where it comes to young girls!*

Adam talked happily as they covered the four miles from their new home to the Edwardses' house, not noticing that Molly sat stiffly beside him, saying almost nothing. Finally he pulled up in front of the house, and the two of them got out of the buggy.

They were halfway up the walk when the front door swung open and a young girl about her own age came sailing out. She was crying out Adam's name and he dropped Molly's hand and stepped forward to catch her in his arms. He spun her around laughing, and said, "Well, I guess you really *did* miss me, didn't you, Mary?"

Molly drew back as he put her down, and as the two of them chattered away, she felt very lonely. Then several other girls came out to greet Adam, but the one called Mary did not turn loose of him, holding on to his hand as if she owned him!

"Welcome home, Adam!" A tall man and a beautiful woman came out, and they both shook his hand.

The entire family swarmed around Adam, all talking and laughing, Molly drew farther back, wanting to run to the buggy.

"Well, who is this young lady?" The tall man separated himself from the group and came to stand before her. There was a kind light in his eyes as he put his hand out, saying, "I'm Rev. Edwards, child."

"Oh, this is Molly Burns, Rev. Edwards!" Adam moved to come to where they stood, but Mary held tightly to his hand, so he stood there and explained. "She's come all the way from England, and I've told her so much about you and your family."

"Why, we're so glad to have you, Molly," Edwards said.

"Come inside and we'll let you try to learn the names of this mob!"

One of the older girls, who looked about fourteen, came up and smiled. "I'm Jerusha, Molly. You come on and tell us all about England." Molly looked up and saw that there was a gentle look on the girl's face, so she let herself be led inside.

They went into the parlor, and for the next hour Molly's head swam, for she had never been around such a group of talkers in her entire life. They wanted to know all about her, but she was too shy to talk, so she listened while they chattered.

She looked around several times for Adam, but at first he was off in the next room talking to Mr. and Mrs. Edwards. Then when they came back, Mary pulled him off and made him sit down in a chair and was right up in his face talking as fast as she could.

Finally, they went in and sat down at a big table, Mr. and Mrs. Edwards on one end, and the children opposite each other. Molly sat next to Jerusha, whom she had trusted at first sight. She heard the names of Esther, Lucy, Timothy, Susanna—and Mary, of course, but her head was swimming with all the talk.

Adam sat across from her between Mary and Mrs. Edwards. He smiled at Molly, asking, "Isn't this nice, Molly?"

She forced herself to nod, but she had wanted him to sit by her, and she blurted out, "Oh, yas, Mr. Adam, but this 'ere 'ous ain't nowhere as big as ours!"

Mary stared at her, then covered her mouth with her hand and laughed merrily. "She talks so *funny*! Is that the way everyone talks where you come from, Molly?"

"Mary!" Mrs. Edwards looked displeased. She turned and gave the visitor a smile. "Mary is very rude at times, Molly. You must forgive her."

That incident served to seal Molly's lips; she would have allowed herself to be torn to pieces rather than be made fun of again. Jerusha and her parents saw the tears form in her eyes, though Adam did not.

After they left the table and the children all went into the parlor, Mrs. Edwards detained the young man long enough to say firmly, "Adam, you split wood very well." He stared at her blankly. Then she smiled and said, "That child is very frightened, and you must be very careful. She's far more fragile than a log of oak. Didn't you see how frightened she was at the table?"

"Frightened?"

"Yes! You left her and talked with others and then you didn't sit beside her. She's very much afraid—as anyone would be in her situation."

Adam's face flushed, and he said, "I—I guess I wasn't thinking. I'll be more careful."

She stared at him with apprehension in her fine eyes. "Adam, I don't think you have any idea of what you've done. Oh, it was noble of you, from what you've told us, and I honor you for it. But it's so much more than having a *servant*! She's a bound girl for ten years, but she's a small girl who's very much afraid. And her future is in your hands, Adam. You've taken upon yourself the responsibility of her life—do you understand what an awesome thing that is?"

Adam Winslow stood there twisting his hands, his eyes suddenly cast down. He shook his head slowly. Then he looked up and there was sadness in his dark blue eyes. "I'm always doing some fool thing! Guess this is just another one, Mrs. Edwards— I must have been an idiot to think I could help the girl!"

She touched his cheek, looking at him with a soft light in her eyes as she shook her head. "No, you did what very few men would have done, and I'm very proud of you, Adam. But you must always remember that from now on *you are Molly's family!*"

He stared at her, swallowed hard, then nodded. "Yes, Mrs. Edwards. I—I'll remember that."

"We'll help you, of course. But I must warn you of one thing."

"Yes, Ma'am?"

"Mary is very possessive, Adam! She is the brightest of our children—but not the kindest. That's Jerusha. Do you understand what I'm saying?"

Adam looked blank, then said bluntly, "No, I don't."

"Men!" Mrs. Edwards snorted. "Well, let me make it plain for you: Molly needs you—but you've let Mary monopolize you ever since you've been in this place. You're a big toy to her. All she has to do is snap her fingers and you jump. Well, that may have been all right before, but you must be more careful now."

"You mean, my first responsibility is to Molly?"

"Exactly! Now, it will all work out, but you must be careful, Adam!"

She said no more, but Adam was downcast. He said little, but he saw that Molly was unhappy, so half an hour later, he said, "We must be getting back."

"Why don't you let Molly come over on a regular basis and begin her schooling with the girls?" Edwards asked.

Jerusha saw the fear in the child's face and went to her at once. "Why, that'll be fun!" she said, putting her arm around the girl. "You will come, won't you, Molly?"

It was a kind and tactful thing to do, and Molly nodded, saying, "Yes, if you'll 'elp me, miss."

"We all will!" Jerusha said gently, and Mary added, "Why, I'll teach you better than anybody, Molly!"

They left then, and Adam tried to find out what was going on in Molly's mind, but she answered his questions shortly. Finally he said, "Molly, I'm sorry if you didn't have a good time."

She bent her head and he was startled to see a tear run down her cheek. "Oh, Molly, you mustn't do that!" he said in dismay. Stopping the team, he turned to her, and in an awkward display of affection, he put his arm around her, saying, "Molly, I know I'm thoughtless sometimes, but you mustn't be angry with me. It's just that—well, I've never had anyone to—to take care of, so I don't know how to go about it." He felt her shoulders shaking, so he sat there helplessly, not knowing what to do or say— wishing that he'd left her in London, wishing that someone else could step in and take over, but knowing there was no one else.

Finally he said huskily, "I know I neglected you today. I shouldn't have left you alone. But I want you to know one thing—look up at me!"

He pulled her face up, appalled to see her small defenseless features contorted with grief. She had her eyes shut tightly, and was biting her lip to hold the sobs back.

"Molly," he said quietly, holding her fast with one arm, "I

want you to know that I love you very much—and as long as I live I'll take care of you. That's all I can say!"

She opened her eyes suddenly, and he saw the fear that had been in them all day replaced by a sudden flash of joy. She smiled tremulously and whispered, "Will yer now? Will yer truly allus take care o' me?"

"Yes!"

Molly Burns—bound girl—did not say anything, but he saw that his promise had driven away the despair that had filled her. She nodded once, then grabbed him in a wild embrace, the first time she'd ever done such a thing. And as she held on to him, Adam Winslow thought, *God help me if I ever let this child down!*

As they sat there holding one another, Adam realized that it was not the child that was "bound"—*he* was the who was bound by his promise!

Ten years! he thought wryly. *Some of those who came over on the Mayflower were bound for that long—I guess I can do it, too. After all, how much trouble can one small girl be?*

PART TWO

NORTHAMPTON

★ ★ ★ ★

1745–1750

CHAPTER NINE

A BROOCH OF SILVER

★　★　★　★

A sudden movement caught Molly's eye, and she held the goosequill pen off the sheet of paper, glancing out of the single window of her bedroom at the antics of a pair of purple martins. As they sailed acrobatically to a landing at the birdhouse, a smile turned the corners of her wide mouth up. It was the third time she'd watched a family of the connubial birds raise a family, and she suddenly remembered how Adam had built the birdhouse and set it outside her window during her first lonely months at Winslow House. She cast an involuntary glance at the forge, noting the smoke pouring out of the chimney, and her eyes softened at the memory of Adam sitting beside her for hours as the birds had come that first March. He'd held her in his lap, pointing out the antics of the martins, and a warmth filled her as she thought of how he'd drawn her out of her solitude during those days.

She sighed, lowered her eyes and, noting that her pen was dull, she cleaned it with a small cloth, trimmed it with a silver-handled knife Adam had made for her for that purpose. A small stack of papers was neatly stacked on the desk beside her, with *Molly Burns—Her Journal* written across the first sheet in a careful childish hand. Dipping the pen in a bottle of ink, she began writing in an even hand across the sheet:

28 May, 1747

Yesterday Adam's brother, Rev. William Winslow, preached instead of Rev. Edwards. I liked his sermon very much, and afterwards he came home with us to take dinner. Mrs. Stuart and I cooked a good meal. I made some blackberry tarts and he liked them as much as Adam. He asked me how old I was, and when I said *thirteen years old*, he seemed much surprised, and said many nice things, like "My! what a fine young lady Molly has grown into during the last two years!" He is so handsome—much taller than my master, I'm afraid, and Jerusha says that every young woman in his parish is dying to marry him!

The sow gave birth to fourteen pigs yesterday, so with the two new calves, we will have plenty of meat. The garden is much better than last year! The new kind of tomatoes are already so big the stalks are bending double, and the potatoes are doing well.

I am very excited about meeting Miss Jerusha's young man. We are going to the Edwards' house this afternoon for supper. It is Mary's birthday, and I made her blue blouse out of the silk that Adam had bought at Boston last month. Mrs. Stuart helped me, but I did very well, Adam said.

I hear Mrs. Stuart calling me, and must end this writing, which I do with a prayer of thanksgiving to God for bringing me to this place. When at times I wake up at night after one of my bad dreams, almost crying out with fear as I do when I dream of my childhood at home, how wonderful it is to suddenly know that I am here at Winslow, with Seth and Beth almost like parents—and of course with my master, Adam Winslow, who has shown nothing but kindness for these two years!

Beth Stuart had been calling urgently. Molly blotted the sheet, carefully added it to the others, then slipped the journal into the lower drawer of the small chest beside her bed.

"I'm coming!" she called out, then ran out of her room and down the stairs.

"Molly, I've been calling you for ten minutes!" Mrs. Stuart said sternly. "If you're going to get Mr. Adam to that party, you'll have to go drag him out of that shop right now!" She spoke harshly enough, but there was a light in her eyes that betrayed her affection for the girl, who was not in the least frightened by her frown. The Scotswoman had been a mother indeed for the past two years, showering her with love such as she had never known, and teaching her many skills—cooking, washing, canning, sewing, and a dozen other arts of the country housekeeper.

"I'll get him—but will you finish hemming my new dress, please?" Molly did not wait for an answer, but patting Mrs. Stuart fondly on the shoulder, skipped out of the back door and ran lightly to the large wooden building a hundred yards east of the main house.

Pushing the door open, she entered and saw Adam standing with his back to her at the wooden workbench. He did not hear her enter, and when she said, "Mr. Adam. . . !" he gave a sudden start, and wheeled to meet her with a frown on his dark face.

"Molly! Don't sneak up on a man like that!" He turned and swept something into a soft leather bag, then blew out the large lamp that served as a light for the fine work he did. Turning again to face her, he saw that he had driven the smile from her face. He smiled at once, saying, "I didn't mean to speak so rough." He was rewarded at once as her face lit up, and he thought as he had many times, *This child is so sensitive! Have to remember to be gentle*. He put his arm across her shoulders, grinned and said, "It's hard to live with a grumpy old blacksmith, Molly, but you and Mrs. Stuart will make something out of me yet!"

"It's time to get ready, Mr. Adam," she said, pulling at his arm. "You've got to wash and shave and I've pressed your best suit—you hurry up now!"

He allowed her to pull him through the door, and as they made their way across the yard spotted with Black Winslow chickens, he marveled at how she had changed since the first day they set foot at Winslow House—the name that had gotten attached to the farm. She had grown taller, of course, so that now at thirteen she was almost as tall as Mrs. Stuart. He thought suddenly of how much she was like the young colt that frolicked in the pasture across from the house—leggy, awkward, but with the grace that all young things seem to have. *First thing you know,* he thought with a sudden grin at her, *the place will be cluttered up with a herd of young fellows wanting to court her!*

"You wash, now, and don't forget your neck!" Molly gave a warning shake of her finger at him, then left him at the pump, saying, "I'll have the hot water and your razor as soon as you're finished."

He washed his upper body, then his face, then stuck his head under the pump. As he worked up a lather with the heavy square of lye soap, he thought of how the girl had lost her early fears. She had been as shy as one of the wild kittens at the barn for the first few months. *Now she bosses me around like I was the bound servant*, he thought as he dried his thick black hair on the towel she'd left. *Mostly Beth's doing—she and Seth have been a god-send for the child!*

He went inside and found the water and his razor and soap waiting. He shaved carefully, then turned and noted his clothes carefully laid out on the bed. He put on linen undergarments, the brown homespun breeches, then the fine white shirt, the buff-colored coat, and finally the fine leather boots he'd bought on his last trip to Boston.

He took a small bag from the pocket of his work clothes, put it in his inside coat pocket, then left the room, calling out, "Molly—are you ready?"

"Yes, I'm coming!"

He met Mrs. Stuart at the bottom of the stairs and said, "We may be late getting home, Beth. You and Seth don't have to wait up." Hearing light footfalls on the stair, he turned; seeing Molly he said, "My word! How nice you look!"

Beth Stuart saw the rosy glow that rose to Molly's neck and cheeks at Adam's words, and she was gratified to think that the hours she and the girl had spent on the dress had not been wasted.

"Thank you, Mr. Adam," Molly murmured breathlessly. Her clear eyes were blue-gray—Adam could never decide which—but the dark blue material of her dress brought out the blue. Her ash-colored hair was combed back into a single heavy strand, and was so thick and heavy it seemed almost to pull her head back. Her figure was only beginning to fill out—just a hint of womanly fullness in her straight carriage. She wore no jewelry, but the bright yellow ribbon that held her hair, and another at the high neckline of the silk dress, added a touch of color to her attire.

Seth had brought the buggy to the front, and as they got in, he gave a spare smile, saying, "Weel, now, I'm thinkin' there's a little vanity in your dress—but ye'll no be the worse for such, maybe." He helped Molly into the seat, gave her a steady smile and said, "Ye watch this one, Molly girl! That Jerusha Edwards may set her cap for your master!"

She laughed and said as Adam released the brake and they pulled out, "No fear there! Miss Jerusha's got herself a minister—she'll not be after a blacksmith like Mr. Adam!"

They drove out of the yard, and Molly felt very grown-up as they made their way along the road, the buggy sending a cloud of dust high in the air behind them. She had been going to study at Jonathan Edwards' house for nearly two years, but this was the first time she'd gone almost as a guest. She realized, of course, that she was expected to help with the serving, but all of the other girls would be doing that as well. She sat beside Adam, brushing the fine dust of the road off her dress, and more than once she stole a look at the man beside her. *He's not as handsome as William*, she thought, then looked at his square jaw, the dark blue eyes that were now mild, but could set off sparks when he had one of his fits of fierce anger. She thought contentedly, *He may not be handsome, but he's strong and he's good!*

"Looks like you'll be losing your teacher, Molly," Adam said mildly. "I look to see Mr. Brainerd carry her off pretty soon. You'll be pretty sad, I reckon."

Jerusha Edwards was being courted at the age of sixteen by Rev. David Brainerd. Molly had been closer to her than anyone in the world except for Mrs. Stuart, and she gave Adam a sorrowful look. "Are they really going to get married, Mr. Adam?"

"I think so." Adam gave the girl a look, and added gently, "She's young, Molly, but lots of girls no older than Jerusha have families. And Mr. Brainerd is a good man—a famous one, too."

"I know."

Jerusha had met David Brainerd a year earlier, and after

Molly's lessons, she had spoken in glowing terms of the young minister who had attracted her. He had left Yale after a stormy career to become an evangelist to the Indians, and in a short time, every church in America was buzzing with his activities. He had walked into the woods at the forks of the Delaware River with no training, not speaking a word of the Indian language. Not a few had told him he would perish in the wilderness—that he would either die of starvation or be butchered by the fierce tribes that still made that area their home. Instead, he had encountered a young Indian with the unpronounceable name of John Wauwaupequuaunt, who happened to know English, having been raised by a minister in Longmeadow, Massachusetts.

From that time on, Brainerd had driven himself, ignoring the frightful hardships of the wilderness, and his success with the savages had sped about the Colonies. He had emerged from his labors with the Indians only long enough to preach on a tour. On his engagement at Northampton, he had met Jerusha Edwards. Their courtship had been swift as lightning, stunning the Edwardses and everyone else.

"I wish she wouldn't do it," Molly said wistfully. "I think he's too old."

Adam cast a quick glance at her, then said gently, "Why, he's only twenty-six or so." Then he laughed and threw his arm around her, giving her a rough hug. "I keep forgetting what a child you are, Molly! Guess folks as old as Mr. Brainerd and me seem old as the hills to you!"

"*You* don't seem old!" she said instantly, then flushed and looked away, adding, "He's so thin, though, and looks sickly."

Adam nodded. "You're right there, Molly. Mr. and Mrs. Edwards are real worried about that. Mr. Edwards told me that the man's spent too much time exposed to all kinds of weather—and he wasn't too strong anyway." Shaking his head, he said a few moments later, "I don't see how they can make it. Marriage is hard enough, and I can't see him draggin' Miss Jerusha into the wilds. That'd be hard enough on a strong man, but for a woman . . . !"

They talked little on the rest of the journey, and it was midafternoon when they pulled up in front of the Edwards' house.

Several buggies were drawn up at the hitching rail, and Adam said, "Looks like Judge Dwight is here—and most everybody else!"

They dismounted, and the younger children came in a rush to greet them. "Molly!" Susanna Edwards cried, pulling at the girl's dress. "You come and play with us!" She was six, the youngest of the Edwardses' girls, and a favorite of Molly.

"I have to go help with the food, Susanna," Molly said, giving her a pat on the head. "We'll play later."

"Adam!" A huge young man stepped out of the house, coming down the steps to meet them with a smile on his broad face. He stood six feet four and weighed 250 pounds. He stood over them, dwarfing Adam, but there was a mildness in his hazel eyes. "Been waiting for you. You want to take a look at the spring on my buggy? The stubborn thing won't stay together!"

Adam smiled up at the genial giant, nodded and said, "Sure." The two were acquaintances, though not close friends. Everyone in the area knew Timothy Dwight, the strongest man; and Adam Winslow was almost as well known for his genius for making things work. "You go on in, Molly," he added.

"You look real nice, Molly," young Dwight smiled down at her. Then they turned and walked toward the buggies, and Molly went up the steps and into the house.

She was met by Mrs. Edwards, who gave her a relieved look. "Oh, Molly—what a relief! We're absolutely *buried* in here." She gave Molly a quick squeeze and smiled. "I have to talk with Mrs. Dwight and the others. Would you help Jerusha and Esther with the food?"

"Yes, Mrs. Edwards," Molly smiled. She went quickly to the kitchen, which was a beehive of activity. Jerusha and Esther welcomed her with cries of relief. Molly felt as much at home in this kitchen as she did at Winslow House, and though the others were older, she had an efficiency about her that soon made itself felt. For two and a half hours she worked with the other girls, Mrs. Edwards popping in to check on the progress of the meal, and finally at four o'clock, Esther said with relief, "I think it's all ready. I'll go tell Mother to get everybody seated."

There were too many guests by far to seat them all, even in

such a large dining room. The children and the younger people were herded into the parlor, while the Edwardses and their guests ate around the large dining room table. Molly, wearing a white apron over her dress, served the adults. Carrying in the large platter of sliced beef, she saw the Edwardses seated at the head of the table. To their left was the guest of honor, David Brainerd, and seated beside him was Jerusha. Across from them sat Judge Dwight, a large man with a florid face, and his wife, a thickset woman with silver hair. Their son Timothy sat beside his mother, and Adam beside him. Two other ministers and their wives from nearby parishes completed the table with one exception—Mary Edwards, the only child present, who sat beside Adam.

Molly was surprised, but not greatly. Mary was the one child who seemed to be able to manipulate her parents. And after all, it *was* her birthday. She was looking even prettier than usual in a beautiful white dress with green ribbons at the shoulders, and her glossy brown hair gleamed in the candlelight. She caught Molly's eye, gave her a saucy wink, then turned to pull at Adam's arm, drawing him away from a conversation he was having with young Dwight.

The meal lasted a long time, for it was far more of a social event than Molly was accustomed to. At Winslow House they sat down and ate steadily, then got up and went to the parlor to talk. That night the meal went on for an hour and a half, with over six courses, then coffee or tea with cakes as the talk rolled on and on. Molly was in and out of the room constantly, or else standing beside the wall ready to carry a plate away or fill a glass, so she heard it all.

She was most interested in David Brainerd, and she noticed that he ate practically nothing, merely picking at his food. Jerusha would lean close and urge him to eat, and he would give her a smile, but did not eat enough for a child. He was a slight young man, with a thin face and very fine hands. Molly noticed as she bent over him to pour tea that his fingers were bony, and there were two red spots on his cheeks—not a healthy red, but feverish and sickly.

He did take part in the conversation after sitting silently for the first thirty minutes. He had a high voice, not strong at all, as most ministers, but as he spoke of his love for the Indians and made little of his own hardships, Molly warmed toward him.

Judge Dwight said when Brainerd had finished, "Ah, Reverend, would that a little of your good spirit were abroad in our Colonies!" He shook his heavy head sadly, then continued. "There's a coldness among us spiritually that makes the physical cold of the wilderness seem as nothing!"

"The Revival has lost its fire," one of the older ministers said sadly. He looked at his host and said, "Brother Edwards, you must be heartsick over the lukewarm condition in our churches, are you not?"

Edwards nodded sadly, and there was a fatigue in his face that had not been there, Molly noticed, when she had first come to Northampton. "Yes, it is tragic to see a revival fade—and I must admit that we are in decline."

"I remember back in the early thirties," Judge Dwight stated. "My, it was nothing to see a whole congregation falling to its face before God, convicted of sin and ready to repent. Now we seem to be frozen."

"Well, there are exceptions, of course," Edwards returned, "and we must not give up hope, Judge. The Spirit of God will move when His people respond."

Timothy Dwight picked up a large tankard that looked like a toy in his huge hand, emptied it, then remarked, "Well, it seems to me there are more church members busy fighting their pastor than fighting the devil."

"Timothy!" his mother admonished instantly with a warning look.

"Oh, it's no secret that many of my church members are unhappy with their pastor, Mrs. Dwight," Edwards said with a faint smile.

"The sermons you preach against the Half-way Covenant have made you no friends," Adam said. The Half-way Covenant was a compromise agreement that allowed the children of church members to become a part of the church without a conversion experience of their own. Edwards had taken a strong stand against it, insisting that every individual must have a conversion experience.

"When Jesus said, 'Ye must be born again,' " Edwards smiled at Adam, "that eliminated any other options."

Judge Dwight looked uncomfortable, shifted in his seat, then said bluntly, "Rev. Edwards, you know that I stand with you on this issue, but many of our churches do not. And your controversy with Charles Chauncy has hurt you."

"Charles Chauncy is a good man, but not at all sound," Edwards stated without anger. "He believes that some of the unfortunate cases of emotional excesses of the Revival prove that the entire move was not of God. I must demonstrate that despite these errors, the awakening was a move of God. If he wins people to his way of thinking, Judge, we will never see God move in a mighty way among His people."

Molly listened carefully, for she was aware of the opposition Edwards was facing. It had gotten so bad, Jerusha had told her, that many church members refused to speak to the pastor or to any of his family. Her heart ached, for she loved the Edwards family dearly, and she had seen the strain grow as the situation worsened.

Finally the talk dwindled, and just as Molly waited for them to get up and go to the parlor so she could clear the dishes away, Rev. Edwards got to his feet. His tall frame seemed even taller in the flickering light of the lamps. There was an expectant expression on his face as he spoke, "We must not forget the dual purpose of our coming together, friends. We have said little about our guest, but Mrs. Edwards and I would like to express our joy in the coming marriage of our daughter Jerusha to Mr. David Brainerd."

There was a time of congratulations and toasts, during which Jerusha blushed and Mr. Brainerd nodded his thanks with a smile.

"Now, it only remains that we owe our youngest guest a happy birthday," Edwards said with a smile. "Mary, on your thirteenth birthday, we wish you many returns!"

Again applause and laughter ran around the room, and Mary rose to her feet, poised and beautiful, to open the gifts that were placed before her. The children all crowded in from the parlor as Mary began opening the presents, making a witty comment about each.

She's so beautiful! Molly thought, hanging back in the shadows. Mary had always been the brightest of the children, the natural leader. She had been cordially kind to Molly most of the time, although there had been moments when she ran roughshod over the English girl. The most obvious of these times had involved Adam, for Mary felt she had first claim on him, and Adam had not always been careful to keep his promises to Molly when Mary had other plans.

Finally, after all the packages had been opened and Mary had thanked everyone, Adam rose and suddenly said, "Here's one more, Mary—a small one made by a very clumsy blacksmith."

Molly recognized the leather pouch; it was the one he had had in the shop! Mary took it, pulled the drawstring, and let something fall out into her open palm.

Every eye was on it, and Molly saw the girl's eyes open wide as she held something that glittered brightly in the candlelight.

"Adam!" Mary whispered. "It's the most beautiful thing I've ever seen!"

She held it up to her throat, and they saw that it was a beautifully designed silver brooch with a red stone in the center. It was in the shape of a star, and the silver was worked so delicately that it seemed to be spun of silver thread.

"I got the stone from a peddler," Adam explained, as he stood there enjoying the look on Mary's face. "He claimed it was a blood ruby."

Mary turned and threw her arms around his neck. She was a tiny girl, much smaller than Molly, and looked as delicate as the brooch. Adam laughed and caught her to himself, hugging her joyously.

Molly suddenly whirled and left the room, her eyes smarting with tears. She pushed her way through the crowd, ran to the back door, and almost fell down the steps as she sought the darkness of the outdoors.

She walked blindly along the path that went to the pond, biting her lip to keep from sobbing. How long she walked she never remembered, but when she came back, Jerusha met her.

"I've been waiting for you, Molly," she said, then took the younger girl in her arms. She said nothing, but held her quietly as the child sobbed, giving way to the tears that could not be held back any longer.

Finally Molly drew back, ashamed, and wiped her face with a handkerchief. "I—I'm sorry, Jerusha. I don't know what's wrong with me."

Jerusha smiled strangely; then she said, "You're growing up, Molly," adding quietly, "Mary is sweet, but she's careless of others' feelings. And Adam is not tactful."

"I don't care what he does!" Molly snapped quickly. "I'm just a bound girl to him—just a servant!"

She whirled and raced away from Jerusha, who stood there for a long time staring into the darkness. Then she sighed and went into the house.

CHAPTER TEN

TRIP TO BOSTON

★   ★   ★   ★

"Adam, will you be going to Boston this week?"

"Why, yes, I will, Brother Edwards. My father sent word for me to come, so I figured to go right away." Adam noted the strain etched on the pastor's face, and asked tentatively, "Is there anything I can do for you while I'm there?"

"Actually, it's a little more than that I'm asking—perhaps it will be more than you'd care to do."

Adam's tanned face lit up and he said strongly, "No, I owe you more than I can repay, Brother Edwards. You and your family have been so good to Molly that I'm beholden."

"Why, that's been no burden, Adam. As a matter of fact, it was Molly who told Jerusha you were going." He hesitated, and there was a stoop to his shoulders as if he bore a burden. Adam knew of the opposition Edwards had been having in his church, and he thought at first that the request had something to do with that; however, it was something quite different.

"David Brainerd is quite ill, Adam," he said heavily. "I've been concerned about him for some time, so I asked Dr. Mather to stop in and see him earlier this week."

"What did he say?"

"He—could not give him any encouragement." Adam

stared at Edwards, knowing that this was more serious than any of them had thought.

Edwards suddenly gave Adam a peculiar look. "I can see that bothers you, Adam."

"Why—of course, sir!"

The minister bit his lower lip—something Adam knew he did only when he was struggling with a knotty problem. He looked directly at Adam again and said, "It bothers you, my boy, because you are not ready to meet God."

That blunt announcement caught Adam off guard. He reddened deeply, unable to answer. Edwards was the kindest man he knew, and unlike many of the hell-fire-and-damnation preachers that abounded in the country, he seldom spoke so plainly. Perhaps it troubled him as well as Adam, for he went on quickly. "I'm sorry to be so direct, Adam, but I think you must know by this time how Mrs. Edwards and I feel about you. We couldn't think more of you if you were our own son—but I feel that I've done you an injustice by not speaking on the matter long ago."

Adam's flush deepened, and he stared at his feet. Finally, he lifted his eyes to meet those of Edwards', saying, "You think I'm not a Christian, sir?"

Edwards said simply, "Ye must be born again." He put his hand on Adam's shoulder and added, "I would be very glad if you could tell me that you are indeed a new creature in Christ. Can you say that, my boy?"

Adam struggled with his thoughts, but finally whispered, "No, sir, I can't say that."

"I was afraid not—but that could change! You have heard the Gospel for quite some time. Do you believe the Word of God? Well, I feel certain that you do."

"Yes, sir!"

"Then you know what God requires—repentance, faith toward God in His Son the Lord Jesus. All that remains is for you to obey the scripture. The trouble in my church is tied to this. I say that men must have a personal experience with God—they must be born again, as the Scriptures clearly state. Would you like to call upon the Lord, Adam?"

With all his heart, Adam longed to say *yes* but there was something blocking this impulse. He stood there, torn between the desire to do exactly what Edwards asked—and the fear that rose up in him like a black cloud.

Finally he said sadly, "I—I can't do that, sir."

Edwards did not press the point. He said only, "I have faith that you will find Christ as your Lord very soon, Adam. I'll pray for that!"

"Mr. Brainerd—he's going to die, then?"

"We all must do that, Adam," Edwards said with a shake of his head, "but David is in critical danger. He insists on going to Boston to wind up his affairs. He feels he must put his missionary work in good hands, so that if he does pass away, the work will go on. Jerusha wants to go with him, and Mrs. Edwards and I have agreed. But it's out of the question for a young woman to make a trip like that alone with a man. It's asking a great deal, but would you be willing to take them? He says he can get the business done in two or three days."

"I'll be glad to." Adam shook his head sadly. "Wish I could do more." A streak of fatalism flashed in his dark blue eyes, and he stared off into the distance, thinking about Brainerd. "Not much anyone can do when something like this hits, is there, Pastor?"

"No, there isn't—but you'll give us some comfort if you watch out for David and Jerusha, Adam." He put his hand on the younger man's shoulder, and there was a warmth in his eyes as he said before he turned to leave, "Take Molly with you. She'll be a help to Jerusha."

Two days later Adam drove slowly along the road to Boston with Molly on the front seat beside him while Brainerd and Jerusha sat in the back. When he had told Molly that she was going to Boston with him, her face had glowed with pleasure, but he had felt it best to tell her the truth, that Brainerd was dying. She had stared at him; then tears had risen to her eyes. "Poor Jerusha! She loves him so much!" she had said quietly.

They had stopped overnight twice, and Adam was glad that Molly had come. She was cheerful and a great help to Jerusha. Brainerd was frail in body and had a bad cough, but he smiled often and his calm acceptance of the dark shadow that had risen to touch his life made a deep impression on Adam.

The last day of their journey, Brainerd had looked out at the wildflowers that crowded the fields outside of Boston and said with a smile at Jerusha, "God appears excellent, doesn't He?" Adam had actually turned around and the serenity on the sick man's face was genuine. "His ways are full of peace."

Adam felt a touch on his arm, and glancing down he saw Molly looking up at him. A smile trembled on her lips, and her gray eyes were moist—the first sign of grief she had allowed to escape on the three-day trip. Dropping his hand to her shoulder, he gave it a squeeze and whispered so quietly that the two in back could not hear, "Miss Jerusha's got herself quite a man, Molly!"

They arrived in Boston at midday and deposited the couple at the home of one of his friends. "Stay as long as you like, Mr. Brainerd," Adam had said after he carried the luggage in and stood there at the door with Molly. "I'm in no hurry at all."

"You have been an angel in disguise, Mr. Winslow," Brainerd said with a smile. "Jerusha and I are in your debt."

"An angel?" A quick flash of humor swept across Adam's face, and he shook his head in wonder. "I've been called lots of things, sir, but no one ever put *that* one on me! Send word to my father's house when you're ready."

Jerusha kissed Molly goodbye, and Adam turned the horses toward the outskirts. The two of them said little as they made their way through the city and down the dirt road. Finally, just before they arrived at the house, Molly said in a quiet voice, "Mr. Adam?"

"Yes, Molly?"

"You said Mr. Brainerd is going to die?"

"I think he is," Adam answered slowly.

"He's not afraid, is he?" Molly turned to look up at him, her thin face tense with strain. "I'd be afraid if I was going to die— wouldn't you, Mr. Adam?"

The simple question caught Adam off guard, and he dropped his head as he tried to find an answer. Her own honesty prevented him from making a quick, easy answer. He suddenly realized that with one simple question, she had released something he'd kept buried deep in his spirit—a fear that he'd kept caged within, like a dangerous animal locked in a dark place. Now Molly had loosed the beast. He remembered when Jonathan Edwards had preached about sinners being held over the pit of hell, like loathsome spiders, how he had quaked inwardly with a fear that stripped away every thought but terror. He had almost fallen to the ground, as so many others had done that night. Now he suddenly realized that the fear that had eaten at his heart that night had not vanished over the years. He had only managed to muffle it by shoving the issue into a dark corner of his mind.

"I'd be afraid, too, Molly," he said slowly.

"But you go to church all the time—and you aren't bad!"

They were at the front of the house now, and as they pulled up to the iron ring driven into a huge oak, Adam shook his head, saying only, "I guess it takes more than that to satisfy God, Molly. And David Brainerd, he's sure got something inside him that most folks don't have!"

Not wanting to continue the conversation, he jumped to the ground then helped her down. "You can talk about it to Rev. Edwards, Molly—" his broad mouth grew hard, and he said as they went to the porch, "And that's what I ought to do, too!"

They were met at the door by Charles, who grabbed at Adam and pulled him roughly inside. His bright blue eyes sparkled and he grinned as he cried, "You Indian, you! Come into the house—and you, too, young lady!" Laughing, he leaned down and gave her a kiss on the cheek, then laughed louder at her rosy confusion. "I never miss a chance to kiss a pretty lady, Molly. And you're growing up to be a beauty!"

Adam allowed himself to be pulled into the parlor, saying little. He saw at once that Charles had grown into a different man, for there was an ease and assurance in him that many men twice his age lacked. He spoke easily of his travels, of meeting important men; and large sums of money seemed small when he talked about them. He was wearing expensive clothes, and a large diamond flashed as he cut the air with his hand to emphasize a point.

He was charming in a way that Adam knew he could never emulate. There was an easy grace in every move, and as Charles hovered over them, pouring tea into bone china cups, he radiated charm. He let just enough drop in his narration of the venture in Virginia to let it be known that he had become a full-fledged member of Saul Howland's firm. When he spoke of Winslow House at Northampton, he somehow made the high praise he gave to Adam for his efforts there seem—not unimportant, exactly, but at best a minor side issue.

Finally he pulled a gold watch out of his waistcoat pocket, glanced at it, then said in surprise, "I've kept you too long! I'm beginning to talk like a woman!" He got up, and nodded at the study. "Better go and see Father."

"How is he, Charles?"

"Well, not very well, I'm afraid." Charles bit his lip in a worried fashion, shaking his head sadly. "His rheumatism is bad right now, you know. Mother does her best, and Aunt Rachel helps out when she can. We've had to move him from upstairs and make a bedroom out of the study. Look, I must go now, but we'll have plenty of time to talk. You'll be here for several days, won't you?" He acknowledged Adam's nod, then smiling down at Molly, he left the house.

"I've got to go see my father, Molly," Adam said. "Come with me." He guided her to the door leading off the hall, knocked softly, then opened it as his father's voice called out, "Come in!"

Miles was sitting up in bed with a large book on his knees. A smile of pleasure crossed his lips as he looked up at his visitors. "Adam! Come in, my boy, come in—and you too—Molly, is it?"

"How are you, sir?"

"Why, you can see I'm sentenced to this bed!" Miles' face was drawn with pain, but then his old eyes sparkled and he said, "I'm like an old bear chained to a log, Adam! Terrible patient! Snap at everyone."

Adam sat down in the chair beside his father's bed, hiding the shock he felt at seeing his condition. Age had fallen with a heavy hand on his father: the once strong, upright frame was shrunken into a smallish bundle of bones. The eyes were sunk back in the sockets, and the skin was dry and fragile—parched like old paper.

"Tell me about your place, Adam," Miles urged. He pulled himself up with an effort, and for the next hour Adam told him of the progress at Northampton. Realizing how hungry his father was for talk, he went into great detail on the innovations that Seth Stuart had made, then spoke of the work he'd done at the forge. It was pathetic to see how greedy the old man was to hear of a work that he'd never see.

Finally, Adam ran down, then grinned. "I'm getting to be quite a talker, Father! But what we've done is pretty small compared to what's happening in Virginia. When Charles was leaving, he told me what great things were happening there."

"Hmmm, I suppose so," Miles shrugged. "But all that's speculation, Adam. Could all vanish like a vapor. If the French decide to flow into the Ohio Valley, we'll lose our shirts. Now, your place, why, it's *real*! Never be worth a penny less—probably a lot more. I'm proud of you, Adam. Rachel and I both are; you've done a fine job!"

Adam's tanned cheeks flushed at his father's praise. He ducked his head, muttering, "Why, that's kind of you, sir! Most kind!"

"No, it's not kind!" Miles snorted. "Just plain truth. We'll have a meeting now that you're here. The family has to go on, Adam, and I'll not be around to see to it."

"Sir—!"

"Don't be foolish, son." Miles gave an impatient shake of his head, his voice suddenly strong. "I'm old, Adam. I've had a good life—a good life! God has blessed me, and I'm thankful to Him." Suddenly he reached out and said, "The one thing I'm most grateful for, I think, is that you and I have come closer. We have, haven't we, son?"

Adam's throat tightened, and as he took his father's thin hand, he could only nod, saying in a choked voice, "Yes, sir— we have!"

The two looked into each other's eyes, and suddenly Molly (who had been quietly watching them) saw that despite the many differences in the two men—they were somehow *alike*. Not in appearance, she thought, but there was the same look in their faces.

Then Miles seemed embarrassed. He touched the book he was holding, saying quickly, as though to get away from the emotion that had risen to engulf them so unexpectedly, "I've been reading Grandfather's journal quite a bit. You must have it, Adam! Here, I've got this one for you—best leather Franklin could find in the Colonies."

"Thank you, sir," Adam murmured, taking the book. "I've read some of it."

"It's more than a book, Adam. It's a life, and it makes most of us look pretty small. The Winslows have had some pretty good men, if I have to say so myself!" The old eyes grew warm with humor, and then a light of speculation glowed as he peered at this son who was so unlike him. "I have not been a good father to you, but I have a feeling that you're going to be the best of us, son!"

"Oh, sir, not me!" Adam flushed, and said uneasily, "Charles—he's the one who'll make us all proud."

Miles said nothing, then lifted his head, but as he was about to speak the door opened, and his wife came in.

"Adam, I'm sorry I wasn't here to meet you." His step-mother looked no older than the last time he'd seen her, but there was still a hard-edged expression around her thin lips, though her words were civil enough. "Charles told me you were here. I've made up the south room for you, and your servant can have the little room off the back porch."

It made Adam uncomfortable, the way she said *your servant*, referring to Molly. Technically it was true, of course, but he was so accustomed to treating her like a young sister or cousin that he never thought of her as a bound girl. He glanced quickly at Molly, noting her pale face, but she said nothing.

"Why, that's kind of you, ma'am," he acknowledged, "but I thought we'd impose on Aunt Rachel." He made up a story quickly, not wanting his father disturbed over the arrangements: "I'll be doing quite a bit of business in town, and it'll be more convenient to stay there. And I wanted Molly to spend some time with her, too."

"As you will, Adam." She looked at Miles, who had missed none of this, and said, "Charles told me you want the family to meet tonight?"

"Yes."

"I wish you'd tell me these things, Miles," she said evenly, and there was an edge in her voice that gave Adam a hint of what his father had to put up with. *The old witch!* he thought.

"Sorry, Martha," Miles said quietly. There was something about the helpless manner in which this strong man lay that cut Adam to the heart.

"I'll take Molly over to Aunt Rachel's, sir." He got up and Molly followed him out of the room.

They drove back to town, and when they arrived at Rachel's house, she greeted them warmly. "Of course you can stay here! You're always welcome. We just rattle around in this big old barn of a house." She showed them to their rooms, and when Adam left to conduct some business, she took Molly into her own bedroom and talked with her for over an hour.

At first Molly was withdrawn, but Rachel was adept at drawing people out, and finally the girl spoke freely. She talked about the Edwards and the Stuarts, of the way she'd learned to read and of the life on the farm. She found herself telling of her life in London—the first time she'd shared it with anyone—and most of all she told Rachel of Adam.

Rachel sat listening, her heart going out to the young girl, who so obviously leaned on her nephew body and soul. Finally Molly seemed to realize how much of her secret self she had allowed to let slip, and she reddened and grew silent.

Rachel did not attempt to touch her, much as she longed to draw her into her arms. She merely said, "You've done well, Molly. I know Adam is very proud of you—as we all are." The praise drew the color into the girl's fine gray eyes, and she drew herself up, giving a rare smile. "Now," Rachel exclaimed, "let me tell you all about Adam when he was a boy! Did he ever tell you about blowing up almost a whole flock of his father's pet chickens. . . ?"

They all assembled in the parlor. Miles was sitting in the large chair, looking around at his family. There had been much talk of Virginia, the fur trade, the danger of French invasion. Adam had given a brief report on the farm in Northampton, with a touch of heat in the discussion between Saul and Miles concerning some future developments. Saul wanted to spread out, buy more land in Virginia. "This country is filled up, Miles!" he exclaimed. "Can't make a profit unless there's room to grow."

"You can lose your shirt, though!" Miles snapped.

"But, sir, don't you think it's important to move with the times?" Charles spread his hands eloquently, a smooth persuasion in his whole manner, one which most had found difficult to deny. "After all, Adam's farm can never get much larger—while those tracts on the Ohio, why, they'll be worth a fortune someday!"

"We've not seen any great profit yet, Charles," Rachel said quietly. "Your expenses, as a matter of fact, have been so high lately that it has set the project back considerably."

Charles suddenly turned pale, and Adam saw a streak of raw anger flash in his eyes; however, he mastered it, saying smoothly, "You're correct, Aunt Rachel. I stand rebuked, but let's look to the future."

Adam looked at the faces around the room, and realized suddenly that tension was in the building. Charles, he sensed, had done something that had disturbed the rest of them, but they did not speak of it again.

Finally Miles said, "Some fools wait until they die to let their family know what they intend to do with their property—but I'm not one of them!"

His words cast a silence over the room, and he grinned, adding, "Well, *that* got your attention, didn't it! But, there'll be no surprises in my will." He looked at his wife, who was staring at him suddenly with suspicion, and said, "It's a man's duty to see to his wife, and I have done that. William, because of his position in the church, will receive a cash endowment rather than property. Mercy will be given a generous trust fund and a suitable dowry. The rest of the property will be evenly divided between my other two sons."

Adam glanced at the faces around the room, and even as shock ran through him he thought, *Charles is shocked—he expected more!* But the face of his brother was a smooth mask. Charles smiled easily, saying, "Why, that's just as it should be, eh, Adam?"

"Yes, it is!" Rachel said strongly. She nodded at her brother, saying, "I approve, Miles. You always did have good judgment."

Then suddenly it was over. After the goodbyes Adam drove his aunt back to her house. It was quiet, and the cries of the owls sounded ghostly as he guided the buggy down the road.

"What did Charles do, Aunt Rachel?" Adam asked finally.

"Nothing very admirable." Rachel paused for so long that Adam thought she was finished, but then she added wearily, "Charles didn't show much originality in sowing his wild oats, Adam. Gambling, drinking—and a very large sum went to a young woman who was quite expert in such things!"

Adam stared ahead, unable to accept what he was hearing. Finally he shook his head, asking, "Does Father know all this?"

"I'm afraid so."

"It's a wonder it didn't kill him! Charles has always been his fondest hope."

"It did nearly kill him—but it made him look more closely at his other son, so it wasn't all bad."

"I'm afraid they don't like it—my getting a half interest."

"No. And I want to warn you, be very careful in your dealings with Charles, and with Saul, too! My son is a good man, but he bends things to get his own way."

"No, you're wrong about that, Aunt Rachel. I trust them to do the right thing."

"Well, let *me* be a little suspicious," Rachel said firmly. Then she changed the subject. "I like your Molly. She's going to be a beautiful woman. And she's bright, too."

"She's all of that!" Adam was glad she liked Molly, and he went on recounting the girl's good points the rest of the way home.

When Rachel repeated some of those things to Molly the next day, it brought a glow to her cheeks.

"But, he'll always think of me as a bound girl," she said with a droop in her shoulders. "And he likes small girls—like Mary Edwards—not a big old thing like me!"

"Adam Winslow is a man, and therefore sometimes quite blind!" Rachel said pertly. Then she smiled and patted Molly on the cheek, and her eyes looked amazingly young in her withered face as she whispered, "One day, Molly, he'll open his eyes and see what I see!"

When Adam got home that night, he was taken aback when Rachel said with no warning whatsoever: "Adam Winslow—you can make pretty things, but you're blind as a bat!" She stalked off, her back rigid, and Adam stood there staring at her helplessly.

"I think Aunt Rachel's getting old," he said finally.

CHAPTER ELEVEN

A VALENTINE FOR MOLLY

★ ★ ★ ★

For a week Adam and Molly stayed with Rachel, and during that time the girl learned more about the Winslows than Adam himself knew. When Martha was called away to visit her sister in Philadelphia, Rachel came to the country to take care of Miles. Adam was gone a good deal of the time working with a gunsmith named Simms, but Molly accompanied Rachel. There were plenty of servants to do the menial work, so Rachel spent a great deal of time in the sick man's room.

Miles and Rachel had not been together much in recent years, and with Martha gone, they enjoyed going back over the old days. When Rachel left Molly there alone, Miles often asked her to read from Gilbert Winslow's journal, and all through the long afternoons she lived the adventure of Gilbert Winslow and his odyssey on the *Mayflower*.

Miles lay there watching Molly's eyes widen as she read of his grandfather's duel with Lord Roth, his romance with Lady Cecily North, and his adventures with the intrepid band that planted Plymouth so long ago. "Was Lady North *really* in love with your grandfather, Mr. Winslow?" she asked breathlessly.

"I think she must have been, Molly. She sailed all the way from England to America to find him."

"And then he fell in love with a poor girl and married her?"

Miles smiled at her. "Sounds like a fairy tale, doesn't it, Molly? But my father told me many times how his mother—who was Humility Cooper, you know—told him she never had a thought that Gilbert would turn from a wealthy and beautiful woman to marry her."

Molly looked down at the book, then lifted her eyes. She was, Miles reflected, a strange child—not at all like other children her age. Part of it was her background, but even beyond that, he saw in her something of the maturity and quiet beauty that the Scottish women frequently have. "You're happy here, child?" he asked suddenly.

"Oh, yes!"

"What do you want to do—I mean, when your period of indenture is over and you'll be free?"

A startled look crossed her face, and he realized that the question had taken her off guard. "Why, I don't think about it, Mr. Winslow. It's not for a long time."

He smiled suddenly, thinking of what an eternity that was to her—and how short it was to him! "It'll be here sooner than you think, Molly. Now, read some more." He lay back on his pillow, and she picked up the story of the Winslow clan again— she, intent on the words, while the old man watched her face.

Word came from Jerusha that they were ready to return home, and on Sunday the 19th of July, Adam and Molly picked the pair up and started their journey. They made slow time, only about sixteen miles most days, and by the time they reached the Edwards' house, Brainerd was so weak that Adam had to practically carry him in.

The sick man was unable to climb the stairs, so the Edwards' maid had prepared a bedroom downstairs. Adam shook off the profuse thanks of Sarah and Jonathan Edwards, saying only, "It was nothing." Then he looked at Mrs. Edwards, who was pregnant again, noting that her face was pale with strain. A thought came to him, and he asked, "Maybe Molly could stay and help with things. You wouldn't mind, would you, Molly?"

Mrs. Edwards' face brightened, but she said, "It would be asking a great deal of Molly. . ."

"Oh, I don't mind—really I don't!" Molly said at once. She had looked forward to going home with Adam, but her heart was touched by Jerusha's pale face. She said only, "Would you bring my things, Mr. Adam?"

"Of course I will—and I'm mighty proud of you, Molly," Adam said, and the light of approval in his dark eyes brought a flush to Molly's face.

8 October, 1747

I have not written here in so long! The last three months have been dreadful. Mr. Brainerd has gotten weaker day by day, and all of us cry when we are alone. I heard the doctor tell Mr. Edwards that Mr. Brainerd won't live a week longer.

Last night Jerusha was sitting with him, and I was beside her. He'd been unconscious for a long time; then he opened his eyes and said, "Dear Jerusha, are you willing to part with me?" And she couldn't do anything but cry, so he said, "I'm willing to part with you, though if I thought I couldn't see you in heaven, I couldn't bear it."

I couldn't stand it, so I ran out and cried. Then this morning, he called all the children in and said, "When you see my grave, children, remember that there lies the man who wants to see all of you in heaven."

9 October, 1747

Mr. Brainerd died today. He said goodbye to every one of us, even me. And then he raised up and looked around with a smile and said, "It is another thing to die than people think!" And then he put his head back and closed his eyes.

12 October, 1747

Mr. Adam brought me home after the funeral. The church was full, and Mr. Edwards preached on "True saints, when absent from the body are present with the Lord."

Miss Jerusha cried when I left, and when we got home Adam said, "This place has been lonesome without you." And he gave me a hug and kissed me on the cheek. And I don't know why, but as I write this, I can't see to write for crying. Not for Mr. Brainerd, but for some reason I can't even say.

The shock of David Brainerd's death passed away for people, as such things do, but the Edwards family did not get off so lightly. Jerusha had worn herself down caring for him, and in the weeks that followed she began to develop severe symptoms. Winter was bitter that year: in January she got drenched in a freezing winter rain, and the next day took to her bed.

Adam brought the bad news to Molly and the Stuarts one Friday evening. He had come in after dark, stomped the frozen ice and snow from his boots, then gone to stand by the fireplace.

Molly brought him a tankard of hot cider and asked at once, "Did you go by Mr. Edwards'?"

"Yes, and Jerusha is sick." He took a sip of the scalding drink, made a face, then shook his head. "I didn't see her, but Pastor Edwards was real worried."

"And Mrs. Edwards with a baby coming on!" Mrs. Stuart said. She set a plate on the table, piled it high with ham and eggs for Adam. "I don't see how they make it, Mr. Winslow! Nothing but trouble. First, that fine young man, and now their own daughter."

"God's been gude to them, tho'—" Seth said, puffing at his pipe. "Most families lose a child, or more than that. And they got ten leetle ones, all alive!"

"Maybe I better go help nurse Miss Jerusha," Molly said. "There's not much work around here."

Adam took a bite of ham and stared at her. "If you feel like you ought to do it, Molly, it'll be fine with me."

She nodded and said, "I can help a lot. Esther's the only one who's any help to Mrs. Edwards."

"Except for Mary, of course," Adam added. He did not see the sudden frown on Molly's face, and it was gone by the time she looked up. "I'll take you over tomorrow—and I can cut some more wood for the pastor."

The next day Molly packed and came down wearing her warmest clothes. Mrs. Stuart was in the kitchen, and Molly said, "Let me help with breakfast."

"It's ready. Go down to the shop and get Mr. Winslow."

Molly walked across the packed snow to the shop, opened the door, and saw that Adam was not there. He had been, however, for a fire was glowing on the forge. She went over to hold her hands over the burning coals, and as she stood there soaking up the warmth, she saw a small box on the workbench. Adam was always showing her things he made in the shop, and she opened it curiously, then she caught her breath—for a flash of gold picked up the light of the forge, glowing dully in the darkness!

She pulled out a gold necklace, marveling at the tiny links and at the delicate round pendulum, not more than an inch in diameter, but marvelously worked to look like tiny strands of golden cords. It was a beautifully done piece, and she stood there gazing at it when she heard footsteps. She quickly put the necklace inside the box, closed it, then moved to the door.

"Molly?" Adam stepped inside, and seeing her, said, "I was in the barn hitching up the team. Let's eat breakfast."

"All right."

They ate and were soon on their way down the hard-packed, icy road. Adam had made special shoes for the horses and converted a small buggy to a sleigh by pulling off the wheels and putting steel runners under it. As they raced along, Adam grinned at her. "Beats any ride I've ever had!"

"Oh, yes! I wish we could ride like this all the time."

"It would be hard to do in August, wouldn't it—without snow." He glanced at Molly and said suddenly, "I'm proud of you for helping the Edwardses."

"Oh, I don't do much."

"I don't agree. Means a lot to them." The runners hissed as the sleigh raced along, and they were soon at the house. As he pulled up, he said, "Won't be long 'til Valentine's Day, will it, Molly?"

"Well, this is January 15, isn't it? Just about a month."

He helped her down, then held on to her shoulders and said, "Well, you've got a real surprise coming, Molly."

She stared at him, and his eyes were gleaming. "What kind of surprise?"

He laughed and said, "No need to pester me. You'll just have to wait—and don't go poking around in the shop looking for it, you hear?"

"I—I won't, Adam. I promise!" Molly's heart was swelling, and a joy such as she had seldom known came to her at the thought that he would give her such a gift.

He cut wood all day while she helped with Jerushà, and

when he left that afternoon, he smiled and said, "Now, don't forget about Valentine's Day!"

As he drove off, Mary came to stand beside Molly. She watched as Adam waved, then drove down the road. "What was that about Valentine's Day, Molly?"

"Oh, nothing," Molly said. "He always gets me something on Valentine's Day."

"Really?" Mary said nothing more, but she could not disguise the envy in her voice as she added, "I'll bet he'll get me something, too! Something nicer than my silver brooch!"

Molly only said, "He probably will, Mary." Then she went up to sit with Jerusha. But all day long, she thought about Adam's promise, and it made her smile when she thought of the delicate golden necklace.

She stayed with the Edwardses for a week; then Jerusha seemed to be getting better, so Adam brought her home. He said nothing more about Valentine's Day, but the next day while he was out hunting with Seth, she went to the shop and found the box on a shelf. Carefully she drew out the necklace, then carried it to the door so she could see it clearly. It was even more beautiful than she remembered! Carefully she put it around her neck, and it made her feel somehow *precious* in a way she couldn't explain. Then she carefully replaced it, and did not look at it again.

On the 8th of February Adam suddenly spoke of his promise for the first time. They were eating supper when he said, "There's going to be a little Valentine's Day party at the Edwardses on Friday; we'll go over there. Mrs. Edwards thinks maybe Miss Jerusha will be able to sit up for a little of it."

The days seemed to drag by for Molly, and finally on Thursday he took her to the Edwardses to help cook for the party. "See you tomorrow, Molly." He winked and was gone.

She worked hard all that day, not only cooking but helping catch up with the washing and ironing. She was tired when dark fell, but she went to sit with Jerusha.

"My Molly!" the sick girl said with a wan smile. She coughed with a hollow sound, and Molly got her a glass of water. "Tell me all you've been doing, dear," she said. "I get lonesome for news lying here all the time."

Molly never intended to tell anyone about the necklace, but she let it slip before she thought. As soon as she realized what she had done, she gasped, "I—I didn't mean to tell *anybody* about it!"

Jerusha had large dark smudges under her eyes, and there was an ominous leanness in her cheeks, but she smiled and said, "It means a great deal to you, doesn't it, Molly?"

"He's been so good to me—but he's never given me any-thing—anything just for *me*!"

Jerusha had known for a long time that Molly was in love with Adam Winslow as only a very young girl can fall in love with an older man. She had thought, *It will pass as she gets older.* Now she said, "I'm glad for you, Molly." Then fatigue washed over her and she drifted off to sleep in that sudden fashion that had come to alarm them all.

If telling Jerusha was a mistake, Molly made a more serious one the next morning. She and Mary and Esther were making little cakes in the kitchen, and Mary had been chattering on about the party. She had a new dress and had been describing it to them for the third time. Molly was only half listening, her mind on the necklace. Then she heard Mary saying, "I've got my silver brooch to wear—it's too bad you don't have a nice piece of jew-elry to wear, Molly. I'll let you wear my brooch sometime!"

"I don't need it! Mr. Adam is giving me a gold necklace of my very own!"

Mary and Esther stared at her, and Mary at once began trying to discover more, but Molly set her lips and would say nothing. Finally, Mary sniffed and said, "You're just making that up, Molly Burns! Adam wouldn't give a servant a gold necklace!"

Had it been possible for her to leave, Molly would have fled, but there was no way. She kept as far away from Mary as pos-sible, and she knew that the girl had told others what she had said.

When Adam came that afternoon, Timothy Dwight was with him. The two had been replacing a timber in the church, and they both got washed up just in time to join the party.

It was a simple party with just a few young people who lived closeby. They played a few games, sang songs, and spent the evening enjoying one another's company.

Jerusha was brought in when it was time to exchange valentines. It worried Molly to see how sick she looked. She went and sat beside her, and saw that her face was flushed with fever. "You need to be in bed, Miss Jerusha!" she whispered.

"I'll go as soon as you get your necklace," Jerusha smiled. "I couldn't miss that!"

It was a loud time, squealing and laughing, and finally when they all had their valentines, Adam said, "I've got a valentine here for every Edwards on the place!" He began to hand out small items he had made—such as a pair of tiny tongs for Sarah Edwards, a spoon for Jerusha, small toys for the younger children. He had pewter cups for Mary and Esther, and there was a broad smile on his lips as he passed these gifts out.

Finally, he looked around and said, "Well, that's all, I guess."

"What about Molly?" Mary said loudly. She smiled saucily around and added, "You didn't give her anything."

Molly wanted to fall through the floor, and she shrank into the chair, wishing that she were anywhere else in the world!

Adam looked surprised, then shrugged. "Well, as a matter of fact, I *do* have something for Molly, but it's outside in the sleigh. I'll go get it."

While he was gone Esther said in a whisper, "See, Mary? He did get her a necklace!"

Mary said nothing but her eyes went to the package that Adam had in his hand when he came back. He came to stand in front of Molly, and smiled as he said, "Well, here's your valentine, Molly. And if there's another like it in the country, I'll eat my boots!"

Molly stared at the package he placed in her hands, and could not say a word. It was much too large for the necklace. *Maybe it's in a larger box,* she thought. As she unwrapped the paper, she felt Jerusha bending close to see what it was.

Then she pulled out a black metal container of some sort and stared at it. It was a round pan about a foot in diameter with a sturdy metal clasp on the side. She stared at it, and he reached down and said, "It opens like this," and he lifted the top.

There was a silence, and Molly could not lift her eyes. Finally Mary asked loudly, "Well, what in the world *is* it?"

Adam smiled. "We've all gone to bed with our feet freezing. But Molly won't have any more cold feet, because she's got the first footwarmer ever made!"

"A—a *footwarmer*?" Molly whispered.

Adam did not see the distressed look on her face. He was so pleased that he took the pan from her and held it up, saying, "Look, you put hot coals in here when it's time to go to bed. There's a frame with it that goes under the bed. You put the footwarmer on it, and you've got nice warm feet no matter how cold it gets!" Then he looked at Molly, who still had not lifted her head, and he said, "Well, didn't I tell you you'd get a valentine like you never dreamed of?"

Mary laughed. "Well, it's very nice—but it'd be hard to wear it around your neck."

"Around your neck?" Adam asked. "That's not what it's for, Mary. It's to keep your feet warm. Do you like it, Molly?"

Molly sat there, and suddenly the room seemed very quiet. She raised her head slowly and he saw that there were tears in her eyes. "Thank you, Mr. Adam. It's—very nice."

He stood there, aware that something was terribly wrong, but having no idea what it was. Then Jerusha said, "I'm very tired. Would you help me to bed, Molly?"

Molly's eyes were filled with tears, but she instantly got up and led Jerusha out of the room. When Jerusha was in bed, she reached out and took Molly's hand. "Try not to feel too bad. He was thinking of a way to make things easier for you."

"I know." There was a dead sound to Molly's voice. She had dried her tears, and she said, "I'll stay with you tonight."

"No, you must go home. Come tomorrow—and don't be angry—"

She dropped off into a restless sleep, her face flushed from the high fever. Her mother came in, looked down and said, "We shouldn't have let her get up, but she wanted to so much!"

"I want to stay with her, Mrs. Edwards!"

Mrs. Edwards had heard from Esther about the necklace,

and she went and put her arms around Molly. "If you want to," she said quietly.

"I'll go tell Mr. Adam." Molly slipped away and found Adam standing beside the door, his face pale. "I'd better stay with Jerusha, if you don't mind."

"Molly, Mary told me about the necklace. I—I never thought—!"

"It's all right. I should have known better." There was something different in Molly's voice, and her lips were thin as she said, "It wasn't your fault. I'm stupid!"

"Don't say that! I—I just didn't think, Molly. I made it for Aunt Rachel, but you can have it—!"

"I don't want it. Bound girls ought to have better sense than to expect gold necklaces from their masters!"

"Molly, don't—!"

He reached out to touch her, but she pulled back, her face pale as paper. "I won't make a mistake like that again, Mr. Winslow."

She turned and walked away without another word, and Adam suddenly left the house just as quietly.

Jerusha died early the next morning, hemorrhaging without warning. It was a difficult time for Molly, but she forever looked back on that night as the time she left childhood behind.

19 February, 1747
   I have tried to pray, but nothing happens. When Mrs. Edwards told me that Jerusha was dead, I died, too.
   I can't love God, even though I try!
   Why did she have to die? Or Mr. Brainerd?
   Adam brought me home, and he tries to tell me about how sorry he is about the necklace. It doesn't matter. I don't care!
   One thing I promise! I'm a bound girl, and I'll never forget that—not as long as I'm his! Never!

CHAPTER TWELVE

CHARLES FINDS A WOMAN

★ ★ ★ ★

Fall came late in '49, the soft grasses stubbornly keeping their emerald color all through September. The leaves, ordinarily trodden under foot by the end of the month, still clung tenaciously to the oaks, and the winds, though cool, did not bite and freeze the fingers. Even in October the brooks were not skimmed with ice, and the morning sun warmed the earth by noon.

Molly caught the first trumpet of fall on the morning of the 15th as she was sitting at her small desk writing in her journal. At this time of day, the house was quiet, so Molly had formed the habit of spending the early hours of the morning writing. But now her journal had thickened. Suddenly a sharp breeze swept through the window, scattering some of the loose pages. Picking them up, she glanced at the date, then let her eyes run down the page.

It was the page she had written two years earlier on the day of Jerusha's funeral, and although time had blurred the sharp pain and bitterness, her lips grew soft as she thought of her friend. Then she read the last comment on the page: *One thing I promise! I'm a bound girl, and I'll never forget that—not as long as I'm his! Never!*

She leaned over, shut the window, then got up and slipped

out of the flannel nightgown, thinking of that time of her life—something which she rarely did. *I was thirteen years old when I said that—now I'm fifteen*, she thought as she pulled a gray cotton dress from a peg and slipped into it. The fact that it was too small made her realize how rapidly her figure had developed the past year. She and Beth Stuart could not seem to keep up with her wardrobe. *Fifteen—and he still thinks I'm a child!*

She looked down at herself, not at all happy that she was five feet nine—taller than any girl she knew and only an inch shorter than Adam. A year earlier she had begun to stoop trying to disguise her height, but Beth had railed at her: "Sit up straight, girl—you look like a worm all bent over! God's given you a tall, strong body, and you go creeping around like a cowering slave!"

She had been bullied into a good carriage, but now she thought rebelliously, *Why couldn't I be small and dainty instead of a giant?* Then she stooped and peered into the small mirror on her desk.

What others saw was a face with rather high cheekbones, the planes sweeping down to a firm jaw totally feminine for all its strength. The eyes were calm, a strange blue-gray color, large and wide spaced. Thick black lashes curled over them, and the brows arched gently under a smooth broad forehead. Her lips were full with a hint of stubbornness, yet soft and red, and when she smiled, a dimple appeared on her left cheek, making her look almost saucy. When she let her thick ash-blond hair down, it cascaded down her back like a smooth waterfall, but usually she wore it up in a crown of braids that framed her face.

She went downstairs and cooked breakfast. As she was taking the bread out of the oven Adam came in. "Winter's in the air—maybe snow," he said.

He sat down and she put a bowl of hominy and a pitcher of cider in front of him. "Charles should be in this afternoon," he said, pouring a stream of dark molasses over the hominy. He waited until she sat down; then they bowed their heads and he said briefly, "Lord, we thank thee for this food, and ask you to grant thy mercy over us this day in Jesus' name."

"Is he going to stay long?"

"No, I don't suppose." He took a pull at the tankard of cider she had put in front of him, looked at it and said, "That's a good cider, Molly." Then he shrugged, saying mildly, "Charles doesn't stay anywhere long, I guess. He's been all over Virginia, even went to England last year, according to Aunt Rachel."

"Did he say why he's coming?" Molly cut a thick slice of fragrant bread, adding a thick layer of yellow butter. "He's never come before."

"I think he wants to see that we're making money—or maybe why we're not making more."

She was suddenly indignant, and her sharp white teeth snapped off a morsel of bread; then she said, "This is the best farm in the colony! And that new plow of yours has made a good profit, Adam!"

He looked across the table, grinned at her, but only said, "I guess this operation is pretty small potatoes to Saul and Charles. They've been buying land like crazy in Virginia. Can't think what he'd want to tell me, though. He and Saul are the businessmen, and I'm just a plain blacksmith."

Molly started to deny his statement, but she had learned long ago that while there was no man more confident in working with metal, Adam Winslow saw his brother and his cousin as being superior to him in every way. It infuriated her that he put himself down so, but she only shrugged and watched him finish his breakfast.

He was twenty-two years old, and looked much the same as he had the first time she'd seen him. Among the Winslows, where all the men were uncommonly tall, he seemed small, not over five ten, but the years at the forge and on the farm had molded him into a solid shape. He did not look large, but she had seen him without his shirt, washing at the pump, and the swelling chest, the heavy muscles of the shoulders and arms, and the massive development of the muscles in his back made other men look frail. In a land of strong men, only one man was his superior—Timothy Dwight. But Dwight's strength was massive and ponderous, like a heavy draft horse, while Adam's was quick as a cat.

I wish he wouldn't feel so inferior around Charles, she thought, then gave it up as she always had in the past. Only once had she mentioned this to anyone. Mrs. Stuart had listened while Molly burst out, complaining how Adam always saw Charles as being better at things. Beth Stuart had shocked her when she'd smiled and said, "You don't like that, Molly, but I can tell you something—you do exactly the same thing with Mary Edwards!"

The memory disturbed Molly. She rose and began to clear the table. "We'll put him in the downstairs bedroom—oh, yes, we're invited to the Lindons' day after tomorrow. A last fling for Tom, I think."

"I'm not sure if Charles will want to go to such a small party," Adam said doubtfully.

"Well, let him stay at home and stare at himself in the mirror then, because I've already told them we'd be there!"

He grinned at her, amused at the fiery response. "You don't like Charles, and you don't even know him, Molly. And you better watch that temper of yours. What if the preacher heard you?"

She ignored him, and later that day when Charles got off his horse and came inside, she greeted him with a smooth countenance. He filled the doorway, his eyes alive and dancing, and after greeting Adam with a bear hug, he turned to her, and with a startled expression he said, "This isn't *Molly*?! Why, you're not a snub-nosed little brat anymore—let me see!"

"She's grown up a bit, Charles, hasn't she?" Adam grinned.

Charles was looking at Molly strangely; she felt uncomfortable, yet at the same time it pleased her. He was, she decided, the best looking man she'd ever seen, even more handsome than she remembered him. He had filled out a little, and his eyes, blue as cornflowers, seemed to look right inside her. There was a boldness in his manner that was lacking in Adam, and she knew instinctively that he had had much experience with women. He reached out to take her hand, and she saw the sharpness of his expression, heard the smooth ease in his voice as he said, "Miss Burns, I'm glad to meet you. Always a pleasure to see a young woman blossom into a beauty."

"Enough of that, Charles!" Adam laughed. "Don't give her any ideas along that line. I've warned her about your worldly ways."

"Ah, too bad!—but how do you know I haven't repented, Adam? I assure you that my feeling for Molly is strictly honorable." He still held her hand and added with a wide smile, "Just think of me as a big brother, Molly. Come to me with all your troubles."

"I'm afraid that'd be like putting the fox to guard the chickens!" Adam said wryly. They all three smiled, and Molly saw at once that Adam was incapable of believing any wrong of this flamboyant brother of his.

They spent a good afternoon, sitting around the kitchen table, with Charles telling them tall tales of Virginia. Adam and Molly sat drinking in the talk, for the man was a born storyteller. He made the dark forests and the painted savages come alive, and finally he said, "It's not so much my world as yours, Adam. I've liked seeing it, but I'm a city man. You'd do well there, as much as you like the out-of-doors."

Adam was stirred. "I don't guess I'll ever find out, Charles. Someone has to mind this place."

"I suppose, but as much as you know about guns, you'd make a place for yourself. All Virginians are sportsmen, and they'll swap their sisters for a good rifle—pardon the loose talk, Molly! There's a family named Washington close by, and they're good enough farmers, but they live to hunt. Ride to the hounds, of course, but the youngest son, George, he loves a good gun. Wish you could come and see the country there."

"I'd like to."

Later that day, Charles brought out a leather case and extracted a sheaf of papers. "We've managed to get an option on a large tract over the mountains, Adam. I couldn't believe the price!" he exclaimed. "Saul and I are spread a little thin, but you know how it is—you have to take opportunities when they open up. Saul's figured out a way to keep what we have, get a loan on some of it, and buy this section. It's really pretty involved—but we can't lose. It's all tied up with the general estate, so all of us have to sign it."

"What did Father and Aunt Rachel say?" Adam asked. He felt uncomfortable dealing with papers and lawyers, and wished that he'd gone to Boston so that his father could explain it all.

"Oh, you know how they are, Adam," Charles shrugged. "Getting on, I'm afraid, and old people are all conservative. Took a lot of talk, but Saul finally got his mother sold, and she talked to Father, so that's all right. They've already signed, and so have I. Your signature is all we need—but we've got to move fast or The Hudson Bay Company may get wind of it; then it'd be a lost cause!"

Adam stared at the papers, then nodded. "Well, if they signed, I guess I will, too."

"It's going to make us all a pile of money, brother!" Charles said. He took the papers after Adam had signed his name, and put them back into the case with an air of satisfaction. "Now, maybe you'd like to show me the place. Rachel thinks you've done something unique here."

For the rest of that day, and all the next morning, Adam and his brother walked over the entire farm and Charles showed a quick intelligence that went beyond his indolent manner. He commended Seth Stuart for his work in managing the crops, but he was most interested in what Adam was doing at the forge.

"This is fantastic, Adam!" For the past few years Adam had been experimenting with muskets, and Charles was holding his brother's latest effort. It was something of a cross between the old style musket and the Kentucky hunting rifle. "This is beautifully balanced; is it accurate?"

"Well, I hate to brag, but it'll do very well against most competition," Adam shrugged. "You know how the old flintlocks are—the Brown Bess that English soldiers use. Anything over fifty yards and you might as well forget it! The soldiers just aim in the general direction and blaze away. They don't even have a front sight! But they're easy and quick to load and the powder and ball aren't too critical—just about anything will work. Now the Kentucky rifle, why a good marksman will knock a squirrel out of a tree at a hundred paces—but the balls have to be specially made, and so does the powder, and they take three times as long to load—so massed troops can't use them."

"And what's this you've done?" Charles sighted down the gleaming barrel of the rifle.

"Well, I'm trying to find a weapon that's got the best of both the rifle and the musket. Quick and easy to load, but accurate. This is better, but the powder and shot is still critical." He hesitated, then said, "I've got an idea, Charles, but it's still just that."

"Well, Adam, after seeing this piece of work, I'm convinced you can do anything! What's the idea?"

Adam faltered, taken off guard by the praise, but he said, "Well, the obvious answer is a breech-loading mechanism, of course. Lots of men have tried, but nobody's hit the answer yet."

Charles's wedge-shaped face was alive with excitement. "You think you're on to it? Adam, if you could get that thing made, why, it'd be worth millions! Every army in the world would sell their souls for it! Why. . . !"

Adam laughed, and held up his hand in protest. "Hold on now—it's just an idea, Charles!"

"You work on that, you hear me? Why, the Winslow rifle will make our name famous!"

Adam laughed suddenly. "Remember how we blew up Father's chickens with my first gun? This may turn out like that!"

Charles threw back his head and roared. "And I ran away like a rat and left you to take the blame, didn't I, Adam?" he said finally. "You must have hated me for that!"

"Why, no!" Adam's open face showed surprise, and he added, "I couldn't fault you for anything, Charles."

The remark moved the tall young man, yet he seemed disturbed. "You're too trusting, Adam. You've got to learn to be a little more careful about people."

"You're not people," Adam smiled. "You're my brother."

Charles stared at the smaller man, and there was a light of wonder in his face. Finally he shook his head, saying, "I shall have to watch out for you, brother!" Then his face changed and he said, "Saul will be interested in your rifle, but now tell me about yourself."

"Myself?"

"Yes, not the farm or the forge, but *you*. Are you in love?"

"In love?"

"Confound it, don't be such an echo! You must have done *something* all these years besides grow turnips and make rifles. Come on, now, tell old Brother Charles all about it!"

There was a light of expectation in the face of Charles Winslow, and Adam was speechless. He opened his mouth, closed it, then finally said, "Well, I haven't had much time for such things, I guess."

Charles studied him, and there was a sharp light in his eyes. "But I think there's somebody special, right?"

"Why, she doesn't really know how I feel. . ."

"Why not?"

Adam flushed, and biting his full lower lip, he cleared his throat, saying, "Charles, I've never told anyone about this. There's only one woman I've ever felt anything for, but it's not easy. She's very young, and I've been like a big brother to her."

"The best thing in the world!" Charles grinned. "Why, all you've got to do is let her know that you're *not* her brother!"

"But she's only fifteen years old, and she's the daughter of the best friend I've got in the world."

"Well, who is this paragon of youthful beauty?"

"Mary Edwards!"

"Ah! The plot thickens!" Charles stroked his chin. "The famous preacher, I take it?"

"Yes."

"Well, I don't care if she is a preacher's daughter, she's just like any other woman! See here, I've got to give you some help in this business!"

"Oh, I don't think—!"

"When will you see her again? Soon?"

"As a matter of fact, Molly says we're invited to a party at some neighbors, and Mary will be there. But I didn't think you'd want to go, Charles. It's really a rural affair."

"Lead me to it!" Charles laughed. "Country matters are what I crave. And by the time I get you fully instructed, you innocent young Hercules, Fair Mary will fall into your arms helpless with young adoring love!"

Over thirty young people had gathered to celebrate the coming wedding of young Tom Lindon and his bride-to-be, and with the older guests, well over fifty people were present. They were hard-working people, these children of the Pilgrims, and they delighted in donning brightly colored clothes and having a time of relaxation.

Molly had drawn an exclamation from Charles as she came down the stairs in a new dress that she'd been saving for a special occasion. It was a simple blue-gray gown with a cluster of red ribbon at the high neck and sleeves and a wide red sash. It showed off her maturing young figure well. "Good heavens!" Charles breathed, taking her hand, "let me look at you!" He made her turn around, and there was a flush on her creamy complexion when he kissed her hand and said quietly, "You look very beautiful, Molly—very beautiful, indeed!"

Adam, taken aback by Charles's attention, said nothing, but he stole several glances at Molly as they went out to the carriage. He was quiet on the way to the Lindons', but Charles kept the conversation flowing, eliciting a giggle from Molly several times as he described some of the amusing happenings at parties he'd attended in Virginia.

They arrived at the Lindons' late, and Charles was immediately the center of attention. There was an exotic air about him, and his stunning good looks and fine dress would have marked him if his elegant manners had not.

Adam introduced him to the senior Lindons, then to the guests of honor, and he won the bride's favor by saying fervently to young Tom Lindon, "Zounds, Mr. Lindon, I'd advise you to keep this beautiful creature away from the city! She'd cause a stampede there, I vow it!"

Timothy Dwight came in a little late with Mary Edwards, and Adam whispered, "That's Mary!"

"Who's the elephant with her?" Charles grinned. "I hope you don't have to fight it out with him for her fair hand!" Then he looked at Mary, who was elegant in a green silk dress with white brocade, and said, "Well, she's a beauty, old boy!"

On being introduced, he kissed Mary's hand and said, "Miss Edwards, I'm honored. Your father is a man I cannot presume to praise too much. Would you object, sir, if I stole this lovely creature for a time? I've read every book her father has written! He's quite an idol of mine, you know."

As Charles walked off with Mary by his side, not at all disturbed by the thundering lie he'd just uttered, Timothy looked at Adam with a smile and said, "Well, I'm glad his charm doesn't run in the family, Adam."

Adam looked up at young Dwight, and realized that there was more in his words than the others around knew. For the last few months the two of them had been bumping into each other constantly, usually at the Edwardses, often at church or at functions like this. Adam was so accustomed to having Mary claim his attention, as she had done for years, that he only now realized, although nothing was said, that he and Dwight were engaged in some sort of rivalry.

Now staring at Timothy, Adam knew that the big man's constant attention to Mary had awakened him, making him realize that he no longer felt like a brother to her—not in any way!

Timothy read Adam's expression and said, "It's taken me a year to get Mary's eyes off you. Matter of fact, I almost gave up! Worst case of a girlhood love I ever saw!" He smiled as Adam gave him an incredulous look. "Oh, you're too dumb to know it, Adam, but everybody else did!"

"In love with me?"

Timothy laid a heavy hand on Adam's shoulder, the weight of it enormous. "Too late, old man. I've managed to cut you out pretty well, but if you were a man who knew women—as that dandy of a brother obviously does!—why, I'd have had no show at all!"

Adam felt as though he'd been kicked in the stomach by one of his mules! His mind reeled as Timothy walked off, and his thoughts tumbled wildly. *Mary in love with me? But I've never even kissed her! Never really courted her!*

For the next hour Adam was stunned. He was still able to function, but his movements were automatic and his thoughts were fragmented. He managed to play some of the simple games that the young people engaged in out in the yard, but he could not have told you a thing that happened. *Mary in love with me!* The idea shook him, but despite his confusion, he did notice one thing: Dwight was never far from Mary, and the smile she gave him was not that of a little girl, but of a woman aware that she was being pursued!

Adam Winslow was a slow-moving, easy-going sort. He smiled and was amiable in most things. But from time to time, he fixed his eye on something and, with every ounce of determination in his spirit, said, *I'll have that or die trying!*

The thick cords of muscles in his solid jaw suddenly bunched up, and his eyes narrowed to slits of royal dark blue. He stood there like a cat watching a bird, getting ready to pounce! Then he forced himself to relax, but there was something in his face that Molly saw at once—for she knew him well enough to recognize the tenacious look he had when his mind was made up.

He said little, but he began moving closer to Mary, and she recognized at a glance what was happening. Her bright eyes flashed, and all afternoon, young and inexperienced as she was, she managed to play them off against one another.

Charles had been drinking cider with Molly, and he said, "That young woman is a menace, Molly! Look how clever she is with those two!"

"Mary's clever enough," Molly answered. "She's always been able to get anything she wanted."

Charles stared at her in surprise, for there was an edge in the girl's voice. "You don't like Mary, do you, Molly?"

"Yes, I do. She's a fine girl, Charles, but she's hard on people. She's so much smarter than the rest of the world, she can get what she wants without trying. That would be bad enough in a plain woman, but she's beautiful as well—and that could be terrible."

He stared at her, a sudden flash of approval in his eyes. "You're a very observant young woman, Molly. I like that." Then he stared at the trio across the yard and said, "My word, he's huge! No man could stand up to him in a fight! I hope Adam's got sense enough to know that—but then, Adam never had any sense! He'd tackle a grizzly bear if he got mad enough!"

"I wish we'd go home," Molly said suddenly.

"Why? The party's just started!"

"These parties are pretty much the same, Charles. Sooner or later the young men will start having contests. Running, jumping, wrestling—that sort of thing." She looked up at him, and bit her lip, murmuring, "I've never seen Adam so aggressive! He usually stands on the outside and just smiles—but look at him now!"

Charles saw what she meant. Adam and Timothy were both practically hovering over Mary, looking for all the world as if they wanted nothing better than to fall on each other.

"I don't think wild horses could drag him away," Charles said. He looked at Molly and said tentatively, "Adam and I have not been very close, but he confided in me yesterday. He told me he was in love with Mary."

"He has been for a long time." There was no emotion in Molly's voice. She said it as if it were not very interesting, but he saw her lips were pressed tightly together, the small blue vein in her forehead pounding.

"Well, let's hope they don't lock horns! That fellow's a bull!"

But they did. Just as Molly indicated, the young men soon began to engage in athletic contests, and as always it turned into a tournament, each of them determined to prove to the young women how strong or fast they were.

It began with a shooting match, and Charles took part in that himself. They blazed away at a target, moving farther and farther back. They were all good shots, but soon it became evident that young Dwight and Tom Lindon were the best. Charles was eliminated, and then Dwight hit dead center, while Lindon missed.

"What about you, Adam?" Timothy asked with a challenging smile. Adam had taken no part, although several had urged him.

Now he saw that it had become a personal thing, but still he shook his head. "I guess not today."

Mary smiled and said, "Oh, I wish you would, Adam."

He lifted his head and smiled, "You want me to, Mary?" He looked at Dwight with a strange smile, then said, "I'll take a shot."

He got the rifle that Charles had admired, and came to stand beside Dwight. "You can set the distance, I guess."

Timothy looked somewhat uneasy. "That's a new rifle, isn't it, Adam? Well, I guess we can set the target back a little." He waved the young man back who was setting the white piece of board onto a tree. "That's a hundred yards. Suit you, Adam?"

"Fine."

Timothy shot first, kneeling and taking careful aim, the flint-lock steady in his huge hands. He took a long sight, then finally fired. The young man ran over, looked at the target, then yelled, "Almost a miss. Touched the outside corner!"

It was a good shot, considering the distance, and Dwight smiled, "Your turn."

Adam swept the rifle up and pulled the trigger. There was no appreciable pause between the time the gun rose and fired. The young man looked, then yelled, "Dead center!"

A sudden cheer went up from the crowd, and Mary joined in the applause. Adam's face reddened, and he should have stopped there, but he had been stung by Dwight's attitude. "Move back!" he called, and twice more he waved the man back. "Right there."

"Nobody can hit that mark!" Lindon exclaimed. "That's over two hundred yards."

Adam had reloaded, and now asked, "You want to shoot first, Dwight?"

The big man looked at the distant mark and shook his head. "You're showing off, Adam. Tom is right."

Adam raised the rifle, and this time he steadied his piece. It was, they all saw, as steady as if it were fixed in rock. Adam fired, and the call came back: "A hit—to the right."

Mary ran over and took Adam's arm, her face a picture of delight. "Adam, I never knew you could shoot like that!"

Molly said loudly, "He made that gun, Mary. Why wouldn't he be able to hit with it?"

The young men instantly crowded around, demanding to see the rifle, and Adam, for the first time, was the center of attention.

"Dwight's not happy," Charles said quietly to Molly. "I'd guess he'll try to top that shot."

And he was right. For a while there were foot races, but neither Adam nor Dwight entered into that, both of them far too heavy to challenge the striplings.

Then someone cried out, "Let's toss the stone!" They chose a stone that weighed about fifteen pounds, a round one, slapped smooth in a stream, and the young men took turns seeing who could heave it the farthest.

Adam and Timothy were deliberately placed last. Everyone in the crowd realized that Adam was tremendously strong, but young Dwight's strength was proverbial. Everyone in the village knew of the time when as a very young man he had crept up to a farmer who was driving a yoke of oxen hitched to a cart. Timothy had tiptoed up behind the cart, yanked the oxen to a halt, then held them as the farmer urged them on, their hooves skidding and scrambling as the young giant held them in place.

As Adam picked up the stone, hefting it in one hand to catch the balance, the crowd held its breath. He crouched and sent it sailing twenty feet past the best attempt.

Then Timothy walked over, and just the way he picked up the stone in his huge hands, as if it *had* no weight, brought a whisper from the crowd, and Adam bit his lip. He came back to the mark, turned ponderously, then sent the stone flying through the air! It went far beyond Adam's mark. Everyone gasped.

Every eye turned to Adam, and there was an eager light in their eyes, for the thing was turning out to be a personal contest between the two men. It happened often that two young men would pursue the same girl, and most of them realized that Adam and Dwight were actually competing for Mary Edwards.

Adam glanced at the stone, shrugged, and smiled briefly, "No man in the world can beat *that*, Timothy."

"I hope that's all of it—they're even," Charles muttered, but it was not to be.

"No, they'll wrestle," Molly said grimly. "They always do. But Timothy never has. He said once he was afraid he'd hurt someone."

"Adam has more sense!" Charles protested.

"No. He doesn't!"

Molly's bitter words were prophetic, for when all the others had wrestled, someone cried out, "Timothy, what about you and Adam?"

"No, it wouldn't be fair," Dwight answered.

Adam's face burned at the implication, and he said at once, "I'll take a fall with you, Timothy."

A cry of excitement went up and a circle formed instantly around the two men.

To Charles it was incredible. He stared at the bulky form of Timothy Dwight—six foot four and 250 pounds of hard muscle. Then he looked with apprehension at his brother. Adam had taken off his boots and was circling his huge opponent; he looked small. Charles had laid his hand on Adam's shoulder once and been amazed at the thick sinews, but he still had no hope. *A bullet in the brain! That's what would stop that big ox!* he thought.

Everyone saw at once that Dwight's tactics were simple. He could not hope to match Adam's quickness, but if he got one hand on the smaller man, the contest was over; no human could pull free from a grip such as his!

Twice Adam feinted, and twice Dwight was faked out of position. Both times Adam could have gotten a hold, but he knew full well that if he missed, he would be as helpless as a baby in Timothy's hands.

Then as Adam moved close, Dwight's hand shot out, but he caught only the fabric of Adam's shirt. It tore away like paper, and the crowd drew a sudden breath, for none of them had ever seen such a man as Adam. His body was smooth with muscle, tapering from a trim waist to enormous pectoral muscles, and with every move, the tremendous power of his arms was revealed.

It could not last long, and it didn't. Adam moved to his left, drawing Timothy after him, and as the large man went for him, he shifted, agile as a cat. He reached out and jerked Dwight even more off balance, and for one second, the giant's back was to him. Adam leaped high, whipping his arms around Dwight's throat, and locking his powerful legs around his waist.

A cry went up, and Molly saw that Adam's eyes were blazing, and she put her hand to her mouth.

Dwight tried desperately to reach back and get his hands on Adam, but the smaller man ducked his head and clung like a burr. His right forearm was pressed against Dwight's windpipe, and his left locked that arm in place.

Dwight's face grew red as his air supply was cut off, and a terrible whistling noise came from his tortured throat. Charles suddenly ran to the pair and pulled at Adam's arms, but they were like iron bands. "Adam! You're killing him! Let go!"

Adam did not relax and Charles saw madness in his eyes. He reached out grabbing Adam's thick hair and pulling his head back, at the same time yelling in his ear, "You're a Winslow, idiot—not a murderer!"

The words got to Adam, and he loosed his grip at once, and stood there, a dazed look on his face. He stared at Dwight, who was gagging and trying to get his breath; then his face turned deathly pale. He went over and stood looking up at the big man, saying, "Timothy, I—I didn't mean to. . . !"

Dwight glared down at him for a second; then the inherent good nature of the man took over. He forced a grin, slapped Adam on the shoulder nearly driving him into the ground, and said in a raspy tone, "Well, Adam, you'll have to admit one thing—it's been the most *interesting* party we've ever had in our whole lives, ain't it now?"

Molly saw Mary Edwards smile and come up to stand between the two men, and she turned and went into the house. Charles followed her and as they went inside, he said, "Well, they didn't actually kill each other that time for her—but it's not too late, is it?" There was no one in the parlor, and he suddenly stopped. Putting a hand on Molly's arm, he swung her around, and before she could think, he drew her close and kissed her firmly on the lips!

He released her at once, and she stood there gaping at him.

He laughed at her and said, "It won't kill you, one little kiss, Molly. And if those two fools had any sense, they'd be fighting over you instead of that little mouse!"

He had thought little of the kiss, but when he looked at her, he was taken aback by the flashing anger in her eyes. She was pale, but her voice was steady as she said, "Mr. Winslow, don't you *ever* do a thing like that again—not ever!"

And as she whirled and left the room, he took a deep breath, shocked to discover that her anger had shaken him!

CHAPTER THIRTEEN

"THE BEST OF THE WINSLOWS!"

★ ★ ★ ★

Charles went back to Boston, telling Adam before he left, "You can beat Dwight out, Adam. These preacher's daughters are pretty hotblooded! Grab her, kiss her soundly, and she'll wilt in your arms."

Adam had smiled, but had done no such thing. During the three months since Charles's visit, he had worn a path to Mary's door, but he usually found Timothy there, so the two of them spent most of the time trying to wait each other out. Neither of them referred to the wrestling match, but Mary did from time to time. She delighted in the contests, encouraging both of them, but seeming to favor neither.

Once her father came and sat with them, on one of the rare occasions when Timothy was not there. He had a sober look on his long face, and Adam's heart sank, for he was fully ready to hear Rev. Edwards tell him to leave his daughter alone. But that was not what was on the minister's mind.

"Adam, I'm afraid you've not been helped by your friendship with us."

"Sir?"

"We've become very unpopular in this place, as you've noticed."

"Why, there are some malcontents, Brother Edwards," Adam said quickly. "But they'll come around."

Edwards sighed, and he looked suddenly old and worn in the yellow candlelight. "I fear not. My stand on the new birth has alienated many of them."

"Not a single person has joined the church in three years!" Mary said indignantly. "They're jealous of Father's fame. All they want is someone to visit them. They don't understand that it's an honor that he gets calls to preach all over America!"

"I'm not a very good pastor, my dear," her father sighed. "I can't seem to make small talk." Then he smiled and said, "If we have to leave this place, Adam, you'll be one we'll miss the most."

"Leave? Why, it can't come to that!"

Edwards shook his head sadly. "It may, my boy. There is much dissatisfaction with me in the church."

"Father's been so worried," Mary said tearfully after her father left. "With ten children and a new baby, you can see why."

A proposal leaped to Adam's lips, but before he could speak, Mrs. Edwards came in with Elizabeth, the new addition, and the moment passed.

Adam stayed long hours at the forge, working on the rifle, but his temper grew short. It leaped out when people spoke harshly of Rev. Edwards, and when he offered to thrash the next man he heard speak critically of the pastor, everyone was careful to keep quiet about the matter when he was around.

His bad temper flared out at home. For the first time, he was short with the Stuarts, even with Molly. Seth had endured one of his rare outbursts, then said, "Weel, now, Mr. Winslow, I think you're yellin' at the wrong man. I dinna' think ye'll go too far wrong if ye look in the mirror. Ye'll see there whose t' blame for your troubles."

Adam had stared at him, then stomped off with his eyes smoldering.

Molly came in for her part of his wrath one Tuesday evening. A young farmer named Robert Wells had been stopping by the place quite often. His father owned a large tract of land, but it was mostly the son who operated it. He and Seth were good friends, and often they exchanged ideas, but lately he had come over several times in the evening and talked. The kitchen was the warmest room, so all of them sat around the table.

He was there when Adam came through the door with a glum look on his face. He'd had another failure with the breech mechanism, and his bad temper was obvious to everyone but Wells.

For several hours the young man sat there, talking some to Seth and speaking at times to Adam, who only grunted. He and Molly were reading some book that Adam had never heard of, and they grew animated, laughing at their wildly differing interpretations of some of the poems. Beth Stuart sat near the fire sewing, her face expressing pleasure in the visit.

Finally she and Seth went to their quarters; Adam expected Wells to go, but he did not, for he and Molly were sitting together on the bench, laughing at one of the poems. Time ran on, and Adam grew more irritable until finally he stood up and said, "Well, it's late. We'd all best get to bed."

Robert jumped to his feet, his face red with embarrassment. "Oh, I—I'd forgotten the time! Sorry, Mr. Winslow!"

Molly walked with him to the door, handing him his heavy coat, and saying, "It's been a wonderful evening, Robert. I hope you'll come again."

Wells gave a quick glance at Adam, who was shifting impatiently, and muttered, "Why—I'd like to! I'll be more careful of the time in the future, Mr. Winslow."

He left and Adam went over and latched the door. "I thought he'd never leave! Why can't he talk business with Seth at a decent hour?"

Molly wheeled to face him, her face rigid with anger. There was a tremble in her voice as she said, "He didn't come to see Seth—he came to see me!"

Adam stared at her stupidly. "You?"

"Yes, Mr. Winslow—me!" She was on the verge of tears, but her eyes were flashing as she stood facing him. "Is it completely incredible to you that a young man would want to come to see me?"

Adam stared at her, but he was still uncertain of what she

was saying. "Wells was here to *see* you? You mean *calling* on you?"

"Yes!"

Adam's anger flared out. "Well, he can't do it!"

"Why not?"

"You're too young, that's why not!"

"I'm as old as Mary Edwards!"

He floundered, trying to find an answer and, knowing he was making a fool out of himself, finally blurted out, "Well—I'm the master here, and *I* tell you he can't come hanging around you any more!"

"That's it! You're afraid of losing your bound girl! You're afraid Robert will pay off my indenture and you won't have a slave anymore!"

He grabbed her by the shoulders and shouted, "That's a lie, Molly Burns!"

His grip was so strong she winced, but she looked straight into his eyes. "You're hurting me—why don't you go ahead and beat me, Mr. Winslow? That's what people do with bound girls!"

He dropped his hands as if they had been burned, and for a long moment the air was charged with the violence of the scene that had exploded without warning. Then he said with an effort, "Molly, I never think of you like that—never!" Then, perhaps because he knew himself to have been unkind, he could say no more. Wheeling quickly, he left the room, leaving her standing there in the silence; as soon as he was gone, she gave a small cry, then collapsed at the table, her face in her hands, weeping as if her heart would break, crying, "Adam! Oh—Adam!"

The next day he was gone when she got up, and for three days she watched the road to no avail. She asked Seth, and his only reply was, "He took his gun and went on a hunt. May be a good thing for him, too."

When he did return, he came to her at once and said, "Molly, I'm sorry about Wells. See him as much as you want."

He stayed late at the forge every night for a week, and as she listened to the clanging of his hammer all day long, she felt cut off, but did not know how to mend the situation.

On Saturday morning, Adam and Seth were standing in

front of the house when a messenger came riding up on a lathered horse. "That's Henry Caldwell," Adam said to Seth. "He works for my cousin in Boston."

"Must be bad news to wear a horse out like that," Seth said dolefully.

Adam felt the same, and said quickly, "What's wrong, Henry?"

"Your father's taken bad, Mr. Adam. You'd best come at once."

Adam stared at him, then said, "You rest your horse, Henry. I'll leave at once." Then he called out, "Seth, saddle the bay for me!"

He ran into the house and met Molly, who asked, "What's wrong?"

"Father—he's dying, I think!"

"Oh, Adam!" She put her hand on his arm, and her lips trembled as she said, "Let me go with you!"

"No, it'll be too hard."

"I won't complain," she said quickly. "Please, Adam!"

He stared at her, then smiled briefly. "All right; we'll have to take the buggy. Get your things!"

She scurried off and fifteen minutes later Adam sent the team off at a hard gallop. "Me and Beth, we'll be praying for you!" Seth called out.

The horses played out halfway there, and Adam changed teams at a smalltown blacksmith shop. "Keep them 'til I get back with yours, but I don't know when that'll be," he told the owner.

They pulled into Boston a little after midnight, and Adam drove straight to the house, which was lit up. Several buggies were tied at the post, and Adam hurried up the steps.

He was met by Rachel, who looked almost dead herself. "You made good time, Adam," she said as she put her arms out. Adam held her close. She was nothing but skin and bones, but she clung to his neck with a fierce grip. She finally released him and reached out to embrace the girl. "Molly, I'm so glad you came! Miles has spoken of you so often these last days!"

"How is he, Rachel?" Adam asked.

She stared at him, her dark eyes sunk deep in the sockets.

"I think he's only holding on by a thread, Adam." She smiled as she added, "He always was a stubborn man, you know, and he told me yesterday, 'I won't go 'til I see my son—you can bet on it!' "

Charles came out of the parlor with his mother behind him, and said tersely, "Better go in, Adam. He could go any time— and he wants to see you."

Adam nodded but did not fail to notice the bitter look he received from Martha. He started down the hall, then turned and said, "Molly, come with me."

She nodded to Charles and followed Rachel and Adam down the wide hall and into the same room where she'd read to the dying man from Gilbert Winslow's journal. The room was dim, only one lamp burning on the table, and the sound of Miles' breathing was raspy and erratic.

Rachel walked to his side, bent over and said clearly, "Miles—Miles?"

He stirred, moving his head from side to side, then slowly his eyes opened. "Adam?"

"He's right here, Miles."

As she moved back, Adam stepped forward and saw the recognition in the old eyes. A smile touched the shrunken lips, and he whispered, "You cut it pretty fine, boy. I didn't know if I could wait . . . who's that with you?"

"It's me—Molly!"

He reached out and she took his hand. He held it tightly, then smiled, "We had quite some times, didn't we, Molly?"

"Yes, sir. I—I've never forgotten a word!" She leaned forward and kissed his hand.

Feeling her hot tears on his hand, he reached out and touched her head with his other and said, "You remember how my grandmother kept on believing?"

"I—I remember." She hoped he wouldn't say more, for he referred, she knew, to how Humility Cooper had believed for a husband named Winslow.

"You must always believe, Molly," he whispered. "You have a gift for that, you know!" Then he seemed to catch his breath and a look of pain raked across his face. "Adam?"

"Yes, sir?"

Miles released Molly's hand and took Adam's. The dying man's grip was surprisingly firm; he said, "Rachel?" and she moved to the other side of the bed to take his other hand. He lay there quietly, then said, "Rachel, you remember how all of you were in jail at Salem? All of you—Father and Mother and Grandfather?"

"I remember, Miles." Rachel leaned over and brushed her brother's long hair from his forehead. "You used to bring us food every day. And you and Robert would cheer us up. You never let us down."

Miles whispered, "I always felt bad that I wasn't in there with you. I would have been if I could."

"No, you kept us going. I remember Grandfather said once, 'We'd all be dead if it weren't for Miles.' "

"He said that? You never told me."

"He was always very proud of you—we all were."

Miles smiled then, and the tension left his drawn face. He held on to their hands and seemed to sleep. Finally his chest rose and he strained for breath.

"Miles!" Rachel cried, and stared at Adam. "He's going!"

But the eyes of the old man suddenly opened, and he said in a firmer tone than they'd heard: "Yes, I'm going—it's time!" He turned his face to Adam, and stared at him open-eyed. His chest heaved and he blinked, but then he opened his eyes and gasped, "Adam, my son! I have loved—have loved you greatly— these last years!"

"And I have loved you!" Adam said, tears flowing down his face.

"Have you? Have you? Then I am happy! For you—" he coughed and half rose in bed, and his grip tightened—"you are—the best of—our house!" he gasped. "The best of the Wins- lows. . . !"

He expelled his breath, closed his eyes, and then his head fell back. Adam lowered it to the pillow and stared at Rachel.

"He's gone, Adam," she whispered. She put her brother's hand to her cheek and whispered, "He's gathered to his fathers!"

The room was silent. Adam heard only the labored sound

of his own breathing and Molly's sobbing.

Then he looked at Rachel and said, "Aunt Rachel—I feel so alone!"

She nodded, her old face shrunken and tired. "He was so much of my world," she whispered as she placed his hand down carefully. "Somehow the world seems empty to me without him!" Then she said softly, "Goodbye, Miles. . . .I won't be long!"

They turned and left the room, but Adam paused for one last look. He heard again the words he did not himself believe: *You are the best of the Winslows!*

His lips formed the words, *I'll try to be!*, and then he left the room.

CHAPTER FOURTEEN

BROTHERLY LOVE

★　★　★　★

"Weel, it's a fair pleasure, Wife, to get oot of the house and fight weeds." Seth Stuart straightened up, gazed down the row of beans he'd hoed, then glanced at the house. "It's my guess what we're adoin' to these blasted weeds is what Adam would love to do to young Mister Robert Wells!"

"You think they're tellin' him about getting married?" Beth gave a troubled glance at the house, then shook her head sorrowfully. "She told me last night that Robert had worn her patience down and she'd agreed just to make him hush."

"She don't love him?"

"Not a bit of it! But she's sure that Mary Edwards will be mistress of this house soon—and she'd marry any man rather than stay here under the same roof." She chopped viciously at a weed, missed, and cut a thick bean stalk down. "Oh, it'll be a good match, I suppose. And Adam Winslow's been enough to drive a saint crazy these last six months! Since his father died he's done nothing but run around in circles after that girl!"

"Weel, I guess he'll let Molly go—and sorry I am for it."

Inside the house Molly looked out the window to see Robert come riding down the road. He'd gotten off his horse with a bound, and there was a determination in his face that made her wish she had never agreed to marry him.

She turned to Adam and said, "Robert is coming."

He looked up at her, and the restraint that had built up between them was like a wall. He stared at her bleakly; then when the knock came, he moved across the room and opened the door.

"Mr. Winslow." Wells stepped inside, saw Molly standing there twisting her apron nervously. "I need to speak with you."

"Come in, then." Adam stepped back, and the young man went over to stand beside Molly.

"I'll not take much of your time." He nodded at the silent girl, and there was defiance in his voice as he said, "I suppose Molly's told you about us?"

"No."

The blank look in Adam's eyes and the single monosyllable offered no encouragement, so Wells said bluntly, "Well, I want to marry her. I'll pay whatever is owing on her paper, so that's no problem."

Adam did not speak, but turned his dark eyes on Molly. She met his gaze defiantly, but there was a tremor in her lips and a vulnerable expression in her eyes.

"Is this what you want, Molly?"

"I think it would be best."

"That's not what I asked." He wanted to beg her not to throw herself away on a man she didn't love, but he had no right to interfere. "Do you love him, Molly?" was all he could ask, and the words came hard. This girl was precious to him in a way that was somehow confusing. He could never quite think of her as a woman ready for a man, despite the full erect figure and the quick mind behind the calm blue-gray eyes. His mind carried a memory of a tiny frightened child, dirty and thin, that he'd held in his arms long ago. For years he'd protected her, loved her—so much that this beautiful woman who stood staring at him still evoked the sharp memory of that child.

She hesitated slightly before she spoke. "Robert and I have agreed, Mr. Winslow," she said evenly. "You know his reputation in this place. He's a good, hard-working man, and he's offered to make me his wife. I'm most grateful for your many kindnesses." Her voice trembled slightly, but she pressed her lips together and added. "I'm sure you'll be able to replace me without any trouble."

Adam's lips were dry, and he longed to find some way to deny their request, but there was nothing he could say except, "There'll be no money in this, Wells. I've never considered Molly in any other light than as a dear sister. I—I wish God's blessing on you and your marriage."

Molly's eyes burned and she said quickly, "Thank you."

Wells nodded, relief in his voice. "Thank you, Mr. Winslow! You may be sure I'll be very good to her!" He put his hand out to take Adam's.

Adam shook his hand, then said, "I suppose you two have plans. I have a lot of work, so you'll pardon me."

As Adam left the room, Robert turned quickly and put his arms around Molly, kissing her fervently. It was not the first time, of course, for he was passionately in love with her, but she was not responsive to his kiss, so he released her at once. He stepped back and asked quietly, "When will it be, Molly?"

"I'll—think on it, Robert." She mustered up a smile and said, "You get on now. Come back tonight and I'll have some of that apple tart you like so much."

The Stuarts had been watching the house furtively, and as Adam left, his back straight as a ramrod as he stalked to the shop, Seth said, "Adam's not happy." Then a few moments later when Robert Wells came out and rode off down the road, he added, "Aye, woman! It's likely things won't be too happy around here. Hate to see it come—it's been a bonny place up to now."

Stuart's words were prophetic, for from that time on there was an air of unhappiness in the Winslow House. Adam continued his single-minded pursuit of Mary Edwards, never coming to blows with Timothy Dwight, but both of them working at their courtship with desperate intensity.

Robert came almost every night, often to eat, and when Adam was there, he made every attempt to be a good host. He talked to the young man of farming, hunting, politics; everything, in fact, except what Wells wanted to talk about—his marriage to Molly Burns.

The weeks went by until finally Timothy Dwight came striding up to Adam, his cheerful face marked with strain. "Adam, I'm sick of all this business!" He groaned and shook his massive head. "I thought courtship was supposed to be *fun*—and it's making a wreck out of me!"

Adam smiled up at the big man. He had perversely grown more fond of Dwight during the tiring struggle for Mary's favor, and he knew the feeling was mutual. "Well, I guess sooner or later one of us will up and die, Timothy." He scowled then, and shook his head. "I agree with you, though. You got any ideas?"

"Well, not a wrestling match!" They exchanged grins remembering the last match. "But I've had enough, Adam!" Dwight's face grew serious. "I'm going to tell Mary tonight I want to marry her. I think you ought to do the same thing. Then we can both stand back, and the whole thing's in her lap."

Adam stared at him. "I think you've got a good idea, Timothy," he replied, smiling. "You know what I've been thinking? I've thought that if there'd been only *one* of us—and I mean *either one*—Mary would have been married by now. What time are you going over?"

"Thought I'd drop over early, maybe about six."

"I'll be there at eight."

They suddenly grinned and shook hands. "One way or the other, Adam, one of us is going to get hurt—but if Mary chooses you, I'll not be able to hate you like I would nearly any other man!"

"Same here, Timothy."

They parted, and at eight o'clock Adam seated himself in the large parlor of the Edwards' house. Mary started to speak brightly of a quilting party she'd been to that afternoon, and Adam asked bluntly, "Dwight came over earlier, did he?"

"Why—yes, as a matter of fact. . . !"

"He have anything important to say, Mary?"

Her face flushed, and for one of the few times he'd known her, she was confused. She started to speak; then her lips trembled and she stumbled as she said, "Well—Adam—he said that. . ."

Adam smiled at her and nodded. "Yes, well, I've come to

say the same thing he did. I love you, Mary. I want to marry you, but I can't keep up this game we've been playing anymore."

"Game?"

He was suddenly impatient with her, and reaching out, he pulled her close and kissed her firmly. She tried to resist, but he ignored her struggles. Finally, he released her and said, "Me or Timothy, Mary. You can't marry *both* of us!"

Wide-eyed, she looked at him, breathing hard. His kiss had stirred her, and she whispered, "Why, Adam, you're angry!"

"A little bit, Mary," he confessed. Then he took her hand and said quietly, his eyes warm as he looked at her. "Mary, I know a young girl has to have a time of courting. But it's gone too far! Why, the whole country's laughing at me and Timothy, and your parents are embarrassed. It's hurt me to see them having to endure this farce."

She sat there and tears welled up in her eyes. She was a girl of deep feelings, although she seldom let them show. She was so bright and full of fun that things came easily to her, and now these two strong men who wanted her had offered themselves honestly. "I know I've been frivolous, Adam, with you and Timothy. I love you both, of course. But Timothy said the same thing—the time's past for this."

"He's a fine man, Mary—none finer!" Adam stood up suddenly, saying, "I love you, Mary, but you'll have to choose."

She stood up, and there was no foolishness in her as she looked at him. Reaching up to place her hands on his broad shoulders, she whispered, "I—I know I don't deserve to have two men love me, not men like you and Timothy." Her eyes filled with tears, a rare thing for this girl!—and she said, "There'll be one happy person come out of this thing, Adam."

"Just one?"

"Yes, because no matter which one of you I marry, I'll grieve for the other!"

Timothy and Adam proposed in early June, but as July and August went by, Mary said nothing definite. Both Timothy and Adam shrugged and stayed away from her to a great extent, knowing that sooner or later she would make a choice. Both of them yearned for it, yet dreaded it.

Molly and Robert went on much as before, though at times he grew impatient with her. She refused to name a date, and once when he pressed her, she looked at him and said calmly, "Would you rather we called it off, Robert?" Her readiness frightened him, so he fought down his impatience and said no more about it.

A letter from Saul came in September, so confusing that Adam could not make head nor tail of it. It was an involved matter of business that required Adam's signature, and since Rachel had agreed to the deal, he signed it and mailed it back.

Scarcely a week later, Molly came to the forge to get him. "Charles is here."

"Charles?" Adam stared at her, and saw something in her face. "What's wrong, Molly?"

She hesitated, then tears filled her eyes. "It's—Rachel."

He put down the hammer he was holding on the anvil, then looked at her. "Is she dead?"

"Yes!" Then her face broke and tears flowed down her cheeks. She turned from him, bringing out a handkerchief and trying to stem the flow.

He stood there, tense, feeling as if life had been drained from him. A great emptiness filled his heart. Unable to believe what he was hearing, he finally murmered, "She was very good to me. Never gave me anything but love." He pulled off his apron and stated calmly, "We'll have to go right away for the funeral."

"She's—already buried, Adam."

He stared at her, then said, "I'll talk to Charles."

He found his brother in the parlor, and went straight up to him with a blunt question, "Why didn't you come and get me for the funeral?"

Charles looked startled. He was weary, and it was the first time Adam had ever spoken to him with such obvious displeasure. He licked his lips, then said in a conciliatory voice, "Adam, there wasn't time!"

"It's not that far to Boston!"

"No, but she died of some sort of plague," Charles said

quickly. "Nobody knows exactly what it is, but it's all over the city. There's a new law—bodies have to be buried within twenty-four hours."

Adam relaxed, and he shook his head. "Sorry to be so sharp, Charles—but she meant a lot to me."

"Yes, I know. I wanted to come, but there was just no way."

"Did she suffer much?"

"No, thank God! She was taken on Monday and the terrible thing works so fast that by Wednesday it was over." He put his hand on Adam's shoulder. "Her last words—she spoke of you."

"Of me?"

"I was with her. She'd been unconscious, but before that she'd said goodbye to everyone—Saul, and Esther and me. Then she woke up and she said, 'Tell Adam that Miles was right!' "

You're the best of the Winslows. That was what she was saying, and she'd managed to pass it along without offending her family.

Adam blinked, then said, "I'll miss her, Charles."

"Yes. You were always her favorite."

They stood there in the grip of that paralyzing helplessness that comes with death—struggling to say that which can never be said, to express that which can never be framed in words. Charles sensed that Adam did not want to talk about Rachel, so he excused himself as soon as he could.

All afternoon Adam walked through the woods, seeing little, but going over and over old memories. He startled a mule deer and watched as it went sailing smoothly over logs in a motion that was as much like flight as any animal ever achieves, but this time the movement did not provoke the admiration it usually did. He could almost hear Rachel's voice telling the tales of Matthew Winslow, of his fight to the death with an Indian to save her life. She had not been a dramatic woman in her Christian life, but as he looked back, he realized that her iron-ribbed convictions to her God were part of what he had loved. She had never wavered, and now he thought of all the times she'd spoken so confidently of this very time—for her belief that she would see Gilbert and Lydia and Matthew again was unshakable.

It made his own intellectual acceptance of faith look scanty and foolish, and he wondered how she and others had come to such belief. Finally, he looked up, overtaken by dark, and made his way back to the house.

Molly met him at the door, and he tried to eat, but could only nibble at his food. Charles sat there, watching him furtively, but said little. Finally they went to bed, but Adam lay there most of the night thinking of his aunt.

The next morning Charles said, "I have to talk to you, Adam." He hesitated, and there was a lack of assurance in him that puzzled Adam. "I know it's a bad time. . ."

"It's all right." Adam got up and led the way to the parlor. He stood beside the window, but Charles paced back and forth, his face strained and his voice higher than usual.

"Adam, it's an awful time to come to you with this, but there's no way it can be put off!"

"What's the matter, Charles? Bad news?"

"No!" Charles paused abruptly, and said the word so quickly that Adam at once knew he was not honest. "Well, Adam, to tell the truth, *you* may think so, but somehow I've got to show you it isn't."

Adam stared at him curiously. "Why don't you just tell me what it is and let me decide if it's bad or not."

Charles paused, bit his lip, then shrugged and said uneasily, "I wish Saul were here, Adam! This thing is so complicated that I'm not sure I understand it myself. And I wish that we'd got it all settled before Rachel died! You'd have believed her!"

"And I'm not going to believe you?"

"I'm hoping you will, Adam! I really am!" The tall man began pacing again, and said, "I wish we'd been closer, you and I. Oh, it's my fault, I suppose—or maybe it was inevitable, with Mother feeling like she does." He halted abruptly and rushed on hurriedly, "I—I didn't mean that like it sounded, Adam!"

"I've never been Martha's favorite, Charles," Adam said. "That's no secret. Look, what's the matter? Something gone wrong with the business? Come on, let's have it!"

"All right, here it is. . ." Charles stated, a bead of perspiration rising on his upper lip. Then he said in a rush: "Adam, the whole picture has changed—everything! The fur trade has picked up so much in the last year that Saul and I *had* to increase that side of the business. And that meant that we had to have money, so we shifted as many of the assets as we could to get the cash."

Adam said doubtfully, "But that's pretty risky, isn't it? I mean, what if the French invade the Ohio Valley? Where does that leave us?"

"England will never let that happen, Adam. Look at the map, and what do you see? We're pinned in here along the coast right up against the Appalachian Mountains. The whole continent lies over those mountains, and if you think King George is going to let the French have it, you're just not thinking!"

"Well, we haven't done much so far," Adam argued. "We've had two wars over that territory, and there's another around the corner."

"And we'll win this time!" Charles' face gleamed with excitement. "France may keep Canada, but never in a million years will the Crown let this New World go! Not if she has to fight a full-scale war for it! And if that comes, whoever owns that land in the Ohio Valley will control the country!"

"I don't know politics, Charles," Adam shrugged.

"You've got to see it, Adam! A whole new world over those mountains, and it's ours for the taking!"

Adam grinned at him and remarked, "You're trying hard to sell me, Charles. You must want something from me pretty bad. Well, you're going to *have* to tell me sooner or later what it is."

"Adam," Charles stated quietly, "it took all of it. That's what it cost to get in on this thing."

Adam looked at him, doubt in his eyes. "All of what?"

Charles took a deep breath, then answered quietly, "I mean we had to liquidate everything, Adam—we had to sell this place, too."

"This place?" Adam stared at him. "You can't sell this place, Charles. It's part of the general estate. We'd all have to agree and sign."

"You *did* sign, Adam."

Then it finally dawned on Adam, and he said slowly, but with a growing rage beginning to swell up in his chest, "Those papers you brought last time you were here, and that letter from Saul? That was what I signed?"

Charles saw for the first time the dangerous light in his brother's dark eyes, and said hastily, "It—it all happened so *fast*, Adam! Why, we had no idea at the time that we'd ever sell this place—or anything else—but when the thing came up, we had no choice!"

"Rachel knew about this?"

"Y-yes."

"You're a liar, Charles," Adam stated with a deceptive calm. "You lied to her, too, didn't you? You and Saul arranged this, and you knew we wouldn't be in favor of it. So you lied and got our names by fraud."

"I tell you, Adam, there wasn't time—!"

"How long does it take to get here from Boston, two days? And was Aunt Rachel all that far away? You're lying again, Charles!"

The easy assurance of Charles Winslow had fled, and he wished with all his heart that Saul had come, or that they'd put the thing in a letter as he'd suggested. But Saul had said, "You'll have to face him sooner or later, Charles. Might as well meet him head-on with it."

Now staring at Adam's face, Charles tried vainly to make the thing look better, but the more he talked the worse it sounded even to him.

Finally Adam said, "I want an answer from you right now— and don't beat around the bush. Father left his property equally divided between the two of us. What do I have and what do you have?"

"Why, it's not that simple, Adam!"

"Nothing is ever simple to a crook, Charles! You sold this place that I've poured my life into—what do I have to show for it?"

"Don't worry, Adam," Charles said swiftly. "We got a good price, and you've got one of the finest tracts of land in Virginia."

Adam stared at him. "A plantation?"

"N-no, not exactly!"

"It's just a patch of wilderness land, isn't it? That's what you've sold this place for?"

Charles said, "Well, it's wild land, but—!"

Then with a cat-like spring, Adam was on him! He caught his brother by the throat, and though Charles was much taller and a strong man, the iron hands of Adam Winslow held him as though he were a child.

"You're a thief!" Adam roared, his dark face contorted with rage. He ignored the gurgling sounds that emerged from Charles's throat, and his voice rose as he shouted, "Liar! I trusted you! And you stole this place. . . !"

Charles's tongue was protruding, his face a dark crimson. His hand beat ineffectually at his brother, but the room was exploding into flakes of light.

Adam was cursing him, blinded by rage, and then he heard a voice scream, "Adam! Let him go!" He felt small hands beating on his back and pulling at his hands, and he suddenly saw Molly standing there crying.

He loosed his grip, and Charles slumped to the floor, his oxygen-starved lungs gulping in air in great swallows.

"What is it, Adam?" Molly asked. When he didn't answer, she took his arm and moved in front of him so she could see his face. "What's he done?"

Adam took a deep breath and forced himself to relax. He looked down at his brother, who was slowly pulling himself up. Reaching down, he plucked him off the floor, stood him up, and said quietly, "He's robbed me of my inheritance, Molly." Then his lips twisted in a parody of a smile and he added, "Brotherly love, he'd call it."

"No!" Charles gasped. He put out a hand to touch Adam, and he tried to explain. "It's still yours, Adam! More than ever!"

Adam stared at him, and Charles saw a door close inside his brother. "I'll never believe you again," he said quietly, then he turned and walked from the room.

"Molly! You've got to talk to him!" Charles groaned. "He's gone crazy!"

"Did you take this place from him?" she asked abruptly, and he found it as difficult to face her as it had been to look at his brother.

"Molly—Molly, it was a matter of business! We did it for his good as much as ours. Adam needed us! He hasn't got the head for this sort of thing!"

Molly stared at him, contempt in her eyes. "No, he's not as smart as you are, Charles. He's so simple-minded he believed in you, trusted you. I heard you tell him once, 'You've got to learn to look out for yourself, Adam!' Well, he didn't listen to you, did he, Charles? He didn't look out for himself—so his own family destroys him!"

"It's not *like* that!" he tried to reason. Taking his handkerchief out of his pocket, he wiped his face using the time to regain his composure. Finally he calmed down. "Molly, this place is gone, but nobody has *stolen* it from Adam! I—I see now that we should have come to him, but there's nothing to be done about that now. But he can have *ten* places like this in Virginia!"

She looked up at him and studied his face. Finally she said, "Are you telling me the truth, Charles? With you I can't tell."

"I know I'm no good," he said quietly, then smiled at the look on her face. "You think *I* don't know that, Molly? Adam, he's the one who's like Gilbert and Edward and Father!" A look of pain touched his light blue eyes, and he whispered softly, "I've wished a thousand times that I didn't just *look* like a Winslow—but that I *acted* like one!"

Molly felt a sudden touch of pity for this tall, strong man, for she had not seen this side of him. "I—I believe you, Charles— and maybe you're not as bad as you think."

He straightened his shoulders, smiled wryly, then said, "Let us pray that I am not—but in any case, as much as Adam hates us—and as much wrong as we've done him—he's got a great opportunity. He was made for Virginia, Molly! And you've got to see he doesn't let his hatred for Saul and me let him miss out on it!"

Molly looked away from him, thinking of Adam; then she sighed and replied, "I'll not be a help, Charles. He's going to marry Mary Edwards."

The thin veneer of sophistication that covered the cynicism in Charles suddenly slipped, and he stated with a grin, "Not likely she'll marry a man who has no big farm here. She'll go for that other fellow!"

Molly thought about Mary, and Adam's pursuit. "No," she returned, shaking her head, "I don't think so—but I'll certainly pray in that direction!"

"Well, I trust your prayers work. But just in case they don't, here's what we've planned."

For the next hour Molly listened as Charles explained to her how it was going to be.

CHAPTER FIFTEEN

"AND THE WALLS CAME TUMBLING DOWN!"

★　★　★　★

The mood of New Englanders is delicately hinged to the weather; nowhere else is winter so trying, the mud season so endless, spring so giddy, summer so brief, fall so glorious. Tuned to the caprices of weather, New Englanders' moods swing as the climate does. Perhaps that was why Jonathan Edwards was hounded by the Northampton church in 1750.

The whole year had been one of spooky extremes. The winter was unusually severe. Mill River had frozen over by early October. The town was smothered by six feet of snow that lingered monotonously for months. The gray weeks dragged out, chill rains slanted over stubble fields, maples gauntly swayed in the harsh winds.

To make matters worse, Edwards grated on his people in a campaign against taverns—an old struggle that he fanned into new fury. He intimidated people, quite unintentionally, with his intelligence. He tried to be less awesome, but it was difficult.

The antagonism against him increased, and finally two hundred parish members signed a petition for his dismissal. The council was dominated by a man named Joseph Hawley, who read a diatribe against the pastor, and the council voted 8 to 7 to dismiss Jonathan Edwards.

Adam Winslow had scoffed all along at the idea that his friend would be voted out, and when he got the bad news it was coupled with a second blow.

He heard of it early in the morning, and late that afternoon he rode over to the Edwards' and went directly to the pastor.

Edwards was calm, his face was pale, but it was obvious to Adam that the man was deeply hurt. He listened quietly as Adam raged against those who had raised their hands against him; then when the storm ceased, Edwards said mildly, "It's not the end of the world, Adam."

"But—what will you do?"

A smile broke across Edwards' face, and he said with a look of wonder on his face, "Judge Dwight has offered to share half his income with me—if I will start a new work with those who did not agree with the decision to release me."

"Good!"

"No, it would be divisive. It wouldn't do at all."

"Then what? Where will you go?"

"I'm not sure. God is not finished with me, I'm sure. I may become a teacher at a college. Write some books, perhaps."

He was so calm that Adam marveled, but he was still angry enough to say, "I despise those cowards who fought against you!"

"You mustn't say that, Adam! Jesus said, 'If you have aught against any, the Father will not forgive you.' "

Adam said no more to Edwards, but as he left, Mary was waiting for him. She took him off to the small parlor, and he told her of his anger. He did not notice that she was saying nothing, nor did he see that she was nervously twisting her handkerchief into a rag.

Finally he ran down, and started to rise, saying, "Well, it will come out all right somehow."

"Adam. . . !"

There was such a strain in her face that he sat back down, thinking that she wanted to talk more about her family's disaster. She sat there, looking very small in the large chair. Finally she bit her lip and said, "Adam—I've got something to tell you."

He stared at her, noting that she looked more miserable than he'd ever seen her. Suddenly he knew.

"It's Timothy, isn't it, Mary? You wouldn't look so miserable if I were the one."

"Oh, Adam!" she cried out, throwing herself at him and clinging to him as she had done when she was ten years old. Sobs racked her body, until finally she had no more tears. Drawing back she mopped at her eyes, then said pitifully, "How could I do this to you? I've loved you all my life!"

Adam felt nothing, but he knew the pain and loneliness would come later. He was not in the least angry, and discovered to his surprise that he had known all along it would be this way. He patted her shoulder, saying, "You must never grieve about this, Mary. It wouldn't be fair to Timothy."

That set her off again, but he said firmly, "Come now, I want to see you smile. I may have lost a wife, but I've still got a friend, haven't I?"

She could not stop crying, so he left. He was so much in shock that he got a mile down the road before he realized that he'd forgotten his horse. Going back, he mounted and went straight to Judge Dwight's house. There was a determination to finish the matter as much as possible, so he was glad to find Timothy at home.

There was a look of alarm on the big man's face as he opened the door, but Adam said, "I haven't got a gun, Timothy. I just came to wish you well."

Dwight stood there, his vast body filling the room, a sad look on his good-natured face. He looked at Adam, and a heaviness filled his voice as he said, "I wish it hadn't come to this, Adam."

Adam mustered up a grin, and put his hand out. It was swallowed by Dwight's huge fist. "You're the one for her, Timothy. I just told her I couldn't afford to lose a friend like her— and that goes for you, too. All right?"

"Adam—I guess you know. . ." He tried to put his feelings in words, and finally said, "Looks like the world is breaking up for you. I know you're taking it hard about losing your place—

and it hurts about Brother Edwards—and now this."

"It's been a bad month, Timothy," Adam agreed. "Guess I feel like the folks inside Jericho when the walls started falling down."

Timothy Dwight stared at him, started to say something, then seemed to change his mind. "I started to give you some good advice, maybe quote some scripture. But that's apt to get on a man's nerves, ain't it, Adam? Never could stand to hear somebody preaching at me about trusting God when *I* was hurtin' and *he* wasn't!"

Adam grinned, and turned to go. "Got to get back. All the best to you and Mary."

"Wait," Timothy said quickly. "You got to move off your place? Where you goin'? You can get a place close around here, Adam. Everybody knows what a good man you are."

"They know Seth Stuart has made that place a farm," Adam shrugged. "I'm just a blacksmith."

"But what you going to do? Where you goin', Adam?"

Adam considered the question, then looked up at Dwight and said directly, "Why, I'm going to get drunk, Timothy."

He wheeled and left, and Timothy Dwight sighed and said under his breath, "Well, under the circumstances, I'd say that's not a bad idea, Adam!"

Adam had not been serious about drinking. He had just used it as an excuse to get away from Dwight. He rode back home, and for the next two days he kept to himself.

On Wednesday the final straw came. A man drove up to the front yard, talked to Molly, then came to find Adam at the shop. "Hello," he said as he entered. He held out his hand, a big man with buck teeth and a shock of black hair that fell over this eyes. "Name's Royal Taylor. You're Winslow?"

Adam took the man's hand, nodded, then asked, "You're the new owner?"

"Sure am. Just stopped by to see what your thinkin' is on this thing."

"My thinking?"

"Why, yes." Taylor seemed surprised. "Didn't your cousin tell you what I said?"

"No. I haven't talked to him."

"Well, I been talkin' around, did some before I bought the place and some after. Winslow, everybody I talked to said what a good thing you made of this place." Taylor took off his hat and pushed his hair back. "I got to have me a man, see? I won't be here much, and I told your cousin to ask you to think on it."

"Stay on here?"

"Sure! Why not? I ain't a hard man to get along with. I reckon we can agree on the money."

Adam leaned against the forge, his face still, while Taylor waited. Finally Adam shook his head. "I'm grateful for your offer, Mr. Taylor, but I'll be moving on."

Taylor did not protest. He stared at the young man, then said, "Sorry to hear it. Been sort of countin' on it."

"You don't need me," Adam said quickly. "Seth Stuart is the one you've got to have, Mr. Taylor. I do the forge work, but Seth—he's the farmer. You ask around, then talk to him. Folks around here will tell you he's a good man."

"Sure," Taylor nodded. "I already heard that. Guess I'll talk to him." He put out his hand and said, "You stay around here long as you like, Winslow, you hear?"

"Mighty nice of you—but I'll be moving on soon. You'll find Stuart in the east pasture, I think."

All that day Adam walked around the farm, avoiding Stuart, who was taking the new owner on a tour. He had several jobs started on the forge, but knew that he'd never finish any of them. All day he roamed, and every foot of the farm brought some sort of memory: here he had to pull the ox out of the mud hole; there was the thicket where he'd shot a panther eating the carcass of the colt; there was the deep hole in the creek where he'd caught his big catfish.

It was long after dark when he returned, and the lamp was still burning in the kitchen. He looked around, then went to the cabinet and pulled out the jug of whiskey. Everybody kept whiskey; even preachers sometimes took their pay in it. He sat down, poured a generous amount into a cup, and stared off into space.

He thought about his father, then drained the cup. Filling it to the brim, he thought about Rachel, then drained it again. He was not a drinking man, and the powerful liquor went to his head. He sat there thinking of his life, and somehow it didn't add up. He'd come to nothing.

How long he sat there, he could not have said, but the jug was half drained and his head was swimming when he heard a voice say, "Adam?"

It was a hard job just lifting his head, and he had to blink his eyes and strain to see clearly. "Molly—zat you, Molly?"

He concentrated on focusing his eyes, and when he saw her face, he blinked and said, "Late—you'sh be in bed." He knew that his tongue was thick, so he pronounced every syllable carefully, the way a drunk will do. "I—am—having myself—a—party." He was proud of having said the words right, and grinned at her.

"Yes, I see you are." She sat down across the table and put her chin in her hands.

"Wouldja lika drink?" he asked, peering at her owlishly.

"No, thank you."

"Everybody—Molly—gotta' believe—in something, right?"

"That's right, Adam."

He peered at her, then said solemnly, "Right—I believe— I'll have a drink!"

She said quietly, "Maybe you've had enough."

He considered her words thoughtfully, then said, "No, I doan think—so."

She watched him try to pour, but he missed the cup. The clear liquor ran onto the table then to the floor. He sat there staring at it, and she got up and mopped it up with a cloth from a rack.

She came to his side of the table and asked, "Mary chose Timothy, didn't she, Adam?"

Adam slammed the jug on the table and asked pugnaciously, "Well—why not! He's—good man! Make—her good— husband."

The room was whirling and he suddenly felt very sick. He got up to head for the door, but the room reeled, and he fell headlong to the floor. The jug broke as it fell, and as he started to throw up, he was aware that someone was holding his head, trying to help him.

When he opened his eyes, he knew that he'd been asleep. A shaft of sunlight hit him a blow that made his head pound. His mouth was dry as dust, and he had the most terrible taste in his mouth he could remember. He was still on the floor, but a blanket was over him, and somehow a pillow was under his head. He threw the cover back, sat up, and almost cried out, so great was the pain that struck him in the back of his head.

"You might want to wash up and change clothes."

He squinted up, and there was Molly looking down at him. He got to his feet, holding on to the wall, and then he ducked his head and went to the porch. He stripped off his stained shirt, washed in the basin, then put on the clean shirt she hung on the peg beside the washstand.

He walked slowly back into the kitchen and she had a cup of cold tea poured for him. He took it, stared at her, then drank it down. It felt good in his parched mouth, but made his stomach roll.

"You'll feel better after awhile."

He stared at her, then tried to smile. "That's good. I'd hate to think I'd feel this bad the rest of my life."

"You'd better try to eat something."

He shuddered at the thought, but when she fixed him a soft boiled egg, he ate it and to his surprise felt better.

"Sorry to be so much trouble."

"You had it coming," she said. "Most men would have been drunk long before this."

"I hate drunks," he said quietly.

"You're not a drunk," she insisted. "You *got* drunk, but you're not a drunk."

He sipped at the cold tea and said, "Mary's going to marry Timothy."

"I know. You told me."

"I did?" He tried to remember, but couldn't. Then he said, "I'm leaving, Molly. But you can stay here."

"I'm leaving, too."

He stared at her. "You can't leave! Your time's not up."

"You going to have me put in jail?"

"Of course not!" He looked at her, and his head hurt. "Where you going?"

"I don't know—where are *you* going?" she shot back, then smiled at his confused look. "I want to talk to you, Adam—about Charles."

"I don't want to hear it!"

"Will you get that mulish expression off your face?" she said sharply. "You're acting like a child!"

He shuffled his feet, and looked into her eyes. "What do you know about all this?"

"I know a lot more than *you* do, Adam Winslow," she said pertly. "You were so set on feeling sorry for yourself that you went off pouting. Well, I want to tell you what you'd have heard if you'd been sensible enough to listen to Charles."

"He's a crook—and so is Saul!"

"I guess they come close, but now that you've finally come to see that, you can take care of yourself."

He stared at her, then stated humbly, "You knew it all along—so did Aunt Rachel. I was just too dumb to see it!"

"Not *dumb!*" Molly said sharply. "You—are—not—dumb! Can't you accept that? You *trusted* your family, and that's not dumb. But it would be if you didn't keep your eyes open from now on."

He sat there admiring her. She was wearing an old robe he'd seen a thousand times, but there was a light in her clear eyes and he could not bear the thought of not seeing her. "All right. Tell me what Charles said."

"Charles said there's a man named Tom Cresap, an old man that all the Indians trust in the Ohio Valley. He came to some of the richest men in Virginia and said he'd get the Indians to trade with them and nobody else—so ten of them formed the Ohio Company of Virginia. One of them is a man called John Hanbury, a rich London merchant who markets the furs, and he's a good friend of the King!"

"How do we fit into all this?" Adam asked.

"Why, Charles has been making friends in Virginia, and some of them are in the company—there's Lawrence and Austin

Washington and George Fairfax, the richest man in Virginia. Anyway, they petitioned the King for 200,000 acres of land on the south bank of the Ohio and they offered to build a fort at their own expense. They had to agree to settle at least 100 families on that land within seven years, and then they'd get another 300,000 acres."

"That's 500,000 acres of land!" Adam exclaimed.

"And some of it will be yours," Molly said. "Saul and Charles used the money from this place—and their own money—to get into the company. So you've really sold this place to become part owner of the Ohio Company of Virginia."

He sat there, trying to take it all in. He had determined never to believe Charles again, but everyone knew the Washingtons and Thomas Fairfax. Those men would not be involved in a crooked deal.

"You've got to go to Virginia, Adam," Molly prodded him.

"Me? Go to Virginia?"

"It's your kind of place—a man's world, Adam," she stated firmly, a wistful smile on her lips. "You can't stay here—this world is lost. This place, and—and Mary." She faltered at that, but he did not flinch. "You've got to go!"

As Adam sat there considering the possibilities, the thing grew on him. Northampton was gone, as Molly insisted. A new world—a big new world, with big challenges awaited him. He could not think of a single reason why he should not go.

Then he looked at her and said, "I can't go and leave you here. When will you marry Wells?"

"Not ever."

He stared at her stupidly, then shook his head. "I don't understand you, Molly."

"I told Robert yesterday I wasn't going to marry him." She smiled and added, "He wasn't too surprised. It's been wrong from the beginning—and he was starting to see that."

His mouth was open, and he stared at her, then laughed. "I can't keep up with you, Molly Burns!" Then he asked, "What are you going to do?"

"I'm still bound to you, Adam," she said quietly.

"You'd come with me—to Virginia?"

She nodded and a smile touched her lips. "I think you have to take me. You can't just run off and leave a bound girl behind." She knew it irked him to hear her speak of the indenture.

But this time Adam held his hand out, and she looked up at him questioningly, then placed hers in his.

"It'll be beautiful in Virginia in the spring, won't it, Molly?"

She suddenly felt her eyes burn, and her hand trembled in his, but she smiled up at him.

"Oh, yes, Adam! I know it will!"

PART THREE

VIRGINIA

★ ★ ★ ★

1751–1755

CHAPTER SIXTEEN

A BALL AT MOUNT VERNON

★ ★ ★ ★

After four years in the backwoods of Virginia, Philadelphia looked huge to Molly. She smiled at Adam's excitement as he pointed out buildings he remembered; then she thought of the letter in her pocket. "Adam, can we post this letter to Mother?"

"Sure—let me have it."

As he took it and stopped the team long enough to run into a small office, she thought over what she had said to her mother:

14 March, 1754

Dear Mother,

I know I have not written as I should, especially since you have been in poor health. Please forgive me! It is impossible to tell you how life is here—how it has been for the last three years since we left New England and came to Virginia. As I told you when last I wrote, Mr. Winslow has prospered in his trade of making guns. He has a small shop in a small village, and one helper, who with his wife lives with us.

I am well, very well. Virginia is very different from England. It is rather wild, with large tracts of woods like nothing in England. Our lives have been very simple. We work, we go to church, we visit neighbors.

One problem occurred some time back. Some of the women in the village said it was wrong for a woman full grown—can you believe that I am grown up, Mother?—to live

202

with an unmarried man. But the pastor of the local church, Rev. Terry, is very understanding. He shut the gossips down by pointing out that Mr. and Mrs. Tanner live in the house and are adequate protectors. He is very fond of Mr. Winslow.

I must close, for we leave in the morning for Philadelphia—the longest journey I've made since we moved here three years ago.

I suppose you remember me as a little girl—and I still remember you with love. You asked in your last letter if I would marry—and you hinted at the possibility of marrying Mr. Winslow. My time of indenture will be up soon, and I will marry, I suppose. But Mr. Winslow gave his heart to another young woman, and when it did not work out, I think he resigned himself to remaining single.

I enclose a small gift. Use it for yourself and for the children.

Your loving daughter,
Molly Burns

She sat with thoughts of sadness over how her mother had endured such hardness. It had been easier after Tom Burns had died, and Molly had been generous with her—for Adam insisted on helping. But London seemed far away, and she thought of her mother and brothers and sisters like characters in a book she had read rather than as real people.

Adam came back soon, mounted the wagon, and they continued down the busy street.

"Look, Molly!" There was excitement in his eyes as he pulled the team to a halt in front of a plain white building, and he pointed up to a sign that read: BENJAMIN FRANKLIN, PRINTER. "He's still here."

"Do you think he'll remember you, Adam?" Molly asked.

"Why, I don't reckon so. That was—let's see, this is 1754 and I was only thirteen, so that'd be—why, it's been fourteen years ago!" He shook his head, then got out and helped her down. "No, Mr. Franklin's now a famous man; I don't think he'd remember me."

He led her into the shop and was surprised to see that very little was changed. He had remembered it as being much larger, and now there were at least five men working a series of presses that lined the walls instead of the single one that had stood in the middle of the floor.

"Help you?" a tall man asked, leaving his press to come and stand before them.

"Is Mr. Franklin in?" Adam asked.

"Yes, but somebody's with him. He ought to be able to see you before too long."

"We'll wait."

The tall man eyed the long rifle case that Adam carried easily under his arm, and said, "Don't guess that thing's loaded?"

"No."

Reassured, the printer went back to his press, and the pair stood there watching the work for ten minutes. The door to the inner office swung open and two men walked out talking. Adam recognized Franklin at once, for the man was little changed. Indeed, except for a larger girth and a hairline that had crept upward, the famous man looked almost the same as he had at their last meeting.

He stopped abruptly, took a look at the pair, and there was a puzzled look in his small brown eyes. He stepped forward saying, "I know you, sir—but the name is gone."

"Why, I'm surprised you remember me, Mr. Franklin. It's been a long time ago—fourteen years. I'm Adam Winslow, and you printed a book for my father—"

"Of course!" Franklin slapped his high forehead with his palm, and a smile spread over his round face. "The journal of Gilbert Winslow, your great-grandfather—why, it's one of the finest pieces of work ever put out in my shop! And your father, how is he?"

"Gone, Mr. Franklin. He died five years ago."

"Ah, well, I'm sorry, my boy!" Franklin shook his head, and put his hand out impulsively.

"I think he got as much comfort out of your book as anything," Adam said. "He was very proud of it."

"Well, now, I'm very happy—very happy!" Franklin nodded his head and there was a smile on his thin lips. "So much of the work I do is ephemeral—much of it not worth a great deal, you know. But *Winslow's Journal* was the first book I was really proud of—and still am! Not only a first-class piece of printing, but the subject matter—oh, my word!"

"May I meet your friend, Benjamin?" Franklin's companion, spoke up suddenly. The moon-faced man dressed in buff broadcloth declared, "I always said that was the best thing you ever put out of this shop. I've read it many times."

"Why, that's so! This is Adam Winslow—great-grandson of Gilbert Winslow. This is Mr. Paul Revere."

"Gilbert was my great-grandfather," Adam said, shaking the hand Revere offered.

"And you have another beautiful young lady with you, I see," Franklin said. He smiled at Molly and added, "The last time, I recall, your lovely sister was with you."

"This is Miss Molly Burns—Mr. Franklin and Mr. Revere," Adam returned. He was always a little awkward introducing Molly, so he said quickly, "I remember we went to hear Mr. Whitefield."

Franklin was admiring Molly with a steady glance, but he looked back at Adam and smiled broadly. "Why, so we did! Twice, if I remember correctly."

Revere seemed amused by the reference. "People can't really understand your fascination with that preacher, Ben. Every time he comes to America, he practically lives with you. You sure he's not made a convert out of you?"

Franklin sighed regretfully. "Unfortunately, not, Paul. I'm still just a seeker after the Lord. But—there is *something* about that man—there really is!" He shrugged and changed the subject quickly. "Well, Mr. Winslow, can I help you in any way?"

"I came to Philadelphia to get some advice on a new type of rifle I'm working on, Mr. Franklin, and I remembered that you were interested in inventions."

Revere threw up his hands, exclaiming, "Heaven help us, Mr. Winslow! You've touched on his madness! If there's one thing Ben dotes on more than politics, it's some hare-brained invention—the wilder the better." He snorted impatiently and added, "Why, right now he's working on some fool thing that'll bring a fire right into the middle of the room without even a fireplace! He'll burn the town down before he's finished!"

Franklin shook his head, and reached out for the rifle. "You're a fine one to talk! Why, you spend half your time tinkering at that shop of yours."

The two men argued mildly as Franklin pulled the rifle out of the soft leather case. But when both men began to examine it, they gave cries of approval. "Why, this is fine work!" Revere said instantly, then added, "But what's this part here?"

"That's the new firing mechanism I've been working on," Adam answered.

Franklin looked at the part Revere was pointing to. "Come back into my office, Winslow," he said, "I want to examine this more closely. Goodbye, Revere."

"I'm dismissed, you see!" The other man laughed and added as he shook hands with Adam, "He's afraid I'll steal your idea—and he may be right. But you'd better keep your eyes open—and you, too, Miss Burns." He lowered his voice so that Franklin, who had walked away toward the office, could not hear. "An invention—a pretty woman—those are Ben Franklin's weaknesses!" Then he winked and left the shop.

Adam led Molly into Franklin's office, and for the next hour she listened as the two talked about frizzens, pans, priming, and other matters. At first Adam was in such awe of Franklin that he said little, but soon he forgot himself and argued loudly over the design of the mechanism.

Finally, Franklin looked up and said, "Why, Miss Burns! We've quite neglected you!" He shook off her denial, adding vigorously, "You must be bored to death with all this technical talk."

"Why, no, Mr. Franklin, I'm not."

"Mr. Winslow, would you mind stepping over to the inn and getting us a pot of tea? I'll entertain Miss Burns."

Adam left and Franklin looked closely at the girl, taking in the clear gray-blue eyes, the golden tan that no woman of fashion would have, the strong hands and erect carriage. He had been conscious of her beauty, but now he began to speak with her, and he was quite adept at the business, his questions seeming quite artless.

Soon, however, she found herself telling the printer all about herself—and Adam. He had asked where they lived, and she hesitated, then said, "Well, we moved from Boston to the Ohio Valley in 1751. Mr. Winslow has a large tract of land there."

Franklin stared at her. "But—that's not a very safe place, or so I understand. And you were with him?"

"Oh, yes." She saw a question flicker in his eyes and knew what he was wondering. "I'm indentured to Mr. Winslow. My time will be up in another year."

"I see," Franklin said simply, "I'm sure that'll be a happy day for you."

Molly had grown accustomed to people being curious as to her rather unusual relationship with Adam, but her face grew warm under the scrutiny of Franklin. "I—I suppose it will. I don't think of it." Then she said quickly to change the subject, "We're living in Virginia now."

"Virginia?"

"Yes, a little town near the Potomac River, Woodbridge."

"I know Woodbridge. It's not far from Alexandria."

"Adam's brother Charles has a large plantation close to there—the family business. Their cousin is Saul Howland—you may have heard of him?"

"The businessman from Boston? Yes, a very shrewd man, so I hear. And what do you do in Virginia?"

"Why, I work." Molly looked up in surprise, and then she added quickly, "Adam's going to have a shop in town. That's all he wants to do, Mr. Franklin—work on guns. For the last few years he's been so busy with the fur business he had to put it off, but then he finally told his brother that he was going to quit— so that's when Mr. Howland and Mr. Winslow agreed that Adam should start a shop close to the Virginia property."

Adam came in just then, bearing a pot of steaming tea. Franklin took the teapot and insisted on serving them. As they drank the beverage, the printer remarked, "I think your new matchlock will not work—not as it is, Mr. Winslow. But it has promise."

Adam flushed with pleasure and replied, "That's my own thinking. I thought you might be interested in doing some work on it yourself."

"I've no time, unfortunately—too many irons in the fire as it is!" Franklin shook his head, but there was a steady light of interest in his eyes. "You and I both know that the answer is in breech-loading rifles—but nobody's been able to come up with a workable model, not yet."

"It's got to come—but if I could just perfect this firing mechanism—why, any army in the world would jump at it."

"Yes, and do you know. . . ?" He paused and seemed struck by a new thought. "Miss Burns was telling me you're going to settle down in Woodbridge?"

"Yes, sir."

"I know some people there who might be of help to you. I had a very good friend, a Mr. Lawrence Washington, who died a little over a year ago. He was very interested in the Ohio land where you've just been."

"Yes, he was one of the founders of the Ohio Company, so my brother Charles tells me."

"Ah, yes. Well, his brother, a young chap named George, has taken over for Lawrence—and I believe you ought to talk with him."

"Why is that, sir?"

"Because he will be very interested in your views on the land in the Ohio Valley, for one thing. He's been there himself. He and a man named Van Braam took a message to the French to clear out of the land claimed by the Crown."

Adam smiled grimly. "You know how much good that did? The French are dug into that country and nothing short of a war is going to put them out!"

Franklin sipped at his tea, staring at Adam, then nodded. "That's *exactly* the sort of view that Washington needs to hear, my boy! He feels the same way himself, so I hear, but the politicians are blind to the situation."

"They won't be when the French turn the Indians loose to butcher the settlers there."

"You think they'll do that! Surely not, Mr. Winslow—I mean, they *are* civilized—the French, that is!"

"They've already done it," Adam shrugged. "That's why I took Molly and cleared out. The Iroquois are champing at the bit! You don't hear about it here, but every month some helpless settler and his family are butchered!"

Franklin nodded. "Yes, you must see Washington. Not only to pass this word along about the French in the Ohio Valley; he'll be interested in this rifle as well. He's a lieutenant colonel in the Virginia militia, and his brother Lawrence often told me how fascinated he was with small arms and cannon."

Molly spoke up suddenly, "Adam, don't you remember that name?"

"What name, Molly?"

"Why, George Washington. Charles mentioned him in his last letter—no, it was the one before last. He said his plantation was called Mount Vernon."

"That's Washington's home, all right," Franklin confirmed. "A fine place, so they say."

"I can't remember," Adam said thoughtfully.

"It's at his home that the ball is going to be."

Adam snapped his fingers, saying, "That's right, Molly!" He smiled at Franklin, adding with a twinkle in his dark blue eyes, "I came to Philadelphia to see somebody about my rifle—but Molly came to buy a dress. My brother tells me we're going to go to a ball, and it's at Mt. Vernon. I'd forgotten."

"You'll be moving in high society," Franklin smiled. "Along with the Hugers and the Lees, the Washingtons are at the top of the ladder."

"Maybe you could suggest a place to get a fancy dress for Miss Burns?" Adam asked.

"And a suit for you, Adam," Molly added quickly. "You can't go to a ball wearing those buckskins."

"I think we can find you something suitable," Franklin offered with a smile. "Philadelphia has quite a few shops, and a beautiful young lady such as Miss Burns will have no trouble." He nodded to Adam, saying, "You tell Washington about those Indians—and make him look at your rifle."

"Don't see myself taking a rifle to a fancy ball, Mr. Franklin," Adam grinned. "Just the thought of *goin'* is pretty scary after being out in the woods for so long. But I want Molly to go. She's not had many fancy things, and I want to see her all dressed up in silks myself!"

Franklin did not miss the expression that swept across the young woman's face as Winslow spoke, but he only nodded and said, "It will be quite good for both of you—that ball at Mount Vernon!"

"You say this brother of yours has been living with the savages, Charles? Can't see how he'll fit into a ball!"

Lord Stirling leaned back against the rich leather of the seat, pulled a snowy white handkerchief from his pocket, and flicked away a spot of dust from his sleeve. He was a big man, slightly corpulent, with large bold eyes in a florid face. He had the air of one who was accustomed to being obeyed, but he appeared indolent as he turned his eyes to the tobacco field they were passing through.

"I dare say you're right, Henry," Charles shrugged. "My brother never was much for things of this sort. A diamond in the rough, you might say." He cast a glance at the large man beside him and added, "He'll be useful, I think."

"How could a bumpkin be useful? Seems he'd be quite out of place and a bore. Don't suppose he's shaved or had a bath for years?"

Charles laughed. "Oh, he'll be presentable, never fear. But he knows that Ohio country like a book—and we've got to convince the others to come into the Ohio Company."

"You've been at me for a month about the blasted company, Winslow!" Stirling complained. "I'm not sure it's going to be as profitable as you say."

"Then I'll have to do a better job of selling you on the thing, Henry!" Winslow laughed. "You made a fortune in the slave trade—now I want to see you make another in the fur business."

"And make you a bundle of money at the same time?"

"Of course!" Charles Winslow shrugged and replied, "I've never lied to you about that. You wouldn't believe me for a second if I told you I was only out to serve you. We're two of a kind, Henry—get rich and stay that way!"

Stirling suddenly threw his head back and roared with

laughter, his large teeth gleaming in his wide mouth. "Now I believe *that*!" he cried. "So we'll have this rural brother of yours to entice the Lees and the other rich fish into the company, eh?"

"Adam may not look like much—but he's spent the last four years working among the fur traders and the Indians out in the wildest part of that country. He knows every inch of it, and somehow he's gained the confidence of some big chiefs—Indians, you know."

"All very well, but you should have sent your man to clean him up—dress him like a gentleman!"

"Oh, I told him to go by a shop in Philadelphia and buy some good clothes."

"It'll have to do, I suppose."

Stirling leaned back and looked over the small town that they were entering. He said nothing until the driver pulled up and asked a passer-by where the gunsmith's shop was located, then moved on down the street.

"I hope he's ready," Stirling grumbled as they pulled up in front of a neat frame building with the sign GUNSMITH over the door.

Charles swung down, saying, "He just moved in three days ago, but I sent word yesterday we'd pick him up early today." He moved to the door and entered without knocking. Inside he saw a room about twelve feet wide and at least twenty feet long. There were weapons of all kinds hanging from pegs, and several large workbenches were covered with parts of rifles, muskets and pistols. A burly man with a shock of thick black hair beginning to go silver stood up and asked, "Yes, sir? Can I serve you?"

"I'm looking for Adam Winslow."

"Ah, yes, sir, I'll just call him for you." He moved to the back of the shop, called through the door, "Mr. Winslow? Can you come to the front?" He came back to stand beside his bench, and said with a smile, "You'd be Mr. Winslow's brother?"

"Yes."

"I'm James Tanner, Mr. Winslow. Your cousin, Mr. Howland, hired me to come and help Mr. Adam. Me and my wife live here with Mr. Winslow." He looked at the back door, then added, "He's a fine gunmaker, sir. But then you know all about that."

Charles nodded and started to speak, but Adam came into the room. "Why, Adam, I wasn't expecting you to look so—"

"Civilized, Charles?" Adam laughed. He was wearing a plain suit of brown, with a white linen shirt and a light blue waistcoat. His muscular figure gave the simple attire a certain air, Charles saw, and he was relieved that he would not be embarrassed over his brother's dress.

"You look very well, Adam," Charles said with a smile. "Are you ready?"

"Let me call Molly."

"Molly?"

There was such surprise in Charles's voice that Adam stared at him. "Yes, she's going with me."

"But—she's a servant!"

Adam settled in his tracks and the familiar stubborn look came to his jaw. Charles knew there was no need to argue, and he smiled, saying, "I'd forgotten about Molly, to tell the truth. Does she look presentable?"

Adam said nothing, but went to the stairs to the left and called loudly, "Molly! Come on—it's time to go!"

She must have been waiting, for they heard her light footsteps as she came down the stairs. Charles looked up and almost gasped.

"Why, Molly—you look lovelier than ever!"

She was wearing a gown made of a light blue material, with lace at the bosom and around the hem. Her ash-blond hair was lighter than he remembered, and her lips fuller. She smiled suddenly at him, and there was little left of the teenaged girl he'd seen in Boston. This was a woman of twenty, with all the fullness of figure and mystery of expression he had rarely seen.

"I'm glad to see you again, Mr. Winslow," she returned, her voice lower than most women's, with a vibrant tone that suggested great power.

"Well," Charles said finally with a smile, "you have grown up—which I believe I told you the last time we met, didn't I, Molly?"

"Yes, you did. You're looking very well."

"Now, shall we go?"

As they came out of the building, Henry Stirling took one look at Molly and quickly limped out of the carriage. The indolence that had kept him half asleep in Charles's presence vanished. As he took Molly's hand and kissed it, there was an alertness about him—a predatory air that he could not quite conceal.

He greeted Adam with a word, then insisted on seating Molly in the frontward facing seat, sitting down beside her and waving the Winslow men to the other seat with a laugh. All the way to Mount Vernon he kept the conversation going, and Adam noticed that Stirling sat closer to Molly than was absolutely necessary.

Charles noticed as well, and he engaged Adam in conversation about business. He told him, in effect, that there were some wealthy planters who were not yet investors in the Ohio Company, but were interested. "We're expecting you to convince them it's a good proposition, Adam."

"Do they know there's going to be a war?" Adam asked.

"Why, no—and neither do you!" Charles said in alarm. "Don't say anything about that, Adam!"

He was so alarmed that Adam stared at him. He said nothing, but as Charles continued to urge him to give a good report to the potential investors, it became clear that he'd been brought in to sell them on the idea. The idea depressed him. For the past few years, he'd lived on the cutting edge of life—one day at a time, all he could be sure of. It had been a simple matter—just stay alive—and now he was being drawn into a complex world of business that he had no taste for—and he hated it.

But it was too late, so he followed the two men and Molly inside when they arrived at the magnificent mansion with the large white pillars in front. When they went inside, Adam had an impulse to flee, for there was an opulent air to the house that was unlike anything he'd ever seen. Everything was rich and gilded, and the dress of the men and women made him feel like a poor relation.

Molly caught a glimpse of his face and knew at once that he was miserable. But Lord Stirling pulled her into the large ballroom and, with the assurance born of much dealing with women, led her onto the floor and began to dance.

It was a strange evening for both of them. Adam lurked on the outskirts of the ballroom, feeling totally out of place. Charles stayed with him briefly, then went off to his own devices. Adam watched Molly, who was like a stranger to him. He was accustomed to seeing her in simple cotton dresses, and this girl in silk, who moved with such grace in the complexities of the dance, was not his Molly at all.

She saw him from time to time, his dark face in the shadows along the walls, but there was no opportunity to go to him. Stirling monopolized her time, and she had seen enough of men to recognize that he was in full pursuit of her. Even though her experience was limited to the rural scenes, men are men, no matter what the station, and she saw the same hot desire in his eyes that she had seen in the eyes of the hunters of the Ohio Valley.

The hours sped by and Adam was almost ready to leave and walk home when Charles touched his arm, saying, "Come with me!"

He led the way to a door at the end of the large room, then as they went down a broad hall, whispered, "Be careful what you say to Washington, Adam. He's a fox!"

They went into a room that seemed small after the large ballroom, but was actually fifteen feet long and almost as wide. There was a long table around which seven men were seated. The man at the end stood up as they entered, and Charles said, "This is my brother, Adam. Adam, I want you to meet Colonel Washington."

"Happy to have you, Mr. Winslow," Washington returned. "Won't you join us?" There was a rawboned look of power about him—blunt features, including a broad nose and heavy forehead. His pale blue eyes looked inquiringly at the young man. "Your brother tells me you've just spent several years in the Ohio Valley."

"Yes, Colonel. In the fur trade."

"Ah, we would be most interested in your thinking on how things are going in that area."

Washington leaned back, and Adam, feeling very uncomfortable, began to speak. He had not gotten far before Washington began to ask him specific questions, and that made things much easier. He found out at once that the colonel knew the area well.

Finally, one of the other men asked, "What about trouble with the French? If we sink our money into this venture, can we expect peace from them?"

Adam felt Charles's intense gaze on him, urging him to deny any possibility of trouble, but he was looking into Washington's face. There was such a power in the colonel's gaze that it could be felt, and he heard himself saying simply, "There will be trouble with the French until the Crown of England settles the matter of who owns the land."

Washington slapped the table so hard that the rest of them jumped. "Exactly what I've been trying to make the House of Burgesses understand!" He smiled at Adam and said, "I'm very happy that you have settled in our area, young man. Would it be possible for me to enlist you under my command in the militia?"

Adam stared at him. "Why, I'm no soldier, Colonel Washington!"

"But you know the Ohio Valley—and you know guns." Washington nodded at Adam's surprise, and added, "Your brother has told us much of your efforts to come up with a superior firing system for the musket. I would very much like to see your work. But I would more like to see you in my company. Can I count on you, Mr. Winslow?"

Adam felt the power of the man, as did the others in the room, and as many others would feel it in the days to come. It was almost perceptible, a tangible thing, the force of George Washington, and Adam found himself assenting.

"Why, I'd be proud to serve under you, Colonel!" When Washington took his hand, he knew at once that something had come into his life—something new and different.

Much, much later, he and Molly were deposited by Stirling and Charles at the shop. James and Hope Tanner were still up as Adam and Molly entered, and Adam thought—not for the first time—how their presence in the house made it possible for Molly to stay there. A young woman living alone with an unmarried man would be impossible otherwise! They got up, said good night, and he turned to her.

"Molly?"

"Yes?"

The candle guttered and threw a golden gleam over her face, and her eyes looked enormous as she faced him.

"You—looked very lovely. I didn't know you could dance like that!"

"Robert taught me years ago. Although he wasn't very good at it, I learned the steps. It just seems to come naturally to me."

"Everybody was watching you. You were quite popular."

"I was disappointed."

"Disappointed?"

"I thought you'd come dance with me—at least once."

"Me?" He seemed shocked at the thought. "Why, Molly, I'd have been a poor show—with all the fine gentlemen in their fancy clothes."

"I—I wish you had come," she whispered. She was standing so close that he could smell the faint odor of the violets she wore, and it made him suddenly nervous.

"Well if I'd known that—maybe I'd have come."

"Will you dance with me the next time?"

He nodded, and suddenly his throat seemed tight. At a loss for words he simply said, "Go to bed, Molly."

"Good night, Adam." She went up the stairs without another word, and for a long time he stood there, in a trance, thinking of her. Then he smiled and shook his head. "Me dance with her! Now wouldn't that be a sight!" He turned and went to bed.

CHAPTER SEVENTEEN

THE BULLETS WHISTLE

★ ★ ★ ★

Molly put down her quill, rubbed her eyes, and picked up her journal to read the entry she had just made. Her fingers, she noticed, were trembling and the lines across the page wavered in a manner quite unlike her usual even script.

April 2, 1754
Woodbridge
Adam left this morning with Lieutenant Colonel Washington. They are part of the force to drive the French out of the Ohio Valley. I was so proud that Washington made Adam his aide! But they are too weak a force, Adam says (and the colonel agrees), to push the enemy out. I pray that he will be safe!

I am glad that Adam is gone, for he was so angry with Lord Stirling that there would have been trouble. Oh, what can I do? I have avoided Stirling, have told him I do not care for his company, but he forces himself on me. I have tried for the past few months to hide this from Adam, but two days ago he came home and found Lord Stirling here—and my face was flushed, for he had been—well, he had been no gentleman! It hurt me, for Adam thought I had been encouraging his attentions—that I was kissing him, when in fact I had just managed to pull myself away from him.

Charles is no help. He *encourages* the man, telling me that

I must be *nice* to him, for he can help with the family business—that's his answer!

Somehow I must free myself of his attentions—I must! My heart pounds even now as I think of how he forces himself on me as if I were a common girl!

And Adam—I cannot bear for him to believe I like the man—yet if I told him the truth, he would beat him. And for a common man to strike a member of the nobility would be a tragedy!

What can I do? Lord, help your servant!

"You're impatient, Adam," Washington said quietly. He had come up to stand beside Adam, who was looking over Great Meadows—an open plot of land in the midst of the forest lush with grass for horses and cattle.

"Well, I guess I'm guilty, Colonel," Adam nodded ruefully. "We've been on the march for two months almost, and we've only been within striking distance of the enemy once."

"I know." Washington looked westward to the gap in the woods that marked the road they'd hewed out, and there was a frown on his heavy features. "If we could have followed the first plan, we'd have been there by now, but when Colonel Fry got lost, we had no choice but to hack our way through." He looked down at Adam with a smile and added, "At least you can tell your grandchildren you had a part in building the first road west—for that's about what this is!"

"We could have taken a party of riflemen through the woods, Colonel."

"I think now that's what we should have done," Washington admitted. "By this time we've been seen by enough enemy scouts to carry the word to the French at Fort Duquesne. They'll be waiting for us."

Adam pulled a weed, bit it off, then asked sharply, "We going on, Colonel—anyway?"

"Yes! You see that hill?" Great Meadows was about 200 to 400 yards wide and two and a half miles long. At a point about 100 yards from a forested hill on one side and 150 yards from another on the other side was a rise. "I've marked off an outline there. We're going to build a fort."

"A fort? Why, that'll take even *more* time, sir!"

"I know—but we may need it, Adam. If we get over-whelmed, we can't run all the way back to Virginia, can we?" A smile touched Washington's firm lips, and he put his hand on Adam's shoulder—an unusual action for him, but he had grown to trust the young scout during the past two months. "We'll call it—Fort Necessity."

Building the fort was not such a big job, for all the men were expert axmen. They simply dug a trench three feet deep, placed logs twelve to fifteen feet long upright in it, and then packed the dirt around it. Loopholes were cut through the logs, and in less than a week, Fort Necessity stood ready for action.

"Wouldn't take but one cannon to knock it down, Colonel," Adam said as the two men stood inspecting it early one morning.

"No, but we could hold it against any massed infantry at-tack—and there are no cannon in this part of the world." Wash-ington turned to see an Indian runner emerge from the trees on the western side of the clearing.

The Indian approached one of the soldiers, who waved an arm to where Washington stood with Adam, then ran at once to the rise. "Colonel Washington?"

"Yes."

"I am Silverheels. Message from Davidson."

Washington took the leather pouch the runner had handed him, pulled out a parchment and scanned it. He looked at Adam, his pale blue eyes alive with excitement. "You won't be bored anymore, Mr. Winslow! Get the men out!"

Forty men left Fort Necessity—with the colonel after less than an hour. As they made their way through the thick woods, Washington said little, but as heavy rain set in, he told the men to rest. "The message was from a man who was with me last December, Winslow. He tells me that an expedition of French-men are on their way to attack. But I don't think we'll wait for that."

"Do you know where they are, sir?"

"The messenger will lead us to their camp."

"How big a force do they have, Colonel?"

"Davidson wasn't sure—but it could be over a hundred."

Adam surveyed their unit, rubbed his chin, and said, "We'll be outnumbered."

"We'll have the advantage of surprise, though—and if we wait for the other men, we'll let them get away!"

Adam smiled at the tall man, for he had learned much about this aristocrat over the past two months. They were facing an enemy that outnumbered them two to one, and Washington was afraid they would "get away." At a time when other men would be thinking of retreat, this soldier feared only the loss of an opportunity to do battle. In years to come, Adam was to think often of this moment, but as they stood there in the dripping rain, he could only think, *He's going to get some of us killed—but he'll be right in the middle of it too.*

It was a bedraggled, hungry lot who saw the sun rise. They marched single file with Washington, who was following Silverheels. The guide led them to a depressed glen, rimmed with rock that concealed the French army. "A perfect hiding place!" Washington whispered to Adam as they circled the camp. Breakfast fires were burning, but the dense overhanging foliage absorbed their reflections.

Colonel Washington glanced around, saw that his men were in position, then yelled, "Attack! Attack!"

The French threw down their eating utensils, grabbed guns, and made a dash for the protection of the rocks. The French commander fell in the attack, but Washington did not rush the makeshift fort because the French put up a furious fight.

Adam loaded and fired again and again; he heard for the first time the cries of the wounded and dying. He fired and saw a shadowy figure drop; then as he stood up to reload, a ball whistled by his head and he heard a *thunk*. Turning around he saw a soldier named Jake Kilrain still standing, but mortally wounded, a musket ball in his forehead. Suddenly the man fell like a tree, slowly, his unbending body slamming into the ground. Adam's heart went out to the wounded but there was no time to tend them. The battle was fierce and he wondered if he would survive.

"Cut them off!" yelled Washington as he walked from tree to tree, ignoring the vicious whistling musket balls. He signaled a sergeant with a small squad to fill in a breach where the enemy was running to escape.

The battle lasted about fifteen minutes, though it seemed much longer to Adam! Finally a cry went up asking for quarter, and Washington bellowed out, "Hold your fire! They're surrendering!"

A tense moment passed, but the French rose slowly, hands over their heads, and their officer, Captain La Force, came forward to stand before Washington. "We will fight no more," he said with tears of anger in his eyes. "You have win these fight—but you nevair get back to your country!"

There was celebrating in the camp that night. Colonel Washington and his small force remained at Fort Necessity to search the forest for signs of the enemy, for they were certain that some of the French troops had escaped to Fort Duquesne with word of their defeat.

A week later, Silverheels departed on a scouting trip and came back at twilight with one of the braves from his own tribe. Washington listened carefully as the Indian spoke, then to Silverheels' translation: "He says that the French with many Indians have left Fort Duquesne—he says they have heard how you beat La Force and they vow to kill all of you."

The colonel believed the report and drove the men to strengthen the fort. The water had become contaminated and dysentery spread through the camp, but a construction crew never had greater incentive to work. Every now and then a man would drop out because of illness.

In the center of the fort was a stockade 57 feet in diameter, loopholed for rifles and muskets. Within the stockade was a hut 14 feet square, roofed over with shakes, which offered protection to the most seriously ill and the dangerously small supply of powder.

The scouts kept them posted as they built, and finally Washington told Adam, "They'll be here tomorrow."

That night it rained, and day broke to reveal the first signs of three French columns advancing on the fort. Their Indian allies had put aside their blankets and came naked in the rain.

"There's too many of them," declared the colonel. Adam

stared at Washington, not believing his ears. He knew the colonel was stating the truth, but he never once considered that the tall Virginian would agree. "There are too many for us, but it won't be very glorious if we don't fight, will it?"

"No, sir."

Washington watched the approaching ranks and said evenly, "I don't think they want to die any more than we do. If we put up a show of force, I think they'll allow us to surrender—then they can go back claiming victory."

That, to Adam's surprise, was exactly what happened. He wondered afterward how Washington could *know* such things, but at the time he simply obeyed orders.

The French and Indians advanced, flanking the fort. Washington drew his men into the palisade, stationing them in the trenches, and the battle continued through the afternoon.

Heavy clouds gathered and the rain began, making steady firing impossible. Water soaked into the guns, and the flint sparks only hissed in the wet powder. When that happened, it was necessary to draw out the wet charge with a ramrod fitted with a screw.

"I wish that new gunlock of yours was finished, Winslow," Washington remarked once as Adam's piece misfired. "But at least they're having the same trouble we are."

As darkness fell, the French commander called out, "Voulez-vous parler?" "Do you want to negotiate?" Washington's interpreter met with the French officer and returned after a while with articles of surrender. The French had won, but Washington was allowed to leave on the condition that he and his men would return home.

The next morning the sun was high in the sky when the English, with the wounded supported by able-bodied soldiers, marched out with drums beating and colors flying. As they left Fort Necessity, Washington looked back, and said to Adam, "Though war is terrible, there is something strange about being in the thick of it, Winslow."

"Yes, sir?"

Washington was not a talkative man, and Adam saw that he was trying to find words for something. There was a strange look on his face, and finally he smiled and looked into Adam's dark eyes.

"Those bullets whistling around our heads—" he paused, his eyes lighting up with wonder. Then he finished, saying slowly, "Even when one is in danger of death, there's something quite charming in that sound!"

The morning sun crested the tall elms that shaded the shop as Adam slipped from the back of the leggy gelding that had carried him from camp. He had marched back with the army to Williamsburg, but after two days in camp, had gone to Washington, saying, "Sir, if you don't have any use for me, I'd like to get home."

The Virginian had smiled, shaken his hand and said, "Certainly, Winslow. I'll be leaving myself shortly. Take one of my horses. You can return it to Mount Vernon later."

Adam walked across the plank walk, and was surprised to find the door closed, even more so to discover it bolted. "James! James!" he called out. "Where are you?"

At first there was no answer, but soon he heard footsteps, and then Hope Tanner, James's wife, asked, "Is that you, sir?"

"Yes, it's me, Hope."

The door opened and he went inside, asking at once, "Is James sick, Hope?"

She hesitated, then shook her head, saying, "No, Adam, he's in jail."

He stared at her in disbelief. "Jail! What for?"

Hope Tanner was a middle-aged woman, steady and firm, but there was trouble in her eyes and she twisted the cloth she held in her hands nervously. "Well, sir, it's bad news for you, I'm thinking."

Startled, Adam thought immediately of Molly. "Where is Molly? Is she sick? Is she—" He started to say *dead*, but said instead, "Is she all right?"

"She's not sick, Adam. But she's not here."

Adam stared at her, then cried out, "For God's sake, Hope! Tell me what's happened!"

"Well, you maybe didn't know, Adam, but that English lord,

he's been after Molly real hard."

"I—I knew he was interested in her," Adam hesitated. "And I thought she liked him."

"Never!" Hope cried out indignantly. "She never did! It was him, the dog!"

Adam grew tense, and then he asked directly, "What happened, Hope? Let's have it all."

"Well, he kept coming here, bothering her, Adam. Kept pestering her to go off with him, but she wouldn't do that. Then last Wednesday, me and James went to church, but Molly stayed here alone. When we got home, we seen his carriage in front of the shop, and then we heard her crying out! Like she was hurt or scared!"

She bit her lip, then forced herself to go on. "We run in and he had her pinned up against the wall, pawing at her. Her dress was torn and she was fightin' to get away from him, but he was too strong for her—the beast!"

Adam's temples throbbed, he felt lightheaded, as he always did just before rage came. He listened carefully, his fists clenched as Hope said tearfully, "James jumped at him and when Stirling hit him in the face, James knocked him down, then he picked him up and threw him out of the shop!"

"And next James was arrested for assaulting Lord Stirling, is that it?"

"They come the next day and took him, Adam," she nodded. "I knew he'd come again, so I sent Molly to stay with my sister over close to Alexandria. She didn't want to go, but I couldn't protect her here."

"Thank God you and James were here, Hope!" Adam said fervently. He went over and put his arm around her shoulders. "Don't worry about James; they can't hold him."

"But, Adam—"

"Is Stirling still at my brother's house, do you know?"

"Yes, but he's been here every day to try to get me to tell where Molly is."

"You stay here, Hope."

She watched carefully as he walked over to the wall and took down a small pistol. It was a twin-barreled over-and-under flintlock with a tap action. He loaded it, saying nothing, but there was something frightening about his intensity, and Hope said as he put the pistol in his belt and headed for the door, "I—I'll pray for you, Adam."

He shot her a look from under his narrowed brows, his dark blue eyes frosty and cold. "Pray for his soul, Hope—for he's a dead man!"

He left the shop, mounted, and turned the horse's head toward his brother's plantation. The rage that had fallen on him in the battles at Washington's side had no comparison to the frozen hatred that seemed to eat away at his heart. Not for one moment did he consider the consequences that would follow if he killed Stirling, and if he had any cries from his conscience, he stifled them.

He arrived at the house at dusk, and the short, fat slave who took his horse recognized him immediately. "Mist' Winslow!" he cried out, taking the reins of Adam's mount. "You done been gone a long time!"

"Is Lord Stirling inside, Jim?" Adam asked.

The black face suddenly lost its toothy smile, and Jim swallowed, for he saw something on the white man's face that frightened him. "Yessuh! The gentulmens is playing cards in de den."

Adam walked around the carriage in front of the door, then paused and stared at it. His lips curved slightly in a smile, and he reached out and plucked the buggy whip from its holder, then walked to the front door. He went in, almost running over Minnie, the house slave who had come to admit him. She took one look at his face, then wheeled and left as quickly as she could without a word.

The den was a large room off the hall, and as Adam went toward it, he heard the sound of laughter. He paused outside the door, listening for a moment, then pushed it open and entered.

The five men seated around the table looked up at him, and a silence fell on the room. Charles was seated next to Lord Stirling, and across from him was John Franklin, a wealthy planter. Next to Franklin sat Lawrence Carter, a member of the House of Burgesses, and to his right was a lean man with a pale face that Adam had never seen.

The table was covered with cards, and each of the men had a glass at his hand. Tobacco smoke was thick in the air, and the sudden silence was heavy as Adam stood there, the whip in his hand.

Charles turned pale, but tried to carry the thing off. "Why, Adam, you're back!" He rose to his feet, forcing a smile. "I believe most of you know my brother, Adam—he's just returned from serving with Colonel Washington."

Adam paid no heed to his brother. He was staring at Henry Stirling. The large man had been slumped in his chair, but now he came slowly to a rigid position, for there was death in the eyes of the man who stood framed in the doorway.

Charles tried again, saying, "Adam, sit down and join us. We must hear all about the battle! You're quite a hero around here, you know!"

His words fell flat, and there was a ghastly silence broken only by the sound of a slave out in the yard singing a song about Moses and the Lamb.

"Stirling, you're a dog!"

Adam's deliberate words cut across the nobleman's nerves, and he jumped to his feet, his face livid. "I won't be insulted by you, Winslow!"

Adam's dark blue eyes were unwavering, and his voice grew quiet and menacing. "I didn't come to insult you, Stirling—"

"You'd better retract!" Stirling cried out in rage, striking the table angrily.

Adam raised his own voice, his words cutting like a knife. "I didn't come to insult you—I came to horsewhip you!" He cut the air suddenly with the whip, filling the room with the loud *whishing* sound.

Charles jumped forward, crying out, "Adam! You've gone crazy!"

"Stand still, Charles!" Adam said, not taking his eyes away from the Englishman. "I have a few 'brotherly' remarks to make to you later, but not now."

"Can't you do something, Winslow?" the thin, pale man said loudly. "I can't believe you'd let your guest—especially an honored guest such as Lord Stirling—be insulted!"

"Adam, just let me explain—!"

"I'll do the explaining." Adam bit off the words and swept the room with disdain. "This 'distinguished guest' of yours has assaulted a young woman in my care. He forced himself on her, and when a friend of mine intervened to save her, he had him put in jail."

"I'll see the fellow sent to Botany Bay for life!" Stirling cried. "He'll be taught a lesson."

"He'll be out of jail tonight—or you'll be cut to ribbons right now."

"I won't—!"

Adam suddenly flicked the whip across the table, the tip catching the end of Stirling's cigar, snatching it from his fingers and flinging it across the room.

"Stirling, you can have your choice." Adam's steady voice was almost a whisper. "Either you give your word in front of these men that James Tanner will be out of jail tomorrow—or I'll open you up like hot butter!"

Stirling turned pale. He licked his thick lips, then running his eyes around the room, suddenly stood up. He made a dash for the end of the room, and Adam let him go, seeing what he was attempting.

There was a musket on the wall, a Brown Bess, such as the British soldier used, with a bayonet gleaming on its end.

"We'll see who does what, Winslow!" Stirling yelled venomously as he lifted the rifle high, then lunged across the floor, thrusting the blade at Adam's belly.

Adam waited on the balls of his feet. As the naked steel shot toward his unprotected midsection, he reached out with the whip and forced the blade to one side. With his free hand he whipped a sudden blow into Stirling's stomach. The rifle clattered to the floor, and the big man fell, holding his stomach and gagging.

A movement to his left caught Adam's eye, and he turned to see the tall man pulling at a pistol that was in a coat hanging from the back of his chair. He came out with it, but the fire in his eyes died as he looked down the barrel of the pistol that had seemed to jump into the hand of Adam Winslow.

"Either use that, or drop it!" Adam commanded, and stood there waiting.

The thin man had the pistol almost lifted. Just a little move of the wrist and he would have it dead center, but he could not do it. There was something frightening in the smile on Adam Winslow's lips, and he let the pistol drop hurriedly, his face suddenly ashen.

"Second thoughts are usually best," Adam said quietly, then turned to look at Stirling, who was struggling to his feet. He waited until the man was upright, his face pale as paper, and then he said, "I won't ask you again. You have five seconds to decide if you'll have Tanner out of jail—or if you'll have a horse-whipping. Which shall it be?"

"He'll do it, Henry!" Charles cried out loudly. "He'd do it if he knew he'd die for it two minutes later!"

Stirling took one long look at Adam, then slowly, with hatred freezing his face, nodded once.

Adam said, "These men see that you have agreed." He put the pistol back in his belt, tossed the whip on the floor, then wheeled and went to the door. He paused and looked back at Stirling, saying, "If you don't keep your word—you can ask my brother what will happen."

Then he turned and was gone.

There was not a sound in the room, but Charles said in a whisper, "I can't answer for him, Henry! I know he's my brother, and I'm sorry for it all—but I have to tell you, if you've got any idea of not keeping your word, forget it!"

"Why, I'd have him locked up, Stirling!" the lean man cried.

"It wouldn't help, Ralph," Charles said, shaking his head with a bitter smile. "He'd dig out somehow, Henry, and you'd never have a night's sleep—because you know Adam would get you."

"I'll kill him for this, Charles!" Stirling whispered, and there was an insane gleam in his protruding eyes.

"No doubt you'll try, Henry," Charles shrugged. "But you're too shrewd to do it head-on." He slowly put a cigar between his lips and his hand trembled as he lifted a candle to light it. As the blue smoke rose, he said bitterly, "Let it rest, Henry. For now. He'd kill you out of hand—and I need you." Then he said quietly, "Shall we continue the game?"

CHAPTER EIGHTEEN

"I WANT TO BELONG TO YOU!"

★　★　★　★

"General Braddock, this is Adam Winslow—he served with me at Fort Necessity."

Major General Edward Braddock, a foot shorter than Washington with more fat than muscle in his bulk, peered at Adam from his shaggy brows, his small eyes suspicious. The powdered wig under his winged hat and the uniform blazing with bright decorations and embroidering seemed garish in the plain room where the three men stood.

The stubborn Englishman's nose flared in disdain. "You mean when you were *defeated* at Fort Necessity, before you had even reached your objective."

Washington refused to be humbled. "As you please, General. But you have asked me to be your aide, and it's my duty to tell you that Adam Winslow knows the terrain as well as the Indian scouts; we'll need his kind to guide us."

Braddock grunted and snapped with some irritation, "You mean you need *us*, Washington! Orthodox war, that's what I intend! No games, no hiding behind trees and jumping out at the enemy like children!" The bulldog of a man looked up with his eyes hard as marble. "Put him in uniform if you please—but I want only men who respect my authority!"

He nodded shortly, then left the room, and Washington shook his head, smiling grimly. "I never said he was an *easy* man to deal with, Winslow, but he is one of the most experienced soldiers in the British army. He's a long-time career officer. At the Battle of Culloden he broke the enemy with his headlong charges, much to the satisfaction of the Duke of Cumberland."

"Well, sir, if he tries to charge massed troops into a thick woods bristling with sharpshooters and Indians, it'll be a different story."

Washington bit his lip, then shrugged, saying only, "I have no authority, you understand?"

"A shame it is, too, Colonel!"

After the battle at Fort Necessity, Washington had been awarded thanks by the House of Burgesses for negotiating a surrender that allowed him to bring his troops home. He had been offered a command by Governor Dinwiddie, but the English government had issued an order that officers holding the King's commission should rank above provincial officers. The degradation of being outranked by every whipper-snapper who might hold a royal commission by virtue of being the illegitimate son of some nobleman's cast-off mistress had been more than Washington's temper could bear. He rejected the offer.

But when on February 20 of 1755 Braddock had arrived with two regiments to make a fresh attack on the French, he had decided that the young soldier's experience would be valuable; he had offered him a place on the staff with the rank of lieutenant colonel, where he would be subject only to the orders of the general. Washington had accepted.

Adam had known of this, and resented the treatment of the tall soldier whom he had learned to admire. "Why did you agree to serve under Braddock, sir? He obviously despises all soldiers who aren't regulars in the British army."

"I want to learn," Washington rubbed his chin, and there was a determined light in his eyes as he stared at Adam. "These are the picked troops of England. They have been unbeatable on the Continent. Braddock says they'll sweep the French out of the west—and he must have his chance."

"Yes, sir." Adam pondered a thought, then asked, "You

want me to go with you, Colonel?"

"It would be a personal favor. You will be my aide, not a regular." The tall man smiled and said, "Maybe we can get some of our own back on the French, eh, Winslow? Can I count on you?"

Adam warmed at the thought of serving with Washington, but hesitated. "When will the army move, sir? I need to make a trip to Boston right away. My family is in the fur business, and I've got to freight last year's pelts to our warehouse there—and then I'd be willing."

"You've got plenty of time for *that*! This army doesn't know the meaning of *hurry*! It's been almost a year since our battle, and it'll be another month at least before this army takes a step!"

"With your permission, then, I'll make my trip, and report back to you for duty as soon as possible."

"Fine—fine!" Washington gave one of his rare smiles and asked, "Still working on that rifle of yours?"

"Well, actually, that's why I'm stopping by Philadelphia on my way back, Colonel. I've made some progress, but Mr. Franklin says he has a new idea."

"Benjamin Franklin? Well, tell him I sent my regards," Washington replied. "If we could get a weapon that was accurate, that could be loaded in less time and fitted with a bayonet, we'd be a force to be reckoned with!"

"It's just a matter of time, Colonel."

"Ah, but that's just what we don't have—time! Those Frenchies will be settled so thick in the Ohio Valley in a year or two that we'll never get them out."

"You think there'll be another war, sir?"

Washington smiled grimly. "We're already in it! Remember Fort Necessity? Those bullets we heard whistling around our ears? Now we're going back. And I tell you if we fail, it'll take a miracle of the Almighty to root those scoundrels out!"

Adam asked curiously, "You believe in miracles, Colonel Washington?"

The man's features broke into a smile, and he murmured as he turned to leave the room, "There are precedents!" He turned to smile strangely at Adam. "There are, indeed, precedents!"

Molly never forgot that trip to Boston, for despite Adam's mild objections, she insisted on accompanying him. She gave several reasons, but did not mention the chief one—that she did not want to be left alone anywhere near Henry Stirling.

Months had passed since Adam's humiliation of the nobleman, and on the surface the affair seemed to have been forgotten. Adam of necessity had to go to Charles's home, and it was impossible to avoid Stirling. There had been no way for the man to avoid having Tanner set free, and he nodded and spoke whenever he met Adam, but there was a coldness in his watchful eyes.

"Watch out fer 'im, Mr. Winslow!" James Tanner counseled. "I had me a mule once who'd behave 'imself a whole year jes to get the chance to kick me once!"

Charles had come to Molly once after the incident and pleaded, "Molly, he's not a bad man—just spoiled, you know? Try to get on with him." Charles had suddenly looked haggard, his handsome face tense. "I—I haven't been careful enough, perhaps, in some ways."

"You owe him a great deal of money, Charles?" Molly had asked.

"Oh, I'll get it back when the company starts producing— but until then, I'm tied to the man. He won't bother you again, Molly, so if you could just try to keep things—well, smooth, you see?"

She had seen no profit in offending Stirling, though the thought of his hands on her made her flesh creep. But Adam had been her strength; she had subconsciously made him so, and when he had announced that he was going to be gone for several weeks on a trip to Boston, she had felt a streak of fear at the thought of being at Stirling's mercy—so she had asked if she could join him for the trip.

It turned out to be a wonderful trip, spring setting the frozen brooks free to gurgle in their beds, and the fruit trees shimmering pink and white dresses in the distance. The air was crisp and clean, and after the hard winter both of them relaxed in a way they had not since the days back at Northampton.

They avoided the inns along the way, preferring to camp out beside the trail. Every night they would stop early beside a stream or a spring, bring out the cooking gear and feast on game that Adam killed along the way.

On the last night before they arrived in Boston, they pulled off from the main road farther than usual. Adam shot a buck in a stand of oak and hickory half a mile to the east, and since there was plenty of dead wood and a creek, they made camp early. He skinned and dressed the deer, and by the time Molly had made a fire and they had cooked a choice cut, the sun was down.

"It may be a little cold tonight," he said, staring into the fire. "If you get cold in the wagon, just pull up another bale of beaver pelts."

Molly stood up, stretched, and said lazily, "It's so cozy in there, Adam!" She sat down across the fire, picked up a stick and began to poke the coals, sending up tendrils of smoke. "I wish Boston were another hundred miles away!"

Adam laughed. "So do I, Molly!" He lifted his head and watched as an owl sailed silently across the open field to their right and dropped making a sudden tiny scuffle in the grass. "It'll be strange seeing the house again."

"I think about your father a lot—and Rachel." Molly dropped the stick and watched it begin to glow in the coals. She leaned her cheek on her knee, and by the firelight her eyes seemed large and her lips looked soft as memories stirred through her. "I—I miss them, Adam," she sighed.

"So do I. They were—different." There was a hesitation in his speech and somehow he could not frame his thought. Finally he said, "They were godly people, Molly. I envy them that."

They had not talked much of religion since those days at Northampton, and now she asked, "You were bitter, weren't you, Adam—I mean about the way the church treated Rev. Edwards?"

"Yes! I still am, I guess. It wasn't fair!"

"Nothing much is."

He looked up swiftly, for in all the years he had known her, there had been few times when she had spoken so sadly. He tried to weigh her tone, her words, then asked, "Are you unhappy, Molly?"

She stood up and there was a restlessness in her as she took a few steps away from the fire, then came back to stand over the blaze. "No, I'm not."

He rose and she turned from him, but he reached out and pulled her around, trying to read her expression. A golden wash of light from the fire tinted her smooth cheeks, and her eyes were enormous. "You don't worry about being indentured, do you, Molly? You know that's never *meant* anything."

Suddenly her lips quivered, and he saw tears form in her eyes. She had been thinking of how he had come to her that first time—long ago in England. For years she had struggled to bury the memories of the filth and poverty, the mistreatment she had suffered at the brutal hands of her father. Each time those thoughts rose in her like ghastly phantoms, she had learned to force them deep down—yet all the time she was aware that somewhere they lurked in her spirit.

The last year had been difficult in a way she could not understand. Her thoughts had often been confused, wandering back across the years like ghosts seeking freedom from a dread yet uncertain bondage. Often she had been wrenched from sleep drenched in perspiration with a scream rising to her lips, terrified of something she could never quite understand. Sometimes it was a dream of sinking into some dark pool; she would thrash out wildly, seeking for something solid to grasp, something to keep her from sliding helplessly into the depths.

She had been restless in mind, and her body was changing in some subtle way, so that she was often swept with a vague emptiness—more like a longing—but she could not have said what she sought.

Now here in the darkness broken by the flickering fire below and the cold silver points of brilliant stars, she stood close to Adam in a silence that became almost palpable. All these things seemed to converge, causing her throat to constrict, her breathing to quicken, and her heart to trill like the voice of a small bird.

His face was only inches away from hers as he bent forward, striving to see what troubled her. His dark eyes were warmed by the reflection of the yellow tongues of fire, and every plane of his face was familiar to her in a way that no other had ever been.

Perhaps it was the cathedral-like silence of the forest that seemed to breathe gently, stirring her heart like the tender green leaves high overhead. Perhaps it was the sudden rising of the old fears that loomed like dusky phantoms, but died as she saw the kindness in his face. She remembered how he had come to her years ago, and warmth suddenly filled her as she recalled he had held her in his arms and soothed away the fears, murmuring softly into her ear.

Perhaps it was the long loneliness she had known for years, having no one, of walking alone with her guard held high while her heart cried out for someone to walk beside her—for Adam!

He leaned toward her and asked again, "Molly, you don't worry about being a bound girl? You—you have never *belonged* to me!"

Without volition, her hands rose, and she placed them on both his cheeks, gently caressing the scar that ran the length of his face. She whispered the thought that must have been kept guarded for a long time, but now passed her lips almost like a prayer:

"But—Adam—I *want* to belong to you!"

The words startled him, and his eyes suddenly opened wide. He was caught by the same spell that had caused her to speak, and there was a roaring in his ears as he searched her face, taking in the smooth cheeks brushed now by the thick curling lashes. His arms encircled. Suddenly her lips were under his; in a gesture as unrehearsed as her utterance of trust, he kissed her softly, warmly.

For her, it was like coming into a port after a wild storm. The fears that lay beneath her mind were now no more, for his arms were holding her tightly. Standing there, so secure, so safe, a sudden gust of joy swept through her.

For Adam the kiss was like nothing he had ever known. He had kissed women, but in Molly's response there was a sense of trust—complete and without reservation. She leaned against him, and though her woman's figure stirred him, somehow, for one fleeting moment, she was the small child that he had comforted so long ago.

Molly never knew how that kiss ended, nor did she remember who pulled back. But finally his arms dropped and she took a step back.

"Molly! I—I've never felt like this!" He seemed embarrassed, and uttered a strange half-laugh, saying, "Don't be afraid. I just—lost my head for a minute." Then he bit his lip and smiled, adding in a voice of wonder, "You've grown into a beautiful woman, Molly! I hadn't realized how pretty you are until . . ."

She smiled at his rising color, and said quietly, "I'm not afraid, Adam. How could I ever be afraid of you?"

His head rose and he looked into her face, then relaxed. "I'm glad of that!" He seemed awkward and uncertain of himself, and it was as if he were the small child and she the adult. Finally he said, "Guess I'll take a walk before I turn in."

It was his way of giving her time alone, and she watched him move across the tree line and disappear like a wraith in the silver moonlight. She made her preparations for bed, washing her face and hands in the cold waters of the brook, then climbed into the wagon and lay down. She could see the silver points made by the stars through the rear of the wagon, and for the first time in many years she was not afraid of the darkness. She remembered the firm warmth of his lips, and raised her hand to touch her own mouth. Finally she smiled enigmatically, but she did not sleep until after what seemed to be a long time, she heard him come back to the fire. She listened as he unrolled his blanket, and then she smiled and went easily into a dreamless sleep.

CHAPTER NINETEEN

"YE MUST BE BORN AGAIN!"

★ ★ ★ ★

The trip to Boston was uneventful, but the scene beside the fire had marked both Adam and Molly. She had gotten up at dawn lighthearted, singing cheerfully as she made breakfast. Adam, on the contrary, seemed subdued, and more than once he let his gaze rest on her face, a puzzled expression in his dark eyes.

Although neither of them mentioned the kiss, the moment was a sharp memory to both of them. Once she turned suddenly and caught him looking at her, and as his face burned with embarrassment, she laughed and said, "Why in the world have you been staring at me?"

He gave the reins a twitch, thought about it, then shrugged his massive shoulders. "Don't rightly know, Molly. Guess I ought to know by this time that you've grown up—but it keeps sneaking up on me." It was as close as he would ever come to mentioning the kiss, and he added, "If anybody had tried to tell me the dirty little girl I bought a handkerchief from in London would turn out like—like you have, I'd not have believed it."

Her eyes dropped with pleasure, but she said only, "That was a long time ago, Adam."

They pulled in to the warehouse in Boston, only to discover

that Saul was out of town, so the next day they headed home. The weather held firm, and they made good time, arriving at Philadelphia at midday on Thursday. Adam drove straight to Franklin's shop, but the master of his shop shook his head, saying, "Mr. Franklin's gone to France. Won't be back for two months." He had wiped his hands on his blackened apron, cocked his head and added with a sly grin, "He wanted to stay and hear Preacher Whitefield, but he likes them French gals a leetle better'n hearing a sermon."

"George Whitefield is here?" Adam asked.

"Been here nigh on to a week—and like always, he's got the whole town buzzin'! Ain't no church big enough to hold the crowds, so he's out in a big field the militia uses for drillin' soldiers."

Adam thanked the man, then went back to the wagon and told Molly what he'd learned. "Sure am sorry to miss Franklin," he added ruefully.

"Could we go hear Mister Whitefield, Adam?"

He looked up in surprise, then smiled, "Why not? Soon as we get back, I'll be leaving with the army. Why don't we walk around town, get something to eat, then go to the meeting?"

"Oh, that would be so nice!"

Adam drove to a modest hotel, took two rooms, and after cleaning the dust of the trail off, they walked around town for a few hours. There was a holiday air about Philadelphia that infected them, and when they saw a theater with a sign that offered the latest drama direct from London, Adam bought two tickets, and they went in, feeling rather guilty. Neither of them had ever been to a theater, and the play was a melodrama with singing, romancing, duels, and a happy ending. Sitting there in the darkness, Molly became so tense when the heroine was threatened by a fate worse than death that she unconsciously reached out and gripped Adam's arm.

He looked over to see her large eyes fixed, her teeth biting her full lower lip in an agony of suspense. She was leaning forward, completely absorbed in the action on the stage, not at all conscious that she was holding his arm tightly.

Finally, when the rather exaggerated heroine was saved by

a tall actor wearing a blond wig, Molly leaned back and expelled her breath. Turning to Adam she cried, "Oh, I was *so* afraid he'd be too late!" Then she noticed she was clutching his arm, and a rosy tint spread over her neck and cheeks. She dropped her eyes and pulled her hand back quickly. Noticing her confusion, he laughed, saying teasingly, "You only bruised me slightly!"

After the performance and dinner, they still had an hour, so the two walked along the boardwalks looking into the windows at the new fashions. He offered her his arm, and as she slipped her hand under it, she felt a sense of delight and security. Other couples were walking together, and she watched them, wondering how they had met and if they loved each other. Not once did she see a man who seemed as attractive to her as Adam, plainly dressed though he was.

He was aware of her hand on his arm, and like her, felt a strange sense of delight in walking with her. When they turned and left the central section of town to walk to the drill field, she suddenly looked at him trustingly, "Adam, do you ever think of Mary?"

Giving her a startled glance, he considered her question. "Well, I got a letter from Rev. Edwards last week," he said casually. "Mary and Dwight had a son last month. Named him Timothy, too. They're doing fine, Rev. Edwards says." He took a few more steps, then asked, "Why'd you ask about Mary?"

"Oh, I don't know." The crowd grew as they moved off the boardwalk and took a wide path to the large field that was already beginning to fill up. "You were very much in love with her. I guess you always will be."

"Why, I guess not, Molly." Adam was struck with a thought that seemed to disturb him. He bit his lip and his brow wrinkled as it did when he was intent. She thought he would say no more, but finally, he spoke.

"I wanted her pretty bad—and for a long time it hurt to think about her. But now that's all gone. I just think of her as Timothy's wife, a nice girl I knew a long time ago."

She considered that, then said timidly, "I thought love was supposed to last forever."

"Maybe it does in stage plays—or maybe it really does,"

Adam mused. "Most likely, all it proves is that I never really loved her at all."

At his answer she gave him a swift look, trying to discern his expression, then she smiled and said, "I'm glad you feel that way, Adam. It'd be hard going through all your life loving somebody you could never have, wouldn't it?"

They had become a part of a river of people that came from every section of the town and merged into one stream, already packing the area around a platform at one end of the field. Adam spotted a small rise over to the left where a large oak spread its branches, and taking her arm, he guided her through the crowd. "This is about as close as we're going to get, I reckon."

For the next half-hour they watched the crowd grow until a sea of humanity surrounded the platform. There seemed to be no single type of hearer; many who wore silks and sported diamonds rubbed shoulders with laborers wearing rough clothes. Age was not a factor, either, for though there were many young people with rosy cheeks, there were more with white-hair, and leaning on canes.

The sun was warm, but not uncomfortably so. Finally there was a stir in the crowd over to the left, and someone shouted, "There he is!"

A small group of men were making their way through the massed spectators toward the platform. Adam recognized Whitefield at once as the group mounted the wooden structure. He was heavier than the other men, leaning somewhat to corpulence, but he mounted the platform gingerly and waved his hand to the crowd.

"He looks older," Adam commented, "but not bad for a man who's preached as hard as he has for all these years." Since Adam had heard Whitefield preach, the man had crossed the Atlantic back and forth a dozen times. He had preached before the King, and the Countess of Huntington had introduced him to the nobility of England. David Garrick, the greatest living actor, had said, "I'd give a fortune to have his voice! He can make people cry by saying *Mesopotamia*!"

Whitefield had toured both America and England so many times that he'd lost count, making both enemies and admirers in the process. His remark, "Harvard's light has become darkness," had closed the doors of that school as well as Yale to him. He'd also been refused the pulpits of some of the most prestigious churches in the country, having said that an unconverted ministry was ruining the land.

Yet none of these things had succeeded in dampening the enthusiasm of the common people. No matter where the preacher went, people came by the thousands to stand in the open air to hear him proclaim the gospel of Jesus. Adam marveled at it, trying, as he studied the crowd, to account for such a thing. "I can't understand it, Molly," he said finally. "What has the man got to make people come out in mobs like this?"

"Brother Edwards always said he had the anointing of God, didn't he?"

"I'd forgotten that," Adam mused. "Look, I think it's going to start."

A tall, thin man with a booming voice prayed a long prayer. Then a short, heavy man with full whiskers stepped forward and for nearly an hour led the crowd in singing. They sang psalm after psalm, filling the air with music from the lips of twenty thousand people singing at the top of their lungs.

Finally the singing came to an end, and Whitefield stepped forward. He was bareheaded and wore a black robe. Whitefield knelt immediately and began to pray, looking rather ordinary as he prayed aloud, beseeching God to look down from heaven. He ended his prayer, but did not rise. For a long time he knelt there in profound silence—but it was not a dead silence, for Adam began to feel the same intensity he remembered from the last time he'd heard Whitefield speak. And now there began to be heard from various parts of the crowd, a few cries as people began to weep. A tall, broad-shouldered man just to Adam's right bowed his knees suddenly and began to sob, and farther down a woman raised her hands and with tears running down her cheeks began to cry out, "God have mercy! God have mercy!"

There was something electric about the way emotions were charged, even before Whitefield rose, but when he did stand and begin to speak, at once the power of God began to sweep over individuals.

As he began his address, clouds broke and the afternoon sun streamed down. He laid a solid doctrinal foundation by reading the story of Jesus and the man called Nicodemus, but as he read from the third chapter of John, clouds broke the sun's rays, with alternating bars of light and shade falling on the audience. Suddenly he stretched his arm out, crying in a bell-like tone that carried to the edge of the great crowd: "See that emblem of human life! It passed for a moment and concealed the brightness of heaven from our view. But it is gone! And where will you be, my hearers, when your lives are passed away like that dark cloud?"

"Oh, my dear friends, I see thousands here with their eyes fixed on this poor unworthy preacher. In a few days we shall all meet at the judgment seat of Christ—every eye will behold the *Judge*! With a voice whose call you must abide and answer, He will inquire whether on earth you strove to enter in at the strait gate. Whether your hearts were *absorbed* in Him."

By now the sun had gone behind another cloud, and the sky grew dark; in the distance the rumble of thunder sounded. "My blood runs cold when I think how many of you will seek to enter in and shall not be able. Oh, what plea can you make before the Judge of the whole earth?"

He began to rebuke them for sin, but soon he was on his favorite theme—the new birth. "You were born once of the flesh—but except a man be born again, he cannot see the kingdom of God!" he shouted. "But I have been a good man, you say." He lifted his voice and thundered louder than the rumbling in the distance, "Except a man be born again, he cannot see the kingdom of God!"

And then he began to tear down their excuses—that they had been members of the church, that they had taken communion, been baptized. That they had done no one ill, and on and on. To each of these Whitefield reiterated sternly, "Except a man be born again, he cannot see the kingdom of God!"

The storm was almost overhead. The preacher stood in the eerie light of a thundercloud about to break. "Oh, sinner! By all your hopes of happiness I beseech you to repent. Let not the wrath of God be awakened! Let not the fires of eternity be kindled against you!"

Forked lightning scored the sky. "See there! It is a glance from the angry eye of Jehovah!" He lifted his finger, then paused. Tension hovered at the breaking point, and then came a tremendous crash as thunder pealed and reverberated. As it died away, the preacher's deep voice came from the semidarkness. "It was the voice of the Almighty as He passed by in His anger!"

Adam had expected to hear a powerful sermon, had been prepared to be impressed by Whitefield's oratory. He had heard many sermons, and he had been stirred by many of them—not the least by "Sinners in the Hands of an Angry God" by his friend Jonathan Edwards.

But something was happening to him that he had not counted on.

It had begun when Whitefield had knelt and prayed. That simple act had struck some deep chord in Adam's heart. His knees suddenly felt very weak, and a lightheadedness seized him. He had attempted to shake the feeling off, but as the sermon progressed, he was more and more aware that something akin to fear was rising up in his spirit.

Adam Winslow was not a man who had known a great deal of fear. He had been in danger of death for several years in the Ohio River country, and that had been something he'd learned to control. But now he could not control the trembling of his hands as Whitefield continued to describe the plight of the lost, and his lips were so dry that he could not swallow.

Once he tore his eyes away from the preacher to look at Molly, and he saw that her face was pale, that her hands were twisting her handkerchief into a knot, and that she was beginning to moan.

We've got to get out of here! he thought wildly. But his feet seemed rooted to the ground, and besides that, no matter how disturbing the words of Whitefield were, he could not tear his gaze away from the man!

The sky grew darker than ever, and then Whitefield cried out, his voice like a trumpet: "Oh, will you die? Will you perish? Will you make His blood and His cross as nothing? Why will you trample underfoot the Son of God and do despite unto holy things?"

Then he cried out, "Come to Jesus! Let His blood wash you from your sin and guilt. Ye must be born again!"

He began to move his arm, repeating, "Ye must be born again!"

Adam saw the finger of Whitefield moving relentlessly across the crowd, and then it pointed to him! He felt as if all the air had been drained from his lungs, and he began to pant for breath. Then a great fear, such as he had never felt, grasped him, and the strength left him. He felt himself falling, and as he fell, he cried out, "Oh, God! Help me, for Jesus' sake!"

When he hit the ground there was no sensation of shock, and he felt almost as if he were out of his own body. There was no awareness of the ground, nor did he have any care for those around him. He lay there praying and calling on God for mercy, but he had no sense of time. The voice of Whitefield seemed to come from very far away. He was conscious that many were calling on God in tears and groans, but he was shut off, insulated from it all.

Finally there came a change, and he seemed to come back to the world, as if he had been locked in a dark room and had stepped back into the world of light. He was shocked to discover that he was lying flat on his stomach, his face pressed against the grass. He got to his feet and looked around. Molly was staring at him, her cheeks stained with tears, her eyes large with fear.

He looked at her and tried to smile, but he could not. She came close and put her hand tentatively on his arm, whispering softly, "Adam? Are you—all right?"

He nodded, conscious that he was totally exhausted, so tired he could hardly stand. But he knew also there was something in him that had not been there earlier. He stood with his head bowed, his arms hanging limply by his side, and examined his feelings.

The one thing he was most aware of was that he had a sense of complete and utter restfulness, and he marveled at how he seemed to be totally at ease, almost as if his spirit were floating. He smiled at her and said quietly and with wonder in his voice, "Yes—I'm all right, Molly."

Then he said more strongly, "You know what? I'm more all right than I've ever been in all my life!"

Molly's eyes opened wide and she held on to his arm. She saw something in his face that moved her, and she asked quietly, "Adam, are you born again?"

Adam Winslow looked up to where the skies were beginning to clear, then back to her. He smiled, but his voice was not completely steady as he said almost in a whisper, "I think so, Molly. For the first time in my life, I'm not afraid to think about meeting Jesus Christ."

Then a look of amazement touched his eyes, and he threw his head back and said in wonder as he looked up at the skies, "You know, I'm even looking *forward* to seeing Him! Now, isn't that a strange thing? For a man to actually *want* to see God?" He looked back to her and asked suddenly, "Well, do you think I've lost my mind, Molly?"

She threw her arms around him. He heard her say in a muffled voice as she buried her face against him, "No! I think you've just begun to find out what you are, Adam Winslow!"

Then she leaned back, tears gleaming in her eyes. As they turned to go, she said the one thing that he wanted most to hear, "You know, your father and Aunt Rachel—they must be very proud of you!"

"You think so?"

"Oh, yes! We'll write William and Mercy, too. Think how happy they'll be."

His mind reached out and images of the kind faces of those two swam before him, and he whispered, "They will, won't they, Molly? They really will!"

CHAPTER TWENTY

DEATH AT MONONGAHELA

★ ★ ★ ★

Adam knew as soon as he took one look at Charles that something was wrong, but he had no time to listen to him carefully, for Braddock's expedition against Fort Duquesne was pulling out of Will's Creek even as his brother came riding up.

"Adam—I've got to talk to you!" Charles pulled his horse to a halt, his face tense under his wide-brimmed hat. A big cannon pulled by a span of heavy draft horses lumbered forward, forcing him to pull his mount over to the side of the narrow road, and Adam followed him to where he dismounted under a spreading elm tree.

"I can't talk now, Charles," Adam said impatiently. "Whatever it is will have to wait until we get back."

"I've been trying to catch up with you for a week!" Charles complained. "Where've you been?"

"Trying to help Washington get this army started—and it's a miracle that we're on our way as it is!"

Neither Adam nor Washington could believe the complications that had arisen to delay the expedition—but it was Braddock's fault, for he insisted on a force that was unwieldy, massive, and awkward. He had an army consisting of 1,445 regulars fit for duty, 262 men in 3 independent colonial companies,

30 sailors to assist with block and tackle in hauling the cannon over the mountains, and 449 Virginia, North Carolina, and Maryland troops, as well as a small detachment of gunners.

The artillery train consisted of ten 6- and 12-pounder guns, 4 big howitzers, and 14 small mortars. The heaviest piece weighed well over half a ton, not counting its carriage, a discouraging object to haul over mountains where no road existed. In addition to the guns themselves, shot and shell had to be carried, as well as powder. There was, moreover, a host of necessary artillery supplies that must be taken, about 269 separate items, many of them in several sizes, ranging from a small derrick down to candles and carpet tacks. Food had to be supplied for more than 2,000 men for at least a month and food for the horses, for there would be little or no natural feed in deep woods. No horse could maintain its strength on leaves alone, but part of the time they were to be reduced to that. All this meant many wagons, and only by the aid of Benjamin Franklin, who produced 150 heavy wagons, was the expedition made possible.

"How we'll ever get this train through to our objective, I can't see!" Washington had protested, but he had thrown his energies into the project, and Adam had been hard driven to keep up with the colonel.

Now Adam said impatiently to Charles, "I've been busy— say it quick, whatever it is."

Charles's handsome face was thinner than usual, and he seemed nervous. Finally he said, "We've had some backsets in the business, Adam. I've been wanting to talk to you about it."

"You and Uncle Saul will have to take care of it," Adam said, and then he heard his name called. Looking up the road, now clogged with wagons and marching men, he saw Colonel Washington hailing him. "I've got to go, Charles. You'll have to take care of the problem." Then he paused and asked quickly, "You never wanted my advice before. What's different about this time?"

"Well, to tell you the truth, it's Stirling."

"Stirling? What about him?"

"We've borrowed a lot of money from him, and—well, he's getting anxious."

Adam stared at him, then said with a harsh line around his mouth, "Get free from the man, Charles! And I don't say that because I've had trouble with him. He's not good for us. How deep are we into his debt?"

"Too far," Charles admitted grimly. "He's in a position to make it hard on us if he wants to force it."

Adam stared at him, then shook his head, and swung up into the saddle. "We'll talk about it when I get back. We better go see Saul—find a way to get Stirling out of our hair. Stall him off until I get back."

"But, Adam. . . !" Charles called. But there was no time, and Adam had only a final glimpse of his brother as the young soldier caught up with Washington and the train rounded a turn in the narrow road that had been hacked through the woods by Washington's force a year ago.

"Winslow, ride on ahead," Washington said urgently. "I've tried to get the general to put out scouts and flankers, but he laughed at me."

"You're not expecting an attack this early, are you, Colonel?"

Washington's face was flushed; he had been fighting a fever for several days. He hated sickness, in himself most of all, and now he shook his head, impatient with his weakness. "No, but we'll have to send a crew ahead to clear the road. It gets much narrower up ahead, you remember. Go take a look, then come back and I'll try to get General Braddock to send the axmen ahead to do the clearing."

"Yes, sir!"

Adam wheeled his horse around and rode past the lumbering wagons at a fast gallop. It was hot, and he knew that by noon the soldiers in their wool uniforms designed for the cool climates of Europe would be staggering under the heat, and that the overloaded wagons would pull the strength of the horses down to a walk.

Soon he was far in advance of the army and entering the silent thick forest. The contrast was a pleasure. He had been in the midst of noise and confusion for the past month, and the solitude of the woods had a healing effect on his spirit.

He searched the trees constantly, his head moving from side

to side, but it was with the automatic watchfulness he had learned during his years in the Ohio Valley. He noted soon that Washington had been right, for the road narrowed down to a rutted track not six feet wide—enough for troops to pass, but not nearly enough for the wagons. He kept on for the rest of the morning, then turned his mount back, his head filled with thoughts of the past few weeks.

Since the afternoon Adam had fallen to the ground under the influence of Whitefield's preaching, he had been strangely peaceful. The next morning after his experience, he'd gotten up half expecting that the whole thing would have faded. He'd known enough converts to shout and profess salvation, only to fall away once the excitement was over. Jonathan Edwards had been clear enough on that, for he had insisted strongly that the test of the new birth was not an emotional experience but a new walk with God. "It's not how high a man jumps, Adam," the preacher had said to him once. "It's how straight he runs after he hits the ground! The one mark of the new birth is this: *A new birth will always make a man love Jesus more!*"

And that had been the essence of the days that followed. Adam had been consumed with a hunger for the Bible, and the person of the Lord Jesus Christ had been a reality in his spirit.

Molly had noticed it instantly. "You're different, Adam," she had said when they got back to Virginia. "You were never a hard man, but now there's something new in you!"

He turned and searched her face intently. "You found Christ, too, didn't you, Molly?"

"Yes," she said, and there was a fullness in her smile that reflected a joy in her spirit. "It's so *different*, isn't it, Adam— being saved? Jesus was always just someone in a story to me— but now He's my best friend!"

Adam had stared at her, then a smile had touched his broad lips, and his eyes warmed as he said, "We've got lots to talk about, haven't we, Molly?"

But there had been no time, for as soon as they reached home, he found an urgent message from Washington instructing him to come to Alexandria at once. He had thrown a few things together and said a quick goodbye to Molly. "You'll be all right with James and Hope until I get back."

"Be careful!" she had said nervously. "If anything happened to you, I'd—".

He had smiled at her, a thought coming to him. "You know, you're not going to be a bound girl much longer. What is it, two more months?"

She had stared at him, wondering what was on his mind, and then she'd shrugged, saying, "I don't ever think about it."

"Well, it's something we'll talk about when I get back. I have a thought or two about your future." He'd said nothing more than that, but her head had lifted, and her fine gray eyes had warmed.

Now riding back down the road toward the army, Adam wished he'd told her what was on his mind. "Why in the name of heaven didn't I kiss her—tell her I love her?" he said aloud in disgust. He had thought of it, but one fact had kept him from speaking: he might not get back—or it could be he'd return as a hopeless cripple. Such things happened in war, he knew, and he didn't want her to be the victim of that.

I wonder how long I've been in love with her? he mused as he picked his way along the rutted road. All the way back to camp, he thought what it would be like when he returned home.

But the only time he had to think of Molly for the next few weeks was at night after he'd eaten and lain down on the ground, wrapped in his blanket. The days were filled with work, and the expedition advanced slowly, ponderously through the primeval forest. The soldiers, all wearing swords, left the weapons behind, as well as some of their other heavy gear. The work involved was incredible. The road had to be hacked out, rock ledges drilled and blasted, swamps corduroyed and streams bridged.

The expedition advanced slowly. Small parties of French and Indians continually hampered their progress, entering into skirmishes with the flank guards Braddock had put out at Washington's insistence.

Finally Braddock realized that the rate of advance was far too slow, and a council of senior officers was held; the decision was made to detach a part of the force, lightly equipped, to proceed forward as rapidly as possible, with the remainder, and most of the wagons, to follow at a slower pace under the command of Colonel Dunbar, the officer next in seniority to Braddock.

On the morning of July 9 the advance army was on the south bank of Turtle Creek, which flows into the Monongahela. The scouts urged a crossing by marching to the main channel, which because of drought would be easily fordable.

At the first crossing, Washington, who had been riding on a bed in a wagon, ordered one of his horses brought up and saddled, with a pillow placed on the saddle. The fever had left him, but he was still weak from twenty days of illness.

Adam rode close beside him, worried about the officer, but said nothing. He did point to where the British were crossing the river. The red-coated regulars splashed into the stream, relishing the cool water on that hot July day. The river was so low that it exposed a pebbly beach a quarter of a mile wide. Here Braddock paraded his army with unfurled guidons, drums beating, and trumpets blaring.

"I suppose General Braddock thinks this will impress the enemy," Washington said. "But I don't think it'll have much effect on their marksmanship."

"No, I'd much rather we sent out more scouts," Adam admitted. He bit his lip, shook his head and asked, "Did you talk to General Braddock about the attack—I mean what we spoke of last night?"

"About letting the men take cover if we're attacked? I tried, but he only said, 'There'll be no hiding behind trees!' "

"He's a fool, sir!" Adam exclaimed angrily. "Look at those troops! Why, it'd be impossible for a marksman to miss them!" The brilliant scarlet coats and the high red mitre caps stood out like a flame against the green woods, and Adam shook his head, saying, "If they jump us, we're finished!"

Washington did not answer, but when Braddock led the line of troops into a small thicket lined on both sides with towering trees and intensely thick ground cover, he said, "I don't like this ground!"

He had no sooner spoken than a ragged volley of shots rang

out, and red-coated troopers fell writhing to the ground. "It's a trap!" Washington shouted, and spurring his horse, he drove forward past the line of soldiers to pull up to Braddock. "Sir! There's a walnut grove back there—we can pull back and see the enemy."

Braddock stared at him as if he were insane. "Retreat from this rabble? No, sir! You may now see how the British soldier handles an enemy!" Galloping ahead he ordered Colonel Burton to bring his troops forward, then rode to find the Virginia troops had taken to the trees and the Pennsylvania axmen were doing the same. Some of Gage's men had taken cover also, and Adam saw Braddock's face turn scarlet with rage. Drawing his sword he galloped up and began beating his own men away from the trees, crying out, "Forward! Charge!"

The troops moved forward, but the firing from the bushes became more intense. "Sir, this is the main body!" Washington cried loudly.

"Nonsense! It's just a few skirmishers!" Braddock scoffed. He gave a command, and the British fired into the forest. Their musket balls cut leaves from the trees and splintered saplings, but the enemy was firmly entrenched behind the huge trees. They knew, of course, that the British having once fired would have to reload, so they came zigzagging through the trees like phantoms, firing at will, felling the redcoats like stalks of grain before a scythe.

Suddenly the general's horse reared as a musket ball struck its flanks, dumping Braddock unceremoniously to the side. He mounted again and screamed, "Forward! Charge the enemy!"

The massive force was marching in ranks, officers on horseback, drums beating the cadence. A wall of red filled the entire road as the men walked shoulder to shoulder. Behind them were the others, the entire flying column, the militia and the Virginia blues—all walking into a twelve-foot-wide trap, with walls of trees and underbrush on either side of them.

The woods blazed with musket shots. Bullets hailed from the unsecured heights. Within minutes the outer columns were decimated. Every bullet seemed to find a target. The officers ordered their men to face the right and march in formation into the woods despite the fact that there was no target in sight.

The cries of dying men were everywhere, creating a madness that broke the spirit of the troops.

"Hold your positions!"

It was Braddock's last command, for before he could shout again, a bullet knocked him from his saddle. The shot smashed his elbow and punctured his lungs. He fell to the ground, and a groan went up from the soldiers. Some of them began to run, turning to meet a wall of their own kind marching into the narrow passage.

Mob hysteria took hold, and the road became the landscape of a nightmare. Fallen men were trampled by heavy black boots. Faces contorted with a continuum of emotions, from terror to determination to rage. Commands were ignored; few could even be heard above the curses, bellows, and whines.

It was then that Washington cried out: "Retreat!" He had had two horses shot out from under him, but there was no sign of fear on his stern face. The army fell back in total disarray. They ran like rabbits, and as they fell back, Adam saw the Indians come out of the woods, scalping, looting, and mutilating the dead and wounded, their elated whoops blending with the cries of the living victims.

Braddock had been put in a litter, bleeding from his lungs, as the army fell back. The Virginians and the Pennsylvanians brought up the rear, and it was only the firm hand of George Washington that saved them, Adam knew. He was a marvel, organizing the retreat, sending for help from the troops they'd left behind, taking care of the wounded—he was everywhere at once. Adam was at his side, carrying his orders to this officer and that, and he thought, *We'd all die if it weren't for him!*

The count was sickening. Of the 1,451 who had crossed the river at noon, 456 were left dead and a dozen taken prisoner. Of those who escaped, 421 were wounded. This left only 562 unharmed, and it was likely that no more than twenty of the enemy were killed, if that many.

The next day at noon they met Dunbar and the rear guard, but it was too late for Braddock. He died later that night. The last thing he said was, "Next time we will know how to deal with them."

He was buried, then every wagon and every horse was marched over his grave to conceal it, lest the Indians should dig it up for its graying scalp and resplendent uniform.

Dunbar took command, and before retreating, ordered all stores destroyed, including 150 wagons, many of them valuable. The remnants of the army that had marched out so proudly made its way back to Virginia at a crawl.

Washington and Adam rode together, and only once did the colonel comment on the tragic affair. He repeated to Adam Braddock's last words: *Next time we'll know how to deal with them*. Then he said grimly, "I have learned something, Winslow, and I trust that you have also. European tactics will never win a victory in this country!"

They arrived home, and Adam prepared to ride to Woodbridge, but a message from Charles was waiting for him at Alexandria. It was given to him by one of the house slaves, stating only, "Come here as soon as you can. Urgent!"

"Your master wants me now?" he asked the slave, whose name was Junius.

"Yessuh. He say doan go home 'til you see him."

"All right, let's go."

He found Washington, told him of the message, then asked for permission.

"Of course!" Washington said instantly, and a smile lighted his stern face and he put his hand out. "I am in your debt, Adam Winslow—indeed I am! Come to see me at Mount Vernon. We'll hunt a fox and you can show me your new gun again."

A warmth filled Adam as he shook Washington's hand, a warmth that stayed with him until he got to Charles's plantation. He dismounted wearily, made his way across the yard and up the steps. As Charles came out to meet him, Adam saw immediately that he had been drinking heavily.

"Glad you're home, Adam," Charles mumbled. He stood there swaying slightly; there was a hollowness in his cheeks, and dark shadows underscored his eyes.

"What's wrong, Charles?" Adam asked sharply.

"It's bad news, I'm afraid.

"Business?"

"Well—yes, but not like you think." Charles seemed embarrassed, and he rubbed his face with his palm, then held his hand out in a helpless gesture. In a panic-stricken voice he hurriedly said, "I know you'll blame me, Adam—but it's not my fault!"

"Spit it out, man!" Adam snapped. "I've got to get home."

"Molly's not there!"

Adam stared at Charles, fear gripping him. "What does that mean? Where is she?"

"Well, you remember I told you that Stirling was pressing us on the loans?"

"Yes? Did he call them?"

Charles shifted his feet and could not meet Adam's eyes. "Yes, he called some of them—but Saul and I sold off some land and managed to save most of the important things, but—he had a lien on the gunshop."

"He took that, too?" Adam asked, but was relieved. "Well, it's just a place. We can find another. Did you bring Molly here?"

"No, she's not here, Adam."

Adam lost his patience. "*Where* is she, then?"

"Stirling has her, Adam!"

A chilling silence fell between them. Charles's eyes were filled with shame as he tried to explain. "He—took over the shop, and since she was an indentured servant, he claimed her, too. I tried to stop him—really I did, Adam!"

Adam stared at him. "I guess you didn't try too hard, Charles. But he can't make it stick."

"No, not legally—but he *has* her, Adam! He took her by force a week ago. And he left you a message."

"What was it?"

"He said if you came to his place, he'd kill you!" Charles held out his hands impotently, and added bitterly, "I got the lawyers on it, but what good does that do? You know the kind of man he is, Adam!"

"I know, all right." Adam stared at Charles, then asked quietly, his voice steady, "Do you know where he's holed up?"

"Yes. He's in the house on that tract of land you liked on the Mohawk River—the one we got from Cartwright. It's on the bluff by the old Indian burial ground."

Adam turned and ran to his horse. Charles shouted after him, "Adam! He's not alone there! He's hired a bunch of Indians to guard the place. It'll be like trying to get into a fortress!"

Adam ignored him, and for a long moment Charles watched him ride down the road, and then ran across the yard yelling at the top of his lungs, "Junius! Junius! Saddle my horse!"

CHAPTER TWENTY-ONE

CAPTURE THE CASTLE

★ ★ ★ ★

Summer heat lay like a blanket in the Hudson River valley as Adam led Charles along the eastern foothills of the Appalachians, draining the strength of the horses so quickly that they had to exchange mounts three times before they reached the spot where the Mohawk joins the Hudson. The Green Mountains lay east, and Lake Ontario was directly west.

Charles had managed to stay in the saddle only by dogged determination, for Adam had ridden twenty hours at a stretch, stopping only long enough to eat and rest the horses. Now as they turned west, the younger man called out, "Adam! Wait a minute!"

Adam pulled his horse to a halt, turned in the saddle, his face grim. "What is it?"

Charles drew close, straightening up in the saddle to get the kink out of his back. He groaned wearily, saying, "Adam, we've got to rest these horses or they'll break down on us!"

"They'll make it."

"No they won't!" Charles argued. "Look at this animal—he's windbroke already. Be a miracle if he gets there at all." He looked at the three horses Adam was leading, and added, "Why don't I dump this nag and ride a fresh one?"

"Because these horses are our ticket out of this place, Charles. When we get Molly back, we've still got to get away, and if Stirling has any good Indians hired, we'll need all the speed we can get." He looked at Charles's mount, then at his own, and shook his head. "You're right, though. These two are about finished."

"How far do you think we have to go, Adam?"

"Maybe thirty miles—but there's a settler I know about five miles from here. We'll trade these two animals for fresh mounts."

He spoke to his horse, and as they proceeded at a slower pace, Charles was silent. He had thought he'd known this dark half-brother of his, but since he'd given him the news about Molly, the easygoing mildness in Adam's makeup had disappeared. *I don't know this man*, Charles thought as they plodded along. *He's like an Indian now—and I'm glad he's not on my trail!*

They reached the cabin of Adam's friend, found nobody home, and took fresh mounts—a tall buckskin for Charles and a powerful gelding for Adam. They made a quick meal of some cold beef in the smokehouse, then, after Adam left a note explaining the situation, they plunged immediately along the overgrown trail that followed the twisting banks of the Mohawk.

It was late afternoon the following day when Adam finally pulled up and slipped from the saddle. "The house is only three miles from here. We'll eat and sleep until dark."

"Will it be all right to make a fire?" Charles asked.

"Better not. My guess is that Stirling will be expecting me, and he'll probably have those Iroquois fanned out as scouts."

They had a quick meal, and when they finished, Adam lay down with his head on his saddle and closed his eyes. Charles stared at him, and said heatedly, "Well, are you going to let me in on the plan? After all, I'm all the help you have!"

Adam's eyes opened, and he rolled over on his side to look at his brother. His dark blue eyes were intent, and there was a sudden break in the austere hard cast that had been on his face for days. A smile suddenly broke across his broad lips, and he mused, "I've been wondering about that, Charles." He studied Charles's wedge-shaped face and added, "Didn't expect it of you, to be honest. You can get hurt—I guess you know that?"

"You think I'm an idiot?" Charles snapped. "We can both get killed—probably will. It'd be just my luck!" He picked up a dead stick, slapped his palm with it, then suddenly broke it in two and threw the pieces aside. Glaring at Adam he said with a streak of irritation in his voice, "I don't know what I'm doing out here. Looking out for my own skin—that's been my way. Why'd you get me into this?"

Adam considered the face of his brother, and after a long pause he said, "You fooled me, Charles. I never figured you to risk your scalp for anybody—least of all me."

Charles stared at him, a baffled look in his bright blue eyes. "We Winslows haven't been all that close, have we? Guess I've been jealous of you."

"Why—!" Adam sat up, astonishment in his face as he replied, "That's crazy, Charles! You're the bright one of the family—always have been."

Charles nodded, but there was a disgust in his face as he said slowly, "A man can get too smart, Adam. Like this mess we're in now. I wasn't very smart to let this happen, was I? Guess that's why I'm sitting here waiting for a bunch of Iroquois to swoop down and butcher me. It was my fault—and I always liked Molly."

"We'll get her."

There was confidence in Adam's voice, and Charles stared at him, incredulous. "You're sure of that, aren't you? Wish I had as much confidence."

"I'm praying about it, Charles," Adam said quietly.

"Oh? You've prayed about it, and that settles it?" Charles shook his head in disgust. "Can't believe that prayer's going to get her away from Henry."

"We'll do our part, but God's going to help us!"

Charles stared at Adam, his face a curious mixture of disgust and longing. "Well—you'll have to do the praying, brother. But do you also have a *plan*—something we can actually *do*?"

Adam nodded and sat up. Picking up a stick, he drew a curving line in the dust, saying, "Here's the river—and right about here is where the house is." He drew an X beside the wavy line, and said quickly, "The house is built up on a high bluff overlooking the river—must be a hundred feet or more—and it's plenty steep, Charles. I always liked the location. It's like a fort, see? The house is in a sort of projection with steep gullies on both sides—so there's only one way for anybody attacking the place to hit."

"Just one way?"

"Right! The place is practically impregnable, because there's an open space in front, a high wall closing off the house, just like a fort."

Charles looked at the lines in the dust, then up at Adam. "So, how in the world are we going to take a place like that?"

"I've been thinking about it—and there's one way. They'll be watching the front like hawks, but nobody will be watching the bluff because nobody's ever climbed it—that I know of."

"But—can you climb it?"

Adam clamped his lips shut and shrugged his heavy shoulders. "I don't know."

Charles licked his lips, then asked nervously, "You don't know if you can even *get* to the house?"

"No." Adam suddenly smiled, and added, "And I can't carry a musket with me. Just a knife. Even if I could take a rifle, I wouldn't dare use it. It'd wake everybody up, and we'd never get away."

"You don't know where Molly is," Charles protested. "But even if you can find her, how'll you get out? They'll be watching the gate, won't they?"

"Sure. We'll have to come back the same way I go up—down the bluff."

"Why, you can't climb down a thing like that in the dark! And even if you could, Molly couldn't!"

"We'll jump for it—it's the only way." Adam smiled grimly at Charles's expression, then said, "Here's the way we'll do it: I'll climb up the bluff after dark, find Molly, bring her to the bluff. We'll signal and jump for it. You'll be waiting there with the horses, and we get away as quick as we can."

"It's insane!"

"There's no other way, but if you want out, I won't fault

you for it, Charles." Adam shrugged and said, "Even if I get Molly out of there, those Indians are going to be on our trail—and you know what they'll do to us if they catch us!"

A soft breeze lifted Charles's fair hair. The fear lurking in his face gripped him as he sat there contemplating their chances. Adam said no more, but he could sense that inside his brother there was a war. Charles had never been a coward, but the odds for success in this case were small. Both of them knew that, and while Adam was set like flint, Charles was struggling against a lifetime of selfish indulgence. He yearned to get on a horse and ride away, and for a moment, Adam expected him to do just that.

"All right, Adam—I'll do it!" he exploded in despair. "But if you get me killed, I'll never forgive you for it!"

Adam laughed and got to his feet. "Thanks, Charles," he said gratefully; then he put his hand out awkwardly, and when his brother took it, he stated matter-of-factly, "We Winslows are a pretty tough breed, brother—and although God's on our side, we've got one little asset that might make a difference."

He stepped to one of the horses, pulled a rifle from the pack, then fished a leather pouch out of a pocket. Returning to Charles's side he said, "This is our secret weapon. I want you to learn how to use it."

Charles watched as Adam took out a handful of paper cylinders, then asked, "What are those?"

"Cartridges for these rifles," Adam answered. He held a rifle up, moved a lever and put one of the cylinders into the breech of the rifle, then pulled a plate over it. "Ready to fire," he announced with a smile at the expression on his brother's face. "It's what you've been after me to make for years—a breech-loading rifle."

Charles took it, staring admiringly at the new type of mechanism, and listening carefully as Adam pointed out how it worked. "How long does it take to load up?" he asked.

"Maybe five or ten seconds."

Charles stared at him, then looked down at the weapon. "Why, we'll be rich!"

"If we're not dead," Adam replied with a shrug. "There's

just one thing—I haven't got it all perfected. Usually it works, but sometimes it fails. But even when it does, it's quicker to throw a faulty cartridge out and re-load than to load down the muzzle with powder and ball."

Charles looked at the weapon, then up at Adam, respect in his eyes. "Well, it's plain that *I'm* not the smart Winslow!"

"We'll argue about that when we get back to Virginia. Now, let me drill you in how to load this thing. If we get rushed, I want you to load and let me shoot."

Charles learned quickly, for the process was simple. Then he lay down and just before he dropped off to sleep he asked aloud, "I wonder how much we can get for a Winslow rifle?"

"Lord Stirling, he say you come now!"

The speaker was a statuesque Indian woman, not more than twenty-five years old. She was wearing an expensive dress made in a London shop, and the delicate bows and ribbons set off her primitive beauty. Molly knew her by the name of Alice, and though she had tried, she had been unable to break through the woman's reserve. She had been introduced by Stirling with a smirk as his "housekeeper," but Molly had discerned instantly that she had been his Indian "wife." Such things were common enough on the frontier, and trappers sometimes married such women legally.

Stirling, of course, had no thoughts of doing that but Alice had no way of knowing this; it accounted for the sharp glint of hatred in her ebony eyes as she stared at Molly, saying again, "Lord Stirling say you come!"

Molly tried again to talk to the woman, for Alice was her only hope of escape. "Alice—remember what we talked about yesterday?"

Momentarily hope glowed in the woman's face, then faded as she said with a fatalistic shrug, "You no get away from this place. When he tired of you—then you go."

"But you could get me a horse—I could get away after dark—"

"You think you outride one of my people? No. You stay here."

"Alice, you could hire one of your braves to take me home! He'd be well paid, and then you'd have Lord Stirling all to yourself."

A flash of hatred ran across Alice's face, but the stolid look fell over her features. "You come now."

Molly suppressed an urge to beg and plead with the Indian, but knowing it would be useless, she followed her down the hall to the dining room.

"Ah—just in time for supper!" Henry Stirling came from the window that looked out across the river and put his hands on Molly's shoulders. She tried not to show fear, but he saw it in her face, and it made him laugh. He turned to the woman, saying, "Alice, bring the food in—and you can go to bed early tonight."

Alice shot a quick glance at Molly, hatred in her agate eyes, but she merely nodded and left the room.

Molly walked quickly to the window, looking out in the falling darkness. The view was magnificent, for the dining room projected over the bluff. The river far below was barely visible, catching the last gleams of the dying sun, and throwing up myriad points of light. The land fell away, the valley green and lush, running to the low-lying hills far to the south.

She had no eye for the beauty, however, and the fear that had been her constant companion since Stirling had brought her to this place rose in her throat. As he came to stand behind her, she forced herself to stand very still, for she had learned that any sign of fear not only pleased him, but aroused him to passion as well.

When he had first brought her into the house, he had said, "You'll have your own room, Molly, and I'll give you a little time before we get better acquainted."

He had, in some sort, been faithful to that, not so much as a matter of courtesy, but because he had been away on some sort of business—to look at land, she learned later. She had slept little, staying awake and trying vainly to think of some way of escape, but there was none. The Indian woman, Alice, had been her one hope, but it had become apparent that she knew all too well what Stirling would do to her if she helped arrange an escape.

As the days went by, Stirling returned—to begin a heavy-handed courtship of Molly. He was a vain man, accustomed to easy conquests, and it seemed to be something of a shock to him when Molly failed to respond to his advances. He even went so far as to hint of marriage, but this ploy was so absurd that Molly could not hide her disdain.

On one occasion, after a dinner such as was planned for this evening, he had drunk several bottles of wine, and in a drunken stupor had come after her. She had fought clear of him, and was saved only because he had fallen down drunk.

As Molly stared blindly out of the window, her mind was racing, for there was something in his manner that caused fear to mount and grip her heart. This night was different. Her hands were trembling; as she turned to face him, she saw the intent in his eyes.

"Now, let's have a nice meal, and then we'll have time for some good talk, my dear!" Stirling said. He turned to the table, pulled out a chair, and when she was seated, took his own seat. A bottle of wine was on the table, and he poured two full glasses, handed one to her and urged, "Drink up, Molly." When she hesitated, he commanded with a trace of anger, "Drink it, I say!"

She sipped the wine, and as the meal was served by Alice and a black servant, she realized that he was trying to get her drunk—not the first time he'd attempted such a thing.

The meal went on for a long time. Candles were lit as darkness fell, and there were many courses. Stirling had brought his cook from England, and he pointed out the virtues of the various dishes. As Molly picked at her food, sick with fear, he told her tales of his life in England.

Finally the dishes were all taken away, and Stirling said to the housekeeper, "Alice, you may go to bed—and tell the rest of the servants they won't be needed tonight."

"Yes, Lord Stirling."

As the door closed behind Alice, and Stirling turned to her, Molly was possessed with such a fear that she wanted to run to the door and flee, but she knew that such a course would only give him a warped pleasure.

She could see in his eyes the hunger for her that he did not bother to conceal, and when he came over and put his hands on her under the pretense of guiding her to the sofa beside the wall, she did what she had done ever since she had been made captive: she prayed to God for deliverance.

For the next two hours she did little but try to think of God's promises—and she found that the many scriptures she'd heard Jonathan Edwards quote both in his pulpit and in his home to his own family came to her mind. One especially was so clear that she seemed to hear it spoken in his clear, high voice: *I looked on my right hand, and beheld, but there was no man that would know me: refuge failed me; no man cared for my soul. I cried unto thee, O Lord: I said, Thou art my portion in the land of the living. Attend unto my cry; for I am brought very low: deliver me from my persecutors, for they are stronger than I. Bring my soul out of prison, that I may praise thy name.*

She held on to the verse, repeating it with all her heart; soon it was obvious that, indeed, only God could help, for after several crude attempts at flattery, he cast away all decency and began to paw at her.

"Please!—don't do that!" she begged, but he merely laughed and pulled her closer.

Molly pulled free, leaped to her feet, and made a blind dash for the door, but he caught her and held her fast. Then holding her with one arm, he took her face with his other hand and kissed her again and again.

Struggling helplessly, Molly's mind was paralyzed with fear, and when he lifted his face to smile at her, she cried out, "God, save me!"

"No, God isn't going to save you, Molly," he laughed. "I've waited long enough—and nobody's going to save you—so you might as well be nice to me!"

"Turn her loose, Stirling!"

The voice came so unexpectedly that Stirling uttered a cry of shock and alarm. He loosed his hold on Molly, whirling to see Adam Winslow standing in the doorway!

"What. . . !" Stirling tried to speak, but his mind was not able to comprehend the situation. He had felt so secure with the guards fanned out across the front of his house that the last thing in the world he expected to see was his enemy facing him in such a manner.

"How did you get in here?" he demanded, and took one step to the side toward the wall where a brace of pistols were mounted.

Adam leaped forward like a tiger, a knife suddenly in his right hand. He fell on Stirling, driving the larger man back against the wall. With one hand grabbing a fistful of hair, he pulled Stirling's head back and laid the keen edge of the knife against it. "You make one sound, Stirling, and I'll cut your throat out!"

"Adam!" Molly stood there staring at him, her eyes large with shock. Then she suddenly smiled and said, "I knew you'd come!"

Stirling risked saying, "You'll never get away from here, Winslow! There are twenty braves out there!"

Adam made his mistake then, for he turned to look at Molly, to speak to her, and as he did, Stirling moved suddenly with a speed surprising in a big man. He knocked Adam's knife hand away with one arm, then struck Adam in the chest with a powerful right—a blow that drove the smaller man back across the room.

Stirling wheeled, and in one smooth motion, ripped one of the pistols off the wall. He aimed it and fired at Adam point blank!

Molly screamed, but the shot narrowly missed, clipping a lock from Adam's hair as he drove forward, and in that split second he could have driven the knife into Stirling's heart—but something made him reverse the weapon and he struck the Englishman in the temple with the weighted handle.

Stirling went down in a crumpled heap, and Adam wheeled and caught Molly's hand. "Let's get out of here!"

He did not go to the door, but pulled her to the window. Throwing it open, he said, "We're going to have to jump for the river, Molly!"

He leaped to the ground, reached up his arms and caught her, then in two steps they were standing on the brink of the bluff. It was a dark night, and neither of them could see more than a few feet. He swiftly turned to her, put his arms around her, and asked, "Molly, will you trust me? It's a leap in the dark—but God will be with us."

"I—I'll always trust you, Adam," she murmured, pulling his face down to kiss him. When she drew back, she said, "I can't swim, Adam."

He took her hand and said quietly, "Hang on to me, Molly!"

Then together, they leaped off into the darkness, plummeting toward the water far below, and as they fell, Molly cried out, "Lord, Thou art my refuge!"

CHAPTER TWENTY-TWO

DEATH IN THE AFTERNOON

★ ★ ★ ★

Charles had never considered himself a coward, but the long wait in the darkness beside the river had drawn his nerves tight. For the first thirty minutes after Adam had waded into the river and disappeared in the inky darkness of the night, he had strained his ears for any noise coming from the house high above, but there was no sound save the gurgle of the water. As another fifteen minutes had passed, he had stared up, craning his neck to see the dim, yellow lights that glowed from the windows.

Suddenly there was a splashing to his left, and fear struck him like a blow! He whirled and almost fired the rifle, but loosed his finger when he saw a large buck come out of the river and disappear into the thickets downstream from where he stood.

"Devil take it!" he swore, relaxing his cramped fingers and rubbing his stiff neck. He rolled his head, forcing himself to relax, then moved back from the stream to check the horses. Coming back to the shelving bank of the Mohawk, he thought again of what would happen if the Iroquois caught them—scalped alive, burning splinters under the fingernails, gunpowder in raw wounds set on fire. . . !

"Why doesn't he hurry up!" he muttered under his breath—

then realized that Adam was taking the most dangerous end of the business. He forced himself to stand still, listening to the river and dreading to hear the sound of shots above. *I must be crazy*, he thought—*risking my scalp like this! Here I am, the Winslow who's always looked out for his own—and now I'm risking my life for a girl I hardly know.* He wiped the cold sweat off his brow, moved back a few feet to get a better view of the lights above, and suddenly smiled in the darkness. *Maybe I'm getting religion— that'd make Adam happy, I guess.* But he knew himself too well for that, and being a man not given to introspection, he finally gave up and stood there waiting for Adam's return.

Ten minutes later he heard a sound that brought his heart up into his throat—a single muffled explosion that came from high up the bluff, so low he barely caught it. "Oh, Lord! He's caught!" he thought with agonizing fear, and he almost ran for the horses—but forced himself to wait. *Five minutes! I'll wait that long!*

But it was less than two minutes later when he heard the sound of a loud splash, and he ran forward to the edge of the water, straining his eyes in the darkness. "Adam! Adam!" he cried out quickly. "Is that you?"

He held his rifle ready, but almost instantly he heard Adam call out, "Charles—here we are!"

Charles waded knee-deep into the water, and out of the darkness Adam appeared, supporting Molly with one hand. They stumbled to the bank and Molly said, "Thank God!"

"Amen to that!" Adam said huskily. "Are you all right?"

"I—swallowed some water, but—"

"Let's get out of here!" Charles interrupted. "What was that shot? Never mind—it woke up everybody in the place, no doubt!"

"You're right about that," Adam said. "We've got a mighty short lead, Charles—they'll be down on us in minutes."

He ran to the horses, and as he helped Molly mount a bay mare, he said, "They won't have their horses. They'll scramble down the bluff somehow, and then they'll have to go back and get mounted. We've got to put as much distance as we can between us and here before they get that done."

The two men swung into the saddle, and Adam turned his horse toward the river, saying, "We'll make it a little harder on them. Make sure your horses don't touch the bank!"

The river was shallow at the edge and he led them for over a mile along the edge, then pulled his horse to a halt. "I know this old trail—and I guess they do, too. But maybe it'll take them a few hours to think of it."

"I can't see a thing, Adam!" Charles complained fretfully.

"You don't have to. Molly, your horse will follow mine, and Charles, you stay in the rear. There're some low branches, so keep your head down. By dawn, I want to be far away from this spot."

He drove his horse out of the river, and the others followed blindly. It was a hard ride, for although Adam sometimes warned them "Low limb!" sometimes he did not, and both Molly and Charles had scratches from the branches that clawed their faces.

Some time before dawn they came out of the thick woods, relieved at seeing the open country after riding the Indian trail. At dawn they stopped and rested the horses. Adam pulled some cold beef out of a saddle bag, and they ate hungrily. After they finished, he said, "Molly, I want to show you how to load this rifle." For the next thirty minutes he went over the procedure, then said, "That's good! I hope we get clear, but if we don't I want you and Charles to load for me."

"You think we got a chance, Adam?" Charles asked doubtfully. "I keep expecting those Iroquois to jump us at any minute."

"I think we're all right for now. It'll take a while for them to get organized—and then maybe they'll have to hunt for our trail for a time—but they'll kill their horses to get us."

"Well, I'm going to sleep," Charles said defiantly. He threw himself down on the ground, and was asleep almost at once.

Adam moved out of the glade where they'd tied the horses, and took a position on a small rise that commanded a view of the west country. "You better get some sleep too, Molly," Adam said.

"What about you?"

"I'll keep watch—you never can tell."

"No," she said softly, and then she smiled and came to stand beside him. Her ash-blond hair hung to her waist, and there was a gentleness on her lips as she put her hand on his arm and repeated his words: "You never can tell." Then she smiled suddenly and added, "I prayed you'd come, Adam!"

"Did—did he hurt you, Molly?"

He dreaded to hear her reply, but there was a glad light in her blue eyes, and she shook her head quickly. "No—there was nothing like that." Then she bit her lip and added, "But if you hadn't come—!"

He reached out and placed his hand on her cheek, marveling at its smoothness. The glade was quiet, disturbed only by the sound of small birds and the rustling of green leaves overhead. His hand was rough on her face, but she reached out and covered it with her own, holding it against her cheek.

She was so tall that she had to look up only slightly to gaze into his face, and as they stood there in the silence, both of them felt a strange peace. "Funny," he whispered, "here we are just a moment away from being attacked by Indians, and all I can think of is your eyes."

"My eyes?"

"Yes." He put his other hand on her face and stood there with her face cupped between his palms. Looking into her eyes, he grinned, saying, "I'll never be able to say what color your eyes are! Sometimes they're blue—sometimes gray, sometimes both."

She leaned forward to whisper, "And what color are they, Adam?"

"I'll tell you, Molly, they're just the color that every woman's eyes ought to be."

"That's—the nicest thing you ever said to me, Adam," she whispered.

"Molly, I was so afraid when I found out you were taken! And you know what I thought over and over again while Charles and I were on the way to get you?"

"What?"

"If anything happens to Molly, I'm a dead man!" Putting his arms around her protectively, he said, "I don't know what's going to happen—but whether we get out of this or not, I want to tell you something." He pulled her closer and her arms slipped around his neck as he said quietly, "I love you, Molly Burns! As much as God will let a man love a woman—I love you!"

Then he kissed her and felt a deep stirring; as he held her close, she was aware of the strength of his muscular body. It was for both of them a promise of a love that had not been—but which lay waiting to blossom, to enrich their lives with more than passion.

She stood still in his arms, then pulled her head back and whispered, "I love you, Adam. I—I think I always have, ever since I was a little girl."

He shook his head, and there was a wonder in his dark eyes. "I'll never forget the first time I saw you on that street in London!" He laughed, saying, "If anybody had told me that one day I'd marry that ragged, scared little girl, I'd have thought he was crazy!"

"Marry?"

"Why, that's what people in love do, Molly!" Then he kissed her again and said, "You go sleep while you can, my love. We're not out of this yet."

"All right—but I'm not afraid," she replied, then laughed softly. "I've got too much invested in you, Adam Winslow, to lose you just when I've got you ready to marry me!"

She laughed at his startled expression, then whirled and went back to the shelter of the glade. Adam watched her go, and then turned to face the tree line, and his face grew hard, for he knew, as the others did not, how pitifully slim their chances were. While they slept his mind worked steadily, trying to come up with some trick, some way to avoid the Iroquois, but nothing came to him. He knew once the Indians found their trail, they would sweep forward at top speed, killing their mounts if need be to catch up with them.

There was no fort near enough to seek shelter, and those few settlers in the area offered no protection; they'd be destroyed if he went near their homesteads.

We've got to ride like Satan himself is after us—which is pretty much the case! he thought ruefully, then settled down to watch while the others slept.

Four hours later, he awakened them, saying, "Time to ride."

He kept the pace steady, not so fast that the horses would break down, but swift enough so that by four that afternoon, Molly and Charles were exhausted and the horses were beginning to stumble. The sun was setting when he pulled into a small grove and they all dismounted. "We might as well have a fire and a good hot meal," Adam decided.

Charles asked in surprise, "Won't it be seen?"

"No—not by anyone who counts." Adam spoke shortly, and there was no more talk until they had built a small fire and made a hot meal of beef and coffee.

After they had eaten, Molly studied Adam's face as he gazed into the fire. There was something stubborn about his features. Finally she asked quietly, "Something's wrong, isn't it, Adam?"

He tossed the dregs of his coffee into the fire, looked up at her and nodded, "They'll catch up with us tomorrow."

"How can you tell?" Charles asked quickly.

"I saw them late this afternoon—dust from a big party. Who else would be coming at us that fast?"

"Can't we hide—or outrun them?" Charles asked anxiously.

"Not either," Adam shrugged. "I figure we'll have to be ready for them by tomorrow afternoon."

Molly stared at him, her hand going to her throat in a sudden gesture. "Adam. . . ?"

Adam Winslow was not, in appearance, a flamboyant man; Charles had received that from Miles. But there was a steady strength in him as he sat there looking at them across the fire. His eyes were deep wells, reflecting the firelight, but there was a fearlessness in the man that leaped out, and as he said, "I think we'll make it," Molly and Charles both felt a gush of relief. The fear that had risen in them seemed to flow away—such was the strength of Adam in that hour.

"What will we do?" Charles inquired.

"We'll have to catch them in a spot where their numbers won't mean so much," Adam said. "I know this country—came through it many times with a load of beaver pelts. There's a spot up ahead—maybe ten miles, and if we can get there before they catch up with us, I think we've got a good chance."

"How'll you fight that many, Adam?" Molly wondered.

"I've been thinking on it—and it goes against the grain, what we'll have to do." He picked up a stick, motioned them to his side, and drew a crude map in the dust. "There's a break in the mountains up ahead, a pass that just cuts right through the peaks. It saves lots of climbing, because it's easy to get through— flat and about fifty yards wide. Now, if we get through that pass and set up behind some rocks, we can be sure that bunch is going to come right through after us. Then we wait until they're close enough so we can't miss—but just far enough away so they can't charge easy. If we can do it just right, we'll get enough of them right off, so the rest of them won't be too ready to follow."

"You mean—they'd quit?" Charles asked.

"Sure. Indians do that. They don't have any pride about it— and they don't have any shame when they decide not to fight. They just say their charms aren't right—and off they go. That's why they're no good as troops. You can't count on them to stand fast and take a beating."

Charles stared at him, apprehension in his light blue eyes. "Sounds like a good way to commit suicide to me! If there's a big bunch, they'll swarm us!"

Adam looked at his brother, then stated quietly, "Guess I'll have to admit that if the Lord isn't with us, we can't make it, Charles. But you know there's a line in the Bible, in the Book of Esther. The Jews are about to get slaughtered, and the only one who can save them is a woman named Esther. And it's pretty clear that if she won't help, they're all going to die. So her uncle says to her, 'You have come to the kingdom for such a time as this.' Well, I've been working on these breech-loading rifles most of my life." He smiled and remarked wryly, "Guess they were made for such a time as this. If they work, we'll be able to knock them off quick enough to break up the charge. If they don't work—"

"They will!" Molly nodded fiercely, her eyes bright with purpose. "I know they will, Adam."

Charles stared at them, and then a nervous smile touched his thin lips. "Well, I guess tomorrow will tell the story on the House of Winslow, won't it? You and I, we're almost all that's left of our name. All that Gilbert Winslow started ends here if those guns don't work."

Adam stared at him, then replied quietly, "I suppose that's so—but there's another verse I like pretty well—'Some trust in chariots, some in horses, but I will remember the name of the Lord my God!' If we get out of this, Charles, it'll be God, and not my guns!" He smiled, and to Charles's surprise pulled Molly into his arms and kissed her. Then he laughed and said, "You never saw a man kiss his bride-to-be, Charles?" Then he sobered and said, "We'd better get some rest; we sure won't have any tomorrow!"

Dawn had not broken when he roused them, and they rode hard all morning. By noon the horses were beginning to falter, but this time Adam gave them little rest. "Whip them up!" he cried out to the others. "If we don't make it to the pass, they'll be dinner for the Indians anyway!"

By the time they got to the foothills of the mountains, Adam's mount was so lame that he was forced to go afoot, leading the animal. It was two in the afternoon when he led them into a narrow gap that they had not noticed, saying with relief in his voice, "We made it!"

"Thank God!" Charles said fervently, then laughed a little. "Guess this trip will make a Christian out of me yet!"

Adam smiled at him, saying, "I hope so." Then he turned and led his horse through the pass, which grew wider as they proceeded.

Finally they came to a long straight stretch at least a quarter of a mile long with walls on both sides so steep that no trees were rooted there. At the end of the straight stretch, the pass veered to their left, and Adam instructed, "Put the animals behind there where they won't be seen."

They secured the animals; then Adam continued, "Get all four of the rifles—and all the cartridges." When they had the weapons, he led them back to an outcropping of rock three feet high and not over ten feet wide that lay almost in the middle of the pass.

"You get on my right, Molly," Adam said. "Charles, take the left."

"Why don't I shoot, too?" Charles asked as they waited. "I'm not a bad shot, you know."

"It's going to be close, Charles. We can't afford even *one* miss, and I've been at this a long time," Adam replied. He bit his lip, and then shook his head. "I don't like what's got to be done. It'll be like murder—those first few shots!"

Charles stared at his brother in astonishment. "Why, that's not sensible, Adam! They're out to kill us all!"

"I know," Adam answered. "It's like a war. But I don't like to kill a man—not even an Indian who's trying to take my scalp." Then he managed a smile and said, "Oh, don't worry, Charles— I've already fought this out. Guess every Christian has to settle it for himself, and I'm going to do what I have to do to save our lives."

They said no more, and as it grew hot, they drank sparingly out of the canteens. It was a little after two when Adam stated quietly, "There they are."

Charles and Molly had been sitting down; now they scrambled up and peered over the rock. "There's a lot of them, Adam!" Charles exclaimed.

"And Stirling is with them," Adam said grimly. "I didn't expect that. He hates me more than I thought." Then he asked sharply, "You've got all the rifles loaded? All right, you two stay down. I'll let them get another hundred feet; then I'll kill the first man."

Molly shivered at the coldness of the phrase, but she knew there was no alternative. "Will you—will you shoot Stirling?"

Adam hesitated before he said, "No—not him first. Then he whispered, "They're almost here—don't get up. Load as fast as you can, but don't get so fast you get jerky. Try to think of it as just a job that is a little tricky, but can be done if you're careful."

Then he raised up, put the barrel of his rifle on the rock, and put the sight right on the broad chest of the Indian riding beside Henry Stirling. He did not allow himself to think, but pulled the trigger. As the Indian was knocked backward to the dust, he handed the rifle to Molly, and took a quick sight on another Indian. Their horses were plunging, and he could hear their cries of alarm, but he put a ball through the body of another Indian, and exchanged weapons with Charles. A horse reared as he fired, taking the bullet he had sent at the rider, but with the fourth rifle he knocked another brave from his horse with a bullet through his head.

The whole thing had taken less than fifteen seconds, and there were three dead Iroquois on the ground!

Molly had loaded the rifle in her hands, and he took it, his face like flint. He noted as he sent the shot home that Stirling was standing in his stirrups, his face red with anger, and he drove his horse forward. For one moment Adam hoped that the Indians would refuse to follow, but after a moment's indecision they screamed and came after him.

"Here they come!" he said quickly. "They think we've got to reload!"

Then the action unfolded—and Adam never forgot that explosion of death in the afternoon!

The red bodies of the Indians made perfect targets, and one by one he knocked them from their saddles. Only twice did a rifle misfire, and he was careful to hit the leaders so that those that followed would see their fellows die. Once he let his aim fall on Henry Stirling, and almost blew the man out of the saddle. But for some unfathomable reason, he could not kill the man— though it would have been wise.

"I don't think they're going to stop the charge!" Adam said as he exchanged a weapon with Molly. "I'm not going to let them have you alive! I love you too much!"

"All right!" she replied with a steady voice. Then she handed him the rifle and added, "I love you, Adam!"

He touched her cheek, then rose, knowing he could not miss, so close were the remaining Indians, and a tall, thin brave took a bullet in his throat and fell to the ground trying to scream.

It was the one thing that turned the tide, for as he fell, Adam saw the mark on his chest that identified him as the war chief of his tribe. With his death, his medicine was gone, and the Indians swerved right and left, leaning to the sides of their mounts to avoid the fire of their enemy.

"They've stopped!" Adam yelled, then saw at once that Stirling had not even noticed that he was alone—or if he had seen the flight of his allies, he was too filled with battle madness to care.

Adam threw up his rifle, took a bead on the broad chest, pulled the trigger—and the weapon misfired!

As he reached for the rifle that Charles was handing him, Stirling reached the outcropping of stone, pulled his lathered horse around in a tight circle and was suddenly at Adam's left!

"Now, Winslow!" Stirling cried, aiming the weapon directly at Adam, "I'm going to kill you!"

The man stood out clearly in Adam's sight, so clearly that he could even see his trigger finger whiten as he applied pressure. The muzzle of the pistol loomed large, and he knew there was no chance for a miss at such a short distance.

He wanted to say goodbye to Molly and to Charles, and there was a great regret in him, for all the things he'd never see, for all the times he'd never have, but he was not afraid.

Charles had not had time to reload the rifle in his hands, and as Stirling pointed the pistol at Adam, he had nothing to fight with. He did not make a decision, dared not think what he was doing. Stirling was too far for him to reach, so he did the only thing left to do—he threw his body in front of Adam. As the bullet meant for his brother struck him in the chest, he was driven back against Adam, who caught him as he fell.

Adam had no time to move but even as he saw Stirling pull another pistol from his belt, a shot rang out, and a small blue hole appeared in Stirling's forehead. The man fell dead from the saddle and landed in the dust as his horse shied away.

Adam whirled to see Molly, her face white as flour, dropping the rifle to the ground. She suddenly stared at him, horror in her eyes, then put her hands over her face, weeping.

Adam said instantly, "Molly! Stop that! Help me with Charles!"

She gave a sob, then came to kneel beside the two men. Charles's eyes were closed and there was blood high on his chest.

"Is—is he dead, Adam?"

"No. I think the bullet missed a lung," Adam said. His own

face was pale as he pulled Charles's shirt away from the wound and peered at it. He lifted his brother from the ground to examine his back. "The ball's still there. We've got to get it out."

"Oh, Adam, he'll be all right, won't he?"

He looked at her trembling lips, then laid Charles down and took her into his arms. "Yes, Molly, we're all going to be all right—thanks be to God!"

Charles opened his eyes suddenly and looked up at them, saying feebly, "If you can spare the time, lovers, I'd like to get this thing out of my chest."

His thin voice drew Adam and Molly back to reality. They knelt beside him and Adam took Charles's hand, as he said, "You saved my life, Charles. I guess I owe you my life now, don't I?"

Charles Winslow's thin lips turned upward in a smile that ignored the pain, and looking up in Adam's eyes, he whispered so faintly that they had to lean forward to understand his words: "I guess Father would have been pretty proud—of me—do you think so, Adam?"

"Very proud!" Adam agreed, smiling down at Charles and adding, "You saved the House of Winslow this day, brother!"

EPILOGUE

★ ★ ★ ★

Mrs. Edwards was busy trying to wash the ears of her grandson, so when someone knocked at the front door, she called out, "Jonathan! You'll have to see who's at the door!"

The old rambling house at the Indian reservation had been a haven for the Edwardses, for after the hectic days at Northampton the lazy Connecticut village of Stockbridge had been quiet and restful. Not the least of the attractions for Jonathan Edwards was the huge room he had appropriated for a study. Here he had written the books that were beginning to make him famous, and now as he came through the door, he carried a stack of books in his hands with papers sticking out as markers.

"I'll get it," he called out, and putting the books down on a chair, he went down the long, wide hall and opened the door. For one moment he stood struck dumb, for he had expected to see one of his Indian church members.

"Why! Bless my soul!" he exclaimed, and his long face lit up with a broad smile. "Adam—and Molly! Mother—here's someone for you to see—come quick!"

Jonathan Edwards was not an emotional man, but he stepped forward and embraced Adam, then Molly, all the while beaming and exclaiming, "Bless my soul! I can't believe it's really you!"

Mrs. Edwards came in with young Timothy in tow, asking, "Well, who is it—why, Adam, it's you! And Molly, look how pretty you are!"

They stood there in the wide hall, exclaiming over the young people. Finally Mrs. Edwards ushered them all into the parlor, still towing the boy at arm's length.

There was a babble of voices as Edwards told how they had learned to love the work among the Indians. Finally his wife looked at the child who was pounding on the floor with a stick apparently made for that purpose. "This is Timmy—Mary and Timothy's boy," she said, a hesitation in her voice. She was thinking of how devastated Adam had been when Mary had married Timothy, and she feared that it might arouse bad memories.

Instead, Adam laughed and picked up the boy, tossing him high in the air. "Well, thank God he looks like Mary!" he said with a crooked smile. "But he may be as big as his father! Are they here—Timothy and Mary?"

"Yes, they came two days ago to visit. They're out for a few minutes, but they'll be back soon."

Edwards asked curiously, "And what about you, Adam? What have you been doing?"

Adam gave an abbreviated account of his life since he'd left Northampton, ending by saying, "It's been a good time for me."

"And what brings you to Stockbridge?" Edwards asked with a smile. "It's not on the way to any place else, you know, so you must have come just for a visit."

"Well, not really," Adam said. "You remember that Molly was a bound girl, indentured to me for ten years?"

"Yes?"

"Well, Rev. Edwards, the time ran out on her indenture last month, and it disturbed me."

Edwards gave his wife a puzzled look, then asked in some confusion, "Well, that's the way those things go, Adam. You wouldn't want Molly to be a bound girl forever, would you?"

"As a matter of fact, Reverend, I *would*!"

"But, Adam—!"

"Yes, I'm determined not to let her go free!" Adam announced.

Mrs. Edwards suddenly laughed out loud, and came to Molly and kissed her, then did the same for Adam. Then she looked at her husband and said, "Jonathan Edwards, for all your big words and long books, you are the slowest man on the face of the earth!"

Edwards stared at her, then as Adam put his arm around Molly and smiled up at him, his face lit up. "Oh, my word! You're going to marry her!"

"I am indeed—and we want you to do the ceremony!"

"Why, my dear boy, certainly I will!"

When Timothy Dwight and Mary came in thirty minutes later, they were as surprised to see the couple as the Edwardses had been, and just as happy. When they heard the purpose of the visit, Mary sniffed and said, "Well, it certainly took you long enough, Adam Winslow! I could have told you this would happen years ago!"

"Would have saved us some trouble if you'd made it clear, Mary," Adam said with a straight face.

Dwight put his massive arm around Adam and laughed, "You are a lucky man, Adam!"

"When's the wedding to be?" Mary asked. "I can help you with your gown, Molly."

"You'd better do it fast," Molly smiled. "We want to be married now."

"Right now?" Edwards asked.

"If you will, Reverend." Adam looked down at his bride with a smile and said, "I've wasted too much time as it is!"

There was no little confusion for half an hour, but finally, Adam Winslow and Molly Burns stood before Jonathan Edwards and recited the ancient vows. There was quiet in the room despite the fact that all the Edwardses' children were there, and as Adam and Molly quietly promised to love each other in the sight of God as long as they lived, a sudden ray of sunlight came through one of the high windows, falling across their faces and forming a golden corona that seemed to Mrs. Edwards much like a crown. She looked at the couple and thought, *They are made to love each other.* They reached the end of the promises and Jonathan Edwards said, "You are now man and wife." Adam bent to kiss his new bride, but just before he did, he whispered so softly that only she heard it: "Now, Molly Winslow, you're my bound girl forever!" She whispered back, "And you're my very own— bound forever!" Then he kissed her, and they were one.